The Secret

"I suppose everyone knows . . ." Charlotte began.

"Even Joan?" Eleanor asked. She knew that Joan and Charlotte were not on the best of terms, even though they had once been so close. They both loved John better than Paul, George, or Ringo. They wore the same shade of pale lipstick.

But back in the seventies, for two years, Charlotte and Joan had not exchanged one word. Their mother had been incredulous; what kind of daughters had she raised who would not speak to each other? Eleanor had tried to get them to reconcile. Whatever has happened, it can't be that bad. *Talk to her, Charlotte. Talk to her, Joan.* Things only got better when Joan found her husband.

"Years ago, a terrible thing happened. Really terrible," Charlotte told Eleanor now.

"What do you mean?"

"Nothing really. He's out of our lives now. Joan is still my sister. These things happen in families. Don't they?" Charlotte paused. "I don't know why I was so mean growing up. I was, wasn't I?"

"I don't know," Eleanor replied.

SISTERS and STRANGERS

Eileen Curtis

HarperPaperbacks
A Division of HarperCollinsPublishers

This is a work of fiction. The characters, incidents, and dialogues are products of the author's imagination and are not to be construed as real. Any resemblance to actual events or persons, living or dead, is entirely coincidental.

HarperPaperbacks   *A Division of* HarperCollins*Publishers*
10 East 53rd Street, New York, N.Y. 10022

Cover illustration by Cathy Saska

First printing: May 1996

Printed in the United States of America

HarperPaperbacks and colophon are trademarks of HarperCollins*Publishers*

❖ 10 9 8 7 6 5 4 3 2 1

For Steve
For everything

Of great help to me in writing this novel were Stefan Kanfer's *A Summer World* (Farrar Straus Giroux) and Herbert C. Kraft's *The Lenape* (New Jersey Historical Society).

Thanks also to my editor, Abigail Kamen Holland, and to my agent, Bobbe Siegel.

Contents

1 ELEANOR   1

2 CHARLOTTE   22

3 JOAN   41

4 BACK EAST   68

5 DISCOVERIES   91

6 THE WONDERS OF FLORENCE   110

7 THE RUINS   134

8 A PAPER LANTERN OVER THE LIGHT   165

9 THE ROWBOAT   186

10 PRISONERS   211

11 THE STRONGBOX   249

12 THE EDGAR T. HUSSEY SAND DUNE CAFE   274

13 THE ICE AGE   308

14 CULACINO   336

SISTERS
and
STRANGERS

— 1 —
Eleanor

The train stopped for no discernible reason in the middle of the smooth, open hand of the Hudson Valley. Billowy clouds nestled low, below the line of birch, hemlocks, and maples.

A bearded man wearing a safari hat tapped the woman sitting beside him on the train. Nodding to the ticket collector, the couple gathered a camera, a clipboard, and several maps. One of the maps was very large; it seemed to be folded over again and again. Eleanor glimpsed the word, Geological. The other map was more familiar: Eleanor recognized the pink bits, the black web of roads. Without a word, the maps under their arms, the couple stepped off the train and walked into a grassy clearing. Though the sun was high, they didn't cast a shadow. Or perhaps, Eleanor decided, their shadows fell in front of the couple and therefore she could not see them.

To walk into the sunset—that was something, thought Eleanor. Of course, it was noon, but to get off and walk away for no reason, or no reason that she knew of, that was dramatic indeed. When the train started up again, she looked back and the man and his companion were as small as two fingers, and then they disappeared into the steamy haze at the horizon. She wished that she, too, could disappear, and on a train she almost could. On a train, real life was suspended—she could, for brief moments, be neither here nor there. If only she could spend the rest of her life in a joyful blur, sliding past cornfields, cow pastures, knotted woods and never have to face him again—if only she could lose herself in the journey and never arrive anyplace new at all.

After riding smoothly for about fifteen minutes, the train stopped once more in an open field, again without explanation. Eleanor wanted to ask someone, the conductor, a passenger: What's going on? Are we there yet? She wanted reassurance, a calm voice to say: Don't worry, we're not there yet, you don't have to start your life over yet. But no one said anything. At least no one said anything helpful. She overheard a woman complain to the man beside her: "Yes, it's interesting, but we should have driven." A man's voice, a strong baritone, proclaimed, "Eleven and a half acres." A child wailed.

Finally she felt the brake slip and the train once again pulled along the glinting track. It moved very slowly at first, tugging softly past the crooked gray headstones of a tiny cemetery; then it slid past an old red barn, whose wide-open door revealed nothing but darkness. It was difficult to get to Tylerville without a reliable car, she thought.

Nothing was easy anymore. She was escaping Manhattan and her copywriting job—and Rene, especially Rene. As the train climbed the mountain, she thought: he's back there somewhere, he's smaller than an atom, which made her feel slightly better. Still, she needed to do some hard thinking at her country house—well, *their* country house. Her plan was twofold: to forget Rene and to comfort her beautiful sister Charlotte, who was flying in from Los Angeles. Charlotte had a lot of problems—

and pregnancy was one of them. A husband was not one of Charlotte's problems, for Charlotte didn't have one. For a moment, Eleanor thought: *Why does she have to come? Why? Don't I have my own problems?* Charlotte could be abrasive, unpredictable. But Eleanor quickly banished these thoughts. She wanted Charlotte to come. Of course she did.

Beyond the Wurtsboro Mountain, in the thick of the southern Catskills, the countryside was like something out of the past, an archaeological site of sorts sprinkled with ruins. The natural beauty—the groves of maples, the shiny black lakes—had survived, but the old bungalow colonies, the forgotten hotels, the gas stations that had never pumped unleaded fuel, had crumbled. Without inhabitants, the buildings' joists gave way, nails rusted and snapped. One by one, brittle roof tiles slipped and fell. The Catskills, she decided, were somehow haunted, for here people spoke as much of the past as they did of the present. The man who bagged her groceries bragged about Jerry Lewis and Sid Caesar, manic kids with chutzpah who'd gotten their big breaks in the mountains.

Now, passing the remains of an old hotel which had burned to the ground, the woman beside Eleanor said, "How could this have happened? You young people, you don't go to the hotels anymore. You fly off to Europe, you forget your roots. This was the Borscht Belt, you know." She was plump, gray-faced, and, Eleanor decided, unaccountably perturbed. "Did you know," she demanded, "there used to be a thousand hotels here. A thousand! How many are there now? Fifty? Twenty? Ten?"

"I have a house," said Eleanor.

"A second home, am I right?" The woman lit a cigarette.

Eleanor removed her glasses and rubbed her eyes. Her allergies were really bothering her today. She blew her nose. The woman sucked on her cigarette, exhaled. Eleanor coughed quietly. The woman inhaled again. Finally, Eleanor summoned her strength: "I'm really sorry, but I don't think they allow smoking."

"*You don't think?*" the woman asked in a vapor of smoke.

"I don't think it's allowed." Eleanor gripped the metal bar in front of her. She had a terrible headache. A day did not go by when she did not have some ailment—a stomachache, a backache, a headache, a cold.

The woman laughed, "*You* don't want me to smoke. I'll stop if you ask me to."

She sighed. "Okay."

"Come on, ask me!"

Before Eleanor could respond, the woman clasped Eleanor's forearm. "Did you see that couple, the couple who walked off the train? Anyway, they got off for no reason at all, in the middle of nowhere. Of course, the trains are ridiculous. They stop for no reason, and they never tell you anything. What would it take for someone to explain? Years ago, they were so much better."

The woman sighed. "Well, that's a lie. You won't believe what we used to go through. My parents and I used to take the trolley from Canal Street to Fortysecond, then we transferred to a crosstown bus. Then we grabbed the Weehawken Ferry, rushed to the train—us and the rest of the stinking city. We were little sardines— we smelled as bad. My mother would scream, *'Luft, gibt mir luft.'* I've got to translate: no one speaks Yiddish anymore. *Air, give me air.* Then there was a changeover in Summitville—that's back at the Wurtsboro Mountain. We had to drag all our suitcases off and wait for a through train to Monticello. But once we got there—well, we were in paradise. But why did that couple get off?"

"I wouldn't mind trying it myself."

"What, walking off a train in the middle of nowhere? Are you crazy or something?"

"Just a little run-down," said Eleanor, pressing down on her unruly red hair. I'm more than a little run-down, she decided; I'm depressed, I'm hollowed out. I'm thirty-four and going nowhere. And though she knew it, she could not will herself to be happy. She had tried. She'd read that if you smile when you're depressed, you'll soon be happy. She was smiling now, but to no avail.

"You should go to one of the hotels. The Silverman is great, or used to be—that's where I'm going. I wouldn't mind meeting someone. My Morris is dead. Well, not literally. He's dead in my mind. Anyway, I could go for a few laughs. I once saw Zero Mostel at the Silverman. Funny man. Of course, he's dead—literally." She stopped for a moment, then smiled brightly. "I hear the food isn't what it used to be—it's poisonous. And the portions are so small."

Eleanor massaged her temples. "I see."

"That was a joke, honey. Boy, are you gullible. Or are you just polite?"

Eleanor thought, *Yes, I'm polite—too polite*—or was she? Shouldn't she be polite? Was there any sense in being nasty to people?

The woman was silent for a moment. "Can I ask you something?"

"I guess so," said Eleanor.

"Are you married?" Eleanor frowned. "I'm just curious. Because I know a nice man—he's about forty. Married twice before. But he's available." She hesitated. "Are you Jewish?"

Eleanor, too, hesitated. She wondered whether the woman really had a man for her at all—maybe the woman just wanted to know whether she was Jewish or not. Either way, it didn't matter. "I'm Catholic," she said.

"I really didn't think you were Jewish, but it's so hard to tell these days. My nephew, he doesn't look Jewish. Do you know what I mean? My father's name was Mordecai, everyone called him Mo. His grandson's name is Matthew. Do you see what I'm saying? I told Matthew I was going to the Borscht Belt. And he looked at me like I was a meshugeneh and said, 'Oh, right. Beet soup.' "

"I'm Catholic," Eleanor said again, "but I'm not really practicing."

"Who practices anymore? Tell me that? Everybody thinks they're perfect, who needs to practice religion?" She pulled on her charm bracelet, little mock-Egyptian coins. "This trip reminds me of my mother and father. Our tenement on the East Side. The fire escape was the only decent place," the gray-haired woman was telling her. "From my perch, I took it all in—the people screaming, selling smelly fish, the women desperate to fill their baskets. No wonder my mother used to scream. Someone once asked her if she had passed through menopause. 'I ain't even been to the Raleigh yet!' she said. My mother, Ruby, her name was. A character. A pain in the ass."

A pain in the ass—Eleanor knew about pains in the asses. Rene was a pain in the ass. A friend had once told her, "You know what the problem is with you and Rene? You and he are in love with the same person."

Six months ago, Eleanor and Rene had been at a party at a friend's loft, and she'd gone into the bedroom to find her purse and put on some lipstick. Eleanor felt ugly that night, although people told her she was quite pretty, with her wide, open face, and small, pleasing features. Eleanor, however, did not believe the kind people who complimented her. She lamented that she did not have eighties features, that she could not adjust to contacts and had to wear glasses. She believed her lips were too small, that she had too many freckles. It didn't surprise her that Rene called her "Miss Glass Half Empty." So that night, six months ago, she had gone into the bedroom in search of her pocketbook and lipstick. The room was dark except for a small strobe light that curved on flexible metal above the bed so that one might read without disturbing one's partner.

But Rene and Marlena weren't reading. Marlena, resplendent in a silk blouse, was lying on the bed and Rene was curled up beside her, whispering in her ear.

". . . Rene?"

"Oh, no," he said quietly.

But Eleanor knew he didn't really regret what he'd done—or almost done. He nearly always did what he wanted. She believed it had a lot to do with the life he had lived on his father's Lancaster farm. Summers, the sun seared him raw as he rode his father's tractor between narrow rows of corn. All he ever wanted to do was paint, but his father wouldn't allow it. When he left Lancaster to pursue his art, his father told him, "I knew you were a faggot. I knew it."

"Oh, God, I'm really sorry, Eleanor," Marlena was saying, smoothing down her blouse. "This really isn't anything important." She looked at Rene. "It was really a mistake. It just happened. To be honest, I don't really even like Rene all that much." She stood as straight as she could, as if to undo how horizontal she had just been. Rene, too, stood up. In the other room she heard a woman shriek, "Oh! Your wine!"

Marlena shrugged, stared at the floor, left them.

Eleanor sat down on the bed. The window was open and the breeze rattled a delicate metal sculpture of an elongated man. He held a tiny golden scale in his right hand. Eleanor wondered what he stood for. Justice?

She smoothed the blue bedspread, then abruptly stopped, as though she'd been shocked. *It's happened,* she thought. For a minute, you pretend. The minute is over and there is not enough air. There was something putrid about the room. The wind had brought in the scent of something frying, of carbon monoxide. Speaking more to herself than Rene, she said, "You can't do this. You were happy." Outside, she heard someone shout, "I can't get no hot water out of this shower!"

Softly, Eleanor said, "I thought this would never happen."

"I love you," Rene told Eleanor.

"You love everybody," she said.

"Let's just go home," he said, steering her down five flights of stairs. The night smelled faintly of sulfur, like the minute before rain. They passed three Asian women who spoke in pleasant singsong voices. They watched a man holding a briefcase buy a bouquet of flowers at the Korean grocers. They heard a small boy ask his friend, "Where is it, fucker?"

Back at the loft, Rene said, "Let's just lie here." He fell back on the mattress they kept on the floor. Eleanor did too. She decided she should clean away the cobwebs, right there, in the cracks of the high ceiling. But how dumb could she be to think about doing household chores at a time like this?

"I don't want to lose everything just because of what happened with Marlena," Rene was telling her. "I mean, to lose you over this— Eleanor, please, it's ridiculous."

Eleanor was having trouble catching her breath, and for a moment she wondered if there was enough oxygen in the room. It seemed to have been overrun with nitrogen, with helium, with gases that made her want to screech loudly in a high-pitched wail. But this she did not do. Rene pressed his lips on Eleanor's. He tasted like wine and—something she couldn't place. The first time she'd kissed him, she'd noticed it. He tasted vaguely sweet, like strawberries. After hundreds of kisses, he tasted like her own mouth.

Now, he was a stranger. Gasping, she pushed him away.

"Eleanor," he told her, "I'm so sorry. You know I love you."

"How stupid do you think I am?"

"Come on. This is ridiculous. We weren't doing anything."

"You were lying on Marlena."

"No. We were having a talk. She's upset about Alan."

It came to her that her marriage had come apart because she'd felt the urge to put on some lipstick. Her insecurities had undone her. But that wasn't really true. She'd suspected him for a while, hadn't she? The way he talked about the women at the gallery, the new waitress at the Broome Street Bar. The way some nights he didn't want to have sex with her. The way other nights she was angry with him about something she couldn't put her finger on. "I'm not in the mood," she'd say, pushing her fears to the side; she tried to forget her uncertainties, as he, the artist, forgot his dried-up paints and ravished old brushes.

Now she did something. She stood on the bed and proclaimed, "Something *did too* happen! You were going to have sex with Marlena!" She stood there in her IBM T-shirt, a client she had once done publicity for. She went to kick him with her bare right foot, but he grabbed it and she fell on top of him. Stretching his arms around her, he laughed. He was pretending nothing was wrong, that he hadn't been with Marlena at all. She felt her face redden as she struggled to free herself.

Soon she was flat on the bed, looking up at the face of her husband. But he didn't look right. It was like looking at a familiar word—"there," for instance—and suddenly it seems all wrong. Rene knelt over her, blocked her view.

It was probably the shock, but she too decided to pretend nothing was wrong; that nothing terrible had happened; that Rene was still hers.

She swept her mind of lipstick and lofts and willed the dull ache in her gut to go away.

Rene kissed her, touched her in the usual places. His smooth skin on hers, she felt her heart beat, listlessly; there was no passion for her here. And she remembered Carlo, a college boyfriend, whom she had slept with finally, after months of his haranguing her. She remembered how she had just let him have sex with her; she couldn't enjoy sex when she didn't trust her partner. And she felt the same thing now: She just let Rene have sex with her. She just pretended. It was easier.

Are you supposed to feel anything?

It hurts a little—not much. It's no big deal—why don't you just get it over with? She opened her eyes for a minute. One of Rene's paintings, black, turned red. She closed her eyes. Eleanor's body grew warm.

There's nothing wrong with it, is there?

She twisted her hips, panted.

There's nothing wrong with it, is there?

It doesn't change anything.

Rene climbed off of her.

"See?" he told her, wiping his forehead. "You were just confused."

When she bounded out of bed, something punctured the smooth sole of her foot, and she fell back down on the bed, cradling her foot in her hand.

"What's wrong?" said Rene.

"Do you care?"

"Of course. Let me see."

"It's nothing."

"No, it's a splinter. Hold on," he said, running off to the kitchen. He soon returned with a needle. Gingerly, trying not to hurt her, he removed the splinter. "I love you," he told her, "no matter what stupid thing I do." And then he added in a thin voice, "There's something wrong with me. I do things—I can't help."

Rene fell asleep. With quaking hands, Eleanor made a pot of tea. The pot, made by Royal Albert Limited, was covered with daisies and lilies, the tiniest flowers in pastels. But all she saw were green stems and they looked like weeds.

The whitewashed Monticello station, topped with an elaborate cupola, was quiet when the train finally slipped in. Eleanor raised her hand to hail a taxi when she caught a glimpse of a man who looked familiar. Yes, it was Mike Zaccari. The idea of seeing someone she knew brightened her, though the sky had turned the color of an old quarter. She felt a drop of rain. She looked up, then scanned the platform for Mike, and in quickly looking up, then down, she tripped over something. "Oh!" she cried, breaking her fall with her right hand. She gazed at her palm: tiny pieces of gravel pierced the skin. Her left knee bled underneath her jeans, a small red stain seeped through. She wanted to cry but held it in. Her throat felt like someone was pulling on it from the inside.

"Jesus, are you okay?" It was Mike. "Can you get up?"

"I'm okay, really." She sat on a bench and brushed herself off. Meeting so unexpectedly seemed to heighten their friendship, so they hugged each other. "Going back or staying?" she asked.

"I'm picking up Veronica."

"Oh, I didn't see her on the train."

"Well, it's a big train," he said, slipping his hands into the pockets of his dirty jeans. "There," he said, pointing. Veronica's cropped black hair looked as if someone had colored her head with fuzzy Magic Marker. She wore skintight black pants and a Chinese-style short coat. What confidence to wear such a getup, Eleanor thought.

"I saw you fall," Veronica said, handing her luggage to Mike.

"I'm fine," said Eleanor. "Don't worry. How's—how's your play going?"

"It's a strain."

Mike offered to drive Eleanor to the cabin. "But first," he said, "stop off at our place. You won't believe the work we did. The place is really coming along."

"Michael put in a skylight," said Veronica, stretching the word sky. "But the rain comes through."

"I guess I screwed it up," Michael said.

There were still some dirt roads around Tylerville and the bumpy ride kept Eleanor awake, even though the long ride and the sudden rain had made her very sleepy. Her head ached. Sinus trouble again. If only she could sneeze! Michael turned on the windshield wipers, but it wasn't raining hard enough for them to do a good job. He kept turning them on, then turning them off.

Just then, a pair of black wings scrambled at windshield level.

"Shit!" Michael said.

In seconds, three perhaps, an ungainly bird managed to untwist its wings and disappear.

"We didn't hit it, did we?" asked Eleanor.

"No, thank God," Mike said. "You've got to feel sorry for a bird like that, you know, losing its way."

"They're not *perfect*," Veronica pointed out.

"Well," said Eleanor, "who is—perfect?"

"Perfect?" said Veronica. "Very few people."

"Not me," said Eleanor.

"Certainly not," said Veronica.

Mike and Veronica's small pond was filled with water

lilies. Perched near the water, their red farmhouse had been transformed since Eleanor had last seen it. A long skylight now cut the house nearly in half. "There's a lot of light now," Mike explained, "for Veronica's attic study." Another addition was a modern redwood deck, covered with soft, new leaves, jutting out over the pond.

Sipping herbal iced tea, Mike, Eleanor, and Veronica squirmed on the kitchen chairs to stop from sticking. No one had said anything yet about Rene. The humidity had actually glued Veronica's *Architectural Digest*s together. "These magazines are ruined," Veronica complained.

Smiling broadly, Michael stepped outside and, after a minute or two, bounded into the house with a bouquet of purple and yellow wildflowers.

"For you," he announced grandly to Veronica.

"Why do you do this?" she asked. She grabbed the flowers from Michael, opened the door, and hurled them outside. "I'm allergic," she said. "I don't know why he does that."

"Because I'm stupid. I do it because I'm stupid. Because I love you."

"Well, that's nice," said Veronica. "But you make me seem like a witch, throwing flowers away. I can't have flowers in the house."

"I have allergies, too," said Eleanor. "To dust, to flowers, but it's okay, I mean, the flowers. Bringing them in."

To break the tension, Eleanor steered the conversation to Veronica's new play, *Prisoners*, which was to be performed in July at the Downtown Theatre on Grand Street.

Veronica sucked on a cigarette, glanced at it, then said, "I'm going to quit. You know, smoking. I don't want to die." Though how much longer she had to live was anyone's guess. She might be twenty-eight or forty-eight. Her pale face was smooth. She said, "The play—"

"The play's the thing," Eleanor said with a laugh.

"The play," said Veronica, as if she were speaking about the Universe.

Mike poured Eleanor another glass of iced tea. "It's a week old—I hope it tastes okay. I made it myself. Brewed it." He added, "I'm really proud of Veronica. Her play is so musical, but not, you know, a musical."

Veronica broke in, "It's my theory that a play, any work of art, should have a musical tempo. Part six of *Prisoners*, for example, is *andante*: in a calm, melancholy mood, it's a brief encounter between a nun and a middle-aged man who have just been released from prison."

"Ah," said Eleanor.

"It's political," she snapped, blowing a thin line of smoke over the oak tavern table.

"The last scene," Veronica went on, "is really a group of smaller scenes: it's *prestissimo*, jumping from the dying nun, the middle-aged man, and the characters from the earlier scenes, the Buddhist monk and Stalin."

"Very symbolic," Eleanor said, thinking the play sounded tedious, and much like Veronica.

"And how is your writing going?" asked Veronica with a smirk. "Any new ads that you're working on?"

"I'm on leave right now. I've got a month off." Eleanor was entitled to a two-week vacation, but Henry, the creative director at the agency, was letting her take two additional unpaid weeks. He told her that she seemed to be "under some great stress." He would probably fire her when she returned. She wasted too much time at work, said Henry. From the twenty-eighth floor of her building, she'd stare for hours at the Hudson. It looked like a gray snake. She'd study it for inspiration, to uncork her mind, which was crammed with chauffeurs, freckle-faced kids, pageboy housewives, bald guys mowing the lawn—the types who found themselves in her commercials. She created them—a waste of time, she supposed. "I've just done a series of tuna fish ads. You might have seen them already, babies on the moon? Parakeets singing for tuna?"

"Do you find writing advertisements fulfilling? I mean, isn't it, well, a bit crass?" Then, "Where's Rene these days?"

Mike's eyes widened. "He's. . . they're breaking up."

"I forgot," Veronica said, opening a magazine.

Eleanor said, "Listen, don't worry. Anyone could forget. Really."

Mike offered to drive Eleanor to the cabin, about five miles away down the Black Lake Road. As they drove, Eleanor watched the tall pines, the flat ranch houses spread far apart, the white satellite dishes. "I wonder what my sister Charlotte will make of Tylerville," said Eleanor. "She'll probably think she's landed in Green Acres."

Mike sang, "Land spreadin' out so far and wide."

"Charlotte's never been to Tylerville before. Well, I haven't had the house for too many years. Rene and I haven't. Well—"

"Does she look like you? Good-looking?"

"*She* is," said Eleanor, waving off any compliment to herself. Breathing deeply, she took in the scent of cool light rain, the sweetness of the nearby dairy farms.

"So you have the two sisters?" said Mike. "Which one's the actress?"

"Charlotte, the one who's coming."

"And the other one is?"

"Joan. She's married."

"That's her occupation?"

"She takes care of her two children. And her husband." Eleanor felt the need to defend Joan, even though Joan didn't usually defend Eleanor. "She works very hard."

Mike's old Chevy carefully negotiated the narrow dirt path leading to the cabin. When they finally arrived, he seemed reluctant to leave. "Good luck," he said. "You know, with everything. I'm really sorry." He shook her hand. "You'll meet someone who, you know."

"Well, whatever."

"Really, hang in there." He kissed her on the cheek. "Really, things will work out." He gave her a little hug, and went to kiss her again, but Eleanor turned away.

Heart pounding, she said, "Mike, I'm really not ready for another, you know, man."

"Well—I'm just trying to comfort you, that's all. Don't get me wrong. Oh Christ, don't cry. Don't tell me you still love that jerk?"

"Of course not."

"I mean—he cheated on you constantly."

When she had walked in on Rene and Marlena, she'd wanted to take a long kitchen knife and drive it through her own heart. But there were no knives, no blood. The idea of killing herself now seemed as unrealistic as Veronica's play. "I know he cheated on me," she said. "But really, he wasn't all bad. Honestly. In the beginning, he was different."

It *had* been good in the beginning. Six years before, when they met, Eleanor had been an advertising copy-writer, but she was having trouble concentrating, even then. She used to write snappy commercials about snappy people. Her women had superior laughs, they caressed tubs of butter substitutes confidently. Now her women giggled nervously, wondered what was wrong with butter anyway. Rene taught an introductory painting class at the Visual Arts Center on Tuesday evenings and Eleanor signed up; she wanted to escape her deadlines and clients, to make her life glow in yellow ocher light or even perhaps to erase herself with turpentine.

It rained that first day, and SoHo is weird in the rain. Its few colors dissolve. There is so little color anyway south of Houston Street; just the leaden grays and blues of old factories converted to lofts. As she ambled down the street, a woman in a long black coat—from her neck to her toes—burst out of a bookstore. She belonged, Eleanor decided. Eleanor did not. With her corporate look, she felt she didn't exactly fit in. Eleanor sometimes thought she looked like a careless airline stewardess. When she stepped into the classroom, a young woman who wore tight black jeans, black boots, no makeup, hair the color of Chianti, snickered, "Gidget goes Downtown."

Rene stood at the podium. He was so beautiful! His gleaming blond hair was cut "Brit" style: an artful S from his high forehead curved level with his right eye. His hair was slightly wedged in the back, the darker brown of it visible at the nape. He looked, Eleanor decided, like an Etonian. In fact, he had a slight British accent, though he was from Pennsylvania. "Tell me about yourselves," he said. "Please, tell me what you want to get out of this class."

The young woman in black—though they were all in black—said, "I want to grasp for something unattainable! To paint some new form into being."

They all had similar ideas; they wanted to take off where Miró and Magritte and Matisse had left off, to work on neogeometric works, and when Rene pointed at Eleanor, she said, "I'd like to do—well, landscapes. You know, trees and lakes, pretty scenes."

"I see. Well, okay then. Have you ever painted before?"

"Well, not really. But I would like to learn."

"No painting experience?"

"Did we have to have that? I didn't realize—"

He smiled. "No, no. No experience necessary."

"Well, I did used to do paint by numbers, landscapes, seascapes, that sort of thing."

When the class let go a collective gasp, Rene said, "Come on now. Let's not be so tough on her. If you were all such great artists, you wouldn't be here in Painting 101 now, would you?"

In the weeks that followed, Rene continued to be supportive, to seek her out in conversation, while the rest of the class bantered about famous artists she had never heard of before. "Don't be discouraged," he told her, staring at her still life of wildflowers, "you paint with. . . abandon," though he cautioned her, "It's not always a good idea to mix so many colors. This is a bit—" Toshi, the class's most brilliant painter, mumbled, "Early Ringling Brothers," but Rene said, "Don't let them get you down. You've got as much talent as they do." Of course, Eleanor knew he was lying, but she appreciated his support.

After class one night, they shared a bottle of wine in a little French restaurant in the neighborhood. "You're really talented," he told her. "Promising."

As they walked back to his loft, the wind whipped their hair; they breathed little ghosts into the darkness. The New York night was highly seasoned with red brake lights, blasts of perfume, the pale, powdered faces of the SoHo women who, as if in mourning, always wore black.

Rene led Eleanor up six flights to his loft, opening countless locks. Eleanor thought of Houdini as she watched him. Inside, large canvases covered with dark paint—largely black, but an important shade of black, according to Rene—hung from the ceiling to the floor. There was a single couch in the center of the loft. Eleanor imagined someone like Gloria Swanson lying on it.

Soon, Eleanor was.

"You're beautiful," he told her.

"No, not really."

"To me you are."

On weekends, they strolled arm in arm through Washington Square Park. She held Rene's warm, sure hand as they crossed under the arch. They tossed bread at the pigeons. They stopped for falafel at an outdoor kiosk. Before she met Rene she'd never eaten anything as exotic as falafel—meatballs made out of chickpeas? He sometimes washed her hair in the bathtub, as her tense shoulders softened. On a crisp fall morning, they drove to the country. "I've always loved the country," he told her. "And I'll always love you."

He played his part—the would-be successful artist—in the SoHo of the mid-eighties, where everything and everyone was bursting with energy, potential. Rich people were investing in art, so it was a good time to be an artist—*if* the critics and gallery owners liked you—which, unfortunately, Rene told Eleanor, wasn't too often.

These were heady times to Eleanor, and when she met Rene she was born again. Under the pounding lights of the Mud Club, they danced to the music of Bowie, Blondie, the reedy voice of David Byrne. No more Folgers for Eleanor—on weekends she drank frothy cappuccino, dusted with cinnamon, at a swanky cafe near the loft as smoke poured over the wild hair of the women, the blue pallor of the men. It was dreamy SoHo, the Paris of the States. No more Agatha Christie novels for Eleanor. *Murder in the Vicarage?* Rene had cringed. Wanting to please him, and, of course, improve herself, she'd turned to Anaïs Nin, the poems of Emily Dickinson. She'd felt somehow magical holding in her hands *The Complete Poems of Emily Dickinson.* She'd bought the book herself and, after polishing her nails, opened it. Her painted fingernails surrounded the page like so many fake red stones. With a sudden realization that she would never bloody them again, she studied the cryptic poems; she became the person her beautiful artist wanted to be with.

After they were married, Eleanor would grab a bottle of Palmolive at the grocers and say to herself, "Nine bottles. Not bad."

"We've been together eight months" was as dry as algebra, but the liquid that cleaned dishes conjured warmth, intimacy. Especially since Rene did the dishes.

"I don't mind," he'd say. "It gets the paint off my hands."

They'd gone through nearly twenty bottles of Palmolive before the trouble came.

Now she was alone.

After Mike left Eleanor took a good look at the cabin, which was really more like a house, painted white. Originally, the house had been a hunter's cabin, but Eleanor and Rene had renovated it and added an upper floor when Rene's paintings began to sell. In addition to two bedrooms, there were two small rooms for Rene and Eleanor to paint in, a tiny kitchen, a living room, a bathroom, complete with an old cast-iron tub, even an outdoor shower. Now it would have to be sold, and the profits divided between them. To somehow rouse herself, Eleanor kicked the tires of her 1972 Plymouth Valiant resting beside the cabin on the overgrown grass. She didn't trust the car for rides to and from the city, but it was good enough for driving around Tylerville.

She dragged her overnight bag into the cabin. She felt Rene's presence. Couldn't she get rid of him? She felt him in his empty workroom, the floor splattered with yellow ocher, titanium white, cobalt blue. She felt him in the bathroom—his razor blades still lined the medicine cabinet, along with his extensive collection of vitamins. She felt his presence in the living room, where her favorite of his artworks hung above the couch: a woman's face (not her own), sketched with a few charcoal lines. Its economy was admirable. *This* was the kind of work she wished she could do—a few carefree lines and, perfection. This sketch was simple, airy, light—quite unlike his heavier abstract work, his black squares layered on brown triangles. Though, she admitted, maybe she just couldn't appreciate good painting. Rene had told her, struggling to put it kindly, that although she was a good draftsman, had a decent sense of color, she'd never get anywhere in the art world. If she wanted to paint representational daisies, mountain ranges, that was fine. She could sell that kind of work. But it was not, he said, important work.

Now, as if to exorcise him, Eleanor opened the windows in the bright, rose-colored living room, in the small blue-and-white kitchen, in the tiny pink bathroom, in their workrooms upstairs. She listened to the snap of curtains, like flags fluttering around the house. Downstairs, she sat on the sofa, which was covered with rows of tiny roses. And then she did what she had done every day for six months: she broke into tears. She couldn't help it, but really, one of these days, she'd have to stop. To divert herself, she decided to read *Pride and Prejudice*, which she'd already read in high school and in college. She wanted to read it because her sister, Charlotte, was playing the heroine's older sister, Jane, in yet another remake of the book. She'd just finished shooting the seven-part adaptation for Britain's Channel 4.

Eleanor sometimes thought she understood people in books better than those in real life—Jay Gatsby, Scarlett O'Hara, Garp, odd man out. She already knew what would happen to the Bennet girls in *Pride and Prejudice*, she knew that Darcy wasn't such a bad guy after all; she knew that if she had any pride, she'd stop loving Rene. What she didn't know was what her life would be like now, alone in the woods. How would it all turn out?

—2—
Charlotte

The California sky was a confusing mix of blazing sunshine and pewter clouds. Charlotte felt a lot like the sky—she didn't know which way to go. She was so wired, she could barely resist the urge to run a mile or two, to lick the sweat from her upper lip, then to lie down, exhausted, on the sand. But underneath the tense energy, she was immobilized.

She sat cross-legged on the living room floor of her three-bedroom house in Culver City, the city in which Sam Goldwyn had produced *Dodsworth, Dead End, The Best Years of Our Lives.* Culver City wasn't the greatest place in the world. Charlotte told friends she lived in the shadow of MGM, though it wasn't literally true. MGM was miles away. She would have liked to buy a house in Beverly Hills, Bel Air, or Sherman Oaks, but a dump in Bel Air, for instance, was over a million dollars.

She peeked through the blinds. The Lowells, who lived next door, were swimming in their aboveground pool despite the threat of lightning and rain. It hadn't rained in six months. She heard Mr. Lowell, a fleshy man with a marine haircut, bellow, "Kids! Watch this!" Then she heard a gigantic splash.

Soft shadows fell on the street. A small boy went round and round, following himself on a red bicycle, squealing with laughter. Watching the boy gave Charlotte a headache, reminded her that she had not slept well the night before. She'd had another strange dream. Since she'd become pregnant, her night world was filled with blood, car crashes, unfinished business. What bothered her about last night's dream was not so much its weirdness, for it was strange, but that she had remembered it in such detail.

She and Mabel Normand, one of Goldwyn's silent picture stars, sat facing each other on a train. Mabel, her long dark hair a mass of corkscrew curls, was screaming. Charlotte couldn't make out what she was saying; the train was too loud. Mabel's huge brown eyes were frantic. The train moved quickly—light and dark, light and dark. Mabel's face changed: her mouth was a wide red slash. What? What? I can't hear you! Suddenly Charlotte's sister Joan was sitting beside her, only they were no longer on the train but in their mother's old Duster. "I don't want to do this. Do I have to do this?" asked Joan.

"Don't forget," Charlotte said, suddenly guilty for having missed Sunday Mass, "we'll have to stop off at church and get a bulletin. Mom will want to know what the gospel was about. Just say it was about Jesus."

"We *stole money* from Mom and Dad," Joan said.

"Well, we had to do what's best for you."

"I'm scared," Joan said, handing Charlotte a puny, bloody baby.

The sight of the baby, who she suddenly realized was dead, drove Charlotte from the car. She scrambled across an open field until she awoke in her bed, sweating, moaning softly. After a few moments, she made her way, silently, to the bathroom.

Maybe she'd take a sleeping pill tonight. She had a few left over—but no, she wasn't *that* screwed up.

At least she had a new house, though it was bare, save for a couple of Aztec-inspired pillows, a dead spider plant, a seven-year-old Siamese cat named Rebecca (her favorite movie), and a black high-tech phone with red buttons. She'd just moved here from a garden apartment in West Hollywood. She needed a bigger place with the baby coming.

Patting her belly, Charlotte sighed. "Well, kiddo, what's done is done."

She picked up her to-do list. Her last entry had been, "Got to get some furniture." Now, she wrote, "Tell him?" She still hadn't told Ian the news. Ian O'Toole, who'd directed *Pride and Prejudice*, was the father of her unborn child. She knew exactly where it had happened: in Longleat House, which lies in rural Wiltshire, near Bath. The ancestral home of the marquis of Bath, rented by Channel 4 for *Pride,* was more massive than the mansions of Beverly Hills, of Bel Air.

A fountain in a sculpted pool bordered the main approach to the house. The mellow golden stone of the home's exterior was matched only by its interior; the walls throughout were of yellow gold silk and cotton damask. The drawing room's carved mahogany ceiling, thirty-two feet high, was inspired by the one in the library of St. Mark's Cathedral in Venice. On the drawing room wall, red velvet adorned a frieze depicting the story of the goddess Circe.

Who would not want to bed down in such a house?

For Charlotte and Ian, Longleat House was a bawdy house—they'd made it their quest to make love in as many rooms as they could manage. They'd sneak away during a break, when the other crew members were in Paris for the weekend, or eating lunch in a smoky local pub. They'd managed to make love in nine of the eighteen double bedrooms; in the main wing's sitting room—where the inglenook fireplace warmed their rear ends; in the Golden Library—named for the color of the seventeenth century Flemish tapestries that warmed its walls; even in the State Dining Room—on the endless mahogany dining table, undaunted by the fact that Queen Elizabeth I, the Virgin Queen, had been the room's first official guest.

To Ian, Charlotte was an unlikely choice for Miss Jane Bennet. He even told her so. First off, she was American, and Ian didn't particularly like Americans. He considered them stupid and fat, with their suntans, their nasal voices, short noses, square chins—chiseled European features somehow stunted. "I was wrong," he told her, laughing. Still, he complained, Americans make so few documentaries.

Charlotte disputed this claim, but realized that Ian was obsessed with the making and watching of documentaries, and since he could name nearly every documentary ever made, she had little success in convincing him of America's devotion to the form. Ian himself had directed a number of pieces: about the Egyptians, about the search for Troy, about the rings of Saturn.

Though Ian was not in love with Americans—until, he said, he met Charlotte—there was some pressure to hire them since the seven-part adaptation would be shown on American Public Television, then on Arts & Entertainment, and was, in fact, funded with American money.

Charlotte knew that Ian thought she'd done a good job. It wasn't that he came out and said it, but he rarely corrected her once she'd gotten over her nerves. She'd been shaky on the first day of shooting. Luckily, she was supposed to look a bit nervous as she danced with Mr.

Bingley. The dance scene had been shot in the State Dining Room of Longleat House, cleared of its endless mahogany table, of course. Charlotte knew her acting was wooden, but it seemed to work. Meanwhile Alyce Snodley, who was playing Mrs. Bennet, was overacting wonderfully: "Oh! my dear Mr. Bennet, we have had a most delightful evening, a most excellent ball. Jane was so admired, nothing could be like it. Everybody said how well she looked and Mr. Bingley thought her quite beautiful and danced with her twice!"

Ian even admitted to a bout of jealousy when Charlotte kissed Mr. Bingley (who was played by a homosexual) good-bye on the last day of shooting. "Ridiculous!" he'd told her. "I'm so jealous when it comes to you!"

When it comes to the six months I happen to be in England, thought Charlotte. She had enjoyed England, might have stayed there had Ian asked her, but he hadn't. And yet during her stay, Charlotte had sensed something missing from the center of her. She felt as if she'd forgotten something, her pocketbook maybe, her watch. More precisely, she missed something gangling and loud, something unrealized, which she supposed, was America. Big cars, big bellies, loudmouths, laughter—not smooth polite laughter, but boisterous cackles, the kind of laughter that unhinges chandeliers. She had gone back to California, to houses hugging the Hollywood Hills, to sunglasses.

Though she was through with Ian, she couldn't help thinking about him. He was forty-one, and his wiry hair was still black. He had swarthy skin for an Englishman, dark blue eyes, crooked teeth—somehow Europeans are allowed them. He was hardly one of Britain's most beautiful men, though he was becoming wildly successful. There was something important behind his eyes, Charlotte told her friends. He'd gone out with dozens of small, quiet blondes in their twenties, been married three times; "thrice," he'd say with a weak smile. Charlotte, nearer his own age (though he was not aware of this), had been more substantial, he told her. There was much more to her vocabulary than *"Love-*ly!" In the tiny beds of the great Longleat House, she'd told Ian what she liked— and didn't.

Far from Longleat House now, Charlotte tapped her stomach. "What a mess, Ian," she sighed.

She was alone and thirty-nine—though she admitted to being thirty-two. She wasn't famous enough for this inaccuracy to be found out. Just because it had taken her so long to get anywhere—why the hell should she list her wasted years on her résumé? Charlotte examined the tiny freckles on her ringless hands. Not liver spots, surely not liver spots. "What are we gonna do, kiddo?"

Lying on her living room floor, Charlotte told herself, all was well.

She'd gone far already, hadn't she? She'd started out playing bit parts on TV: *Oh no, stop that man! . . . Here's the report you asked for. . . French, Russian, or creamy Italian?* Then she'd gotten terrific reviews for a made-for-TV movie about a woman who saves her seven-year-old daughter from a gang of drug pushers. She still couldn't believe she'd gotten the part of Elizabeth Bennet's older sister, though she was a very good actress and did a convincing English accent. She'd been chosen for the part by a casting director who'd seen her as Katharina, the shrew, in *Taming of the Shrew* at the City of Angels Theatre.

Yes, there was no disputing it—she was a good actress. She tried to convince herself that her career would blossom, that she'd be a good mother.

She picked up the phone and dialed the operator. The

television was on and she heard someone say, "At no risk to you, absolutely free."

"I'd like to make a call to London, England."

But Charlotte didn't have the international access number, or the country code for England.

"You must know it!" Charlotte told the operator.

"Please check your directory."

Shaking, Charlotte hung up. She felt so bloated! So irritable! So mean! She had forgotten to turn on the air conditioner, and she was soaking wet. She knew her face must be redder than usual, and lately, it was really much too red. That's what happens, she lamented, when you get pregnant. "My face is *bloody ruddy*!" she screamed in her Eliza Doolittle voice. She began to cry and there was something strangely comforting about the salty tears; it was as though she had been dying for salt, as she used to crave it before she got her period.

Fifteen minutes later, armed with the code for international calls, the country code, and the seven-digit *real* number, she again picked up the phone and dialed.

"Hello?" said a man's voice.

"May I please speak to Ian?" She blew her nose.

"Speaking."

"It's Charlotte."

He was quiet for a minute, then said, "Ah, Charlotte! Calling from California!" English people, she thought, make California sound like an eight-syllable word.

"Yes, it's me. Calling from sunny California. Only, actually, the sun comes and goes. Just wanted to, you know, see how things were going."

"Lovely of you to call! Wonderful!"

"Ian?"

"Charlotte?"

She told him.

For a moment, no one said anything.

The television said, "Tabitha is the best thing that has ever happened to us."

"Bloody hell," Ian said finally.

"I thought you should know."

"Should I do something? What should I do?"

She thought, *if you have to ask*—

He paused. "Will you do anything—? I mean, maybe you should consider, well—"

It was a logical suggestion; they weren't married. She didn't want to get married. She was just beginning to taste some success, yet the question angered her. Whatever she chose to do, it would be her decision.

"No," she said, hanging up. A few moments later, the phone rang. "Ian?" Charlotte was somehow anxious to talk to him again.

The voice on the other end, a woman's voice, said, "No, it's not Ian. Who's Ian? It's your sister, Joan."

"Oh, Joan."

"Mom told me you were . . . you know."

"Yeah."

"You didn't want me to know?"

Charlotte said nothing.

"I understand you told Eleanor. Can I ask you something? Why didn't you tell me you were pregnant?"

Charlotte couldn't deal with her sister Joan. Not today. "I don't know. I was going to. I'm sorry, I've got to go. Really. The doorbell."

Quietly, Charlotte put down the receiver. Someone *was* at the door. When she opened it, Seldon handed her a large manila envelope. Seldon, a police photographer who lived across the street, dropped by a lot—especially when his roommate Anthony, who wrote music for a daytime soap, was composing.

"I told Ian about, you know," Charlotte told him as he came in. Niceties, exchanges about the mostly unchanging

Los Angeles weather, were not required for Seldon. "Maybe I should call him back? But why the hell should I call him back? He's an asshole."

"God, I hope you *like* these," Seldon said in his singsong voice. He spoke with extreme high and low pitches, as if he were speaking Mandarin, though he was of Polish and German descent.

"You're not listening to me," she said, thinking more about her sister Joan now than Ian.

Seldon's bulky muscles shifted under his LAPD T-shirt.

"I was trying to tell you about Ian," she said, leading him into the living room. "I told him that I'm pregnant. And I feel awful about Joan. Christ!" She took the envelope and pulled out some photographs. "Well, they're good," she said. "They really are." She laughed, pleased with herself. "I look great."

"You *al-ways* think you look great."

"Well, I nearly always do . . . You don't know whether to believe me or not."

She spread ten photographs out in a wide circle on the floor and sat in the middle, surrounded by her face. In one of the photographs, she was looking directly at the camera. In another, she was lying on the wizened California grass, her head positioned at three o'clock; her eyes turned ever so slightly toward the top of the photograph, her pale hair billowing around.

"I can see a line here," said Charlotte. "Shit."

"A line?"

"My eyes." Charlotte ate three crackers. She looked at him. "See! It's okay for you. You have a lot of lines around your eyes. But you're a man."

"What a job, last night. I hardly slept at all." Seldon went into the kitchen, grabbed a beer. "Miller? That's all you've got?" He took a sip of beer and said, "What a scene. It was hard to focus the camera. God, the blood.

And, you know, I'm practically immune. It was an awful car accident, tourists from Minnesota. One guy's leg, completely— Forget it."

"Did they die?"

"Very much so."

"What a horrible job."

He put his hands on his hips. "I'm *using* my photography skills. Crime scene photography is not exactly what I want to be doing, but still, I'm taking pictures."

"Well, I'll show these to my agent."

"It must be interesting," he told her, "to be beautiful." He seemed ready to say something more. Charlotte thought, *He's going to say something important*, but walking over to the TV, he merely said, "Jesus, you're watching *Bewitched?*" He turned off the set, which made a cracking sound.

Charlotte frowned, prepared to say something she didn't mean. Still, she played her part with Seldon. She didn't know why she did it. Somehow it made her feel good, knowing someone would put up with the very worst of her. "I didn't tell you you could turn off the set."

"I guess you didn't."

Charlotte laughed, though she tried not to laugh too hard because it was bad for the face, for the delicate undereye area. Nevertheless, she laughed harder. Then the room began to shake.

"Shiiiiit!" she cried as a picture of Carole Lombard fell to the ground. Three coffee cups fell, shattered. A broom struck the floor. One second, two, three, four. Books fell—*A Woman Named Jackie*, LeCarré's *The Little Drummer Girl*, Leonard Maltin's *Dictionary of American Film*. Then there was a louder boom as *An Illustrated History of the Cinema* broke its spine. Dishes rattled. A photograph of Charlotte's grandmother, hunched over a sewing machine in some Jersey City sweatshop fell, but the glass didn't break. Charlotte saw that the clock in the photo was set at 3:10, and though her kitchen clock marked the time as 3:08, she knew she would push the clock ahead if she lived, to exactly 3:10. A cosmic coincidence.

Meanwhile, Seldon grabbed Charlotte and pushed her under the doorway which separated the living room from the bedroom. His body scent was sweet and nearly imperceptible, like marshmallows.

A groan, a rumble. A click, a clatter. Then nothing.

Charlotte lit a cigarette. "I am never happier than in the three minutes after an earthquake."

"You'd think we'd had sex—the shaking and then, silence. And there you are, smoking a cigarette. Which you really shouldn't be doing."

"I can't get used to being pregnant."

Seldon said, "I'm gonna move, man. LA is *his-tory*, it's gonna *plunge* into the Pacific." He took a breath. "I shouldn't tell you this. Anthony worries."

"Tell him to move back to Cleveland."

"Not about quakes."

Charlotte thought for a moment. "I don't understand why he won't get tested."

"No, I mean, yes, he worries about *that*. I don't even like to say *that*. But what he really worries about is me. You know, me and him. He hopes I don't like you . . . you know, like *that*."

"Well, you don't, do you?"

"Not like *that*. I like you though. For sure."

Seldon then left to pick up some Indian takeout from Indira's down the street. When he returned, Charlotte grabbed the food and started eating. "I have such cravings for salty food," she told him. She then handed Seldon a list: water plants, feed Rebecca once a day, let her out, let her in, let the phone ring. "I'll pick up my messages," she told him. "I finally figured out how to retrieve them."

Seldon set Rebecca on his lap. "Is Mommy going to leave you all by yourself?"

"Eleanor is allergic."

"I'll keep her at my house." He frowned. "Will you see Joan?"

Charlotte's hands were fists. The sisters were on speaking terms now, had been for nearly twenty years, but the thought of Joan still made Charlotte feel off-balance. She could still hear her sister's screams sometimes, though she usually managed to shove the memories out of her mind—the trip to the city, the dingy hotel, the old man who told her sister just to relax—there was no use in thinking about it, and it *was* necessary. The right decision. Joan was only seventeen years old. Stewart, Joan's boyfriend, didn't love her anymore, and he wasn't going to marry her. Though he had once told Joan: if you ever get pregnant, don't worry, I'll marry you.

Charlotte had not forced Joan to make the decision: her sister had her own mind. But Joan blamed Charlotte. The sisters kept it from everyone, her parents, even Eleanor. They were from a strong Irish-Catholic family—whatever that meant. Their mother was in the Holy Name Society, Right to Life. At the time, Charlotte had not known what would be worse: telling her mother that Joan was pregnant, or telling her about what they needed to do about it.

Joan hadn't mentioned it in a long, long time, had not brought up Stewart's name, but Charlotte tensed up whenever Joan was around. She therefore avoided her—which was not difficult, because Joan lived in New Jersey.

Charlotte told Seldon, "You should forget about the things that bothered you when you wore bell-bottoms."

"What are you talking about?"

"Nothing," she said, putting down her plastic fork. "I was just thinking about Joan. She thinks I had a thing for her old flame Stewart, but I never did. She's never forgiven me." Charlotte thought for a moment. "My sister Eleanor, she's okay. It'll be good to see her, to relax in the country, to *breathe*. Eleanor minds her own business. Of course, I don't tell her much. Once, when I was fifteen and she was, I don't know, ten, I told her that my boyfriend felt me up. Well, she cried! God did she cry! 'You'll go to hell and I'll miss you,' she told me. Now she's divorcing her sex maniac husband, a painter who talks like William F. Buckley. A real put-on."

"He wants to have sex with her all the time?"

"Well, he wants to have sex all the time—but with other women."

"You?"

"Thanks a lot! No! Though he's tried. Eleanor, she likes books and babies and believes what people tell her. Me, I like men, *Variety,* and I don't believe a word."

The next day, Charlotte met Eddie Carnes, her agent, for lunch at the I Love LA Diner, his favorite, to talk about an audition he'd set up for her.

"How are you? How are you feeling? Anything I can do? Anything you need? A hat? That we can do! A new dress? What?"

"A hat?" Charlotte repeated. Eddie was a very peculiar man, but he found her work.

"This diner," he said, smiling. "Great." He pointed over his left shoulder. "Carl Reiner." He spoke as if verbs cost him money. Charlotte watched him scrape the meat sauce off of his spaghetti and pour ketchup on it. Eddie was smiling. "You bowl a strike. Okay, that feeling. You know how that feels?"

Charlotte, stumped, stared at his toupee.

"Well, that's how you look. Great."

"Like dead pins in a bowling alley?"

Laughing, Eddie said, "You, you, you! I don't know!"

Eddie Carnes wanted to sleep with her. Once, he'd dropped by her old apartment and insisted she do a striptease for him in the bedroom. "Inhibitions. To get rid of them."

"Fuck off," Charlotte had told him.

"That's good. That's the way to be with the casting people. Good."

But now, in the I Love LA Diner, complete with blue plates on the stucco walls, he was on. He was doing his agent bit. "Norma Shearer bungalow. Three-twenty. Great part. Co-lead. The girlfriend of a mortician. They picked him already. Lenny somebody, the mortician, Italian guy from Brooklyn. New pilot, new sitcom. Lucille—she's anorexic. Different show: tragedy, comedy. Like *M*A*S*H*. War and comedy. Death, anorexia, and comedy. Delicate balance. Wear black. Look thin."

The next day, the day before she left for New York to see Eleanor, Charlotte drove to Paramount for the audition. The traffic, as always, was heavy and she drove slowly along Melrose past Johnny Rockets, where good-looking people in their twenties served the burgers and other good-looking people in their twenties ate them.

She passed the Zephyr Theatre, where she had once appeared in *Apocalyptic Butterflies*, glancing at the boutique next door that sold only hats. She then drove by a run-down nursing home that didn't fit in among the trendy shops. An old woman wearing a lopsided auburn wig stood under the tattered nursing home awning reading *Drama-logue*—a newspaper filled with calls for auditions.

Charlotte finally drove up to the Paramount gate and rolled down her window. "Charlotte Powers. Audition with Andy Capino."

Dressed in blue, like an East Coast policeman, the security guard checked a roster. "Okay." He handed her a pass, which Charlotte placed on her dashboard.

She drove slowly, conjuring in her mind the old stars, the luminous faces, the love affairs, and soon she was passing The Paramount Sky, a billboard, painted blue, three stories high, a football field long. The Paramount Sky, which was not needed in the old smog-free days, was bluer and brighter than the rank LA sky surrounding it. The cloudless Paramount sky was, on the surface, perfect, like Hollywood, thought Charlotte.

At last she pulled into the visitors' lot, then walked toward the Norma Shearer bungalow, an old, two-story building next to the Gloria Swanson bungalow. Before she went in, she blew her nose. "Fucking smog," she mumbled.

Inside, twenty women sat in a small office. Most of them wore black. *Shit,* thought Charlotte. *Everybody's thought of it!* She looked up at a dusty photograph of Cecil B. de Mille, thinking he might give her courage, but he looked at her as impassively as she looked at him. After signing in, she picked up a two-page script. Everyone was silently mouthing the lines. Charlotte, too, read silently:

Lucille: All you care about are . . . are . . . DEAD PEOPLE.

Fazio: Well, whad'ya expect, huh? I'm a mortician!

Lucille: I want you to care . . . to care . . . about ME.

Fazio: Fuhgedaboudit!

Lucille: Fazio!

Fazio: (Looks at Lucille with concern) You losin' more weight?

Lucille: I'm beginning to see I've got a problem. Thank you for caring, Faz.

Fazio: Fuhgedaboudit!

Charlotte pulled a cracker from her purse. She wondered what she was doing auditioning for the part of the anorexic girlfriend of an Italian mortician when she was pregnant. She should have told Eddie, but she just couldn't bring herself to do it. If she didn't mention it, she decided, it wouldn't be real. Though she actually did want to be pregnant, or thought she did, until she actually was. It was all so confusing. Still, she convinced herself she would try to get this job. She could act thin, she told herself. After all, she played a toothless gypsy once, and she wasn't toothless. They could shoot her from the neck up as the season progressed. She'd keep her face thin. She then thought: *I hope I don't throw up.*

Everyone was clutching their 8 x 10s, checking each other out.

"I was up for the female lead in the new Stallone film," said the thin woman sitting beside her. "I got a third callback."

"Too old?" said Charlotte.

Another thin woman was talking about her success as Nurse Ratchet in the Grenada Hills Community Center's production of *One Flew Over the Cuckoo's Nest.*

Still another woman said, "Next *Matlock.* I'm the nurse in the operating room. Ben has a heart attack." Lifting up her black veil, her dewy eyes were wide; she added, "Don't worry! Don't get excited. He lives!"

Soon the woman with the veil, who had saved Ben Matlock from death and cancellation, was called in. Five minutes later she emerged, smiling. *Everyone smiles,* thought Charlotte, *even if they faint, or forget all their lines, or the casting director says they're too tall, or too short, which means they're too ugly.*

The secretary said, "Charlotte Powers?"

She walked into a tiny room, where Andy Capino, the casting director, sat behind a large desk, making him seem even tinier than he actually was. "Charlotte," he said, standing up to shake her hand. Reading the back of her glossy, he mumbled, "Good to see you. How are you? I see you were just in London. Good stuff."

"Good. Fine. Thanks."

The cameraman and reader looked very bored.

"Crazy show," said Andy.

"Oh?"

"This. *A Living Mess.* The show."

"Interesting concept."

"Right."

Charlotte's tongue found a piece of cracker wedged between her two front teeth. She tried to dislodge it.

"You okay?"

"Sure." Charlotte stood behind a line of masking tape. She was beginning to feel more than a bit queasy.

Andy Capino said, "Let's do page two. If I hear page one again I'll go ape-shit. Go ahead and slate."

"My name is Charlotte Powers. My agent is Eddie Carnes."

The cameraman fiddled with his camera. He said, "Go ahead."

The reader said, "Your weight, it's a problem. Your lack of weight."

Charlotte spoke. "Fazio, I know you care, but I'm trying. I had fettucini for lunch."

"Do you know how many people die in Brooklyn every day?" asked the reader without expression.

"I'm not sure—it doesn't matter. All that matters is that I need your attention, your love."

"Okay, babe," said the reader.

Don't throw up, Charlotte told herself. "All of these bodies, doesn't it make you think?"

"Fughedaboudit," said the reader in a Midwestern accent.

"I'm going to throw up," said Charlotte.

The reader frowned.

Andy said, "Oh, wait, is that?—"

"I played a toothless gypsy once," Charlotte whispered, or thought she whispered.

The reader said, "I've got the wrong pages."

Through the dirty window, Charlotte believed she saw a man who looked like Ray Bolger walk by. He was thin and gangling with crooked teeth and a big smile. Then everything around her grew very bright and her ears were ringing and in her mind she rested in a lovely field and it began to snow. It's snooowing!

She heard a voice ask, "Are you okay?"

Someone lifted her up off the floor.

"You okay?" asked Andy.

Charlotte sat down in a chair and put her head between her knees. "I just saw Ray Bolger."

Andy looked at the reader. "What? Who did she see?"

The reader hissed, "The Scarecrow. He wasn't even at *Paramount.*"

"I didn't eat breakfast," explained Charlotte.

"That happens," said Andy, frowning. "Low blood sugar."

The cameraman said, "Very anorexic of you." They all laughed nervously.

Outside, the sun was strong, though the billboard sky was still bluer than the hazy backdrop of Los Angeles. As Charlotte made her way back to her car, her long shadow darkened the hot macadam backlot.

Dressed in Confederate grays, a young man with an expensive haircut had his arm around an actress in modern civilian clothes whom Charlotte had seen before, though she couldn't think of her name.

The woman eyed Charlotte. Charlotte heard her ask her companion, "Wasn't she in—? Oh, I can't think."

Charlotte thought: soon I'll rest in Eleanor's country house. No LA sun, no smog. She saw a cloud in the real sky, or perhaps it was just smoke from another brushfire. She thought of Joan, of Ian, and of the baby that grew inside her.

—3—
Joan

Joan sat on the bed. She knew what she was going to do. Nearly everybody did this, she thought, they just didn't admit it. Still, she shouldn't do it. It wasn't right. Many years before, the Sisters of Charity nuns had assured her that what she was about to do was a sin. But she went on with it, as she knew she would, because she was, in the end, human.

She rubbed herself quickly. She didn't touch anything inside her. She couldn't enjoy that now. If Frederick couldn't, wouldn't— At first she felt nothing. She thought about an article she'd read which indicated that women's orgasms normally last twelve minutes; she knew that had to be wrong. That was too long. Or maybe something was wrong with her? Now, something was happening, she felt a twinge; she felt swollen; she tingled.

She rubbed harder, more quickly, saw her husband's naked body, but not his face; his hand caressed her neck. And it is now, now is the moment—her hairbrush, the vanity, the chests of drawers, the peach carpeting, the botanical prints, the silent TV—the whole room rushed away.

She was a sinful woman, she really was, a terrible Catholic, so unlike the women she had read about with longing in *Lives of the Saints*, a book of satiny pages that Sister Grace Marie, thinking Joan might have a vocation, had presented her with in the sixth grade. She was no St. Agatha, a rich Italian virgin-martyr who somehow got sent to a house of prostitution, but because she wanted to remain a virgin, was tortured with steel hooks in the sides, the rack and fire. Amazingly, she didn't die. Her breasts were then cut off by soldiers, but she was miraculously healed when St. Peter appeared to her in a vision. She was finally killed when she was rolled over coals mixed with broken glass. Wow, Joan had thought, swallowing hard. And then: why did St. Peter help her out for a while, then leave her to the thugs? What was his point?

Joan wondered what she should wear to the meeting. Her skirt was wrinkled, so she'd have to change. She stepped into her closet, but the wide array of dresses, skirts, shoes, and handbags, didn't cheer her. Nor did the scent of new leather, or of her favorite perfume, White Shoulders, which had seeped into her clothes, despite the work of expert launderers. She settled on a navy blue skirt, a gray silk blouse, a pair of expensive Italian pumps. She glanced at the mirror. She was not in love with her face; she was not a beauty like Charlotte; she couldn't play the piano or think up snappy slogans for advertising campaigns like Eleanor. Her eyes were large and dark, her brows thin, overplucked—frightened brows. She should leave her eyebrows alone—let them grow in. Her eyes traced the slight curve of her dark fine hair, which fell to her shoulders.

She touched the curling iron. Not hot enough, she decided, so she put on some lipstick, a coral shade, then stroked mascara on her sparse lashes. She tried the curling iron again, keeping her hand on it for a few seconds. The iron should have hurt her, burned her. The trick, she decided, is in not minding. She curled back her bangs.

Bangs, she decided, were not appropriate for this particular meeting, not serious enough.

The sun made bright shapes on the flat green lawns as Joan drove from her Hillside, New Jersey, home to the Davidson Preparatory School nearby. Light gleamed off the passing cars; everyone here in Hillside seemed to have a clean luxury car—a clean Audi, a clean Mercedes, or, like her, a clean Porsche. On Main Street, women wore pleasant silk dresses with flowers on them. Confident men with graying temples smiled at these women. Several people stood in front of the window of Evanson's Department Store, where, Joan imagined, they were admiring the summer wear—the Bermuda shorts, the windbreakers, the cotton polo shirts.

Soon, Main Street, with its clock tower, bright brick facades, and flowerpots disappeared, and Joan made her way along the residential streets of Hillside, past the mayor's red-and-white Georgian mansion. The lawns on Crestview Drive ran smoothly for a quarter of a mile, jumped up at an intersection, then skipped in again. Now she smiled—the Carsons' rose garden was so beautiful— tendrils of pink roses clung to the green lattice; the roses seemed to grow into the Carsons' house itself. The beauty of the flowers made Joan smile, a bittersweet smile; she could not recall smiling for a long time. In a dark memory that smelled like chalk, a nun told her: wipe that smile off your face.

And then—suddenly—something was wrong. Something was wrong with her. She was driving, yes, but something—something was happening to her. She felt outside of herself somehow. Disconnected. She was having trouble breathing, her heart was hammering, and she thought: *I am having a heart attack, I am going to die.* Sputtering for breath, she pulled over to the deep shadows at the side of the road, where she sat, thinking: *No, I am going insane,* though when her teeth began to chatter, she decided she was suffering not from any mental disorder but from some terrible physical ailment. She was not crazy after all. She sat, teeth chattering, as the weatherman on the radio announced that it was eighty-two degrees.

Gradually, however, her jaw relaxed and her heart slowed, though her mouth was dry, kept catching on the back of her throat. She thought fleetingly of going to the emergency room, but she *was* breathing. She was fine, really. She didn't want to be like Eleanor, the family hypochondriac. She had probably eaten something that had disagreed with her, though she didn't think that canned soup and saltines could have provoked such a reaction.

She pulled her car onto the wide avenue. She was alive. The incident was merely a blip. The body wasn't perfect, after all, she told herself. And though she was unhappy—she felt a small pain in her solar plexus, the center of herself—so were lots of other people. Who was she to complain? How could she be unhappy here in beautiful Hillside? How could anyone deny the goodness of the Hillside Golf Club, which rolled green, one second, two, three, four, five, six, until it disappeared from sight? Who could deny the intrinsic rightness of the Hillside Art Museum with its cool Doric columns?

How could she deny the goodness of her husband, Frederick, who didn't sleep with other women? If he did, that would explain things. Instead, Frederick did all that good husbands do—well, almost. He talked Jason into taking out the garbage, or he gave up and took it out himself; he loaded the dishwasher every night. He once told her (typically Frederick, she thought): "I would like to see what goes on inside a dishwasher." He needed to know the steps of things: how the Lunar Module had worked, how it had burst from the surface of the moon, floating upward to the heavens, how his own body had failed him, why he could no longer have sexual intercourse with his wife. Why his erotic thoughts, the touch of her breasts, no longer fired a signal to his penis.

Still, who could find fault with Frederick? Not his business associates in Manhattan. Frederick's supervisors at Cablevision Consolidated adored him. He could push cable like nobody's business, get the subscribers to pay a bit more, interest them in the pay channels, in Cinemax, in SportsChannel II.

He found his job easy. Everyone, he said, wanted cable.

His secretary Marge Papadoupalis once told Joan, "Your husband is the perfect boss. He never forgets Secretaries Week. He never yells."

"Here's my management style," he'd once told Joan. "I don't yell. I don't humiliate."

"Well," Joan had said, "you don't yell at Jason, or Diane."

"It's counterproductive."

Even his breath was never left to chance. Every evening at about eight o'clock, before he signaled the garage door to open, he shot a fine, anesthetizing spray of Binaca into his mouth. "It's only fair to you," he explained. He worked so hard, so late. Well, what could he do? He was vice president of Marketing and as such, he couldn't leave the office at five; he had responsibilities.

Now, driving out of Hillside, passing young couples arm in arm, Joan thought: I have a sweet-breathed husband.

What she didn't have was harder to talk about.

Davidson Preparatory School was shiny and smelled

like Lysol. School would be over in a week, and, in anticipation, students moved along in frenzied clusters. A
skinny boy tossed a maroon cap with a gold tassel into
the air. "All right!" he shouted, reminding Joan for an
instant what it felt like to accomplish something. She
had attended Columbia, studied biology, but had quit
school when she'd married Frederick. Joan overheard
bits of conversation, a teenage girl saying, "If I don't let
him—" Mrs. Levine, the geometry teacher, asked Mr.
DiFelipo, who taught U.S. History I and II, "Who is to
blame?"

In a cramped office, full of leather-bound books, Mr.
Krauss was telling her about Jason. As if, she thought, she
didn't know her own son. She knew her son, inside, outside—his large red ears, his cluck of a laugh, which had
become too rare lately. His thin white legs. His feet without arches. Joan had often thought, with relief: *My son
will never go to war. He's flat-footed.*

"He's stealing," said Mr. Krauss, grasping a coffee cup
which said, World's Greatest Father.

"What?"

"Mrs. O'Hara, your son has been accused of stealing.
This is not a proven charge. But we have strong feelings,
suspicions, that he, in fact, has been stealing for some
time."

"Stealing?" She thought: *It cannot be.* Softly, she said,
"What?"

"He's stealing money from some of the boys, when
they're in gym. One of our teachers, Mr. Veitch, caught
him rummaging through a few wallets in the locker
room."

The room was floating.

"Some action on your part, on you and your husband's
part, we feel, is—"

"Is best," she whispered.

—

"If you don't measure that flour perfectly, Diane, the cake will be ruined," Joan chided her daughter. She then yelled to Jason, who was watching TV in the family room, "You've really done it this time!"

"Done what?" he shouted back.

"Don't you shout at me!" she shouted.

He slinked into the kitchen. "What did I do?"

"You know what you've done. You've been—doing something terrible!"

He looked stricken. "What are you talking about?"

"Never mind. We'll discuss this later, after Grandma and Grandpa leave. We don't want to ruin your father's birthday."

"What did Jason do now?" asked Diane, stirring the batter with all her might.

"Nothing. Just— Never mind. Let's get this cake in the oven."

"Are you mad at me, Mommy? Cause that would be really unfair if you were. Because I got a ninety-seven on my spelling test. I can spell Wednesday."

"I know, sweetie. I know, it's just that I'm a bit tense. I'm sorry."

"You're nervous because it's Daddy's birthday?"

"Um—yes, that's it."

Joan watched her daughter leave the kitchen, her skinny bum sticking out. She, too, was swaybacked. She had once read that being swaybacked can mean that you'll have trouble conceiving. It was an old wives' tale, for Joan had certainly had no trouble conceiving. She hoped that her swaybacked daughter would have a different kind of life than she'd had, not that her life was anything to complain about. Certainly not.

"Happy birthday, Daddy!" Diane said in a sweet

singsong voice when Frederick arrived home. Frederick, this once, had managed to leave the city early, beating the tunnel traffic. She handed her father a complicated crayon drawing which depicted him holding a mousetrap. A royal blue arc was his wristwatch. Frederick had hunted down his prey, which had lurked under the kitchen sink. Smiling at his daughter's depiction of his hunting prowess, Frederick laughed; he was still grasping an umbrella, though it hadn't rained. Still, the weather report had predicted rain, and Frederick, Joan realized, would never disregard a weather report.

But he could not protect himself from the city's more ruthless uncertainties. She knew that Manhattan unnerved him, though he had worked there for nearly twenty years. He often told her how he feared violence, that he knew, just knew, that someday someone would corner him, slash his throat on a dim corner. "One of those men, who sleep on the streets. It'll be one of them."

Now he kissed the top of Diane's head. "You're a real character, sweetie," he said. Nine years old, Diane was a surprisingly large girl; her hands were nearly as large as Joan's. She was five feet tall. Soon, too soon, thought Joan, her daughter would pull the levers in the voting booth, chop onions, pay the phone bill. Tearing lettuce limb from limb, Joan heard Frederick ask Jason how school was. She heard no reply. She heard Frederick say, "Those headphones."

Frederick stood in the kitchen, hesitated a moment, then kissed Joan quickly on the cheek as she stirred the wild rice. "So what did Mr. Krauss want?"

Joan took a deep breath. "He says Jason's stealing." Her hands shook in a swirl of steam. Frederick made himself a drink, scotch and water. He poured Joan a glass of white wine.

"Stealing what?"

Joan shrugged.

"You didn't ask?"

"Money. From some of the boys—while they're in gym."

"Okay," he said, stroking her arms. "I'll talk to him." He took a long drink of scotch, closing his eyes for a second.

"I just don't understand how . . ." She suddenly pictured Jason in a little sailor outfit, then his First Holy Communion suit.

"Don't worry," he told her. "Act normally. Your parents don't have to know about this. They don't need to worry about this."

"But how can I act like nothing's wrong?"

"You can."

No, thought Joan. *You can*.

Joan's parents, Ed and Catherine Powers, finally arrived from Florence, a working-class town about forty minutes southeast of Hillside. Ed shouted, "Happy birthday, Freddie!" Catherine, whose latest self-improvement project was learning Japanese, said, "*O-medeto gozaimasu*. That means happy birthday." She then handed Frederick a book which *proved*, she said, that Kennedy was killed by the Mafia.

"That's quite an expensive-looking skirt," her mother said.

"Does that mean that you like it? That I look nice?"

"Of course."

Her father called in from the living room, "Joan, you're my favorite daughter."

"You say that to all your daughters," she said.

Ed then told Diane, "They're supposed to be on this desert island, but Ginger never runs out of eye makeup or gowns. Their huts have running water."

"Maybe her makeup is, you know, like, organic,"

Diane said. "Maybe it's made out of tree bark or something."

"I may not be the smartest guy in the world, but I've been around. And you don't find eye makeup or gold gowns on a desert island. Or radar equipment—and, another thing, Gilligan's hat looks like it just came back from the cleaners."

Dinner went reasonably well. Frederick carefully blew out his candles. "So, Mom," said Frederick, taking a second helping of Boston cream pie, his favorite dessert, "any news?"

"Well, you know about Eleanor. I hope you've called her, Joan. She's going through a tough time. Thank God there are no children involved. You know, with the divorce. Rene wasn't a Catholic." She squinted. "What was he?"

"Not a Catholic," said Joan, sipping more wine. She had a feeling she was drinking too much lately.

"Well, what was he? I mean, I'm already forgetting, and they're still married."

Jason said, "Seventh Day Adventist. Does it matter? Jesus fucking Christ!"

Catherine gave Jason a shove, a sharp elbow in his skinny ribs. "Watch your mouth!" Joan was surprised that she was not upset to see her mother shove her son. Strangely, her mother's action soothed her.

"*Jason.*" Frederick's voice was steely. "We don't talk like that in this house."

"I used to call my girls guttersnipes when they talked like that," Ed warned his grandson. "Do you want me to call you a guttersnipe?" Then Ed offered, "There's nothing wrong with being a Mormon. I just wish those people wouldn't drop by so often. Though they dress nice. All spiffed-up."

Frederick smiled, touched Ed's arm, attempting,

thought Joan, to deposit some of his own intelligent aura upon his father-in-law. "Seventh Day Adventists and Mormons are members of two quite separate faiths. And the people who knock at your door are Jehovah's Witnesses."

"The thing is," Catherine began, "that only Catholics can get into heaven—"

"I don't think that's true anymore," said Joan, drinking up her wine. "I think they changed that."

"How can you change something like that?" her mother demanded.

Eyes wide, Diane said, "Uncle Rene can't go to heaven?"

"Let's change the subject," suggested Frederick, winking at his daughter.

"Well, let's see," Catherine said. "I already told you that Charlotte's pregnant."

Ed let out a loud sigh.

"People have sex before they get married, you know. These days, anything goes," said Catherine.

"The *kids,*" Ed said.

"We *know,*" Jason said.

Her mother adjusted her red hair, though it didn't move. She still teased it, then lacquered it with hair spray. She still drew little commas at the outer corners of her eyes, creating what she called "the doe-eyed look." She was still beautiful, though you could not prove Catherine's beauty by measuring her features. Her eyes, in fact, were a bit too round. Her full mouth was gently lopsided. Yet no one would, or could, dispute her beauty. Even at sixty-five, her skin was good and clear. There was an aura about her, something intangible, as if she had been somebody, a starlet at MGM perhaps, a former Miss Rheingold—though she had been no one but Catherine Dougherty, then Catherine Powers.

"Joan," she said, "have you talked to your sister? I don't know what will happen when I'm gone. I don't know how you girls will know what's going on in each other's lives. I'm praying to Saint Anthony of Padua, the patron saint of lost causes, for all of you."

"Well, you really don't need to bother him. I already called Charlotte. Of course, I always have to call *her*. She never calls me. But that's okay. I've come to terms with that." She poured herself another glass of wine. "She didn't have time to talk to me, which is fine. That's the way Charlotte is. She's very—well, selfish would be the word. But I went out of my way and called her. I'm a good Catholic, you see."

Her mother was eating her cake, trying to be careful not to get crumbs all over the tablecloth, but they landed on her belly. After three children her stomach would no longer lie flat—no matter how many leg lifts she did. Joan remembered laying her head in her mother's stomach as a child and calling her lap "my pillowbox," confusing, she now realized, a pillow and Jackie Kennedy's hat. "Charlotte is such a beautiful girl," said Catherine wistfully.

"Let's not ever forget that," said Joan through clenched teeth.

"Well, you're an excellent mother," said Catherine. "You wouldn't want to be as beautiful as Charlotte—those kinds of looks put pressure on a person. How can she ever be as perfect a person inside as she is outside? She'd have to be a saint."

"And that she's not," said Joan, who got up and started to take away Frederick's dessert plate. "I'm not finished," he protested.

"You're not?"

"No—see?"

"Oh, yes."

Joan went to take her mother's plate. "Are you trying to get rid of us?" asked Catherine.

"Of course not," said Joan, wishing she were beautiful, lovable.

Of the Powers girls, only Charlotte had inherited her mother's beauty, though unlike her mother, Charlotte was a dark blonde, not a redhead. Now of course Charlotte was a pale blonde. Well, that was Hollywood for you, Joan thought—or more precisely, Culver City. Eleanor, who had inherited her mother's hair, was pretty, but in the way that wouldn't last. Soon, Joan decided, Eleanor's skin will redden, her thin lips will sag at their corners.

The evening had been difficult. Joan had trouble pretending everything was fine. Later, Joan and Frederick did their parental duty and confronted Jason. They knocked on his door, upon which he had pasted a small decal that said "Detour." Jason was lying in bed, eyes closed. He wore his black headphones the way other boys wore baseball hats.

Frederick and Joan stood over their sixteen-year-old son. "*Jason,*" they said.

He didn't move.

Joan tapped him and he opened his eyes. She had never been able to describe the color of her son's eyes accurately. They were a blend of blue, green, and brown. Hazel, she thought, did not describe them.

Jason pulled off his headphones. "Yeah?"

"I had a talk with Mr. Krauss today," Joan told him.

"Yeah?"

Frederick gripped the pineapple-shaped bedpost. "He says you're stealing, son."

"What?" Jason stood up, uncoiling the headphones. "What?" Joan knew he was pretending. He wasn't looking at them—there was a small crease between his eyes.

And then, for some reason, in a flash, she remembered hunting for shells with him when he was five.

"Have you been taking money from the other boys?" she asked him.

"'The other boys?' What, am I in the third grade? Can't you speak to me like an adult?"

"Jason," his father said, "there's no reason for you to take money. If you need money, you only have to ask."

Jason laughed. "Dad, can I have fifty thousand dollars?"

Later, lying in bed, Joan half watched the television. She took a relationship quiz in a magazine: "How Ready Are You for Change?" She racked up only fifty-two points out of a hundred. Frowning, Joan read her quiz analysis: "When opportunity knocks, you aren't anywhere around—the idea of trying something new is too scary. Ironically, being self-protective can backfire." She then started to read "Recipes for Better Sex," but there was really no sense in it. Frederick wasn't interested. They had not had sex in over a year.

Joan sighed. "What are we going to do about Jason?" She knew that Frederick would have no valuable answers, that he would become philosophical, speak in empty phrases of love, support, and openness.

"We told him not to steal," Frederick said.

"He already knew that," she said, annoyed at her ineffectual husband, disgusted with herself for being a bad parent. Her mother had given him an elbow in the ribs. She had to give her mother credit, though she knew that hitting him was not the answer. Not the answer at all.

Meanwhile, while Rome burned, Frederick sat propped up in bed fiddling with his hair. He seemed to be checking his part. Or perhaps he was thinking of ways to get around the FCC, imagining himself beating a Senate committee in a debate on cable television. He twisted his body down to the *Wall Street Journal,* which lay flat on the floor. "He'll come around," he told her absently.

"You look like a contortionist."

"Well, you don't like me to read the paper in bed. The newsprint stains."

Joan thought fleetingly of telling Frederick what had happened to her in the car that day, but she was getting into a bad habit—she'd have something important to tell Frederick, but she wouldn't get around to it. I'll tell him later, she'd think, then never tell him.

Instead Joan said, "Should I call Charlotte again?" Frederick didn't answer. He was already engrossed in an article in the paper.

It was Saturday. "When are we gonna go, anyway?" Jason asked, peeling his face away from the brown leather couch in the rec room.

It would have been nice, thought Joan, if he actually wanted to go with her and Diane into the city, but at least he's *going* to go. They were going to visit Rene while they were there. Rene had called about thirty times, insisting that he meet with Joan and his niece and nephew. He said he didn't want to lose his family. He also wanted Joan to get Eleanor to change her mind, to take him back. The prospect of seeing her soon-to-be-ex-brother-in-law made Joan nervous. Though she rubbed her hands together vigorously, repeatedly, she could not warm them.

Diane was excited about the trip, though Joan took her to the city quite often. She'd taken her children to the Museum of Modern Art, Bergdorf's, Radio City, Rockefeller Center, Greenwich Village.

"Remember when we saw *Cats*?" Diane asked. "Meow!"

Jason rolled his heavy eyes: "Get serious."

On the bus, Jason and Diane were quiet, resigned. They had assured Joan that they didn't want to take the bus, that traveling by bus was a concept they were not comfortable with. Diane had stuttered, "But—I just don't—why can't we just—God, Mom, can't you drive us?"

The bus entered the Lincoln Tunnel. Jason's eyes were clamped shut. Joan wasn't sure what he was listening to on the headphones; she just hoped that the music wasn't too loud, that his ears would not be damaged permanently, although her own hearing had held up despite several Grateful Dead concerts back in the late seventies.

Joan eyed her daughter, who stared at the string of lights along the white tile of the tunnel. She cried: "We're in New York now!" when she saw the block lettering on the tile, which simply said, "New York," signaling that they had passed from one state to the next. Being in New York made her daughter feel "cooler somehow."

Years before, when her own mother had taken Charlotte, Eleanor, and herself to the city, Joan had worried that the mighty Hudson River would burst through the tunnel. And when her mother had told her that they were, in fact, far beneath the water, deep in the earth, she found that thought even more terrifying. She imagined reptilian creatures lurking just beyond the thin tunnel walls and wondered if they could break their way through.

Diane tugged at Joan's blouse. "Wouldn't it be unbelievable if the water started rushing through the tunnel? You know, like, the river breaks through and we're swept all the way to New York in a giant tidal wave." It amazed Joan that her daughter found this thought exciting. Diane's life—her room, for instance, full of pink and yellow Laura Ashley fabrics and cuddly stuffed bears—was so far removed from natural disaster that she could think disaster fun. Children, she decided, are so unafraid these days.

She herself had spent her childhood in fear: she dreaded not pleasing her parents—well, mostly her mother. Joan had been scared at Our Lady of Perpetual Mercy. What is sixty-two percent of one hundred? the nuns demanded. Why can't you do this? Why can't you get this? She feared diagramming sentences on the blackboard while the other children stared. Should "to the store" modify "went"? Is it nominative case? Objective case?

Joan sent Jason and Diane to nondenominational private schools. Her mother hadn't been happy about the decision. "Where will they get their religious training?" she'd asked.

"From Frederick and me, and from religious classes every Saturday morning."

"It's not the same."

Perhaps it wasn't. "You're messed up," Jason was telling his sister for seemingly no reason. Then he asked, "Where are we meeting Rene?"

"At the Hard Rock Cafe," said Joan. She had chosen the spot because she thought the children would enjoy it. She wanted Jason to warm to her, to like her. *If we could talk, really talk, she thought, then I could change him. He wouldn't steal. He would study. He would play football. He would have friends.*

Joan decided they would walk from the Port Authority Bus Terminal, on Fortieth and Ninth, all the way to Fifty-seventh and Seventh.

"God, there are so many homeless people!" Diane whined.

Jason said, "You are so incredibly surface-oriented."

But after five blocks, he too began to complain. "My

feet hurt. Can't we take a taxi? I always wanted to hail a taxi. It would be so cool." Soon, however, they were turning onto Fifty-seventh Street.

"There it is!" cried Diane. "There's the Cadillac coming out of the front of the Hard Rock. That's it, right, Mom?"

Inside, the children admired the high ceilings, the platinum records, the gilded guitars, the Buddha on the wall.

"I read about Buddha," Jason told his mother. "He was pretty cool."

"He didn't steal, Jason."

Jason rolled his eyes.

Soon Rene arrived. There was something unmistakable about his manner. She could see him gesture to the manager, bob his head up and down. His blond hair was perfectly cut, and its perfection made Joan angry. How badly could he feel if he took such care with his hair?

"There you are," he said. He shook Joan's hand, sighed as if to say, "What are you going to do?"

Diane kissed her uncle on the cheek. Jason removed his headphones.

"Rene, it's good to see you," Joan said.

For a moment, no one said a word. Joan wondered if agreeing to meet Rene had been a colossal mistake. She hadn't told Eleanor that she was going to see him, and yet she believed that their marriage could be rescued, that it would be a mistake for Eleanor to give up entirely on Rene. Marriage, thought Joan with some sadness, was a sacred commitment. You had to stick with it, no matter how horrible things got.

"I'm so glad to see you," Rene was telling her. "It's important not to cut off our friendship. I mean, I'm an uncle and now I might not be. The world is a sad place."

When Rene asked Diane, "So what grade are you in these days?" she smiled mischievously. One of her running jokes with Rene was to fool him about her age. "Fifth. No, sixth grade," she laughed, squirming in her seat. "No, seventh!" She twisted her napkin, ripped parts of it away.

Rene said, "Seventh grade?"

Jason said, "Third grade. And let's drop it."

Everyone ordered BLTs. When Rene ordered a Dos Equis, Jason ordered one, too. *He's got to embarrass me in public,* thought Joan.

"Just the one beer, please," she told the waitress, whose purple hair stood several inches above her skull, defying laws of nature Joan had always respected.

Nudging Rene, Diane asked, "Do you like her hair?" She didn't wait for a reply, and instead swept her own hair upward. "Isn't brown a boring color?"

Jason again told her, "You are so incredibly surface-oriented." Then he said, "Why can't I order a brewski?"

"You can't even drive yet," Joan said.

"But isn't that all the more reason to allow me to drink? I couldn't possibly be arrested for driving under the influence. Am I right? Can you refute me?"

"You're too young. Drinking is very bad. It alters your judgment."

"But Rene is drinking, isn't he? And you've been known to belt back a few. I think you're drinking too much these days myself. Not that anyone's remotely interested in anything I have to say. *I'm* the one with the so-called problems."

"Jason," said Joan, "why can't you ever just—just shut up!"

"How's Eleanor?" Rene suddenly asked.

Diane and Jason fell silent.

"She's fine. Up at the country house . . . thinking," Joan told him.

"So she's still considering—?"

"I think she's made up her mind."

"No change?"

Joan shook her head.

Rene continued to smile as they finished their BLTs and ate their gooey Mississippi mud pies, but Joan decided he had lost some of his vigor. He seemed a bit lost, didn't catch some of the conversation. "Oh, Hillside. Yes. The theater." Meanwhile, Jason opened six packets of Sweet & Low and poured the powder into the poppy-seed salad dressing.

"I expect that of Diane," Joan told him.

"Thanks, Mom!" her daughter said. "I wouldn't—"

"That's not what your mother meant," Rene said, taking her hand. "Sometimes people say things, do things, they don't mean at all. You hope you can take things back, but—"

"So," Jason said, "you cheated on my aunt and now she's dumping you."

"That's not quite accurate, Jason," Rene said.

"My aunt is giving you the heave-ho."

"Jason, you've got to learn to—to be quiet!" Joan shouted. And yet she realized that he had an uncanny way of stating the obvious. Jason didn't temper his remarks. And what he said was true: Eleanor was giving Rene the heave-ho. She said she'd never take him back.

Last week, Jason had also been blunt. "Do you love Mom anymore?" he had asked his father. But of course he was wrong on that count, wasn't he? She and Frederick still loved each other, they just didn't have sex. Still, she supposed, the signs of their passionless marriage were visible: she and Frederick didn't hold hands anymore. They didn't snuggle on the couch. They didn't laugh much.

After lunch, Joan asked Rene to accompany them to the Empire State Building, which she wanted the children to see. The four of them, Joan, Diane, Jason, and Rene, made their way toward Thirty-fourth and Fifth. At Fifty-third Street, however, Rene stopped. "I've got some work to do at home. I should get going." It was a windy day and his clothes rippled about his body.

"Are you okay?" Joan asked.

"I'm fine. I'm just a little upset. About Eleanor."

"You should think before you act," Jason said.

Rene shook his head. "I don't know about you, Jason." And then, "It's not so easy to be a grown-up."

"Well," Joan told her children, "it was nice to see Uncle Rene." As she said the words she felt strange. She hoped she wasn't going to have one of those attacks. She'd stumbled upon an article about panic attacks in one of her women's magazines, and had thought: ah-ha. To cure them, the article said, all you had to do was make sure you were breathing slowly and deeply. The article said to carry a brown paper bag at all times. If you breathed into the bag, you would be cured, but she hadn't bothered to bring one with her. She was a strong person and could summon her will to stop any future attack. "Rene's still your uncle, you know," she added. "Now how about the Empire State Building?"

Her children both sighed. "But what's the point of it?" Jason said. "We've been to the Sear's Tower in Chicago, which is much higher than the World Trade Center, which is higher than the Empire State Building. It isn't close to being the tallest building in the world anymore.

"Listen," he continued, pulling several Hard Rock Cafe matchbooks out of his pocket, then shoving them back in, "New York is full of places to go. How about the Museum of Indian Art? Would you go for that?"

"Oh, barf!" Diane said. "You're just trying to be cool, Jason."

"How about Chinatown?" he said.

"Oh, God," Diane winced. "We already saw so many Chinese people last year when we went to San Francisco!"

"Don't be ignorant," Jason told his sister.

They agreed to walk back to Trump Tower, a few blocks away. Inside, a man in a tuxedo was playing "A Foggy Day in Londontown" on a baby grand piano. Beyond him a waterfall fell down a hundred feet of marble.

"Donald Trump is a fool," Jason said.

Joan had had enough. "I insist we go to the Empire State Building," she said, so at last they trudged toward Thirty-fourth Street.

"This is taking *forever!*" Diane complained. "This is *horrible!*"

"You know," Jason said, "people who want to take taxis should be allowed to. It's very unfair to make people who would really like to take a taxi walk. Who even have the money for a taxi. Look," he said, pulling from his wallet several twenty-dollar bills. "I've got the money. I've even seen *Taxi Driver* on HBO."

"Where did you get that money?" Joan asked him.

He didn't answer.

But now the Empire State Building loomed so high that the three of them stopped on the sidewalk and craned their necks to catch the top. Joan tingled with its power, its ordered assurance.

"It *is* really tall," admitted Diane.

"But not the tallest building," Jason reminded her.

"Still," Joan said, "there is something about the Empire State Building."

"Like what?" Jason asked.

Joan was angry. Angry at her son for stealing, angry at herself for being a bad mother, angry that she was unable to hit him. And she wanted to hit him, to make him cry, though at that moment an old image crept into her mind. Why the image came into her mind she didn't know. No one knows these things. She saw Jason, a toddler, hair still blond, cheeks bright, frosting his name on a chocolate layer cake.

Abruptly, she stood against a granite building. Though the building had appeared smooth from a distance, it now felt quite battered to her. Jason and Diane stopped, too, staring quizzically at their mother. Her heart was pounding. Eyes closed, she took several long deep breaths, which seemed to steady her.

Just then, a Japanese tourist approached, asking, in halting English, "But where is this Empire State Building?" Without a word, Joan pointed up.

Joan, Jason, and Diane crowded into an elevator with about ten other tourists, none of whom were speaking English.

"Ready?" Joan asked, feeling slightly better, more at ease.

"Oui," Jason said.

Standing on the observation deck, Joan noted that the sun was like one more window atop one more building. Diane was giddy, skipping around and around. Even Jason seemed mildly impressed. "That's the Chrysler Building," he told his sister.

"No," Joan corrected. "That's the CitiBank building. Keep in mind, we're 102 stories above the ground. You can see the Atlantic Ocean, the Hudson River. See that big green square? That's Central Park. Over there, Jason, that pointed building, cut out like a diamond? *That's* the Chrysler Building. And there's the Trade Center down there—those two giant towers."

"I think it's neat," Diane said.

"It's okay," Jason said.

Joan wanted them to say more, something along the

lines of: There is nothing quite like the Empire State Building. This is a transcendent spiritual experience. She didn't know why she wanted them to say this. Maybe she wanted them to acknowledge that something was worth looking at for a half hour.

But now that her children had seen the view, they wanted to go.

"Already?" Joan asked.

The wind was gusting now. Diane tried to hold her hair down; Jason's T-shirt ballooned away from his body. Joan looked up, and the sun, which had been pale, nearly transparent, was now a rich yellow, stunning the grizzled sky. "Don't you want to stay and take it all in?" she asked. "Think of all the people who have lived down there. The people who are living there right now. Millions and millions of people, millions and millions of lives."

Gazing down from the observation deck, at the intersecting avenues, at the tiny yellow cabs, Joan saw that people were mere dots. They were nothing at all, of no consequence. One dot was indistinguishable from the next. Joan suddenly wanted to confess to her children that she might have had another baby, another dot. But she said nothing; telling them would serve no purpose. It would be cruel, useless, senseless. Plus, her children were uninterested in the past, for they had no pasts. For them, she decided, there was only the ever-changing present, parceled out to them in episodes.

"There's no point," Jason said, "in pretending to see important things from way up here that you don't bother to look at on the ground. I mean, do you ever really look at me? And Jesus, you and Dad are totally screwed up."

They were quiet on the bus going home. Jason seemed lost in his music. Diane, too, was subdued.

Joan's attention floated from the sound of a radio up

front, to the neck of the man in front of her. It was one of those thick red necks with white lines traversing it. She closed her eyes, and caught a bit of the music from Jason's earphones. Joan was surprised, shocked, really, that he was listening to James Taylor.

She wanted to nudge her son and exclaim, "James Taylor! You and I both like James Taylor!" But she left him alone. His eyes were half-closed, the lids shiny. As the bus wound its way through Hoboken, the skyline of Manhattan could be seen through the windows behind him. To see her son silhouetted against this magnificent backdrop made Joan hope he would do well, achieve something, be happy. But somehow that hope made her feel uneasy.

James Taylor's plaintive tenor voice reminded Joan of Stewart, of riding around Florence in his 66 Mustang with the top down. Thinking about Stewart, about what she'd had to do—it was something that happened to her every June. Her sadness was predictable, yet it always surprised her. She and Charlotte had gone into the city in June. Stewart had left her in June. He had gone to Vietnam in August.

She knew Stewart had survived the war; he had come back—not to her, of course, but he had come back, with a slight limp. He'd moved out to San Diego, and she had never heard from him again. She wondered what he was doing now. Was he married? Did he have children? Did he now live in New York, California, England? Beyond the dateline?

Was he now gray? Bald?

Stewart had had barely any hair on his chest when she'd known him, though now it would be thicker, curlier, like Frederick's. She sometimes wondered if he ever thought about her, about Charlotte. She'd be in line at the supermarket, leafing though a magazine, and it would just hit her. She hadn't realized that this would happen.

She'd gotten pregnant a few weeks before they had split up. Well, that was her luck. "No," he had said, crying, "I can't marry you. Yes, I know I said I would. But that was, well, when I loved you. If I could only love you, love anybody, love me . . . You have to understand. It isn't easy for me either." He said, "You're going to have it done in the city? Good. And Charlotte's taking you? Good. Good luck. I'm sorry. It's for the best."

Wasn't he already losing interest in her at the end? Sometimes he barely listened to her; he was always sucking on a joint, listening to the Grateful Dead, talking about nuclear fallout, revolution, lamenting the death of Bobby Kennedy.

"It's been two years, Stewart. He's dead. Life goes on."

"How can you forget so easily? You're fucked up."

He cried about his friend Lincoln. He called his friend Lincoln because, apparently, he'd looked like President Lincoln, Honest Abe. But Lincoln was killed in Vietnam before Joan had even met Stewart. Stewart was screwed up: he hadn't needed Vietnam to screw him up. After a while, all he ever did was cry; he barely ate anything, just cheese sandwiches. He grew transparent—veins and sinew—Joan imagined she could see through him, but she couldn't.

Now she caught the scent of peppermint gum (Diane was chewing it), and she relived another time: when Stewart was nineteen years old, when she was seventeen:

In her mind's eye, she sees her long black hair on his face. She sees them exchange gum from his mouth to hers, laughing. She feels him, his mouth on hers in his apartment. She has fringes on the bottom of her jeans. So does he.

He is fire and rain and the retainer he still wears at night. He is the whir of the helicopters, Danang.

She is pliant, full of nothing. She is Love's Baby Soft. Still he has pinned her to the bedroom wall and he loves her.

Joan sensed Frederick beside her, felt his foot. The voice of James Taylor—she heard it over and over again in her mind. "Ohh!" She wondered who was talking in their sleep, then realized it was her own voice in her mouth.

"Joan?" It was the voice of her husband. He said, "You're having a bad dream." It's the familiar one: she's taking sociology and she hasn't prepared for the test. The classroom is on the fifth floor; she cannot find the classroom.

Where is it? And where is he? Where's Stewart? But now she sees him ambling down the long hallway. She waves, but he doesn't seem to know her. He's with another girl, a beautiful girl. Charlotte. Her sister.

—4—
Back East

The trees were a blurry blob of green.

"Put those glasses back on!" Charlotte commanded Eleanor. "You don't have to impress me! You look fabulous!"

It struck Eleanor that only truly beautiful people have the confidence to tell other people how great they look—they don't need to hold back. Charlotte's hair was long and golden, the color, Eleanor decided, of Midwestern cornfields, or Catskill cornfields, why not Catskill cornfields? Charlotte said it cost $150 every four weeks to color her hair. Her green eyes, of course, were genuine, a soft blend of yellows and blues. Her eyes were stunning, but the hollows under her broad cheekbones defined her face.

Eleanor relished Charlotte's embrace. No one had hugged her, really hugged her so that her ribs ached, in nearly half a year. Eleanor thought it sad, and yet somehow hopeful, that people needed to be touched, that without the arms of family and lovers, one lost something, grew cold.

"No, it's you who's so beautiful," Eleanor said quietly, holding her glasses in her hands. She decided she wouldn't put them back on yet. She'd made up her eyes and wanted Charlotte to see her handiwork—the carefully shadowed lids layered in gradations of mauve. Though maybe mauve was the wrong color: the color of injured eyelids. And they were in fact injured. She'd been crying earlier. Rene had called.

"Please, Eleanor, we can work this out. You've got to take me back," he had said.

"You know I can't."

"I've made a terrible mistake. You know that."

"You've made a lot of mistakes."

"I don't even like Marlena."

"At the party, it looked like you liked her a lot!"

"I wish you understood how much I love you—it was just something that came over me. I made a terrible mistake, and I'm sorry."

Charlotte would be good for her—a happy diversion. "Nice place," her sister was saying, though Eleanor could tell she was far from convinced. Eleanor pulled at some weeds struggling through the cracks of the slate walkway, but the weeds were stronger than she was.

"Are you okay? You look so pale," said Charlotte, unpacking in the little bedroom at the back of the cabin. Charlotte had brought five bags. Eleanor wondered how long she planned to stay.

"I'm fine. It's just Rene is coming up in two weeks to hear my final verdict, though I keep telling him I'll never take him back."

"Why are you allowing him up here at all?"

"This is still his house."

"But you don't have to be here when he shows up."

"We have to talk about selling the place."

"If you take him back, you're crazy."

"Well, I'm not crazy. I don't love him anymore. Honestly."

Eleanor had always loved the solitude of the country

house, in the days when she and Rene felt like one person. Now Charlotte was here, to tell her what she should do, what Eleanor knew she would have to do. And knowing that she would be alone soon, that she would no longer wake up mornings with Rene beside her, made Eleanor catch her breath. Recovering, she said, "I'm so glad you're here, Charlotte. I'm making you a special lunch."

"Oh?" said Charlotte uneasily. "You're not the greatest— Never mind."

"I'm not the greatest what?"

"Well, you *are* the greatest person."

"I'm just not a good cook—that's what you mean to say."

"It's just that you really have to cook chicken all the way through. You can't serve it rare. I might have just had a virus, of course. That's possible."

While Charlotte showered, Eleanor prepared lunch. Their last Christmas together, Rene had bought Eleanor a cookbook. At first, she'd felt guilty. "I'm really sorry. I haven't been much of a cook. I'll do better."

"Christ, you really are my Miss Glass Half Empty. I buy you a cookbook, and you decide I think you're a failure."

Yesterday, she'd read it with breathless interest.

Smoked salmon tartare. Oh, God, no. Too difficult to make, and what is it? Crawfish regal. Eight puff-pastry shells! She turned the page. Chicken and sausage gumbo. Too many ingredients. Shrimp and crab bisque. Too complicated. Turkey breasts with lemon and capers. All right, she had decided. This I can make. Pound the meat between a heavy plastic sheet. Oh, God. Okay, I'll do it. Charlotte's always watching her weight, and turkey has a lot of protein. Now, a soup? Or a salad? Salad she could handle. Ripping lettuce and chopping celery and carrots were tasks she could manage. And to drink?—a good white wine, a California Chardonnay. Or wait, maybe a New York State wine. Yes, a New York State wine. She has California wines all the time.

Wait a minute: she's pregnant and can't drink! Okay, don't panic. Iced tea. No—caffeine. Oh, God. Ice water? It came to her: grape juice. Charlotte had loved it as a kid. Charlotte would pour grape juice in three crystal wineglasses: one for herself, one for Eleanor, and one for Joan. They would touch glasses, cry "Cheers!", and Charlotte would feign drunkenness. Once she pretended to be Eva Braun. (Sister Anne Marie had just covered World War II in History). "Oh, *mein Führer!*" Charlotte had cooed. "Von't you buy your little *liebschen* a Mercedes?"

Eleanor, choking back giggles, fist in her mouth, suspected that Eva Braun was no laughing matter.

Now, listening to the hiss of the shower, Eleanor dipped the turkey breasts into an egg wash and then into bread crumbs. She fried two pieces at a time in some olive oil. The cookbook said two or three minutes on each side. But what about salmonella? She didn't want Charlotte to get food poisoning again. She therefore cooked them for fifteen minutes on both sides.

Deglazing the pan with some chicken broth, Eleanor—a first-time deglazer—added the capers, parsley, finely chopped garlic, and lemon juice. She took the pâté out of the old Frigidaire (she and Rene—mostly Rene—had thought the Frigidaire more "country" than a modern model). She then sliced some fresh bread, baked by Mr. Lassiter of the Catskill Bakery. She poured grape juice into two fragile wineglasses. She'd made the salad in the morning, refrigerated it, and now, staring at the stiff greens, worried that the salad would be too cold.

Like she was. Too cold. All the time.

—

While Eleanor fretted about lunch, fine lines of warm water caressed Charlotte's body. She rubbed her stomach, which was still flat, thank God, though her breasts were heavy, sore, and, as she lathered up, she avoided touching them—it was just too painful. Charlotte wished she could wash that bloated feeling out of her. Shampooing her hair, she sang, "I'm gonna wash that bloat right out of my hair." She felt increasingly as though she had been injected with saline solution and, though she urinated constantly, she only seemed to grow more bloated.

Eleanor, on the other hand, looked reed thin, pale. Her baby sister looked like a heroine in a Victorian novel, stricken with consumption. Dealing with Rene, however, would drain anybody. Eleanor didn't know all there was to know about Rene—or did she?—and telling her, thought Charlotte, would only make her sister feel more insecure than she already did feel—which was definitely too insecure.

When she turned toward the showerhead, she saw one of his paintings above a plastic rack that held shampoo and a loofah sponge. It was a small painting, about five by seven inches. Most of Rene's paintings were immense; their size, thought Charlotte, corresponded closely, but did not match, the far-reaching dimensions of his ego. Beneath a sheet of foggy glass was a pattern of black squares layered over a multicolored background, though the background colors were dull—dull blue, dull yellow, dull green. Looking at the painting, she covered her body with her arms. It reminded her of last Thanksgiving.

Charlotte had flown back East and had gone to Nana's Jersey City house for Thanksgiving dinner. They'd all been there—her parents, Eleanor, and Rene, Joan (as cool to her as ever), her husband Frederick, plus Jason and Diane, whom Charlotte loved unconditionally.

Nana, who at ninety-two was finally losing her verve, said she had dinner under control. But her mother and Joan, ever domestic, kept watch in the kitchen, hovering over steaming pots.

Charlotte and Eleanor slipped outside. The rain had let up a little, yet the sky was heavy, undulating. The sisters huddled under one bright red umbrella. Their grandmother's tall row house had a very small backyard, like a vegetable patch. Through a few sparse trees, Charlotte could see the golden arches. "McBeautiful view," she told Eleanor. Then, "God, you look really pale."

"Really?"

"But, Christ, I shouldn't mention it to you, or you'll think you have some incurable disease. You really are ridiculous. I've got to cheer you up." So Charlotte sang, "There's a bathroom on the right," instead of "There's a bad moon out tonight," which she knew would make Eleanor laugh. And then they sang their infamous duet, the theme song from the old *Patty Duke Show*: "Meet Kathy who's lived most everywhere, from Zanzibar to Barclay Square," and, in a thin voice, Eleanor sang, "But Patty's only seen the sights a girl can see from Brooklyn Heights."

Together: "What a crazy pair."

Ad-libbing, Charlotte sang: "But they're *sis-ters,* incredible sisters, and you'll find . . . one's sleeping with directors and one thinks she has a heart condition . . . "

"You could lose your mind!" Joan shouted down, perfect timing, from the kitchen window.

Later, everyone sat down for a dinner of pot roast with gravy, carrots, peas, and mashed potatoes, plus some Italian Chianti that their father swore by. As Charlotte swallowed her peas, she felt someone kick her gently under the table.

Rene winked at her.

Meanwhile, intent on proving her latest Kennedy assassination theory, her mother Catherine said, "It was Lady Bird who arranged it."

"What kind of a bird is she?" asked Jason. "Is she a robin red breast? Are her breasts GIGANTIC?"

"Jason," said Joan.

"I never knew that Kennedy had Addison's disease," Eleanor interrupted. "Or about his back."

"Always the clinical eye," said Charlotte, who hoped Eleanor hadn't seen Rene giving her the eye—for he was giving her the eye. He continued to smile at her, a broad, white, even smile. *Is he aware he is smiling?* wondered Charlotte. She wanted to kick him—in the balls—but instead she shot him a deadly look. And yet her deadly look was false somehow—not sinister, not threatening enough. In response, he merely raised his left eyebrow, continued to smile—a reflex it seemed. Her look, she decided, had not shamed him, because, in her heart, for a minute, less than a minute, a moment, a second, she had wanted him. For a split second, she wanted to run her hands through his thick, shiny blond hair, to kiss his pouty mouth. It was only a moment; she was responding only to his beauty.

Still on the warpath, Catherine, her Kennedy-obsessed mother, was saying: "I'm telling you, it wasn't the Mafia or the FBI or Castro who did JFK in. It was Lady Bird. You don't think she wanted her husband to be president? She was obsessed with her gardening schemes. She wanted America beautified, and she wanted to take it over with her flowers. She was like a Panzer division, plastering pansies over every last patch!"

Soon it was time for cake and coffee. The women—always the women, Charlotte lamented—did duty in the kitchen, gathering cups and saucers, lighting the kettle.

Catherine cut a beautiful lemon cake that Nana had made from scratch. "I have a lot of trouble grating lemons anymore," Nana said, rubbing her blue knuckles.

At the table, Ed said, in a mock brogue, "Now isn't it wonderful that the womenfolk are doing the work today?"

Frederick said, "Actually, I love to cook."

Meanwhile, in the kitchen, Charlotte asked Eleanor, "Do you think I'm a terrible person?"

"What are you talking about?"

"Do you think I'm awful?"

"What did you do? I don't understand."

"She's always doing something," snapped Joan.

Ignoring them, Eleanor said, "If Rene and I have children—" She paused for a moment. "Well, if we decide to. If we can— Anyway, I hope all of this tradition doesn't get lost."

Charlotte scanned her grandmother's kitchen, at what Eleanor hoped would not be lost: the worn-down linoleum, the old casement window in the kitchen from which a sudden band of light appeared, tossing flickering patterns on the old linoleum. For a moment, Charlotte thought she caught a human shape—an arm, a torso—dancing in the grayish light, but it was just the trickery of the sun.

"Well," said Joan, placing a stack of dirty dinner plates on the counter, "I think it's important that my kids be around Nana. I mean, how much longer?"

The sisters shook their heads. Nana's house contained memorabilia of another age, and because these things were locked comfortably in the past, they were reassuring—the ancient wallpaper, lilacs lined up in neat vertical rows, the heavy black telephone, the dark bedrooms beckoning with brooches and empty hatboxes.

Eleanor carried a tray of sugar cookies into the dining

room. Joan set the table with cups, saucers, dessert plates, clean napkins, silver forks and spoons.

Charlotte was washing her hands at the sink when quickly, so quickly, making Charlotte wonder if it happened at all, someone came up to her from behind. She felt something wet and warm—a mouth—on her neck.

Turning, she said: "What's—?" And then, "You asshole!"

Rene said, "I didn't mean to startle you. Honestly. I didn't mean that in any, well, sexual way."

"You asshole!"

He offered her a little smile. "I'm sorry."

After lemon cake and coffee, Eleanor sat perched at Nana's old upright piano.

Diane squirmed, covering her face with her hands. "Are you gonna play that song you always play? 'Oh Danny boooooy?'"

"Are you up to it, Eleanor?" her father Ed said, winking. "Not too weak? Heart not skipping?"

"*Palpitating*, Dad," Charlotte corrected.

Eleanor said, "Dad, if I ever do have a heart attack, you're going to feel horrible, really guilty. I'm not a hypochondriac. Really." She raised her fingers over the keyboard. Everyone gathered around. Eleanor's fingers traced over the old yellow keys, and the melody that issued forth was so lovely, so incandescent, that Charlotte caught her breath. Here was her wonderful sister playing so beautifully, while for a moment, Charlotte had fantasized about sleeping with her husband. What a terrible person she was! She caught sight of her grandmother's softly etched profile, and she appeared as more a vision than a person; she might vanish in a kitchen breeze. She thought she might cry, but she held in her tears. Joan's chin shook. Her mother sobbed. Rene, alone, appeared aloof. He stared out the window at an abandoned factory. Charlotte decided once and for all that she hated him.

Far from the old gray city on the Hudson, Charlotte wiped the condensation from Eleanor's bathroom mirror. She opened the window and heard the squall of birds, the hum of a tractor in the distance.

Eleanor had not missed the fact that Charlotte had some difficulty swallowing her turkey breasts and capers, but her sister, for once, hadn't complained, though Eleanor apologized again and again. After lunch, the sisters took a slow walk around the pond. Charlotte broke into a James Taylor song, a song about the world spinning around. Though Eleanor enjoyed listening to her sister sing—her voice was a clear soprano—she dreaded it, too, because Charlotte was never content to sing alone. Still, Eleanor jumped in, though she was unsure of the words. She hesitated before asking, "When will you see Ian? Will you see him? Sorry, if you don't want to talk about it—"

Charlotte tore a tiny branch off a birch tree. "I think he wants me to get an abortion."

"Oh?"

"He didn't actually say it. Forget it." Charlotte picked up a stone and hurled it toward the pond, but it fell short. "Enough about me. God, I can't believe I said that. Anyway, who are you sleeping with?"

"Sleeping with? Me? No—I'm not ready for that."

Charlotte sighed. "Time's awastin', kiddo. I'm nearly forty. That you know, but don't tell anyone. *Remember, I'm thirty-two.* Anyway, I wasn't even dating anyone. I mean, there comes a time when you just say, 'Go ahead, make me pregnant.' Only you don't *say* that, or the guy will run off to Burma. Wait a minute. I've got a joke for you. Do you know how to get rid of your cockroaches?"

"I don't have cockroaches."

"It's a joke, stupid. Ask them for a commitment, the cockroaches."

When she was with Charlotte, Eleanor felt humorless, inept.

Charlotte went on, "I knew I was ovulating. I'm not sure I do ovulate every month anymore, so I was lucky. Still, I wake up in the middle of the night and think: what the hell have I done? I mean, I want to make it as an actress."

"You will," Eleanor said, plucking three dandelions from the brush and tossing them into the pond. The dandelions created gentle, rhythmic circles. The pond accepted flowers, rocks, frogs. Eleanor hoped that Charlotte would accept the baby, motherhood. All her life, Charlotte had been torn, unsettled.

First she was going to be a beautician, but Catherine had nixed that. No daughter of hers, especially the most beautiful one, was going to get varicose veins from standing ten hours a day for a few dollars an hour. Next, Charlotte was going to become a musician, a guitarist with a rock band, but she never practiced. Then, at Glassboro State College in central New Jersey, she'd studied drama. "This is what I was born for!" she'd declared. Drawn by the promise of Hollywood, she moved out to California when she was twenty-two. Still, show business was tough, and she ended up working as a secretary for a long time, typing letters for the Union Pacific Oil Company.

Charlotte sat cross-legged at the edge of the pond and dipped her hands in the water. Eleanor warned, "Don't! Bacteria! Germs!"

"You're scared of the *pond?* I'd be afraid of prowlers. How far are you off the Black Lake Road?"

"Just a quarter of a mile." Eleanor smiled, though she

did indeed worry about prowlers, about strange men with bad teeth who'd tie her to the bed, rape her. She worried about everything—about work, about the job she had probably lost, about Rene (too much about Rene), about not pleasing her parents—though she didn't know anyone who wasn't concerned about pleasing their parents, whether they admitted it or not. Eleanor worried that people didn't like her. Maybe they just pretended? She worried, too, when her hair didn't turn out right, when she got those palpitations, though four doctors had told her there was nothing wrong with her. She worried that she was losing too much weight, and insisted her doctor do an AIDS test, but it had come up negative.

"Really, I don't have it?" she had asked.

"I'm pleased to report that you do not have the AIDS virus."

"Are you sure?"

"Positive. I mean the test was negative."

"Do you ever worry about supernatural beings descending upon Tylerville?" Charlotte asked her now. "Lions and tigers and bears."

"Oh my! Remember how you used to pretend you were an alien, just to scare me to death?"

Charlotte's eyes widened. *"Pretend?"*

When the sun was gone, the sisters sat on wide Adirondack chairs at the edge of the pond. The moon cast ripples of light on the water. The cicadas droned in the dark trees. "There's the Big Dipper," said Eleanor, pointing at the huge sky.

"It's like being at the planetarium. I could live here, you know, it's so peaceful. I wish we didn't have to go to New Jersey this weekend. Why can't Mom and Dad and everyone come up here?"

"They hate to leave Florence."

"Oh, sure, Florence is so lovely, the Paris of New Jersey."

"They always find something wrong with my house, anyway," said Eleanor. "Why don't I have wall-to-wall carpeting? Why don't Rene and I spring for a modern bathtub—instead of the ancient one."

"Does Mom say anything to you about my—pregnancy. About my being a lousy Catholic?"

"No, not really."

"Come on."

"Just that she hopes you'll get married, to the father of the baby."

"She can forget that."

At midnight, Charlotte was doing sit-ups on the wide-planked pine floor.

"Your stomach, it *will* grow," said Eleanor. "Why don't you just rest? It's been a long day."

Ignoring her, Charlotte groaned, touched an elbow to her knee. "I suppose everyone knows . . . I'm pregnant."

"Did you speak to Joan?"

"She. . . called."

"You'll get to see her again on Saturday. That'll be great." Eleanor, however, knew that Joan and Charlotte were not on the best of terms, but she hoped they one day would be. After all, they *had* been so close for many years. They both loved John better than Paul, George, or Ringo. They wore the same shade of pale lipstick. They played Barbie and Ken together for hours. Charlotte proofed Joan's book reports. She drilled her with flash cards. "What's seven times nine, Joannie? Come on, you can do it." One day, Joan packed two pairs of culottes, two T-shirts, a polka-dot bathing suit, and several pairs of cotton underwear in a 45 record case. "I'm running away," she said. "With Miranda." Miranda was her imaginary friend, whom no one believed in.

"Suit yourself," her mother said.

Eleanor couldn't see Miranda. "I wish I could. Maybe it's something with my eyes."

Charlotte believed in Miranda. Or said she did.

But back in the seventies, for two years, Charlotte and Joan did not utter one word to each other. Catherine had been incredulous; what kind of daughters had she raised who would not speak to each other? They'd stopped speaking when Charlotte started to see Joan's old boyfriend, Stewart. Joan and Stewart had been broken up maybe a week when Charlotte was suddenly spending time with him, though Charlotte insisted he was only a friend. Eleanor had spoken to both of her sisters, tried to get them to reconcile. *Whatever's happened, it can't be that bad. Talk to her, Charlotte. Talk to her, Joan.* They made up, an uneasy reconciliation, when Joan found Frederick.

"Years ago, a terrible thing happened. Really terrible," Charlotte told her.

"What do you mean?"

"Nothing really. Stewart's out of our lives. Joan is still my sister. These things happen in families. Don't they? Anyway, what's today's secret? We used to play that game as kids, remember? You'd tell me something you thought I didn't know about you. I used to make you come up with something or someone, or I'd make you smell my feet."

"I hoped I'd just imagined that."

"I don't know why I was so mean growing up. I was, wasn't I?"

"I don't know. You hit Tommy Kroner over the head with your book bag when he stole the bra I'd just bought at Newberry's. You were mad because he spray painted 28AA on the side of the school. I was more than a bit depressed." Eleanor thought for a minute. "You know, come to think of it, I do have a secret. About two years ago, I thought I was pregnant."

Charlotte stopped exercising. "Really?"

"I haven't thought about it in a while. I was late, about six days late, so I sent Rene out to get one of those pregnancy tests. We couldn't figure out if the test result was pink enough. You know, is the answer white or pink? It was sort of in between."

"That's you. Almost pregnant."

"I wanted him to get another test, but he said we should wait and go to the doctor. But I went out and got another kit. Anyway, I saw a plus sign appear—that means you're pregnant. I swear a plus sign appeared, but when Rene finally looked, the test had turned black."

Charlotte hummed the theme to the *Twilight Zone*. "DA-da-da-da, DA-da-da-da."

"Rene decided that I was pregnant. He even came up with some names—Leonardo, Vincent, Pablo. Famous male artist names."

"He would."

"I was sitting there watching a movie on TV, *Monkey Business*, with Marilyn Monroe. It's funny that I still remember the name of the movie."

"Monkey business—I guess that's how you got pregnant. Or sorry, didn't."

"For the first time in my life, I felt voluptuous—like Marilyn. I'd done something amazing. But then I started to get bad cramps. Really bad."

"Jesus, are you crying? You might not have even been pregnant."

"Maybe I wasn't. Anyway, I think there's something wrong with me. Scarred tubes or something."

"You don't know that. You read too much. You're a hypochondriac."

"I started to bleed, but not like I usually do. I had horrible pains . . ." Shyly, Eleanor placed her hand on her sister's belly. "You're lucky," she told her.

"Am I?"

The next morning, Charlotte stood ankle deep in the pond, wearing an unusually modest one-piece bathing suit—a concession, Eleanor supposed, to pregnancy. Charlotte liked bikinis, and everyone, men actually, liked Charlotte in bikinis.

"I really don't think you should swim," Eleanor called out to her. "It's only June."

Charlotte said, "What do you mean it's only June? I want to swim! It's hot!"

Eleanor warned Charlotte about giardia, a parasite infection that people can get from swimming in mountain lakes. She herself had had it two years ago. The diarrhea had seemed endless, and her nausea had been palpable; everything had tasted like metal. Rene had been kind to her—that she had to admit.

The first day, he guided her to the bathroom, soothed her brow with a cool washcloth, bought her magazines, even made her chicken soup, which she could not stomach. Finally, he had called a local doctor, who prescribed medicine that had worked in less than a day. But pregnant women, Eleanor told Charlotte, couldn't take the medication.

Charlotte glided through the water. Every few minutes, she'd sink beneath the surface, then her glistening head would break through.

Eleanor shouted out to her: "It's a parasite infection, carried by beavers, and the beavers carry the infection into the water and humans can get it! You're *pregnant*, Charlotte."

Charlotte shouted back: "What—is this a third-world country or something?"

"I don't want you to get sick. Really, be careful."

Before she went under again, Charlotte called, "You were always so careful, Eleanor."

The next day, Eleanor and Charlotte drove into town. "This car is ancient," said Charlotte. "How old is this thing?"

Eleanor gripped the wheel. "About twenty years old."

"I wouldn't be caught dead in an army green Valiant in LA. But I guess people in LA care more about appearances. Which reminds me. I'm going to give you a makeover."

"I don't want a makeover."

"Well, don't get me wrong, but you could look better. Your hair—well, it's a mess."

Arriving in town, the sisters strolled Main Street. A refreshing breeze tousled the American flag, which flew high over the village green. The weather here was nothing at all like Los Angeles, thought Charlotte. Her eyes weren't bloodshot. She could breathe. "So this is it—this is Tylerville."

"Doesn't seem like much," Eleanor said. "But I like it."

Charlotte thought it was perfect. On one side of the street were Reynold's Hardware, Marty's Bar and Grill, and the brick-faced Tylerville Post Office. On the other side, Skinner's Drugs, the First Methodist Church—a whitewashed building with a dainty spire—plus Harper's General Store and Amanda's Diner.

"Oh, look at that," said Charlotte, pointing down the street. "The Sunshine Hall Library—what a great name. I want to take out a book."

Inside, two elderly white-haired women sat at an old card table.

"Vacationing here?" asked the smaller woman.

"Well, I have a house," Eleanor said, "down the road. Only I've never been in here." The women stared. "I always meant to, but we, my husband and I, well, anyway, I always brought books from the city."

"New York City," the small white-haired woman explained. "Now," she continued, "what kind of book are you looking for?"

Charlotte said, "I don't know exactly."

"How about a book about pregnancy?" said Eleanor.

"Oh, isn't that wonderful," said the larger woman. "Just wonderful." She stared at the sisters. "Which one of you is pregnant?"

Charlotte mumbled, "Me."

The smaller woman stared at Charlotte's belly. "Doesn't look like she's pregnant at all."

"I am, though."

The woman directed the sisters toward the back wall. Charlotte spotted a copy of *Pride and Prejudice* on an old oak table. "Damn that Ian," she muttered. The tiny woman ran her crooked index finger along the spines of a row of books. "Here we are." She handed Charlotte a thick copy of *Motherhood: Everything You Need to Know*. On the cover, a woman in a blue knit sweater held a well-nourished infant. The woman's cheeks were as rosy and full as the baby's. Behind mother and child, stood a tall dark-haired man, wearing a conspicuous gold wedding band. His right hand rested on the woman's shoulder.

"I don't want the book," said Charlotte.

Flipping through it, Eleanor said, "It looks very good, Charlotte. Very thorough."

"I don't want it."

"No?" said Eleanor, rummaging through the stacks. "Let's see, there must be something else. Here, what

about this. *Single Parenthood: The First Twelve Months.*
Or how about this one: *How to Coach—*"

"How to coach what?" said Charlotte, hands on hips.

"Never mind. It doesn't look like a very good book."

"What—you said something about a coach."

"This book is for the coach, of the pregnant woman."

"I don't have a coach." She did have Seldon, but she craved sympathy.

"I'll be your coach."

"You're going to move to Los Angeles?"

"How about a nice mystery?" offered the other woman.

"Let's just pretend I'm not pregnant," said Charlotte.

Back at the house, Eleanor set up her easel near the apple trees. Not that she wanted to be away from Charlotte—or yes, admit it, she needed a break from Charlotte and her blunt—rude?—comments: "Your hair is a mess; you're a nut if you take back Rene; I know all about Rene." (And how did she know all about Rene anyway?) Paintbrush in hand, Eleanor stared at the sky, which, though blue, was filled with clouds. One of the clouds looked like a chicken. She could make out the beak, the scratchy legs. Not a poetic vision, she decided, spotting chickens in the clouds. Of course, she was a chicken; she was afraid of living without Rene, bad as he was.

She gazed at a blank canvas, propped up on her easel. It was a very good easel, made of oak. Rene said it was important to have good equipment. Rene said knowing your subject matter was more important, however. She knew he would frown at the idea of her painting clouds.

Clouds? she could hear him say. Well, okay, clouds. But are you going to paint clouds *as they really are?* Rene insisted that painting things as they really were, photo-graphic painting, was perhaps a waste of her time. Don't do what a camera can do better, he often told her.

Still, she stared at the sky, at—she counted—one, two, three, four, five, six, seven, eight, compact clouds, one of which looked like a chicken. The cloud next to the chicken cloud was strikingly beautiful—the quintessential cloud—billowy, crested with a yellow-white light, soft gray on its belly.

She grabbed a pencil and lightly outlined the clouds. Next, she considered the color of her sky: blue. She frowned. Why not violet? Or red? Or green? Why not? She glanced again at the sky and the sky was blue, and she would not betray its blueness. There was truth in that blue. So she mixed two curls of Prussian blue with one curl of titanium white on her palette and applied the mix-ture to the canvas with a palette knife. Rough clots of color appeared. She tried to smooth the clumps with the knife, but the result was a canvas buttered with blue streaks. She wasn't much good with a palette knife, so she tried a large brush, which worked nicely. She swirled soft blue around the pencil outlines of the clouds, and when she was done, she sighed. Should she paint in the clouds?—they were already white. But the clouds were flat; they had no depth, so she mixed titanium white and a touch of yellow ocher light, and just a dab of thalo crimson, and went to work on the beautiful cloud.

She was so pleased with the result that she shouted, "Charlotte! Take a look! Charlotte!"

A few minutes later, Charlotte stumbled out of the house, rubbing her eyes. "I was sleeping, you know." Then, peering closer at the canvas, she said, "Clouds in the sky."

"What do you think?"

"Decent."

"Does it give you a sense of the real sky?"

"Yes."

"Really?"

"Right off, I knew it was the sky."

"Rene says I'm not much of an artist. I mean, he doesn't say it outright. But I know."

"Well, Rene is a jerk."

"Still, I'm not much of an artist."

Charlotte sighed. "No."

"But I like to paint. Why do I like to do something that I'm so terrible at?"

"If you enjoy it, it doesn't matter."

Eleanor asked, "Is acting very difficult for you? You make it look easy."

"Sometimes I hate it," she said, yawning. "I think: I'll never get these lines straight. I'm so wooden sometimes. And I'm getting old for acting, a bit long in the tooth. When we were filming *Pride,* I thought for sure Ian would fire me. I was awful until the second week. I kept forgetting my lines, screwing up my accent. I was so nervous. Now I'm so . . . tired. I could sleep for a million years."

"That's supposed to happen. You should have taken out that pregnancy book."

"A book isn't going to solve my problems. And I'm aware of the long parade of pregnancy symptoms: fatigue, bloating, varicose veins, palpitations, nausea. Nausea— I'm just beginning with that one. I could throw up right this minute. But I'm not going to think about it. Come, let's do that makeover."

Charlotte all but dragged Eleanor into the house.

"You know, I'm allergic to a lot of cosmetics, so I'm not sure about this," said Eleanor, sitting down at the kitchen table.

Charlotte unscrewed a jar of cold cream and smothered Eleanor's face with it. Then she tissued the cream off. "Your skin can breathe now."

"I hope I'm not going to have a reaction to any of this."

Charlotte fingered Eleanor's hair. "You could use a deep-down conditioner. Now, let's see what we have here." Charlotte stepped back and considered her sister's face. Her features were very small. Her eyes were very blue. She had quite a few freckles—and those dark circles. Charlotte would banish those circles.

"Do you wear foundation?"

"No."

"You should."

Charlotte slathered Eleanor's face with an ivory beige lotion and, according to Charlotte, her freckles vanished. Then, with her little finger, Charlotte dabbed concealer cream over her sister's circles. Charlotte said, "How many hours do you sleep a night?"

"I sleep enough."

"How many hours?"

"Eight. Maybe less."

"Six?"

"Maybe less."

"You've got to get over him," Charlotte said, stroking her sister's eyelids with a soft brown shadow.

"Well, it's not as easy as that. He could be very kind, and generous, and he's very good-looking."

"He is good-looking, I'll give you that. But that's not enough."

"I know he's got a problem, but I still love him. Am I a masochist? Anyway, I can't sleep."

With a small brush, Charlotte painted Eleanor's lips a glossy pink. "Now you look almost as good as he does."

Eleanor pressed her lips together. "Did he ever—?" she began.

"Ever what?"

". . . Nothing."

"Did he ever what?"

"Well, you're very beautiful."

"So?"

"Did Rene ever?"

"Of course not! And if he did, which he didn't, I'd never be interested. For a minute! For a split second! And I can't believe you asked me that question!"

—5—
Discoveries

Eleanor and Charlotte waited for Aaron Silverman, the farmer who lived next door, to come over and help Eleanor build a small water garden. Eleanor said Aaron's family owned the Silverman Hotel.

"This is how I picture it," Eleanor told Charlotte, "a cool black pool with soothing, colorful flowers: lilies, irises, water hyacinth, parrot's feathers. Wouldn't it be wonderful? I want to build something, to do something physical. Maybe it would help me sleep."

Charlotte didn't understand how Eleanor knew the names of all those flowers. Had she missed something in the fourth grade? Had a case of the mumps wiped out her knowledge of the plant kingdom? Charlotte thought building the water garden was a good idea, too, though she wouldn't join in the work. Eleanor wouldn't want her to.

In fact, Eleanor had told Charlotte that she didn't think she was taking care of herself, complaining that Charlotte didn't take her vitamins. Eleanor said that drinking white wine, even just a little, was irresponsible. Hadn't Charlotte ever heard of fetal alcohol syndrome? Charlotte decided that for Eleanor to actually call her irresponsible was like her calling Eleanor a psychotic serial killer.

Charlotte watched her sister lug two large shovels outside. Tucked under her arm was the plan for building the water garden, which Eleanor had clipped from a magazine. Sitting on the grass, sipping her coffee, she offered her face to the sun, which, though strong, was still low. The steam from the coffee tickled her nose.

Eleanor called, "Are you drinking the decaf?"

"Of course."

"Really? It's the decaf?"

"I can't help myself. I need a jolt of java."

"You're a hard person to handle."

Eleanor, as always, was wearing a large, tightly woven straw hat to protect her from the sun. She claimed she was allergic to sunscreen, but Charlotte wondered if she really was, or if she merely was afraid that she was. "Do you remember the time, the golden era, before we knew the sun could give you cancer?" asked Charlotte.

"You were the one who told me. I was lying on the beach at the Jersey shore and I saw a shadow, which was you. You told me, 'This day on the beach will kill you.' "

"I was only kidding."

Eleanor looked very sad, very small today, Charlotte thought. Her hat was too big for her body. There was no substance to her. She had always been thin, but she seemed thinner than ever. She barely ate, a few bites, a shrug. Rene was ruining her sister's health.

Shielding her eyes from the sun, Charlotte saw a man bounding up the dirt path. "Is that him? Aaron?" He wore blue jeans and a black T-shirt, which, as he drew closer, Charlotte saw spelled out, "Woodstock," in bright yellow letters. The massive 1969 music festival, Charlotte knew, had been held just four miles away. Although people generally believed that the festival was held in Woodstock, New York, an hour and a half northeast, it was moved at the last minute to Yasgar's Farm, near Tylerville.

"That's him," Eleanor said.

As Aaron approached, Charlotte could make out his delicately boned face, framed by dark curly hair. His eyes were dark blue and he was, thought Charlotte, better-looking than she thought a Catskill farmer would be. She'd learned about small gene pools and their ugly consequences in her Introduction to Genetics class at Glassboro State College. Aaron shifted back and forth on his mud-encrusted work boots, though it hadn't rained since her arrival.

"How are you?" he asked over and over again. He didn't appear to listen for the answer. He seemed nervously happy and smelled faintly of after-shave.

"So you're not involved in the hotel?" Charlotte said, shaking his warm, rough hand.

He had been, he said, but wasn't anymore. His great-grandfather had originally been a farmer here before he'd founded the Silverman Hotel. "I guess I've gone back to what the family first had in mind. Though I worked at the hotel until I was twenty-five, waiting tables. I also had to dance with the ugly girls." He hesitated. "Sorry. That's chauvinistic. Ugly girls. I didn't mean that. Or," he laughed, "maybe I did. I don't know." He fumbled with his pockets.

"You know," said Eleanor, "I sat next to a woman on the train who was going to the Silverman. She thinks it's terrible, how the hotels are falling apart. Not that the Silverman is, I don't mean it that way."

"Well, it is. The roof leaks. The floors are uneven. The showers are rusting out. The hotel is always three-quarters empty, except in the summer. My brother, Micah, runs the place. He's trying to, as he says, 'Gentify' the Silverman. That's what he calls it. He says he's going to put mayonnaise on the tables. He thinks if he can get the Gentiles to come up, everything will turn around. I'm sure my grandfather is having a conniption in his grave."

Eleanor and Aaron decided to dig the garden about fifty feet from the house, near a group of limestone boulders. Eleanor wanted the garden placed just beyond the largest boulder, a huge piece of naturally sculpted rock that formed a rock-shelter, a small cave of sorts, about five feet wide at its mouth, gradually narrowing out at the rear; the vaulted ceiling was about six feet high. They decided to dig the water garden under the shelter overhang.

"Wouldn't it be great to relax, sheltered from the rain, and admire the flowers?" Eleanor said. "I think I could unwind then. I'm so uptight lately."

"Lately?" Charlotte said. "Eleanor, you've always been uptight. Aaron, she used to cry when she got a B plus. 'I know I failed the geometry test. I know I failed.' And then she'd get an eighty-eight and be really upset. Honestly, Eleanor is the kind of person who never really believes she'll break her way through stop-and-go traffic."

"That's not true. I'm not that uptight. Am I? Do you honestly think I'm that uptight?"

"What do you think, Aaron?" Charlotte asked.

"Oh, I don't know," he said, staring at the ground. "I don't know her that well. I mean, I know her. I know you, Eleanor. But not, you know, real well. Not real well. I suppose Eleanor seems nervous, but she seems relaxed, too."

Eleanor adjusted her wide-brimmed straw hat.

"At least when you're sitting in the rock-shelter admiring your water garden," Charlotte told her, "you can get rid of *that*."

"Maybe I should wear it just in case. I think you can get burned in the shade, too."

"You *can* get burned in the shade," said Aaron, who was a bit sunburned.

Eleanor and Aaron began to dig. It had grown quite hot—a haze was stalled at the line of mountains to the north—and after two hours, they managed to dig down only about six inches. They kept coming upon pebbles and smooth round rocks. They even dug up an old Coca-Cola bottle, the old green glass kind, with the fancy Coca-Cola script. All the while, Charlotte kept thinking that there had to be a machine that could do this. A steam shovel, maybe. There had to be an easier way. Eleanor's back was really going to be in bad shape. Eleanor often complained of sciatic nerve pain radiating down her left side.

Charlotte watched them plunge their shovels into the dirt, ripping away the grass, casting away pebbles and stones. She felt a bit guilty watching them huff and puff, so she went inside for a while. Out of sight, out of mind. Sitting at the kitchen table, she ate an orange, slowly spitting the seeds into her hand. She was eating something decent, something healthy for once; she patted her belly with a sticky hand. Eleanor and Aaron were busy digging, talking softly. Above them the sky was blue, a few flat clouds swirled; from the window, Charlotte noticed the residue of a jet, a long thin white line, which reminded her of California, of her real life.

She knew that reliable Seldon would take good care of her cat, take the mail in. She sucked the last of the juice from her fingers, then picked up Eleanor's phone to retrieve her messages. Thank God it was a push button; she half expected a rotary up here in the boonies. The first message was from her agent, telling her she didn't get the part. "You sick or something?" The next call was from her mother: "Sorry I missed you! I thought I'd catch you before your flight! I'll see you over the weekend! I'm doing so well with my Japanese! Listen to this: (slowly, deliberately) *kono sebiro o osoide dorai kuri-*

iningu shite hoshii no desu—I want this suit dry-cleaned in a hurry!"

Then there was a beep, and the voice of Ian O'Toole. "I've been thinking," he said. "We need to talk. Please give a ring back." The way he put it made her think of returning a wedding ring, and that upset her, for there had been no ring. Although, to be fair, she didn't really think she wanted Ian, at least not on a permanent basis. She'd wanted his sperm, to take her last chance, to have a baby.

He once said to her, as they strolled the Roman ruins at Bath, "Obviously I'm a failure at marriage. Won't do it again. Not four times." The ruddiness of his face had not been reflected in the dark pool of the Roman bath. Only his outline—like an emperor on a coin—had been copied in the water, and this outline could have been any man's.

In her mind's eye, she imagined the Roman men who had bathed at this spot; she called up the images of the women who had loved them, women with long black curls, carefully arranged robes. Her gaze followed the jagged, ancient columns rising from the pool, up to street level, up to the pedestrians, to the medieval stone Cathedral of Bath. Ian had told her that the magnificent cathedral, grander than the Roman baths—though not nearly as mysterious—had been built by thirteenth-century Christians more than a thousand years after the Romans had quit the dark mists of Britannia.

The Romans and the Christians—they'd both prayed for love, for luck. The Romans had tossed little fragments of stone into the bath, stones inscribed with messages such as, "Do not let the evil Levidia take my husband." Two thousand years later, the bath was full of bacteria. Now people were not to put their hands into the water.

Two thousand years later, she was pregnant and alone—what on earth had she done? Charlotte felt her eyes moisten. The taste of orange bitter in her mouth, she held her throat tight. She hated to cry, to lose control, to show she cared about things too much. If you showed you cared too much, the gods would take action. She could hear the faint voices of her sister and Aaron. Eleanor was thanking him again and again; Aaron was saying not to worry, he didn't mind. The two were working so hard, complaining so little, that Charlotte decided to make them some homemade iced tea.

When she came back out, balancing a pitcher and three glasses in her hands, Eleanor and Aaron were breathing hard with open mouths. They had dug down another foot.

"Take a break," Charlotte said. Aaron took a long gulp of tea, then placed his glass on the small picnic bench they had dragged over.

Eleanor told Aaron, "I want to show you something. Pick up the glass."

"What?"

"Please, just pick it up. I'd like to show you something. Do you see that wet mark from the glass?"

"Yes . . ." he said slowly.

"The Italians have a word for that mark: *culacino.* Isn't that interesting? I mean, we don't have a word for it."

Aaron wiped his forehead. "I suppose you're right. That is interesting. Yes, very interesting."

Softly she added, "I have no word for how I feel. Sad, mad, shaky: no one word will do it."

There was an uneasy silence and then Charlotte, unable to curb her need to shock, said, "She also likes to study the sexual behavior of neighbors."

"I do not!"

"Really?" asked Aaron, shyly smiling. "Really? No, no, I'm sure she doesn't."

Charlotte wondered whether or not Aaron was married, so she simply asked him.

"No," he said, catching his breath. "It's no big deal. Well, really, it was a big deal. Yes, I guess it was. My wife left me about two years ago."

She waited for him to say something more, but he didn't. "Well, tell me about the family hotel," she said. "You know, how it got started. In case I play a hotel owner's wife."

"Oh, you're the actress. Right."

How, Charlotte wondered, could people forget such interesting things?

"Well," he began, "my great-grandfather—they called him Aaron the Jew—"

"That's terrible," Charlotte said. "I mean, that's like saying Mickey the Mick."

"My great-grandfather," Aaron went on, laughing. "I guess you could say he turned his back on the Lower East Side. He'd had it with being a peddler. I mean, who would want to peddle?"

Charlotte imagined a hot city sidewalk, a bearded man in black pushing a cart that clanged with metal: old cans, heavy irons. Meanwhile, Aaron was saying, "In Russia—Minsk, I think, or Pinsk?—he'd been a farmer and the Lower East Side tenements depressed him. Of course, Russia had been worse, much worse. They say he didn't really talk about it much, but his mother had been raped, Cossacks, the whole deal. It must have been a terrible life, though they say that my great-grandfather was the most cheerful person, a kind person, in spite of everything."

Charlotte smiled at him. He smiled back. He was really very good-looking.

He continued, "Anyway, a new czar came along, Alexander III. He asked his religious adviser to come up with a solution to the so-called Jewish problem. His answer: one-third conversion, one-third emigration, and one-third starvation. My grandfather opted for emigration. Smart choice."

Aaron gulped some tea, wiped his mouth. "At first, the Lower East Side was the promised land. No Cossacks, no raids. Still, for all Russia had hated him, he'd loved Russia. He missed the fields, the trees, his father's farm."

Aaron told them how his great-grandfather had heard you could buy a farm in the Catskills for a few dollars, so he packed his wife, his four sons, one awful oil painting—though how he knew it was awful she didn't know—and an ornate cherry bureau, into a wagon and made another fresh start. But the soil was bad. Too many rocks. Here Aaron smiled, picking up a rock. "See what I mean?"

Poking the ground with his muddy boot, Aaron said, "The growing season here isn't that good. Too short. The only thing that grows well here is corn. But everybody grows it and the price goes down. Anyway, that's my problem. Though my great-grandfather's bills were piling up, he really believed he'd found his true home. He compared the Catskills to the mountains around Jerusalem— not that he'd ever seen the mountains around Jerusalem. At any rate, he wanted to show his land to his Lower East Side relatives. I still have a letter he sent to my great-aunt. It says, 'Live a little.' So she came—her family and friends came. Soon my great-grandfather was earning a little money—not from the farm, but from the money he charged people to stay at his farmhouse."

"This is really something," Charlotte told him. "You actually know the history of your family. What do we know about ours, Eleanor? We used to ask our grandfather, who was born in Brooklyn, where *his* father had come from. Dad said he'd come from Belfast, but

Grandpa insisted his family came from Belgium. He was always putting us on. Anyway, Grandpa thought it was odd that we wanted to know about the past."

Aaron, apparently, didn't think it was odd—he was tied to his past. "What had been a seven-room farmhouse," he said, "evolved into the Silverman Hotel. In the fifties, a woman would wear a different outfit for breakfast, lunch, and dinner. The hotel commandment," added Aaron, lifting fist-sized stones from the pit, "was 'thou shalt not draw an unorganized breath.' Unfortunately, I had to do a lot of socializing, dance with the girls who didn't find dates. I remember one night, I think it was Spanish Armada Night, I was only fourteen, but my father made me dance the night away with Sadie Cohen." Shaking his unruly black curls, he said: "I will never erase her name from my memory."

"So what happened?" asked Charlotte.

He hesitated. Eleanor looked up from the pit. It was now a three-foot circle tucked under the rock-shelter overhang.

"I'd rather not say." He pressed his foot on the shovel, lifting away the dark soil, then tossed it on a growing mound of earth. They had dug down only about three feet, perhaps less. The magazine article said you had to dig down *at least* three feet; four or five would be ideal. Aaron frowned. "This soil is dirty-looking here, this layer of soil." He touched it. "Ashy, like charcoal or something."

"Give us the real dirt," said Charlotte. "What did this broad do?"

Wiping the soil on his blue jeans, Aaron said, "Well, she tried to French-kiss me on the dance floor. Sounds funny now, but I was terrified. Here was this fifty-five-year-old woman shoving her tongue down my throat. I had never French-kissed anyone in my life. My father came over and said, 'What are you doing to Mrs. Cohen? What in the world do you think you're doing?'"

"He didn't stick up for you?" said Eleanor.

"He wanted the Silverman to be the best hotel in the Catskills, you know, like the Crown View, like the Concord, like Brown's. So a happy guest was his number one priority. Some of the more established hotel people looked down on us, or so my father said. He said he overheard Morry Klein of the Crown View say our place was like a garage with drapes."

"But it sounds like so much fun!" said Charlotte.

"No future in Catskill hotels these days," Aaron said. "Even the Crown View went bankrupt. *That* my grandfather would smile about. The Silverman survives and the Crown View goes kaput. Still, hotel life wasn't for me. Fourteen years old, up until dawn, packing up dinners for the guests to nosh on later—my parents never hired enough people. My father thought he'd make enough money so I could go to Harvard and become president. The first Jewish president. Today my father, with some regret, calls me Mr. Green Acres. 'So how is my son, Mr. Green Acres, already?' He thinks farming is essentially a Gentile profession, but not a lucrative Gentile profession, like insurance, or being the Prince of Wales."

They laughed, an excuse to take another break. Charlotte sat with them on the warm grass.

"Did you always have a theme, for every night?" asked Eleanor. "Before you said 'Spanish Armada Night?'"

Aaron stretched out his loose lanky legs. "Theme nights were mainly Thursdays. We had guests staying three or four weeks at a time. The *tummler*, you know, the social director, how many routines could the guy come up with? We had to have the themes, and they got pretty wacky after a while. Our *tummler*, Benny, thought them up. He was an incredible guy whom my parents somehow distrusted—'All he does is eat!' But Benny gave me chewing gum and taught me how to do the twist. He shared with me his most treasured saying: 'More than man desires to marry, woman desires to marry.' Anyway, Monday night was game night—shuffleboard, Simon Says. Tuesday was usually campfire night. My father used to tell me to jump in the campfire, to get things going. Wednesday was cabaret night. Thursday, that was theme night, when the guests got involved. Benny came up with Gemini Space Flight Night. He made a capsule out of papier-mâché and silver mylar and shoved a single guy and a girl in it."

Aaron poured the sisters more iced tea. "Charlotte," said Eleanor, "you're not supposed to have any caffeine, because you're preg—"

"Tell us more about the hotel!" cried Charlotte.

Aaron said: "Way back in the thirties, Sophie Tucker, the Last of the Red Hot Lovers, dropped by one night and sang 'My Yiddishe Momme.' They say she wore this huge plumed scarlet hat and shattered wineglasses when she opened her mouth, and that the guests gave her a standing ovation. When I was little, my father made me watch Edward R. Murrow interview her on *Person to Person*. She showed him her linen closet. My father told me, 'If Edward R. Murrow can be interested in Sophie Tucker's linen closet, anything is possible. This is the promised land.'

"My father kept the guests pretty happy, putting them in Gemini space capsules. The whole object was to get the females together with the males, who were outnumbered two to one. If someone back in Brooklyn said, 'My Rebecca met a doctor at the Silverman. They're getting married soon,' we were booked up the following summer. My mother actually had a billboard put up on Route 17 that said: I Found a Husband at the Silverman."

Aaron paused. "Charlotte," he said, "are you married?"

"No."

"I didn't mean to pry, I was just wondering. Eleanor, I haven't seen Rene in a while. That's his name, right? Your husband?"

Eleanor sighed. "Oh, he's—"

Charlotte said, "They're thinking about getting a divorce."

"We *are* getting a divorce," said Eleanor.

Aaron and Eleanor went back to work. A few shovels-ful of dirt and Aaron suddenly stopped. He had been digging directly under the rock-shelter's overhang. "This layer of dirt is really hard, crusty." He crouched down, fingering the soil. "What's that?"

Charlotte wished that he'd continue his story. It took her mind off Ian. So, he wanted her to call him. She'd call—but she'd make him wait.

Reaching into the pit, Aaron picked up a piece of stone, encrusted with lime. Shaped like a tapered leaf, it was slightly constricted near the base; the bottom corners flared out to form little ears. It was about three inches long, maybe half an inch wide, and an eighth of an inch thick.

Aaron handed it to Eleanor.

Her sister held it in her open hands, then gave it back to Aaron. For a moment no one said anything. Then Aaron said, simply, matter-of-factly, "An arrowhead, I think."

Charlotte said, "You mean, an *Indian* arrowhead? What do we do with it?"

"Bring it to the Sullivan County Museum," he said. "I found an arrowhead when I was plowing my field two years ago. The man at the museum, Mr. Simmons, told me it wasn't really an arrowhead. He called it a projectile point. Arrows were used with a bow. Projectile points were tied to spears. The one I found was about a thousand years old. The bow and arrow weren't around then."

"Spears? A thousand years old?" said Charlotte.

"No big deal. They find arrowheads all the time around here. Though"—he frowned at the newly found artifact in his palm—"this one is weird. I never saw one that looked like this. This one looks very . . . unusual. It's heavy."

Eleanor took off her hat and bent over his hand to examine it more closely.

Meanwhile, Charlotte spotted something else in the pit. She stretched down and grasped something gray, about half an inch wide and six inches long, gently curved. "This looks like . . . bone?"

"Bone?" said Eleanor.

On the way to the Sullivan County Museum, Charlotte talked incessantly. Eleanor wondered where her sister got her energy. A lot of pregnant women were quiet, exhausted, but Charlotte was going on and on; her voice boomed from the back of Aaron's pickup: "An incredible thing has happened! Nobody in LA will believe it! What do you think we've found?"

"I guess it could be something important," said Aaron. "Though nothing important has ever happened to me. But why not?"

"Why not!" said Charlotte, who clutched the plastic baggy filled with the projectile point and a piece of what they thought might be bone.

Aaron said, "It makes you feel part of something."

"Still," said Charlotte, "it might be nothing at all. What's the use in finding artifacts if they're not incredibly old? I hope they're incredibly old. But they probably won't be. Things are never as good as you think they're going to be."

"Mr. Simmons will hope they're old," Aaron said. "He's been looking for something prehistoric for a long time. When I brought in my projectile point, he rolled his eyes. 'This isn't all that old, my boy,' he said. He can tell just by looking at a projectile point about how old it is."

"How?" said Charlotte.

"I'm not exactly sure. All archaeologists can do it."

"He doesn't think a thousand years is old?" said Eleanor.

"About twenty years ago, Simmons was part of a dig in Pennsylvania, in a quarry cave there. He was digging in the back of the cave when he found a projectile point. Beside it was a piece of bone from a mammoth, a kind of prehistoric elephant. They can date bone, but not anything made of stone. The bone turned out to be about fourteen thousand years old. Simmons said the projectile point must be that old, too. But most other archaeologists said the projectile point must've slipped down to a lower level of the cave because a man couldn't survive then— the ice sheet and all that. But Simmons is convinced that people did live around here fourteen thousand years ago, though no one's ever found anything older than ten thousand years."

Eleanor felt a strange lightening of the spirit. For a few moments, she forgot about Rene. She believed that her girlhood wish had been, in a strange way, fulfilled. Enamored of archaeology, Eleanor had been thrilled when her father presented her with a book about ancient Egypt, with photographs of monuments carved into rock, vistas of the great pyramids, a rendering of the magnificent city of Thebes as scholars imagined it during the Eighteenth Imperial Dynasty.

Inspired, she had buried some Beatles bubble gum cards in an old flowerpot in the backyard, hoping it would someday be unearthed and that she, along with the

Fab Four, would gain some immortality. She had hoped that the future inhabitants of what had once been Florence, New Jersey, would, when digging some new futuristic metropolis, come upon the crooked smile of George Harrison, the doe eyes of Paul McCartney.

"What are you doing?" her mother had asked, shaking a dust mop on the porch.

"Nothing." Eleanor was embarrassed to admit she was planting an archaeological find. People already complained she was an egghead.

"Did one of the goldfish die?"

"It's just . . . an experiment."

"An experiment?" Her mother stopped shaking her mop. "For school? Science?" School, Catherine Powers often told her daughters, was the key to success; a good report card would open the door of a center hall colonial on an oak-lined street in Short Hills.

"I'm doing archaeology."

Eyes gleaming: "Keep it up!"

Eleanor decided that when she and Charlotte visited her parents on Saturday, she'd attempt to unearth the Beatles.

Now they passed the Silverman Hotel, a large four-story stucco structure, very rectangular, very green, with no architectural accents, no columns, no portico; the windows were placed too evenly, making the hotel look a bit like an institution, a minimum security prison, perhaps.

"There it is," said Aaron.

"I've never been inside," said Eleanor.

"We'll have dinner there," he said. "I mean, if that's okay. And Charlotte, you come, too. Yeah, that'll be great. But, you know, it isn't what it used to be. Don't expect too much."

Finally arriving at the museum, the three walked slowly through the foyer. A photo exhibit, titled The

Borscht Belt, adorned the walls. Eleanor peered at Sid Caesar, his eyebrows raised mischievously; Jerry Lewis, eyes crossed; Alan King and his cigar. In an old photograph, a huddled mass of people—women guarding large trunks, men topped with straw hats—stood waiting for a train, a black smudge in the distance. "Eden in the Catskills," the caption said.

Mr. Simmons was found, sitting at a dusty, cluttered desk. Eleanor felt the compulsion to write her name in the dust. That's what her mother had done on the mahogany bureaus her sisters had shared to point out that it was time to dust. "Kilroy was here," her mother would write, though the sisters didn't know Kilroy from Adam.

Charlotte placed the arrowhead and a piece of what she believed to be bone before Mr. Simmons.

Aaron said, "I told Eleanor—she lives next door to me—to drop this off. I dropped off a projectile point a year or two ago, remember?"

Mr. Simmons nodded. Though his thinning hair was black, his eyebrows were nearly invisible.

"Well?" Charlotte said.

Mr. Simmons's eyes narrowed. "Where did you find this?"

Aaron said, "Well, we were digging a garden, a water garden. And, we just stumbled upon it."

"Was it in a field, near a pond? What?"

"It was just beneath a rock-shelter. Eleanor thought the water garden would look good there."

Mr. Simmons measured the projectile point with a small metal ruler. He stared at the point for a long time. Eleanor could hear him breathe as he picked up the other prize: a piece of what Eleanor believed must be bone. Human bone, perhaps?

"If I'm not mistaken," he said, seemingly more comfortable with the bone, "this is a section of an antler of some kind. Maybe deer. It's good to find bone. Crucial to find bone."

"Is it human?" said Charlotte.

"I don't think so. But it's good you found it." He again measured the projectile point. "This is very odd. I can't place it. Too large." He went to his bookcase and pulled down a thick book. Eleanor stared at the opened pages, and read: Major Aboriginal Projectile Points in New York State. There were about thirty points illustrated. Some were bullet-shaped, somewhat like the one they had found, others were more triangular, and the ones on the right-hand side of the page were made of metal, not of stone.

The one in the lower left looked a bit like the one they had found, though it had a groove running from its base to midway up its shaft—and the one they had found had no groove.

"Is that it?" said Eleanor. The point in question was labeled Clovis, and it was the oldest point on the time line, ten thousand years old.

"The dimensions are wrong," said Mr. Simmons. "Clovis points aren't that large. This one is about an inch off. Though there are variations, human variations."

Charlotte grabbed the book. "How do they know how old these different points are if they can't be dated?"

"We can't date them directly since they're stone, but we can date the wood and bone found alongside them. We've been finding these projectile points for generations, so when we find one, we already have a good idea how old it is. People got better at making them as time went on. Projectile points changed over time much as, say, automobiles changed. A model T is older than an Edsel, which is older than a Mustang." He picked up the point. "But this. . . I'm not exactly sure what it is."

"Will it be named after us?" asked Charlotte. "Is Clovis someone's name?"

"Points are usually named after the area in which they're found: Cumberland, Bare Island, Otter Creek."

"But they could be named after people, couldn't they?"

". . . I suppose so."

Mr. Simmons then showed them an article, which looked very scholarly. "This was written specifically to say I'm wrong. That man did not live in this area more than ten thousand years ago. They say it was too cold then, because of the ice age. If the bone you found is older than ten thousand years, they'll know that my find was not a fluke. At the least, we may prove them wrong."

"And at the most?" asked Charlotte.

"Well," he said, "it couldn't be much older than fourteen thousand years. The ice sheet didn't retreat until fifteen thousand years ago. I don't want to get too detailed right now. Or too excited. I don't want us to be disappointed. I'll have to check this out further. There's no point in getting excited. I mean, not yet." He rubbed his invisible eyebrows. "I'd like to bring a few colleagues along to check out the site. You're just off the Black Lake Road, right? How about Monday? By the way—cover the site with plastic, something. Keep it dry."

"Monday is fine," said Eleanor. "We'll be back from our parents' then."

"No use getting excited," Mr. Simmons told them, knocking over a small tin of paper clips.

−6−
The Wonders of Florence

Visiting her parents' Florence, New Jersey, home always reminded Joan of how far she had come. She now lived in a sprawling center hall colonial, had a successful husband and two beautiful children, although Jason was a bit—well, and Frederick was, well—no use dwelling on the negative. She had indeed come far for a woman who wasn't beautiful and who had dropped out of college. The house in which she, Eleanor, and Charlotte had grown up was only five minutes from Newark's notorious North Ward, where Council President Tony Perenza performed citizens' arrests. He liked to corner the criminals, the black ones, hoping, he said, to keep the neighborhood "safe," or, more aptly, "Italian."

For years, Joan wished that she, too, was Italian for a reason she couldn't quite put her finger on. Now she knew it was because Italians could say what was in their hearts.

All her life, Joan had been surrounded by Italians: the man in the pizzeria who could barely speak English called the people who could speak English "Me-di-*gan*," which meant, "American." The cafeteria ladies at school spoke English and Italian—at the same time—as they spooned tater tots and lasagna on thick white plates. *"Mangia. Too skinny."* Florence had been, was still, the place where mothers with heavy dark hair screamed at their children in the grocery store and it didn't mean a thing.

"You stupid idiot!"

"Shut up, Ma!"

Joan could not tell her mother to shut up, though once, whimpering, she had told Catherine, "Why won't you let me be who I am? Your ugly daughter!" and Catherine had said, "I never said you were ugly. I don't know where you get these ideas. I never told you that. You're pleasant enough looking. Don't make me feel guilty for no reason."

"You never said I was pretty. Couldn't you lie? Just once? Christ, sometimes I hate you!"

"Who do you think you're talking to in that tone of voice!" shouted her mother, and then she'd given Joan the silent treatment—the worst treatment of all.

The Powers girls, therefore, did not talk back to their mother, nor did they enjoy the ultimate embraces of the feuding Passaro family.

"Get over here, you give me a big hug!"

Most of the homes in Florence were small, one-story bungalows built after the Second World War.

Her parents' home was no exception, a small one-story bungalow with three tiny bedrooms. Well, their father was not the most successful plumber Florence had ever seen. Joan felt she would break right through the plaster walls. She shared an eight-by-ten-foot room with Charlotte. Eleanor, the baby, had her own room, but since it was about as big as a broom closet, it didn't really bother Joan. Still, Catherine had always spoiled Eleanor, let her get away with everything. Eleanor was allowed to shave her legs in the seventh grade—she didn't have to wait until ninth grade, as Joan and Charlotte had. Joan had worn knee socks, like a protective mask, to hide her gorilla legs.

The Powers' house was not private. Still, it was this lack of privacy that honed Joan's ability to keep her secrets locked inside. Her secrets—what other people didn't know about her—became her power, her *self*.

When Joan, meticulously dressed in a silk floral dress, stepped into her parents' house with Frederick and the kids, Catherine announced, "Eleanor and Charlotte are archaeologists! Can you imagine what they have found! What treasures!" Her father, too, seemed happy, though he still half watched the television. "Those gals," he said. "My daughters."

The house smelled of turkey and lemon furniture polish. Outside, it was eighty-six degrees, a warm, humid June day. The backs of Joan's knees were moist. The warmth reminded her of a time when living rooms, offices, lobbies, were stifling—before air-conditioning squelched the subtle aromas of friends, family, teachers.

The house echoed with voices out of the past, with Eleanor's piano scales, though Eleanor and Charlotte had not yet arrived. Diane was playing the piano, though. "Mommy, listen! Mommy! Get Jason away from the piano. He ruins my songs!" Frederick calmed them: "Now, come on. Let Diane play. Let your sister play."

Joan had had to listen to Eleanor master the piano, from "March of the Gnomes" to Chopin's slow lyrical "Nocturne." Charlotte and Joan, too, had been offered lessons, but they'd been uninterested. They had better things to do. They searched puddles for beautiful ladybugs, insects who seemed to wear eye makeup—or they would play with dolls, pretend Ken was making out with Barbie. Meanwhile, Eleanor's scales became part of the house, up and down and down and up. Her best songs had been "The Norwegian Concerto," which Catherine made her play for company, and "White Christmas," which Catherine demanded she play even as the fan hummed in the background.

Joan's childhood home was full of music and religion. The Blessed Virgin, in fact, sat on top of the old upright piano.

She placed Diane's tiny pocketbook and her own bag on her parents' double bed. The bedspread, bright as a stained-glass window, was splattered with audacious red and blue flowers. Despite the loud bedspread, whenever Joan entered her parents' room, she fell silent, as though the room were sacred, for it had the lighting of a Catholic church, of Our Lady of Perpetual Mercy down the street with its deep shadows, the window light striking dark wood. Her mother had even affixed a large crucifix to the wall and had placed a statue of St. Teresa, the Little Flower, on the bureau. Joan pressed her nose against a loop of Lenten palms stuck behind the bedroom mirror, but they didn't smell like anything. The dried palms, no doubt, reminded her mother of how futile this world really was.

As spiritual as she was, her mother had always craved material things. In 1944, when she was eighteen, the former Catherine Dougherty had landed a job working in the Empire State Building. She worked for Mr. Max Perlow, an importer. Mr. Perlow, she had explained, imported porcelain from China, tea from Bangkok. "He was Jewish, but he was nice," she said. "I typed letters for Max—yes, we were on a first name basis, that's what he thought of me. I made all of his appointments, took shorthand. He was a lovely man.

We worked on the seventy-fifth floor. You can't imagine the feeling—working in the Empire State Building. It still gives me the shivers."

Now her mother was setting the table with the familiar dishes, adorned with navy blue eagles, while her gray-haired father, once a black-haired navy man, watched a movie starring Loretta Young. "Now, Diane and Jason, this is a nice movie. This is TV you can enjoy," said Ed, arms folded as he sat on the couch.

Her cheerful father seemed incapable of moodiness, or even any kind of silence. Still, he was losing his flesh tone; he appeared to blend into the off-white walls. His hair, too, blended in, for it was nearly completely gray, though he did have a lot of it, bearing neat comb marks. He wore a sweet soft smile. Joan felt a rush of love for her father. She wondered if her own children would love her in the same way, whether they would take care of her when and if she needed their help.

Diane wiggled in a large armchair. "I can't wait to see Aunt Charlotte! She's a movie star! She's *beautiful!*"

"And Aunt Eleanor, it will be nice to see Aunt Eleanor," said Frederick, patting Diane's arm.

"Do you want to watch the Mets, Grandpa?" asked Jason, who occasionally offered his grandfather—if no one else—some kindness.

"Those guys make too much money. Stay with me and Loretta Young."

"Who the hell is she?"

Diane said, "I bet you anything she's dead."

"She's someone I used to love."

"Before you fell in love with Grandma at the Commodore," said Diane, who knew the story by heart—well, nearly. "You guys met in 1947, at the Commodore Hotel across the street from—from Grant's Tomb."

"Grand Central Station," corrected Catherine.

"Whenever I had the chance I went over to Grand Central. I went there for the same reason I would have gone to the Colosseum in Rome if I'd had the chance."

Ed said, "I was in town to find someone to back my latest invention."

"Your only invention," said Catherine.

"'I look to the fifties,' I told a potential backer, 'and I see coffee bags.'"

Catherine said, "He walked into the hotel alone. I was there with my girlfriends, and he had on a double-breasted glen plaid suit, and I just fell in love. I don't know what I was thinking of."

Soon Eleanor and Charlotte arrived, bearing a bouquet of tulips and a bottle of French wine. Charlotte, who held the flowers, said, "They're not going to kill you! You didn't sneeze the whole way down!" Eleanor said that the train had given her a terrible headache and she opened her purse to get some aspirin.

"She's like a pharmacy," said Charlotte.

Skipping up to Charlotte, Diane said: "Aunt Charlotte from California!"

Jason even left the Mets—four all in the fifth inning, he reported—to see his Hollywood aunt. Charlotte hugged him tightly; Jason, looking at his sneakers, said "Hi."

Catherine said, "Charlotte, listen to this. Guess what this means: *A ureshii!*: How glad I am! I'm so glad to see you, Charlotte—and Eleanor, and Joan, and Frederick, and my grandchildren." She put her arm around Jason, who was still staring down. Perhaps, Joan thought, he's still mad at his grandmother for giving him an elbow in the ribs. Still, he's got to learn how to control his mouth.

Nana and Aunt Margaret arrived. "Thank God you've got no stairs," said Nana, breathless. She sat quietly on the couch, passively receiving kisses from her brood.

Margaret gave her sister Catherine a hug, then smiled, "What a head of hair you have!"

Pulling Margaret's severe gray ponytail, Catherine shook her head: "This hairdo, does it give you a headache? It does nothing for you."

Margaret only smiled, a smile of benevolent resignation.

Catherine never seemed to get to Margaret, thought Joan. What was her secret? Perhaps, Joan considered, they had never felt competitive, had never wanted to wear the same clothes, had never fought over the same boys—over a guy like Stewart—and therefore had kept the peace. Aunt Margaret, in fact, had been Sister Margaret Joseph, but had cast aside her habit in the seventies. The reasons for this were still somewhat vague: it had something to do with the Vietnam War, with the fact that women could not say Mass or stand on the altar in religious ceremonies, though women could clean the altar before and after these ceremonies. Joan thought Aunt Margaret had gone too far. You had to have faith. You couldn't change your religion just to make it the way you'd like it to be.

Joan remembered an argument—the only one she could actually remember her mother and aunt having. Easter, 1972. Aunt Margaret had come to the house in civilian clothes—a long denim prairie skirt and a loose Indian-style blouse. Joan didn't think the outfit suited her at all. Her aunt was pretending to be young, a hippie, and she wasn't. Aunt Margaret had been a Dominican nun, and Joan had loved the comforting look of her white flowing robes: the white ankle-length dress, the white box covered by a black veil. The sleeves of the dress were so wide that Aunt Margaret hid presents in them, like the girls' favorite books: *Little Women*, Nancy Drew mysteries, even shiny pencil boxes and candy canes.

That Easter, the family ate dinner with the black-and-white TV on. Joan wished her father would break down and get a color set, but he was waiting for them to be perfected. A voice on the television reported casualty numbers. One hundred and ninety-one today. Joan bit her lip. It was over with Stewart, but she wanted him to live. He was somewhere in the swamps of Vietnam. He had flunked out of college and been drafted.

Catherine announced, simply, matter-of-factly, "They should just bomb—bomb and bomb some more."

Her aunt's face flamed.

"Are they like us?" said Catherine. "No. They're not white."

"What kind of victory—" Aunt Margaret began.

Catherine motioned to Ed, who had served in the Pacific Theater during World War II. "If it weren't for the A bomb, where would you be? Dead probably."

Joan wondered: *where would I be?*

Then: *where is Stewart?*

The thought of Stewart scrambling in napalmed villages where children ran naked, where mothers collapsed on their knees, made it hard for her to eat the broccoli and rice casserole. The rice made her think of Stewart, of death, of what she had had to do in the city that dreadful day with Charlotte.

Aunt Margaret did it suddenly, no warning. A preemptive strike.

She hurled a forkful of rice at Catherine's nose.

No one spoke. Well, Joan didn't speak to Charlotte and Charlotte didn't speak to her—neither of them said much at the dinner table.

A minute went by. Helicopters whirred on the television.

Aunt Margaret began to cry. "I'm sorry," she said, turquoise bracelets chiming.

Catherine wiped the rice from her face. "I don't know what's happened to you."

"To me—?"

"You used to be so good, so quiet, so dependable—a good nun. I could *strangle* you—but I won't. I wouldn't strangle a nun, even an ex-nun. I'll tell you this—I put the whole thing down to a spiritual crisis—you'll come back to the Church, I know you will."

"I'm still a good nun, in a way. I just can't be one the way they want me to be."

Catherine's difficult alcoholic father, whom they called Whiskey Demon, said, "Religion—it's for the dogs."

Nana's face stiffened. "He doesn't know what he's saying." She had had to support the family for years. Whiskey Demon was always too drunk.

Nana now lifted herself from the couch, away from the full-color photograph of President and Mrs. John F. Kennedy on the wall. "Are you going to play?" she asked Eleanor.

Eleanor thought: *No. Please don't make me play.* Playing the piano required, at the most, a great passion—at the least, a glint of spirit. And she felt hollow. She hadn't practiced in a while. Back at the loft, she played every day on an old console. But she had no piano in the country.

"Come on, now," said Nana. "You play so well. Your mother sacrificed to give you lessons. She hoped you might become a concert pianist."

That, of course, had never happened. Eleanor had failed the audition at Rutgers. She had chosen to perform Chopin's "Polonaise." Her fingers wouldn't move right; they wouldn't stretch far enough apart. The keys felt like unresponsive wooden blocks. She had heard a few students laughing in the audience.

"You weren't concentrating," Catherine later said.

"Why don't you audition at Juilliard? Come on, stop crying."

"Were people laughing?"

"What does that matter? They were probably trying to throw off the judges. They were worried you might take their place in the music program."

Eleanor couldn't seem to explain to her mother that she just wasn't good enough, that she wasn't going to be a star. There was no Juilliard audition. They weren't interested. Eleanor majored in the nebulous field of communications at Seton Hall University on a partial scholarship.

"Give Nana a break," Charlotte was saying. "Play something."

Eleanor struck a few languid chords: A major, D minor, then an F major arpeggio. She then played a dirge-like rock-and-roll ballad popular back in the seventies.

Joan said, "Please don't play that song. It's too sad."

Charlotte said, "I've always loved that song."

The tension. This house—always the tension. A statue of the Blessed Virgin, broken and glued back together at the knees, stood atop the piano and was evidence of the slow boil, which had erupted—finally—one afternoon more than twenty years ago, when Joan confronted Charlotte about Stewart. Joan had seen her sister holding Stewart's hand in the back of the Florence Inn, a favorite hangout.

Lifting the statue, Joan said, "Remember, Charlotte?"

"Can't you ever forget? Anyway, you missed me. And I didn't go out with him. I was his *friend*."

"I missed you—that's right. Anyway, let's forget the past—after all, I have my Frederick now." Joan squeezed her husband's arm. "Let's bury the hatchet."

"Okay," said Charlotte, "as long as it's not in my back."

To negotiate painlessly through this awkward

moment—and through the years there had been many such moments—Eleanor quickly played, "I've Grown Accustomed to Her Face." She didn't have to concentrate too hard to play it. Her father sang along, arms flailing.

When the song was over, Eleanor tinkered with a Cole Porter song while the family talked. Joan and Charlotte, however, didn't talk to each other. Instead, Charlotte joked with little Diane: "No boyfriends, sure you do!" Joan spoke to Aunt Margaret and Frederick about interest rates. Nana spoke to Catherine about the crisis of vocations in the Church. "So few priests!" Nana said. "And nuns!"

Eleanor half concentrated on her playing. Her fingers moved, but her mind stilled until everything seemed extraordinarily real. The familiar voices rose and fell. She could hear the chattering whole, yet pick out each individual voice: Jason's groans, Charlotte's sighs, Ed's unlikely proclamations— "There were never two guys better in this world than Toody and Muldoon on *Car 54, Where Are You.*"

"Seventies songs—bad memories," Joan was saying, sipping a vodka gimlet, though Eleanor was now playing Schumann's "Remembrance."

"Should she play something by—I don't know, Barry Manilow?" Charlotte asked.

Joan said, "I know people consider him a joke, but Frederick and I enjoy his music. Right, Frederick?"

A small smile from Frederick, eyebrows raised. "Correct."

"You used to like good music," Charlotte said. "You used to like Dylan, the Dead."

In an exaggerated nasal whine, Jason imitated Bob Dylan.

"You're so weird," his sister told him.

"Eleanor, do me a favor, don't play 'White Christmas,'"

Charlotte said. "If I hear you play that song one more time I'll lose my mind. In Saigon, in 1975, 'White Christmas' was the signal, broadcast over Armed Forces Radio, that it was time to bail out."

"It happened in June," said Joan. "Play it."

Ed said, "Play it! Hey, I remember that line, from that movie, let's see . . . *Tangiers!* That colored piano player. Remember?"

"*Black* piano player," corrected Charlotte. "*Casablanca*. You can't remember the name of that movie? Are you for real? We're not amused."

Joan said, "I love 'White Christmas'—it's the most popular song of all time."

"Girls," said Catherine. "I don't know why you can't get along. My sister and I always got along."

"Eleanor, why don't you play 'Danny Boy'?" said Ed.

"I'd really rather not."

"No? You won't play 'Danny Boy'?" He looked at his wife. "Catherine, she won't play 'Danny Boy.'"

"Why not?"

The last time Eleanor had performed it, at Nana's last Thanksgiving, she had worn a new dress; it fit her snugly, showed off her petite figure, but Rene hadn't remarked on it. It seemed such a minor thing now—ridiculous, callow.

Eleanor ached for love, but settled for compliments.

Driving through the Holland Tunnel to Nana's house, Eleanor had asked Rene, "Do I look okay?"

"Yes. Fine."

". . . Fine?"

"Fine is a fine word."

Unconvinced, she took out a small hand mirror, the broken lid of a compact, and held it up to her face. She preferred to catch bits of her face at a time—her nose, her glossed lips, her powdered cheeks. However, in glimpsing her cheeks, she'd said, "Those small veins on my face! What are they? I never noticed them—" She thought that maybe the tiny spider veins were a sign of pregnancy, then decided that the metamorphosis that might have gone on inside her uterus had gone wrong; small signs of life instead had ended up on her face. She'd had the miscarriage more than a year before.

She told Rene, a sudden realization, "We're never going to have a baby."

Now she told her father she didn't want to play "Danny Boy."

"It's as if the Irish was sucked out of you," said Catherine.

"Then why, Grandma," posed Jason, "are you learning Japanese and not Gaelic? Or why, for that matter, not Latin, the language of the Holy Roman Empire?"

Catherine declared, *"Watakushi wa nihonjin dewa-nai,"* which she said meant, "I am not Japanese." Then, as she often did, at the oddest times, she opened up her favorite book, chronicling the funeral of President Kennedy. She turned to the full page black-and-white photograph of John-John saluting his father. "So terrible," she muttered.

"Jeez, Catherine," said Ed, "it was so long ago."

"But what might have been?"

"Catherine," said Nana, "it's a bit like mourning Lincoln, isn't it? All this time?"

Eleanor opened the piano seat and pulled out a song-book called *51 Lucky Irish Classics*, though most of the songs highlighted the singularly unlucky lot of the Celtic race.

"Let's do our other favorite, besides 'Danny Boy,' " said Ed.

Catherine said, "Besides your father's favorite song."

Eleanor glided through "I'll Take You Home Again,

Kathleen" while Ed sang along in a soaring tenor. The song was sad, and in a strange way, she enjoyed being sad. She enjoyed watching sad movies in which the terrible man leaves the innocent woman who sobs, clutching a handkerchief, and everyone, like the handsome working stiff down the street, feels very sorry for her. Eleanor wished she was not thirty-four years old and losing a husband and possibly a job, and somehow letting it all go. Her fingers slowed, the keys blurred, and she thought: *Is Rene so bad? Is there no way to make it work?* He made her lunch on weekends, he walked twelve blocks to buy her the jasmine tea she loved, he worried when she came home late.

Maybe he wasn't so bad.

When the thermometer finally popped out of the turkey, the family sat down at the dining room table, elbows touching. Though she was no longer a nun, Aunt Margaret led the family in prayer: "Bless us, oh Lord, and these thy gifts, which we are about to receive, from thy bounty, through Christ, our Lord, Amen." There was a second's pause, and then bowls were passed hurriedly. Who wants stuffing? Cranberry sauce?

"It's *delicioso*," Ed proclaimed. This pronouncement, Joan knew, meant that Catherine had outdone herself. Despite his easygoing nature, when it came to food, he was known as El Exigente, The Demanding One.

Everyone was impressed with the find up at the cabin. Catherine wanted to know if they could get any money out of it.

"I don't think so," said Eleanor. "I don't think you can make money from things like that."

Eyes wide, Diane asked, "Do you think an Indian squaw lived on your land? Like Pocahontas?"

"You never know," Eleanor said.

Joan glanced at Jason. His chin was greasy from his turkey leg. He had taken the biggest one. "I'm a growing boy!" he said. Then: "Grandma, I have a question for you. Let's consider the Native Americans. Did they go to heaven?"

"I hate to say it, but I think not."

Joan had warned Jason not to talk religion with his grandmother. Aunt Margaret, who Joan figured knew the most about it, kept quiet. Though Joan believed absolutely in the Catholic faith—that there really was a Heaven, a Hell, a Purgatory, that the pope could not be wrong—she knew her son did not believe. Maybe he just liked to get his grandmother's goat.

"So all of these Indians, from ancient times, they go to hell?"

"Well, they weren't Catholic," Catherine said.

"But was that their fault? I mean, what if you were Chinese, born in, I don't know, Canton (Jason liked to show off his knowledge of geography), before the time of Christ, you wouldn't have been a Catholic, would you? You'd be doomed."

"You've just got to have faith," said Catherine. "Greater minds than yours have done your thinking for you." As if to close the subject, she then questioned her daughters' appetites. To Charlotte: "You've got to eat for the baby." To Eleanor: "Divorce is a very hard thing, not that I would know. Your father and I made the best of things. Marriage is a sacrament. But you've got to eat." Promising she would try, Eleanor filled her plate with stuffing and turkey.

Charlotte ate a few bites of cranberry sauce. Aunt Margaret attempted to engage her in conversation, but Charlotte gave her short answers. "England was terrific. California? The sunshine is nice. Autographs? No one has really asked. I'm still a nobody, actually." Charlotte left the table and returned with a box of crackers: "Morning sickness, all day."

Her sister did look pale, thought Joan, though her cheeks were blotchy with commas of pink. Joan said, "I'll get you a glass of seltzer. It might help."

Charlotte took the glass, sipped it slowly, then rubbed her belly.

Joan felt peaceful for the rest of the meal, or almost the rest of the meal, which was something new. When she was with her family, the girls all together, she usually felt off-balance; she didn't measure up: Charlotte was beautiful and talented, Eleanor was pretty and talented—she'd won several copywriting awards and made decent money. And she was, well . . . Joan was eating Catherine's homemade ice cream—her mother was a high achiever in her own way—when the spell of familial contentment was broken.

"Joan, who does your hair?" asked Charlotte.

"Oh, a wonderful man, Rico. He's very popular in Hillside. You have to call a month ahead for an appointment."

"Did you ever think of . . . a change?"

She's doing it to me again, thought Joan, fluffing her hair nervously; *she's making me feel inferior—or I'm letting her make me feel inferior.*

"It's a little too long for your face, I think."

Joan nonchalantly ate a bit of ice cream. "I do think of changing certain things," she said, glancing at Frederick.

"Do you take vitamins?"

"Why?"

"I don't know, your hair looks a little thin. That happens sometimes, sometimes women lose their hair."

Joan felt her mouth twitch. "We can't all be as beautiful as you, Charlotte. Can we, Mom?"

"Unfortunately not," said her mother.

Charlotte said, "Your thinning hair could be a sign of a thyroid condition."

Joan pressed her lips together. She told herself: Do not let her get to you. Do not let her see you cry.

Her father interrupted, smiling weakly, "I can't wait to find out how old those Indian things are."

Joan said, "I think you've done enough interfering in my life. Don't you?"

Charlotte said, "I'm just trying to be helpful. If your own sister can't talk to you . . . ." She eyed Eleanor. "Well, don't you think her hair looks kind of thin? It could be how it's cut. It's too long. She should wear it chin length."

Eleanor said, "Oh, I like her hair. It's so shiny." Twirling a bit of her own she offered, "Mine is frizzy."

Joan barely heard her. She stood up, careful not to look at herself in the gilded mirror in the hallway. Stumbling into the kitchen, she stood at the sink, removing a piece of lettuce from the drain, then looked out at her mother's cheerful garden of marigolds and petunias. She poured herself some water, but didn't drink it. She was going to get her period soon—maybe she was overreacting. Still, Charlotte always knew which buttons to push.

Soft voices came from the dining room—they didn't need her. Then Joan heard a tap of heels, the scent of lilacs, then the heavy footsteps of her husband, who said, "Oh yes, Eleanor, by all means you go talk to Joan."

"Are you okay?" asked Eleanor, peering into the kitchen.

"Of course I am," she said, gazing at her mother's garden. Joan felt Eleanor's thin arms encircle her.

"I don't think she realizes how she sounds."

"Well she should realize!"

"She should."

"But I will take the high road, that's the way I am. She doesn't matter." Eleanor handed Joan a tissue and Joan dabbed at her eyes. Her nose felt fiery.

Eleanor said, "I don't think Charlotte is feeling very well. She's very mixed up."

"That's an understatement." Joan pushed the controls on the microwave oven: on, off, on, off. The oven was empty.

"You've got so much going for you," Eleanor told her. "A husband who loves you, two wonderful children. You live in a beautiful house. Charlotte—she's pregnant, unmarried, she's getting to the point where if she doesn't make it really big, the way she wants to, she never will."

"I hope she never does."

"I think, maybe, I shouldn't say this . . . She's jealous of you."

"Of *me?*"

"Maybe. I'll make us some tea," said Eleanor.

"Don't bother."

Already filling the kettle, Eleanor said, "I'm worried about Charlotte."

"That's what she wants—she wants the attention."

"She's drinking a lot. Wine mostly, more than a few glasses a day. I don't know what to do. And she's exercising all the time. I don't think she should be doing that. And the other day she went swimming in the pond, and really, no one should swim in that pond."

Charlotte's voice drifted in from the dining room. She was saying, in a thin voice, "I'm fine. No problem."

Eleanor was silent for a moment. Finally she said, "Would you come up to the country and help me deal with her? She doesn't listen to me. She thinks I overreact. I don't want to get Mom involved. She deserves some peace."

"We all deserve that."

"Joan, you're better with Charlotte than I am."

"You've got to be kidding. We barely speak to each other. We can't stand each other!"

"She'd listen to you. I'm afraid she's going to lose her baby. You don't want that to happen."

Joan shook her head. "I don't want her to lose her baby. No, I'm not that terrible, that vindictive." But maybe she did want her to lose the baby—it would be sweet revenge.

"Then you'll help me?"

"There's no point. She didn't even call to tell me she was pregnant. She called you and Mom. *Mom* had to tell me about it. How do you think that makes me feel? I tell myself, don't let her get to you. She doesn't matter. But still, I get upset."

"Then she matters," said Eleanor. "You don't really hate her, do you?"

Joan took a hard sigh. "What is hate? . . . I don't know. I don't hate her, no. Of course not. I don't know why you'd ask me a thing like that."

"Then you'll think about coming up and helping me out?"

Joan was silent. Why should she help Charlotte save her baby when Charlotte had helped her . . . oh, God— why couldn't she ever forgive herself? She had confessed her sin to Father Gerrity, who had forgiven her; he had even said, contrary to Church teaching, that life isn't black or white but gradations of gray. "You did what you thought was right at the time," he'd whispered.

"Just think about coming up," said Eleanor.

Eleanor wondered where she had buried it. Near the rhubarb bush, perhaps, but exactly where? With her mother's gardening shovel, she dug down into the earth. Not there. A foot to the left. She dug. Not there. She remembered that she had not buried it deep.

She tried not to rip up too much of her parents' lawn.

Luckily, they kept the grass very short. Her father was forever mowing the lawn. "The outdoors, a little sun, it's the subscription to a long life."

"Prescription," Eleanor had told him.

"Exactly."

She wasn't going to find it. Eleanor sat down on the back stoop. A blue jay screamed and Eleanor watched it angrily circle the yard. Around and around it soared. She tried again. She stabbed the ground with the shovel and felt something, a rock? She pulled away the dirt and saw a hole in the bottom of the flowerpot; she had buried it upside down.

The pot had lost most of its color. Once brick red, it had been bleached the palest shade of peach she had ever seen. As she pulled it from the earth, dirty water trickled down her sleeve. Soggy bubble gum cards clung to the inside of the pot.

Paul's face was gone. John's hair was still brown, but his suit had gone pale, lighter than sand. Ringo's rings were missing. Only George had survived the interment. He smiled at her with crooked teeth; his helmet hair was still brown and shining; he wore a gray woolen suit with black suede around the collar, a black-and-white checkered shirt, and a thin black tie. Turning the card over, Eleanor read:

GEORGE HARRISON: One of The Beatles, the world's most popular singing group. George was born in Liverpool, England, Feb. 25, 1943. He's 5'11" tall, has brown hair and hazel eyes.

The first thing that came to her was to tell Rene she'd found it. But then she remembered.

Joan, Frederick, and the kids soon left. Eleanor and Charlotte stayed overnight, sleeping on twin beds in

Charlotte and Joan's old room. In the morning, Eleanor asked: Are you sorry at all? About your run-in with Joan?"

Charlotte was applying mascara, trying to darken every lash. "Joan's so ultrasensitive," she said. "I only meant to help."

"Do you think she's that sensitive? Do you really think that's the problem?"

"I just said so."

"It couldn't be you? Maybe you don't feel well, maybe that's why you say things you shouldn't say."

Charlotte sighed. "Do you ever think: I'm doing something wrong. This is not the way to act—but you keep doing it anyway? I'm nasty, but I can't stop myself somehow. It's like a drinking problem or something. Well, I have been drinking lately." She scrunched her hair into a ball, then let her hair fall. "I've been sitting here thinking, What a shit I am! I'm bound for change. I called him this morning."

"Ian?"

"He feels guilty." Charlotte rubbed her fingers. "My hands are so bloated. Anyway, he told me that we've got to do what's right. We've got to make the right decision. I asked him if he wanted me to have—you know, to get rid of it. He said that the decision was mine. But isn't the decision his, too? He says he still cares for me. *Cares* for me. I don't know if I told you how far along I am. I told you I was six weeks, but really, I'm ten weeks gone."

"I'm sure he loves you."

"Right, Ian loves me. I love him. We will live happily ever after. You're the one who should live in Hollywood."

"Why are you so cynical? Why *can't* things turn out okay?"

"Christ, if I knew the answer to that!" She ambled

over to the battered bookcase. "Mom kept our books," she said, picking up *Vicky Gets Her Wings.* On the cover, a smiling redhead with large breasts and a skinny waist jutted her chest forward, proud, it seemed, of her shiny medal, shaped like an eagle—or of her breasts, perhaps. Charlotte couldn't remember what the medal was for. Was Vicky a pilot? A stewardess?

Putting Vicky down, she sat on the bed. "I think about Ian all the time. I didn't know that would happen. I lie in bed and think about him. I wonder where he is, who he's with. I figure he's with some airhead. The thought of him— Forget it. Every morning I check the paper to find out the temperature in London. It was sixty-three yesterday." She pointed at the mirror above one of the beds. "Oh God, talk about an ancient artifact!" A framed work of embroidery, sewn by their mother, spelled out Peace & Love in purple cross-stitches and yellow French knots. "The funny thing is, Mom didn't believe in peace and love," said Charlotte.

"She didn't?"

"She was for the war."

"I don't know—"

"Well, she wasn't a proponent of love, that's for sure. Do you remember Susie Hennessey?"

"Sort of."

"She's the one who got pregnant when she was sixteen. You don't remember? Mom was disgusted. 'A sleep-around, always was a sleep-around,' said Mom. Dad got mad at Mom for saying that. Mom kept saying, 'A bun in the oven.' Dad said she wasn't being very nice. Mrs. Hennessey couldn't show her face at the Rosary Society meetings."

Eleanor shrugged. But Charlotte remembered Susie Hennessey. She remembered how Joan, half-watching the TV, had said, "Mom, Susie *loves* Tony."

"So you have sex with boys you love? Doesn't marriage mean anything anymore?" demanded Catherine.

"She wanted to please him," said Joan. "That's all. She wanted him to love her."

Her mother, clearly shocked by the idea of pleasing a seventeen-year-old boy, grabbed Joan by the hair. "If you're sleeping with someone, I don't want to know about it. Is that what you do with Stewart?" Her mother then stopped abruptly and shook her head. "I don't want anything to happen to my girls, that's all. You girls can all go so far in life, and if you have a baby young, well . . . "

After breakfast Charlotte and Eleanor kissed their parents good-bye. Clutching an old missal, Catherine said, "Why not go to Mass with us before you go back? What's forty-five minutes of your life?"

"I never go to Mass," said Charlotte.

"What happened to that wonderful little girl who crowned the Blessed Virgin, do you remember that?"

"Oh, yes. The May Crowning," said Eleanor. "Remember, Charlotte? The whole school stood around that beautiful statue of the Blessed Virgin, next to the convent. And the nuns chose *you* to crown her."

"I don't believe in that crap anymore."

"Well, I don't want to know about it," said Catherine. "But let me ask you this: Do you remember *any* of the prayers you learned?"

In a monotone, Charlotte said, "Oh my God, I am heartily sorry, for having offended thee . . . "

"That's something," said Catherine. She looked at Eleanor. "And if you don't start eating better. . . . Well, I'll pray for both of you. Dear Lord, one daughter's pregnant, no husband, and the other one is getting a divorce. Thank God for Joan, who never misses Mass. I don't know what they taught you in parochial school, but it didn't stick."

"Guess not," said Charlotte.

"We'll drive you to the station anyway," said Catherine. Then, half-smiling, she added, *"Meta ni dete imasu,"* which she then translated: "The fare is shown on the meter."

—7—
The Ruins

After the mild success of her lunch for Charlotte—
Charlotte had actually eaten it—Eleanor decided to
make a tuna casserole, but she wasn't much good at
chopping. She sliced a stalk of celery in less than uniform
pieces; some were tiny and sharp, some fat and ragged.

Charlotte plopped down on the couch, hands clasped
on her belly. "It's so good to be out of New Jersey." Then
she said, "Eleanor, when you think about it, you were
lucky you had your miscarriage."

Eleanor caught her breath. What a thing to say, even
for Charlotte! She stared at the cutting board, cluttered
with celery pieces. Then she walked into the living room,
went to the end table, and swooped away the glass that
Charlotte had poured for herself. She sniffed it.

"It's juice," said Charlotte.

"It's wine." Eleanor paused. She took a deep breath.
"You're killing your baby."

"How can you say that? What I said before, all I meant
was, you're divorcing Rene—so it helps that you don't
have to fight over any kids."

Eleanor stared at Charlotte. "What do you think happens when you drink? That you'll have a healthy baby?"

"Lots of people drink and have healthy babies."

"You don't believe that, I know you don't." Eleanor had never before been so forceful with Charlotte. Eleanor, in fact, was afraid of her oldest sister, afraid of being ridiculed at the dinner table, of having her pimples pointed out, her frizzy hair.

Charlotte shrugged. "Maybe I want to lose the baby."

"Then maybe you should—"

"I couldn't do that. Not on purpose, not now."

Eleanor listened to the chattering crickets, and, layered under the crickets, she heard the low hoot of an owl. She inhaled the heavy sweetness of honeysuckle through the half-open window and sneezed. Charlotte had gone off to bed hours ago. As usual, Eleanor couldn't sleep. She glanced at the clock radio; it was two o'clock in the morning. Her mouth was dry and she thought of going to the bathroom to get a drink of water, to take her allergy pill, but she didn't. The pills made her even more anxious than she already was. She rubbed her eyelashes, which were stiff. She hadn't washed off her makeup. She just wasn't up to it; she wasn't physically ill, just upset about Charlotte, about Rene.

She switched on the bedside lamp and attempted to read a paperback mystery, but the words—black spots on white paper—drifted by without meaning. She turned the lamp off and finally dozed off, dreaming of nothing, until she sat up in bed, keenly aware of some disturbance. Slowly, she got out of bed and stood, heart hammering, in a frozen pose. "Who is it?" she asked nervously.

The door opened. A voice whispered, "It's me. I—I wanted to tell you that I was sorry for what I said about the miscarriage." Charlotte's hair hung limply, and her eyes were puffy.

"My God, you scared me! Are you okay? Are you sick?"

"I'm fine—or no, that's a lie. But I'm not sick. I slept a little."

"My heart is pounding!"

Sitting on Eleanor's bed, Charlotte said, "It was a strange weekend—seeing Mom and Dad, Joan. Me being pregnant. Bad vibes. My boobs feel like they're going to burst. I feel awful, like I need an exorcism." She paused for a moment. "Eleanor?"

"Yes?"

"I was thinking, actually half dreaming."

"Yes?"

"Things come to you at night."

"Is there something wrong? You can tell me—something comes to you?"

"Sometimes, right before you go to sleep, or right before you get up, or when you're awakened. Well, at certain moments, few and far between, there's a small window for truth and you'd better be ready for it."

Eleanor wondered whether Charlotte had been drinking.

Quickly, Charlotte said, "I've got to get it out, get *at it*."

"Get at what?"

"I need to explain things, set the record straight. I've finally realized something . . . I've realized time doesn't just run one way. It runs forward *and* backward."

Eleanor rubbed her eyes—she felt very tired now; she actually might be able to sleep. She didn't know why Charlotte needed to bother her now, when it was so late. And what was she going to confess? Would she explain why she'd gotten pregnant, why she'd never married, why she and Joan still didn't get along? Would she explain why the past is not a pile of discarded artifacts—a lost buckle, a miniskirt, an algebra book—we leave behind us, but a burden we carry on and on?

"I need to talk," Charlotte said again. "It's about Joan—something I've felt the need to talk about lately. Not to Joan, though. I couldn't talk to her."

"Because you're pregnant?" asked Eleanor. "Maybe you feel a new empathy toward her? Because she's a mother, too?"

"I just want to tell you what happened. It's burning at me." Charlotte cleared her throat. "Joan and Stewart really loved each other at first. First love—it doesn't last. Believe me, I know. Things change, people change. Stewart changed, he got radical—well, he didn't want to go to Vietnam. He said he didn't want to die like his friend Lincoln. You never knew Lincoln. His real name was Al, but he looked like President Lincoln. I didn't really know him very well. Anyway, Lincoln was a few years older than Stewart, and he was killed, back in 1968. Stewart never really got over him. It was more than the death of a friend. It was an eerily spiritual event to Stewart, like the crucifixion, only with no resurrection in sight.

"One night I ran into Stew at the Florence Inn—what a dive that place was. A sinkhole. He was sitting there, head down on the bar, surrounded by a row of kamikazes. He was crying. His nose was running—well, he was nineteen. Lincoln had been dead for two years and Stewart was still crying. He stopped crying when he met Joan, but then Stewart started crying again. He said Joan didn't listen to him. Joan was off with her friends somewhere that night. Well, I listened to him. If that makes me a criminal, then I'm a criminal.

"Anyway, Lincoln was dead. Stewart told me that Lincoln never heard the White Album. That he never owned a color TV. That he would never marry. He told me that Lincoln was forever trapped in a hole, the wide hole of 1968. Lincoln had been out on patrol. It was the rainy season. He slipped and a bullet hit him in the chest.

"Joan didn't want to talk about Lincoln, about death. She was seventeen years old—Asia wasn't part of her personal geography. That night, at the Florence Inn, Stewart and I went outside to talk, and that was all. It was nearly spring and I could smell something warm and woodsy, even though the bar was surrounded by garbage cans. Stewart, he was pretty pathetic, sitting there on the back stoop of the Florence Inn. He'd just failed out of Montclair State. He'd done the one thing that would ensure the thing he claimed he didn't want. He said he didn't want to go to Vietnam. But, you know, he did. Guilt.

"He told me he'd learned something in college, not much, but he'd learned something. A poem about President Lincoln—I guess the poem was written shortly after Lincoln was shot. A Whitman poem. Anyway, he recited it; it was a long poem, and I was fairly amazed. The poem was about lilacs and a great star, dropped too soon in the night."

Sitting there on the bed, beside the window, Eleanor spotted the moon. It somehow fit between her forefinger and thumb.

"I didn't really go out with him," Charlotte went on. "I was his friend. But Joan didn't see it that way. There was no talking to her. Joan and her friends dropped by the Florence Inn and they saw Stew and me talking outside." Charlotte sighed—everything seemed to be wrapped up in that sigh. "We never let you get involved. That was the one good thing. You were, what, twelve?"

"I don't know exactly. I remember Joan being upset about Stewart, not speaking to you." Squinting in the dim room, Eleanor asked, "Did something else go on? Was there more to it? That was around the time that Joan got so sick, wasn't it? She was in the hospital, what, for a week or so? Was there anything else?"

Charlotte sighed. "I'm not the one to tell you if there was . . . or maybe I am the one."

But she didn't tell.

"I'm going to be a better person," said Charlotte. Eleanor wondered why she felt the need to say that when her story had cleared her of wrongdoing.

In the morning, a man with longish brown hair and a red beard stood outside Eleanor's house, studying a large map. He had to hold it tightly, for the wind threatened to rip it from his hands. Beside him, a woman with straight blond hair, parted in the middle, scribbled in a stenographer's notebook.

Charlotte eyed them from the bedroom window. She was tired, dead tired. She had unburdened herself to Eleanor, but she had woken up near dawn with cramps—not awful, god-awful cramps, but cramps nonetheless. A few dimes' worth of blood had stained her underwear. Well, that didn't really mean anything, not really. She had borrowed one of Eleanor's sanitary napkins. The intelligent thing to do, she supposed, would have been to tell Eleanor. To call a doctor. But Charlotte did nothing. The pains had subsided, though a heavy feeling remained.

She studied the man and woman, who stood near the pond. Mr. Simmons from the museum stood behind them. He wore blue jeans and a blue work shirt, yet he was unmistakably studious in spite of his laborer's attire. His straight brown hair, neatly combed, didn't move in the breeze. Above them, clouds swirled about the crisp blue sky, and at their feet, the pond was black. Charlotte had felt the bottom of the pond a few days before. Something deadly cold had oozed between her toes.

Mr. Simmons told Charlotte and Eleanor to call him Leonard. "No formalities here. Leonard. Plain old Leonard." But Charlotte knew they would continue to call him Mr. Simmons. He looked like a Mr. Simmons. Not a Leonard, or a Lenny.

The bearded man spoke. His voice was low and modulated. "We've examined your finds. The projectile point— we think it's a very old point, but we're still studying it. We haven't come upon a point quite like it anywhere else. Still, it's close enough to other points for us to take a stab at how old it is." The bearded man introduced himself as Dr. Malcolm Jessup. "We suppose it's in the eight-thousand-year-old category, used by a nomadic hunter to kill big game—mammoth, bison, caribou. It's bullet-shaped so it can penetrate an animal armored with hide, layers of fat."

The woman cleared her throat and in a quiet voice said, "I'm Natalie Fine, associate professor of archaeology at SUNY New Paltz." She pointed down the lawn. "We've set up two tents. I hope that's okay. Malcolm and I will be staying on your property. I see you have an outdoor shower. We'll use that, if it's okay."

Eleanor said, "That's fine." And then, smiling: *"I've seen you two before!"*

"Oh?" said Dr. Jessup.

"On the train! You got off for no reason at all! I'd forgotten all about that, how you stepped off the train, but here you are!"

When Dr. Jessup frowned, as he did now, his eyebrows ran together in one thick line. "Natalie and I did recently get off a train—near Middletown. But it was for a reason, a very important reason."

"The route the train takes was originally an Indian trail," Natalie explained. "We dug up a few test areas, and we think we've hit upon a hot spot."

"It seemed odd to get off a train in the middle of nowhere. It was kind of romantic, though, seeing you two stroll with your equipment into a clearing."

"Our work is scientific," said Dr. Jessup. "But I suppose it is romantic in a way, searching for the past."

Mr. Simmons broke in, explaining that he first showed the artifacts to Dr. Jessup and Natalie, and then sent the bone sample to Dr. Edward Decker of SUNY Albany. "According to Dr. Decker, a paleontologist, the bone is a fragment of a caribou antler. No caribou around here now. It used to be colder, of course. Anyway, Dr. Decker sent the sample to Cambridge, Massachusetts, for carbondating. It will take about two weeks to get the results. That's good turnaround."

"They're doing us a favor," said Dr. Jessup. "Luckily, they're not terribly busy right now." Dr. Jessup spoke in an authoritative, electric way, though he didn't make eye contact; instead he stared at the ground, where, thought Charlotte, his treasures were buried. "I have spent my life," he suddenly announced, "peeling back."

"Peeling back time," added Natalie in a soft voice.

"You've got to realize," he said, "we know very little about 99.99 percent of human history. And what do you know about the Indians who lived right here on your land?"

"Well, I know a little—" Eleanor began tentatively.

"You know nothing, I'm sure. You know the fairy stories, like the one about Pocahontas, and that story is bogus. Pocahontas did not save John Smith's life."

"Oh—that's too bad," said Eleanor.

"Why not learn the tales of the Native Americans who lived here—not the boasts of seventeenth-century Englishmen. John Smith indeed."

Charlotte decided that Dr. Malcolm Jessup was a royal pain in the ass. But perhaps her foul mood had less to do with this tall, all-too-earnest archaeologist and more to do with the heaviness in her belly, her thighs. She took a good look at Natalie, who wasn't wearing any makeup, none at all.

I am losing my baby, thought Charlotte when she felt the cramping again, a gnawing in her belly. *I am losing my baby and I'm doing nothing about it. I don't deserve to have a baby.* Weak-kneed, she followed her sister, Dr. Jessup, Mr. Simmons, and Natalie, over to the rock-shelter pit, which Eleanor and Aaron had dug to create the water garden—and now, Charlotte supposed, it would never be filled with water. As she would never have a baby.

Dr. Jessup touched the shimmering shelter, part of which hung over the outermost edge of the pit like a stone umbrella. He took a small tape recorder from the pocket of his jeans and reported, "Rock-shelter site appears to be composed of carbonate rock, probably of Ordovician age, surrounded by shales and sandstones. The mouth of the rock-shelter faces . . . west." He unhinged his backpack, placed it on the ground, and pulled out a map. "The pond," he continued, "is approximately twenty feet southwest of rock-shelter. Site is at an elevation of approximately three thousand feet, at the southwestern edge of the Catskills, sixteen miles northwest of Monticello, New York." He waved at Natalie. "We'll take more precise measurements later on."

Crouching down, he pulled back the large plastic bags that Eleanor had used to cover the pit, as instructed by Mr. Simmons. As he knelt, Charlotte noticed a few long gray hairs. His hair was quite long, longer than Eleanor's; it was about three inches longer than his shirt collar.

Unaccountably giddy, Charlotte thought: Dr. Malcolm Jessup, artifact from the late 1960s. Hair thinning on top, long on bottom. Messy beard, mustache.

Suddenly he stood up, eyes wide. Such a look of amazement! He said, "Charcoal." Natalie covered her mouth with her hand. Raising a fist in the air, Simmons said, "Now we'll know."

"So you found charcoal," said Charlotte. "Big deal."

Dr. Jessup took hold of her hand. "Here," he told her, the two of them squatting over the pit, "are the remains of a hearth fire. See the black soot, the ashes, the rocks? The rocks form a circle of sorts. Some of the rocks are black, charred by a fire. This is the oldest fire I have ever personally seen—at least I'm hoping it is."

Mr. Simmons said, "Charcoal is the best thing in the world to date—there's a lot of it here, and the dates it provides are very accurate. So if there's not enough carbon in the bone you found, there sure is enough here. It means that at the same level, we've found a projectile point, the remains of a caribou, a species that has not occupied this area in thousands of years, and a hearth fire. It seems clear that a hunter killed the caribou, lugged it into this shelter, then roasted it."

Dr. Jessup stood up, very businesslike now, very Perry Mason. "Eleanor—is this precisely where you found the projectile point and the bone?"

"Yes, just there. I can't wait to tell Aaron about this. He lives next door. He was helping me build the water garden and—"

"Point to the exact spot, if you remember."

"Right . . . there."

He crouched down, pulling from his backpack a small brush and a pair of tweezers. He also pulled out several sheets of aluminum foil. Carefully, he removed the charcoal remains from the pit with the tweezers and placed the ashes in foil. "Eleanor," he said, "what is your last name again?"

"Fox—but I'm going to change it back to Powers."

"I see," he said, labeling the find, Charcoal—Fox site, Tylerville, NY. "By the way," he said, "call me Malcolm." He measured the depth of the pit with a long ruler, and wrote, Three feet five inches deep, on the label.

Meanwhile, Natalie scribbled on a piece of graph paper, sketching in the pond, the shelter, the depth of the find. She pulled from her backpack a first-aid kit, a can of insect repellent, work gloves, three compasses, a giant folding ruler, and something Charlotte couldn't identify from her position leaning against a knobby tree.

"It's a trowel," said Natalie, "for digging." She took out several brushes, a magnifying glass, a ball of heavy twine, plus knives, cameras, plastic bags, and a radio, which she switched on.

Crackly laughter came from the transistor. Fast talk; the temperature was eighty-five degrees.

Charlotte crouched down next to Natalie and murmured, "It's over for me."

Natalie squinted, forced a slow smile. "Excuse me?"

"Nothing. Forget it."

What they had found, Natalie said, was quite important and could indicate that a similar find in Orange County, about thirty miles south, was not an aberration. "We heard about that," said Eleanor. "So Mr. Simmons thinks people lived around here more than ten thousand years ago?"

"That's right."

"Aren't you excited, Charlotte?" asked Eleanor. "I mean, digging back all those years . . . "

"Why is everyone so interested in the past!" Charlotte cried. "Why not just forget the past!"

"But the other day you were so excited. And you said

something last night about time running backward and forward—so it's always here. Just imagine—a lone hunter crouching in the rock-shelter, roasting his caribou. Maybe his wife was with him, his children."

"I bet *he* didn't worry about the past," snapped Charlotte. "He had more important things to do. Like survive." She frowned, watching Dr. Jessup and Mr. Simmons drive wooden stakes into the ground. "What on earth are they doing over there?" she asked.

"They're making a grid," explained Natalie. "They're dividing your property into small sections, as if it were a very large sheet of graph paper. They'll test a few sections to see what's what, then they'll dig up the whole thing."

"I thought they'd just dig around the rock-shelter," said Charlotte.

"Well, we'll do that."

"So, how much money does Eleanor get for this?" she demanded.

"Well, archaeologists feel that a price cannot be put on prehistory. So, there's no payment—I'm sorry, I wish there was. You can, of course, ask us to leave."

"Oh, please stay!" said Eleanor.

"You understand, they're going to rip up your land," Charlotte told her sister. Turning to Natalie: "And, I don't know—you found this stuff three feet down—that doesn't seem awfully deep for something that's supposed to be eight thousand years old." Charlotte felt her uterus cramp into a tight steel ball and her eyes filled with tears.

"In rock-shelter sites," Natalie pointed out, "artifacts that old are sometimes found right on the surface. With a rock-shelter, you have a protected site—there's no erosion, no flooding, no winds to sweep in new layers of soil."

"No money," said Charlotte, taking a long exasperated sigh.

And she thought: *I am losing my baby. Losing my baby. But isn't that what I want?*

Now Eleanor was saying, "I'm sorry. I'm really sorry."

Dr. Jessup said, "Do you know what you've done? Irrevocable! Irrevocable!"

Eleanor: "But we had no idea—"

"Ignorance."

"What's going on?" said Charlotte.

"Do you know what I found in the pile of dirt you left when you were digging the water garden? Have you any idea? Just tossed in, mixed up with no reference to date or layer, I found four hand axes. You probably didn't notice that they were grooved by a *human hand.* You probably thought they were garbage, just rocks. I found bits of animal teeth, claws, choppers, scrapers—God knows what else is in that pile."

"I just didn't know," said Eleanor.

Mr. Simmons patted Eleanor on the back. "He's just a bit upset. He's a genius though. He's our man."

"He's a pain in the ass," said Charlotte. But why was she so unkind? Why not notice his eyes, which were as blue as the sky. She had told Eleanor that she was bound for change. Why not grow kind? What was she afraid of? Why not blossom like Our Lady's roses in May? Our Lady of Perpetual Mercy, hear our prayer.

A holy and shamefaced woman is grace upon grace . . . As golden pillars upon bases of silver, so are the firm feet upon the soles of a steady woman. As everlasting foundations upon a solid rock, so are the commandments of God in the heart of a holy woman.

Suddenly the trees began to whirl in a gust of wind. Eleanor's red hair went round and round.

Charlotte felt something between her legs. Something wet.

—

Jason leaned against the back door, as close as he could to the outdoors, from which he was barred. Three days before, Joan had caught him taking money from her wallet. She'd had one hundred dollars in cash in that wallet; Jason, she was sure, had taken the one hundred dollars. Joan and Frederick had immediately sent him to a therapist—Dr. Joan Silberstein. The whole family had met with her the second time, and she'd coerced them into insights.

But would insight stop Jason from stealing? Joan emptied the dishwasher in the late afternoon light. She gazed at her son. He was thin and tall, taller, it seemed, than even a week ago. His dirty blond hair was too long in the back. She had a sudden vision of her son behind bars, wearing striped pajamas, a James Cagney scowl. Beat it, Ma. Or no, she saw him as a Dead End kid—bad, but with a modicum of wit, good intentions, a delinquent in a malt shop.

He said, "So I presume Dad will be late again tonight."

"Again? I don't know what you mean by again. When is he late?"

"Is quarter to eight early? Shit. You're making it."

"Don't eat it if you don't like it," said Joan. She was trying not to yell at him. Dr. Silberstein said it was important not to make a child feel unloved. "I'll make you a hamburger."

"Don't want one."

"Then eat the meat loaf!"

"Meat loaf—I just don't get it." He picked at the seam of the pussy willow wallpaper. "No one likes it; I don't think you even like it. Why would you make something you don't like?" He looked down at his untied sneakers. "You're caught up in expectations."

"You sound like Dr. Silberstein now. Don't pick at the wallpaper."

"I may become a psychiatrist. I have a gift for insights."

"You'd make a lot of money at least," Joan said, pouring tomato sauce on a mound of ground beef.

"And then," he sighed, pressing down the wallpaper seam, "I wouldn't have to take money from people. I don't know why you're making such a big deal about it. Didn't you ever take any money from Grandma and Grandpa? I mean, don't all kids take money from their parents?"

"They do not!" said Joan, though she remembered the three hundred dollars Charlotte had taken. They had needed the money, for— Don't think about it—no sense in it. "How tall are you?" Joan suddenly asked her son.

Jason looked around, as if someone were behind him. "Oh, are you talking to me?"

"You know who I'm talking to."

"I'm five—I don't know. Eight?"

"I think you've grown," she said, plopping the raw mound of meat loaf onto a baking sheet and sliding it into the oven.

Jason stood erect, back to the door, eyes straight ahead as Joan measured him with a yardstick. It took her a minute or two.

"God, are you math deficient or what?" he said.

"You're five feet . . . nine."

"You look—weird," he said, staring at his sneakers.

Joan wiped away her tears. Last night, she had dreamed again about Stewart. She had rested in the hairless fold of his soft arm, where she was warm and safe. Then, without a word, Stewart had lifted her blouse over her head, unfastened her blue jeans, loosened her panties, then, slowly, undressed himself. He kissed her neck, her belly.

She wondered if Frederick sensed her dreams: perhaps her dreams somehow stopped him from making love to her. Propped up on her elbows, Joan had glanced at her husband. Frederick slept soundly beside her. He used to snore, but he had somehow willed himself to stop. "I don't like to disturb you," he'd explained.

She longed for Frederick to take her. But even in the beginning, Frederick seemed hesitant, set up tentative appointments. "Do you mind?" he'd ask at dinner, before Jason and Diane had been born. "Later, after dinner? Do you mind? About seven-thirty?"

Still, she'd had two children. Diane was watching a rerun in the rec room—a program about a family, two kids, a boy and a girl, and a father who always knew the right thing to do. The mother in this rerun was very confused. Was it *Father Knows Best*? or the last five minutes of *Make Room for Daddy*? or something new? Jason was now upstairs in his room, most likely listening to music, headphone wires coiled around his head. Probably not doing his Algebra II homework, decided Joan, not solving for X.

Joan was checking the consistency of the angel food batter when she heard Frederick's cheerful voice. "Home!" he cried. He kissed his wife. As always, he tasted of Binaca.

Like a sitcom family, they ate dinner in the kitchen together, passing broccoli and ketchup and bits of conversation: Jason, wash the car. Who left all the lights on? They usually ate dinner in the dining room, but Joan wanted the meal to be informal, for Jason to tear down the barriers he erected in conversation; she thought he might be less sarcastic in the kitchen, more apt to talk about baseball and Spanish class. She thought—she knew it was ridiculous—that perhaps the stiff formal curtains in the dining room, the mahogany sidebar, the

Chippendale chairs, the brilliantly colored centerpiece, a rose bowl filled with silk flowers, conspired to make him aloof, to spew nasty quips.

In the homey kitchen, a beautiful American kitchen with oak cabinets and an oak island, Frederick asked his son, "And how is everything going?"

"You don't let me go anywhere," said Jason, branding a slab of meat loaf with his fork, "so everything isn't going. Nothing is going. It's nearly nine o'clock," he told them, "and we're just eating dinner."

Diane said, "Jason is so weird." Then she said, "A circle is 360 degrees, and a right angle is ninety degrees, and I know the names of every single president."

"What's she talking about?" Jason asked, rolling his eyes.

"That's good, Diane," said Joan absently.

"When you were born, Mommy, the President was, um, President . . . Eisenstadt."

"Not quite, Diane, no," said Frederick. "The name is Eisenhower. You're thinking of Dr. Eisenstadt down the street."

Everyone laughed, and then everyone was silent. Finally Jason said, in a voice that was both confused and nonaccusatory, "Dr. Silberstein thinks my parents are to blame. That's what she said in our private consultation."

Joan took a deep breath. "*We* are to blame? How can that be possible?" She actually knew the answer to this. In her own private consultation, Joan had told the doctor that she and Frederick had not had sexual intercourse in over a year, and Dr. Silberstein had shaken her head knowingly: "Ah." The doctor told Joan and Frederick that Jason surely sensed something amiss in his parents' relationship and was "acting out." Frederick had later asked Joan, "Why did you tell her that?"

"It's true."

"I see. I understand. But there is no sense in discussing it. My problem has nothing to do with Jason. I will solve my problem."

Now Frederick said, "I'm going over to the park on Saturday. Perhaps we should all go. We'll have a family picnic."

Joan said, "We'll act like one big happy family."

"Well, aren't we?" said Frederick.

Joan started to take his plate away. "I'm not finished," he told her. "Although I appreciate the efficient way you run this household."

"You do?" she said, gritting her teeth.

"Of course."

She picked up his plate again. "Joan," he said, clutching the plate, "I think you can clearly see that I'm not finished," but still she wrestled with him over the plate—Spring Dream by Mikasa—and during the battle his carrots fell onto the shiny oak kitchen floor.

"Are you okay?" Frederick asked.

"It's probably PMS," said Jason, serving himself some more corn.

"How right you are!" Joan shouted. "How right you are! I'll tell you something: I have Post Marriage Syndrome!"

"Joan," said Frederick calmly, "are you ill? All I said was I wanted us to have a family picnic at the park."

"And I need to talk about—about"—I need to talk about why I may not love my husband anymore, but instead she said—"Jason!"

"Oh, Christ," moaned Jason.

"He's a thief!" said Joan. "How did that happen? How can my son be a criminal?"

"That's why we're seeing Dr. Silberstein," said Frederick, sipping his milk.

"Don't you ever get angry!" she demanded.

"About what?" he said.

"I think I'm going insane!" she told him. "Sometimes my heart, it beats wildly, and I can't breathe, and I— Oh, forget it."

"Could it be the change?" Frederick said.

She stormed upstairs and lay on their bed.

Joan knew that he loved smooth pathways, which was why he liked to steer the conversation in gentle directions, never to talk about anything important, to escape to Hillside Community Park. He'd sit beside the little stream that trickled out from the pond; he'd sit there for hours on free weekends—though with his job, he had very few free weekends.

But when he did, he'd walk over to the park with a small folding chair and some business reports. He'd set his chair a few feet from the stream and read. As rowboats filled with couples sailed by, he'd concentrate on the latest cost figures. Joan sometimes sat beside him, observed his neatly parted hair, his slightly lopsided mouth, the dimples that warmed his otherwise clinical look. His dimples offered a bit of pizzazz to his medium complexion, medium brown eyes, medium brown hair.

He was not exciting but he was good to her, earnest. He often told her, I'm sorry, Joan. Joan, you are right. I'll try to do better.

He was not passionate, had never been passionate—he put his passion, if you could call it that, into his job, as he had put his all into his MBA, which he'd earned from NYU after easily achieving a BS in Economics from Columbia. He paid back his massive student loans on time. He had worried about not paying them back. "I'm not naturally intelligent," he once told her, eyes peering into a macroeconomics book. "But I see to the details. I care about my responsibilities. Well, my parents have always expected a lot of me."

That was something they had in common—Catherine expected a lot from her girls, and Frederick's father expected a lot from him, his only child. His father told him, Don't be a bum. Be a man. Don't waste your life away. There's no free lunch.

Catherine, meanwhile, told Joan, Don't be a beautician. Don't count on men. Don't be a failure. Don't wear purple eye shadow. Don't live in a trailer park. Once she said precisely this (for how could Joan ever forget?): "Joan, you're not the prettiest girl in the world, not like Charlotte, and you're not as smart as Eleanor, so you're going to have to study hard."

Hadn't she? Her son was asking her, "Mom, are you, like, flipping out or something?"

Diane said, "Don't forget, Mommy, you have to make me a crown for *Macbeth*." Joan thought it astounding that Diane would be playing Lady Macbeth in a kiddy production of the play at school.

Lifting her head off the pillow, Joan peered at her children, who stood in the doorway of the bedroom. "I used to take you children to Hillside Park all the time, the both of you. Your father was never around, and now he wants to act like we've always been one big happy family."

"I thought we were," said Diane.

"Dream on," said Jason.

"*I'm* the one who took you there all the time. One day stands out distinctly. I was pregnant with you, Diane—or no, I wasn't. Not yet."

"Was I a good baby?" Diane asked with a giggle.

Jason glared at her. "How many times does she have to tell you? Yes, you were the perfect baby. I was the psycho baby."

"Anyway," Joan said, sitting on the bed, "Jason and I walked around the pond a few times. I held your hand,

Jason. You were a little rocky. Well, you were only four. At pond's edge, a little waterfall slides down through a tunnel—well, you know that. 'I go in there,' you told me. A tall man could make it through the tunnel. But of course, I couldn't allow it."

Diane said, "Did you walk through the tunnel, Mommy? Because if you did, I was with you. I went through, too. Because maybe you were pregnant with me."

"Did you let me walk through the tunnel?" Jason seemed suddenly quite interested.

"No," Joan told him, "I didn't want anything to happen to you. Maybe I should have let you go on through. I could have held you. But I was frightened. I didn't know what was on the other side."

Charlotte opened her eyes and stared at the three flat rectangular lights recessed in the ceiling, and she thought of the Father, Son, and Holy Spirit, which made her angry. Those nuns could be so high-and-mighty—they'd never had to fall in love with actual flesh-and-blood men. She felt something between her legs, a twinge. She glanced at her arm: she was hooked up to an IV.

A nurse came in and said, "You were very lucky."

Dry-mouthed, blurry, Charlotte said, "Was I?"

The nurse, a small birdlike woman, told her about the medicine that had prevented her from going into labor. She told her that the doctor had done an ultrasound, and, luckily there had been no cervical dilation—if the cervix was dilated, or if the baby was dead, of course, they would have gone ahead and let her miscarry—after all, she was only about ten weeks along. Sometimes it's best not to try to save a pregnancy, but this time the doctor had thought it worth giving it a try.

The baby had been saved, but Charlotte would have to

stay in bed for the duration of her pregnancy. She could leave the hospital soon, stay with her sister. Fly? No—no way could she fly back to Los Angeles, not unless she wanted to lose her baby. The nurse reported that her sister had stayed with her overnight, but the nurses had sent her home about five in the morning. "Very concerned about you."

Charlotte stared again at her arm, at the clear medicine hanging in a plastic bag that was going to save her baby. The nurse told her to get some rest.

She closed her eyes, but she didn't sleep. She thought about Joan.

They had gone to Manhattan. They couldn't have it done in Florence, or maybe it could have been done in Florence, but Charlotte never found out where. She and Joan preferred to leave their hometown, to go where the white steeple of Our Lady of Perpetual Mercy could not be seen from every corner. A few months later the law changed in New York, but they couldn't wait that long. Charlotte had said: Too bad you couldn't put a pregnancy on hold.

Charlotte had gotten the name of a doctor, if you could call him that, from a friend. Afterward, she never again spoke to the friend, a girl with long red hair and buckteeth. Charlotte and Joan had taken the bus into the city—they told their mother they were going to Macy's. They were to stand at the corner of Eighth Avenue and Forty-third Street; they had to be there at ten o'clock sharp or the "doctor" said he'd forget the whole thing.

Men clutching amber bottles wove past, women with miniskirts and puckered flesh on their arms jaunted by. Charlotte and Joan, according to the prescribed plan, stood on the gritty street corner, each holding a copy of *Time* magazine.

A middle-aged woman approached them and asked if

they had a problem. As prescribed, Charlotte said, "Yes, we have a problem."

"Can we discuss it?"

But this was only the first stage.

The woman disappeared into a darkened doorway. The sisters then had to sit in the lobby of the Hotel Commodore holding a copy of the *Daily News*, which, thought Charlotte, was kind of ridiculous, since most people carried the *Daily News*. Another woman, who wore a halter top and very short denim shorts, not much older than they were, told them to wait five minutes and then to walk very nonchalantly up to Room 906.

The doctor was old—sixty maybe.

"This is my sister," Charlotte told him.

The doctor, who apparently liked dealing in codes, asked, "Is the ship now full of cargo?"

"Yes," said Charlotte. "And you can cut the B-movie crap."

"This isn't what I expected," said Charlotte, steadying Joan. The man called his apartment a suite. It was comprised of two rooms: a small sitting area stuffed with old magazines and the awful room where he did what he did, which had a sink and toilet and a big leather chair with stirrups.

"This is it," said the man.

He led them to the leather chair. He then put out his right hand, which shook. Charlotte handed him an envelope, which he checked very carefully. "It's not marked, is it?" He laughed. "I'm kidding," he said. The doctor took Joan's hand, and she sat down, though she did not yet insert her feet into the stirrups.

"Well, first," he laughed, "take off your pants and your underwear. You girls always want to leave them on. But you should have left them on earlier, if you get my drift." He tossed her a sheet, then he stepped over to a dirty window at the far side of the room and lit a cigarette. "Can't do it through the pants," he said. "Ready?"

He opened a drawer in a dusty desk and pulled out a bottle of gin. "Have a swig," he told her. "It'll help."

Joan started to cry.

"No gin?" He thought for a moment. "I'll give you a shot." He fumbled in the same drawer and took out a needle that had a place to put your thumb, like a pair of scissors.

Charlotte said, "Let's go, Joan. We'll find somebody else."

But Joan, eyes closed, said, "No. I want it over with. I'm going to get through this."

"Joan! Let's go! I don't like this!"

Joan opened her eyes, looked at her sister, then averted her eyes to the ceiling. "I am going to get through this."

The man said, "Now this may hurt a little bit."

The sisters held hands fiercely, which gave strength only to their screams. Someone yelled from the next room, "Shut up! Jesus, the screaming!"

"You can get dressed now," the old man said. "Leave it in for six hours or so. Then pull it out. You'll bleed soon after that. All done. Like magic. The whole thing— eight hours, tops."

Pain, thought Joan, who had wanted to be a scientist, has a long half-life. You can bury it miles into the earth, but it's still there, glowing, radioactive. She and Frederick sat on the leather couch in the rec room watching the eleven o'clock news. Joan knew that she should have gotten a more comfortable couch, but Frederick had always wanted a leather couch.

He sat dejectedly on the couch he had always wanted, his legs stretched out straight—Joan supposed it was the least stressful position. "Got to be up at five," he told her. He still wore his business suit. She noticed the shadows under his eyes.

She told him, "You work too hard. It's got to stop. How about some brandy?"

Once in a great while they had time to sip brandy. For a few minutes. A rare treat. He took a sip of brandy, put down his glass, and placed his hands over his eyes.

"Are you sick?"

He sighed. "No."

They sat silently, sipping brandy.

Then, for a reason she couldn't account for, the two of them began to whisper, like children.

"Why are you whispering?" she whispered.

"I don't know," he whispered.

She got up and turned off the TV, then put on an old Beatles album, the White Album.

He cringed. "This music makes me feel old."

She had hoped the music would make him feel sensuous, that it would bring to mind mild petting sessions in his old Falcon. They had gone out for months before he tried anything beyond first base. He had been a virgin until their wedding night. And that night, he had slipped his penis under her buttocks, had never really entered her at all. She never mentioned it, and a few days later, he did enter her. She had always wondered whether he realized he hadn't had intercourse with her on their wedding night.

"Got to be up at five," he said.

She took a deep breath. She shouldn't bring it up. It does no good to constantly bring it up. It was the wrong tactic. "You have not had sex with me in a year," she told him.

He shook his head helplessly, as if to say, What can I say? How can I explain? Then he began to cry. His shoulders shook. The sight of him crying made her feel guilty, so she leaned over and kissed his sandy beard. "It's probably me," she said.

He blew his nose, took a long sigh.

Softly, she said, "Something is happening." She wasn't really sure what she meant. Something was happening, something was pulling her from her life, from the hum of the dishwasher, from the large unlit fireplace in the rec room. She opened her mouth to say something, then stopped herself. Finally she said, "I don't think about him anymore."

Frederick sighed. Frederick had never met Stewart— he had only heard about him.

She kissed him gently on the cheek. "You saved me, that I know. I realize that. I'd given up on men and I was so young. When I met you a few years later, I thought, here is someone very different from Stewart."

Frederick stared dead ahead, expressionless. "Why now? Why think about that now? You want to forget those days. Losing a baby at seventeen? You want to forget that."

"Don't you think I want to?"

"Maybe you want to remember. Do you blame yourself? Things aren't black or white. You can't undo it, you can't go back in time. Is it because of Charlotte? Her being home? Is that why you're dredging this up?"

"It's June."

Frederick nodded. "But maybe because Charlotte is home, it's worse. Maybe she set you off."

The idea of being "set off" was not a pleasant one. Joan felt for a moment like a bomb, a device that could be controlled not internally, but by someone else. Charlotte, perhaps, was the terrorist who had started her ticking.

She thought back to that June day in 1970, when she'd driven along the New Jersey Turnpike. Cousin Brucie's radio voice proclaimed, "That was the Beatles with 'The Long and Winding Road.' And the roads are *bad*, Cousins. Avoid the George Washington Bridge." But Joan wasn't going to drive across the George Washington Bridge. She was headed south, to Glassboro. Driving her mother's Duster, Joan's eyes filled with tears. The road quivered. She winked, sniffled, saw sudden blazing colors—verdant lawns, vegetable markets, tall glinting silos alongside old red farmhouses. She drove the endless, monotonous New Jersey Turnpike—on and on and on and on. She blinked back tears again and again.

She had not yet begun to bleed. That awful man said it would take no more than eight hours, but twenty hours had come and gone. She had willed herself to pull out the piece of wire; she held her thighs tight against the searing pain.

She could not wait in her room in Florence, under her mother's roof, to begin to bleed. Her mother was a contributing member of the Right to Life Society. And she hadn't forgotten what her mother had said about Susie Hennessey, who'd made the mistake of getting pregnant. Tony had married Susie, then left her. Susie moved back with her parents with the baby. At night, she cleaned bathrooms in a West Orange office complex.

Gripping the wheel, Joan drove onward, toward Glassboro, toward Charlotte. The day before, Charlotte had held her hand, and whispered in their Florence bedroom, "I have to study for my exams—biology, my O'Neill seminar. I have to. It won't be bad."

"You're leaving me to take your exams?"

"The pains—they won't be bad." Charlotte tucked her golden hair behind her ears. "If it gets bad, call me. Tell Mom."

"If I could tell Mom, I wouldn't have done it!"

But Charlotte assured her that she was too young to

have a baby, even if their mother knew. "Tell Mom if it gets bad," said Charlotte, who finally broke down, shaking with tears, or anger—Joan couldn't decide which.

Joan hadn't told Charlotte she was coming. She told her mother she was visiting Charlotte for a happy Sunday, a sisterly Sunday.

"You look so pale," Catherine had said. "Are you sick? Should you drive? I don't know, Joan."

"I'll lie out in the sun down there. I think it's warmer. Two hours south."

"Yes, well, okay." Catherine liked tans on her daughters. "Maybe the sun will do you good." Holding Joan's face gently in her hands, she said, "I hope you're not anemic. We'll check you out when you get back."

Charlotte lived in an apartment off campus. When Joan got out of the car she had difficulty walking.

Charlotte opened the door slowly. "What's happened? You look so awful!" Haphazardly, Charlotte pulled some letters from the mailbox, then shoved them back in. Charlotte's wet hair clung to the hollows of her cheeks. She wore a long T-shirt; her feet were bare.

"I—I haven't started to bleed yet."

"Why are you here?"

"Did you hear me? I haven't started to bleed yet!"

"Did you drive? Alone? How could you drive?"

Softly, Joan said, "Can I come in?"

Joan sat on her sister's couch, which was covered with cat hairs. A cup of stewed Red Zinger tea, tea bag and all, sat on a crate. The finely honed harmonies of Crosby, Stills, Nash, and Young came from the stereo speaker at her feet.

"When do you think it will happen?" asked Joan, sipping the bitter tea. "Will it happen? I mean, what if nothing happens?"

Charlotte sat down and put her arms around her sister.

"Oh, Joannie, Joannie. What will you think?"

"What do you mean, What will I think?"

"Just believe me."

"What are you talking about?"

And then it happened, the thing that changed everything. What happened next was more bitter than the Red Zinger tea—what happened next blinded Joan more intensely than the glint of silos along the New Jersey Turnpike.

"What's going on?" demanded a male voice, which came from the bedroom.

Joan looked up. There he was. He was pale, his veins were purple. Charlotte said, "It isn't what it looks—"

Joan threw the mug of tea across the room but it only struck Charlotte's foot.

Stewart yelled, "Joan, you've got the wrong impression. I swear—"

"You shits!" Joan said. "You absolute shits!"

"I needed someone to talk to," said Stewart. "That's all. It's tough for me, too!" His sandy hair was longer, just a bit, than the last time Joan had seen him. She was angry that his hair was longer—that he had changed without her. She put her head between her knees. She stood in the center of the messy living room, legs spread, torso bent, her head dangling.

Slowly, she stood upright. "I hate you. Forever, forever, I hate you. Both of you."

Later, hands gripping the toilet bowl, Joan expelled whatever it was that was inside her: a baby or not a baby, she didn't know. It took four hours.

Now Frederick was telling her, "Don't cry. Come on now." Joan could tell he was fed up with her. "All this crying," he sighed. He pulled her from the couch. They stood together in the living room. Soon they were clinging—you could not call it dancing. They moved tentatively, their silhouettes tangling softly as George Harrison sang, "While My Guitar Gently Weeps."

Moving with him, she kissed his neck, and thought about the first time she had done that, the first time she had met him. He had been sitting on the Student Union steps. The sky was gray and thick, like an old nickel. He wore navy pants and navy socks and a navy pea jacket. She had seen him a few days earlier on the bus, and now she went up to him and smiled. "Are you in the navy?"

Slowly looking up, he said, "Excuse me?"

"The outfit, the navy."

"Oh. Yes. I mean, no." He stood up and put out his hand.

"I saw you on the bus," she said, shaking his hand. "You're from Florence?"

"Irvington," he said, "next town over."

He seemed shy, and she liked that. He fumbled with his pockets. "Would you like some coffee?" he asked.

They sat in the cafeteria, and his books were so thick, and he had so many of them, that he had to put them off to the side; otherwise, he would not have been able to see her.

"Study a lot?" she said.

He shrugged.

"There's nothing wrong with that," she told him. "I'm a biology major. I study a lot, too. These days, it's like there's something wrong with you if you study. Everyone keeps saying how irrelevant university life is. I don't find my studies irrelevant. Do you?"

They took a walk over near the gymnasium. Several young men galloped around the track. "Do you do any sports?" she said.

He pointed to the heavy books he balanced on his hips. "No time."

"My sister Eleanor is a cheerleader." She told him all

about her family; though she did not tell him about how she'd gone into the city that afternoon, or how her sister Charlotte had stolen her boyfriend.

"Were you a cheerleader, too?"

"Well, no. I just—well, I didn't have the energy. I've been very— Never mind."

"Please, tell me. You've been very?"

"Nothing."

"Oh."

"Just a bit depressed. But I'm over it. I'm over it now."

"You seem happy," he told her, and hearing his words, she suddenly leaned over and kissed him.

She meant to kiss him on the lips, but instead she grazed his neck. What had she done? She was losing her mind, kissing boys she hardly knew. She sighed heavily and began to cry. "I don't know how to act," she told him.

Now, in the dim, suburban rec room, she held him tightly and wondered when he would check the time and say, Got to get to bed now. She held her breath, hoping this time it would be different—that he would stay with her, make love to her, that she would stop dwelling on that June more than twenty-five years before, that she would stop dreaming about Stewart. That her heart would heal. Next June, she thought, she would be cured.

But he said it. "Got to go to bed. Got to be up at five."

—8—
A Paper Lantern Over the Light

Dear Frederick:
  It seems odd to be writing to you—have I ever
sent you a letter before? *Please pay attention, Frederick.* I
hope you don't read this in a meeting. And don't worry,
you'll manage without me. You'll just have to make the
bed for yourself for a change. Anyway, I'm finally settled
in. Something will happen here—I can feel it. Charlotte
came home today but she has to stay in bed for the duration of her pregnancy. It's hard to be angry with her, seeing her like this—but I can't exactly forget all that's
happened. I want to be a good Catholic woman, I don't
want to hate her. But sooner or later everything comes
out in the wash. Sometimes it's just a very long cycle.
  The doctor says there's a fifty-fifty chance that she'll
lose the baby. I cried the other night because for a
moment I hoped she'd lose it. I felt so awful, so guilty. I
said the rosary before I went to bed, to kind of undo what
I'd thought. Why do I have to have all of these forbidden
emotions? I blame you, Frederick. She's got to stay in bed
till the end, so Eleanor is stuck with her, not that Eleanor
minds—although do you ever really know with Eleanor? I

wonder what she'll do about Rene. I know he's done some terrible things—still, maybe they'll work it out yet. She just doesn't know how to put up with things like I do. I think things would be better for Eleanor if she just paid more attention. I mean, if she had caught him sooner, who knows? If only you were cheating on me—if only that was the problem!

What's it like making your own dinner? Well, you're not actually making your own dinner, are you? You're defrosting them. Don't eat too much ice cream—there's no fiber in ice cream. Please remind my mother that Diane has to practice her piano for an hour every day. I hope Jason doesn't give my mother a hard time, she'll give him a hard time, that's for sure.

Frederick, I don't know how much longer I can stand our . . . situation. I told Father Gerrity about our problem. Take a deep breath, Frederick. He said that a woman has needs, and I said, Isn't the Pope against that? I know I'm not supposed to pressure you, the nuns said I wasn't even supposed to enjoy, well, you know. Did you know that I suffer from anxiety attacks? I told you about my feelings of utter dread, how my heart pounds, and my problem isn't menopausal, so you can give that one up. We used to communicate, or talk once in a while, didn't we? Or maybe not. Stewart was always talking, ranting and raving, and maybe I liked you because you were so quiet.

I'm sitting under a tree—the phlox and violets are blooming, which is why it's so odd that I'm remembering that chilly autumn day, so long ago. The first time I saw you, on the early morning bus to Columbia, you looked like a young scientist. Your hair was cut close to your head, and in those days, everyone had such wild hippie hair. There you were, nose deep in a thick textbook. You didn't look like any of the boys I knew. You looked like someone who had never heard of the Grateful Dead and had never smoked dope. You looked like David Eisenhower without the glasses.

I feel nothing at all like the girl who saw you on the bus that day, who kissed you so brazenly. Can you believe I did that? And if I had never kissed you—would we have ever married? Or would I have remained the girl with her biology books and huge student loans, the girl with the long hair parted in the middle who listened to Bob Dylan to seem cool but who really liked the Carpenters. It was another world, wasn't it?—though I don't think you were a part of it, which is not a bad thing.

Tylerville is not exactly Hillside. The old Borscht Belt hotels are falling apart. We're supposed to go to the Silverman with Eleanor's next-door neighbor soon, which should be interesting. The neighbor's name is Aaron— he's a farmer. I never met a farmer before. He comes over a lot asking for things—sugar, flour. He acts very nervous. He can't stand still. Though, with Charlotte around . . . men never fail to notice Charlotte. This morning he came over and asked for yet another cup of sugar. He's good-looking in a messy kind of way—dark, messy, curly hair, messy clothes, though he has a nice face. He's Jewish, not Catholic. Charlotte says Aaron's wife left him. I wonder why?

I wish I had brought different clothes—my skirts and pantsuits just don't seem right up here. Maybe I'll buy a pair of Levis. I feel out of place. I have trouble communicating with the locals. I was in Amanda's Diner the other morning with Eleanor, and when I ordered my eggs poached, the waitress looked at me like I was from Mars. The eggs were delivered scrambled and I complained, and you know Eleanor, she was no help at all. She just said, "Oh Joan, don't get upset," but I don't like to pay money for what I didn't order in the first place. Oh, and you'll love this, the other night, Eleanor and I, and Aaron and

Malcolm and Natalie (the archaeologists) went for Italian food nearby and when I asked for a glass of Perrier, they told me to check the wine list.

Rene is supposed to come up in a few days. It will be awkward seeing him. I haven't seen him since that day in the city, and he seemed vaguely angry with me, or maybe it's my imagination. He was upset that I couldn't convince Eleanor to take him back. Eleanor doesn't talk about him much, but she does a lot of daydreaming; she walks around the pond with her head down. She asks me, Is my hair a mess? If you didn't know me and saw me walking down the street, would you think my legs were fat? She's so insecure—she still seems so young to me, much younger than I am, though there are only four years between us.

Watching the archaeologists at work reminds me of when I was a student, back in the fourth century B.C. Dr. Jessup explained all about carbon 14 dating the other day. All about the action of cosmic rays forming carbon. He's such an interesting man, Frederick. Brilliant, and *very communicative.*

Love to Jason and Diane.

Joan.

"I'm going to sleep," announced Charlotte. "I'm going to sleep for seven months." And then, "If only I could get out of this bed. I don't know if I can last one more hour."

"Are you sure there isn't anything I can get you?" asked Eleanor, peeking into the bedroom.

"I'll take care of it," said Joan, who sat in the corner of the room reading a book.

"I don't need any help," said Charlotte.

"Well, I'll just sit here then," said Joan.

Charlotte shrugged. "Suit yourself, but I'm not going

to talk. I'm going to sleep. For seven months. I'm going to hibernate."

"I'm going to sit," Joan said.

"Why don't you go into the living room?"

"What difference does it make? You're going to be hibernating."

"It's hard to relax, never mind sleep, with you around. You make me so nervous."

"I don't see why I should. Maybe you can explain it to me."

Eleanor checked on Malcolm and Natalie's progress. It was a dusty day, and watching the two of them hunched under the sun, she thought of Africa, of the wide-topped acacia trees she had seen in books and documentaries. Tentatively, she said, "I was wondering. Can I help? With the dig?"

Malcolm pulled on his beard. "What about Charlotte? Don't you have to take care of her? Will you be able to concentrate?"

"Oh, yes. Don't worry. Joan's here now."

"I'm sorry about the other day. I didn't mean to yell at you. I get a little out of hand sometimes. I hope I didn't make things worse for Charlotte."

"You're not to blame. Honestly."

"Well, we're always in need of bodies. Everyone thinks archaeology is so interesting but no one wants to help. Though a few graduate students will be coming by next week."

"So I can help?"

"We can't pay you, you understand that."

"I'm not doing it for the money." She was doing it to clear her mind of Rene, and of her bickering sisters.

"You take section 7NW," said Natalie, putting Eleanor

to work on a five-by-five-foot square near the apple trees. "It's the section farthest from the pond and ought to be one of the least critical squares, and we've cleared away the grass already."

"What do I do?" Eleanor asked, afraid she would make mistakes. Natalie led her to her square, then handed her a trowel, a pair of pruning clippers, a notebook, and a collection bag.

"All this equipment!"

Natalie said, "Your task is to scrape this square down evenly. You'll scrape down about a quarter of an inch at a time, until you reach four inches. Four inches equals one layer. Then you start working on the second layer, and on and on. Got it?"

"I think so."

Just then, Aaron shuffled toward them, wearing his Yankees baseball cap. "What's up?"

"Eleanor has volunteered to do some archaeological work."

"Really? That sounds great." He thought for a minute. "Can I help? I mean, if that's okay."

Natalie called to Malcolm: "Can Aaron help!" Across the field, Malcolm shrugged, then nodded.

"This is your square, Aaron," Natalie said. "Right next to Eleanor's. Please listen carefully, you two. You'll reach in as far as you can and scrape the dirt toward you. Then you'll scrape the dirt into this plastic container. If you spot anything—a projectile point, any rocks, teeth, anything at all, you've got to label it. Say you find the projectile point somewhere in the first layer, you write Layer One in your notebook, and then, Projectile Point, Number One. And you'll put one of these notes on the point and record, Layer One, plus your plot number. Okay? And then you'll put the projectile point into your collection bag."

"It sounds so complicated," said Eleanor. "What if I miss something important?"

"I'll be here to help. I'm digging the square right over there," said Natalie.

"I'm a little nervous," said Eleanor.

"I am, too," Aaron said. "I don't know why."

"One more thing," said Natalie. "After you scoop the dirt into this plastic container, you pour the soil through this hand sieve to make sure you didn't miss anything. But remember, the idea is to find the artifact in the ground, not in the sieve. So keep your eyes peeled."

"I'll try," said Eleanor.

"Me, too."

Natalie stuck a ruler into the soil, near one of the stakes. "Okay," she said, "dig!"

"Now?" said Eleanor

Natalie nodded.

Eleanor grasped the trowel and scraped the soil toward her. She worked very gently, barely scraping the surface and Natalie said, "Don't be afraid of it. Be careful, but not afraid." Aaron was concentrating hard, his brow furrowed.

Eleanor began to scrape more vigorously, moving the soil toward her. Soon, she filled the plastic container to the rim. She then poured the contents onto the hand sieve and sifted back and forth. Natalie crouched down beside her and said, "I don't see anything. A few pebbles."

An hour later, Eleanor had scraped nearly half an inch of soil, but had found nothing. "I'm not doing too well," she said.

"Still, it's kind of fun, isn't it?" Aaron said. He took off his baseball cap and wiped his brow. His dark hair formed ringlets on his forehead. "Look at the Leakeys, they scraped for a long time before they found what they were looking for. Maybe we'll find something incredible."

"Maybe," said Eleanor.

Aaron laughed. "Probably not."

Eleanor continued to scrape the soil with her trowel. For a moment, she imagined herself in Africa, an archaeologist alone, no husband, no responsibilities, only the deeds of the dead to unravel.

"This is hard work," said Aaron. "Not that I'm complaining. You look awfully warm, though," he told her.

Eleanor took a hard sigh. "Yes." She was hot and thirsty and worried that she would get a sunburn, despite her hat. But she continued to work. She was driven; her right hand gripped the trowel, scraped across the earth. There was something comforting in kneeling over the earth, in taking in its slightly bitter scent. She filled the plastic container to the top once more, then dumped the soil on the screen, and jiggled the sieve from side to side. The dust made her sneeze. But she found nothing, just some pebbles and old roots.

She again crouched over the square of earth, and scraped. And this time she struck something—something solid. "Aaron!" she called. "Natalie!"

But Natalie, who had walked over to the rock-shelter, didn't seem to hear her. Eleanor said, "Should I keep going? Or wait for Natalie?"

Aaron frowned. "You've got to decide, I guess."

"What do you think?"

"I think you should go for it."

She dug gingerly around the object she had come upon. Soon she glimpsed something sparkling, a green jewel in the earth, and she wondered whether she had discovered something astounding—the headdress of an Indian queen, perhaps. She continued digging but her hopes sank when the shape of a bottle emerged. She had found another Coca-Cola bottle, just like the one she and Aaron had found the other day. Still, it was a beautiful bottle, with cool lines and a smooth lip.

"Your first find," said Natalie, strolling back over.

"I suppose."

"Did you record it?"

"Well, no."

"It's a find, Eleanor. It's important."

"It is? Oh, I guess it is."

"I think it's important," said Aaron.

Eleanor labeled the bottle and recorded it in her note-book.

"Let's see what you find tomorrow," said Natalie.

"I can continue working?"

"I told Malcolm you two were doing well. And he said, Who knows what they'll find. He believes in beginner's luck."

Charlotte threw off her blankets. The night was thick and damp; it was an entity, like smoke. She lay spread out, an arm slung across the bed. She wore a long T-shirt that said Universal Studios, silk underwear that Ian had bought her months ago, and ankle socks. She pulled off the socks, then threw them across the room. A sock fell on top of a chest of drawers.

She had been reading a book about Sam Goldwyn and his stormy relationship with director William Wyler on the set of *Wuthering Heights*, but the pages felt limp; they had lost their starch. She placed the book on the night table, hiding the clock radio. Three flying insects, more delicate than flies, hovered about the bedside lamp, drawn to the dangerous yellow light, which would surely singe their wings. To save them, she clicked off the lamp, and for a moment the room was black. Slowly the silver shape of the mirror appeared as did the white outline of the chest of drawers, long vertical lines. Through the window, the outdoors slowly emerged as well, like a photograph in a darkroom. The flowers in the garden were ashen. Eleanor, Aaron, Joan, Malcolm, and Natalie were sitting around a small fire, talking and roasting marshmallows.

A solitary moth danced on the inside windowpane, struggling to escape the confines of the room. Charlotte, too, was a prisoner. She couldn't concentrate. Her mind was fuzzy and she thought, over and over, Would she lose the baby? She'd nearly lost her baby and now she didn't want to lose it. How stupid could she have been? Well, she could be very stupid. She believed it her specialty. She had been insane to drink, to act as if she weren't pregnant at all. This, then, was her penance, to stay here in this room for six months. Eleanor would have to go back to work in a few weeks (if, said Eleanor, she still had a job). Joan, inexplicably, had volunteered to stay at the house with her when Eleanor left.

Charlotte suspected that Joan was a better person than she would ever be. She thought: You're a better man than I, Gunga Din.

Charlotte considered her own moral worth, something she rarely did.

Back in the third grade, Sister Marie Grace had decreed that the soul was like a tablet, marked by Almighty God with roman numerals to keep an accurate tally of sins. She had imagined her own soul with a number like MCMMMMCCC—some gigantic roman numeral.

A short catalog of sins: she had lied to her parents about that math test, always cheated when she played crazy eights with Eleanor, slept with a boy when she was fifteen, and stolen $300 from her parents for Joan's procedure. Her most grievous sin, however, was the sin of pride: Charlotte wanted to get ahead. She was a beautiful girl and there was no reason why she shouldn't rise to the top, like cream.

"You're my cream puff," Catherine often told her.

Catherine wanted at least one of her daughters, if not all, to achieve something big. Catherine thought it a very good idea for Charlotte, her most beautiful girl, to make a career in Hollywood, to be a great and wealthy actress, who, unlike Carole Lombard or Jean Harlow, would not die tragically. Tossing her red unruly mop of hair, sucking in her cheeks, Catherine told Charlotte, "Maybe *I* could have been a star. I could have jumped on a train to Hollywood and made quite a splash."

"You're mixing your metaphors," Charlotte had told her.

One Saturday before Easter, Charlotte arrived home from Glassboro, and while Eleanor dipped hard-boiled eggs in violet food coloring and Joan made out with Stewart on the back porch, Catherine practiced dialogue with her daughter in the sweltering kitchen, the turkey sizzling in the oven. Charlotte was to appear as Blanche Dubois in *A Streetcar Named Desire* at the Glassboro Civic Theatre.

"The heat—it'll be good for atmosphere," said her mother, laughing. She continued, seriously now, reading from her playbook, "Imagine a two-story corner building on a street in New Orleans named Elysian Fields . . . a neighborhood of poor but raffish charm . . . You can almost feel the warm breath of the river." She sniffed, looking up. "I don't smell anything. Just turkey."

Charlotte cleared her throat. "I never was hard or self-sufficient enough. When people are soft—soft people have got to shimmer and glow—they've got to put on soft colors, the colors of butterfly wings, and put a paper lantern over the light . . . It isn't enough to be soft.

You've got to be soft and attractive. And I—I'm fading now! I don't know how much longer I can turn the trick."

Her mother gripped Charlotte's arm. "Remember," she told her. "This is a play. Don't be that way. Don't be soft. Be good in the play so you don't have to be that way, to be—here like it says here, 'depending upon the kindness of strangers.' "

But now she was, and it made her very angry.

Outside, flames tumbled. Branches crackled. Five shadows—Eleanor, Aaron, Malcolm, Natalie, and Joan— huddled around the fire. The sight of them crowded around the flames was an aboriginal vision—reminding Charlotte of caveman films, Westerns. Behind them, the pond was invisible. She imagined sleeping, shimmering trout. She sensed the weakness of the moon and stars. She took a deep breath; the night smelled of impending rain. Malcolm's deep voice rose above the soft cries of insects and unknown animals. He spoke about the Lenape Indians, another name, he said, for the Delaware Indians, an Algonquin people.

He told them that the area in which the Lenape Indians had lived—New Jersey, parts of New York, including Tylerville, and northeastern Pennsylvania— was now referred to by archaeologists as Lenapehoking. No one in the world, he said, knew what the Indians themselves had called their land thousands of years ago.

Joan said to him, "Recite something for us."

"Recite?"

"One of their stories."

"Well—"

"Don't they have some famous poem?" asked Joan.

"You're thinking of the Walam-Olum," he said.

"Actually, I was thinking of 'Hiawatha.' "

"We think it's a fake, the Walam-Olum. It's a pictograph, akin to hieroglyphics, painted on wood, that a Lenape Indian supposedly gave to a Dr. Ward in 1820, for having cured some of his family members. But it probably wasn't really written by a Lenape at all because the picture-writing doesn't correspond to other Lenape samples. It was probably concocted by a white man to make some money. The Walam-Olum is an interesting chronicle all the same. It's the story of the Native American migration from Siberia to the Atlantic coastal region. If you'd like, I can recite it."

"Oh yes!" said Joan.

Malcolm began:

"After the rushing waters had subsided, the Lenape of the Turtle were close together, in hollow houses, living together there.

"It freezes where they abode: it snows where they abode: it storms where they abode: it is cold where they abode.

"At this northern place, they speak favorably of mild, cool lands, with many deer and buffalo.

"As they journeyed, some being strong, some rich, they separated into house-builders and hunters.

"The strongest, the most united, the purest, were hunters. . . ."

And on and on he spoke.

When he was finished, he stomped on the last of the embers. "Glad I could entertain. But you really should know more about the people who once lived on your land. After all, you know about Rome, about England, but you know very little about the people who lived right here."

"Maybe we should know more about people we grew up with," said Joan.

"What do you mean?" asked Eleanor.

"Nothing. Forget it."

Overhearing the conversation, Charlotte thought: If only Joan *would* forget it.

She then picked up the phone and called Ian.

His voice, a recording, said, "Hello, you've reached Ian O'Toole. Please leave your name and message and the time of day when you hear the tone. Lovely. And, as the potty Americans say—have a nice day."

Charlotte said: "This is Charlotte, the potty American woman you have impregnated. I nearly lost our baby the other day. Just wanted you to know."

She hung up

Eleanor and Aaron decided to walk up to the rock-shelter. Aaron wanted to take a look, though Malcolm warned them not to touch anything. As they walked, something slimy jumped on Eleanor's leg and struck again on her shorts. "Ohhh!" she cried.

She went to flick the creature from her bare leg. At the same time, Aaron brushed his hand on her leg. "It's gone, I think," he told her. And then: "I feel, you know, like I had something to do with all this. You know, finding the artifacts."

"Well, you did," she said.

A bolt of lightning suddenly ripped the sky.

Earlier, Malcolm told them that some Native American tribes believed lightning was an immense serpent vomited by the creator, leaving serpentine twists and folds on the trees he struck.

"I suppose God is vomiting!" Aaron called now.

They stood under the sky, lit by sudden zigzags of light. Gazing up, Eleanor saw birds—wings black against the whiteness.

"The sugar!" cried Aaron above the din of thunder.

"What?"

"Come on!" he called, taking her by the hand.

"Shouldn't we go back?" Eleanor had to shout to make herself heard, and for a moment she turned back toward the house, but Aaron kept on going, pulling her along.

When they reached the rock-shelter, he shouted, "Can't see much!" Just then the shelter was illuminated by a lightning burst, and Eleanor thought of a cathedral cut from white stone. Now it was pouring. They scrambled past the shelter, around the pond, toward the dark tangle of trees, brightened by swift arms of light. They continued on toward his house, past the wheels of an old tractor and the remains of a hundred-year-old plow. At last, she could see the soft steady light of his small house in the distance.

Inside, she wiped her muddy sneakers on a small rag rug. After the cacophony of lightning, thunder, the hard rain, everything seemed remarkably still. She started to shiver, which was odd, she thought, because it was very warm in the cottage.

The living room was small—the walls were painted a dull yellow and the ceiling and wood floors were painted the same slate blue as the exterior of the house. A large oak cupboard hugged the far wall. Walking toward it, she saw that it was lined with old unmatched pottery, a bowling trophy from 1966 (she squinted to see it for she'd taken off her wet glasses), and a collection of CDs. On the far wall was a photograph of a very young Danny Kaye, arms around an older man who wore round spectacles and held a fat cigar. "It's my grandfather," Aaron said. "The old Borscht Belt days."

Eleanor sat down on one of two rocking chairs on either side of an old wooden table. Maddie, his Irish setter, jumped up on Aaron, who rubbed his furry neck. The dog then sniffed Eleanor for a second and, seemingly satisfied, shimmied himself under a table.

Aaron went away for a moment and returned with two towels. As they dried themselves off, he said, "I wanted to return the flour, and the sugar."

"I could have gotten it tomorrow. I'm so wet!" But she smiled, shaking her head. "It doesn't matter." Peering at the nearest window, she said, "I hope it stops soon."

"Yes," he said, moving into the kitchen. She followed him into the pale yellow room, which had no cabinets— everything was out in the open on shelves. "Flour and sugar," he said, handing her two heavy paper sacks.

"But I only gave you a cup."

"It's no problem," he said, handing her the sacks.

"Oh," she said. "Thank you."

He also gave her a plastic bag filled with blueberry muffins. "I saved you some. Sometimes I bake. I hope you don't think that's weird."

"Not at all."

"Sit down. I'll make you some tea."

A few minutes later, he was leaning against the sink, watching her drink it. "Awful night," he said.

"Terrible." She walked toward the window. "I think it's let up a little."

"Do you have to go?"

"It's late. I don't want to wake up Charlotte."

"Well, let me walk you back. It's late, and dark, and muddy."

She felt something close in on her—an odd feeling. She didn't know whether it was something to embrace or escape. "Don't be silly," she said. "I'll be fine."

"It's silly for you to go back alone," he said.

"But then you'll have to walk back alone from my place."

"That's no problem. I don't know why you won't let me walk you back."

But she insisted on walking alone. Gazing up at the

sky, she noticed a small brightening where the moon would be.

Half-aware of the sounds of chirping, Eleanor dreamed of small delicate birds with green beaks and purple plumage. She opened her eyes thinking of birds, and saw that it was day. She glanced at the clock: 5:56. Something was different, but she didn't know what it was. She concentrated. One thing was certain: she had actually slept for a few hours. And then the other different thing occurred to her: she hadn't thought of Rene. She waited for the familiar wave of despair to envelop her, as it did every morning when she opened her eyes. A darkness in her gut. But she felt nothing.

Morning light came up behind some misty trees. A strong urge to paint the pond, her country life, came over her. She didn't bathe but quickly dressed, fastened her floppy hat to her head with a long hat pin, and gathered her paint supplies. Setting up her easel near the pond, she watched Natalie and Malcolm crawl out of their tents.

"What are you doing?" Malcolm asked, rubbing his eyes. "Are you an artist or an archaeologist?"

"Both."

"Why not," he said, stumbling toward the shower. Natalie, too, went to talk to her, but, raising her canvas, Eleanor said, "Got lots to do." She didn't want to talk—she wanted to work. She opened her paint box and went to pull out a liner brush but instead grasped the palette knife. She always had trouble with the palette knife, but she willed herself to use it.

She worked quickly, didn't censor herself. In the foreground, she stroked blue and green lines on canvas—a clear, open lake, with verdant trees in the background. With the tip of the knife, she flecked the trees with gold.

She smudged green-black shadows beneath the trees, blurring them into the lake. And then, just below the trees, cutting into the shadows, she painted a thin line of tan—a beach. She highlighted the beach with curls of white, suggesting the water's wake. Her heart was pumping, her eyes were wide. She had not had her tea yet, much less breakfast, and she had completed a painting.

Stepping back, she considered it. Something wasn't right. She pondered the problem. Something was missing. She told herself: Don't think too hard, and quickly she sat down and painted another grassy shore in the foreground, and with Indian yellow she painted a small dusty road, one that did not exist; yet her painting was truer with the road.

Again she stepped back, and this time she smiled. She had done it. She had created a perfect picture. It was perfect in the sense that it was her painting. And if Rene didn't like it—tough.

Later Eleanor had a headache. After concentrating so hard on her painting, and the sun glaring down on her, her temples throbbed. She rubbed her temples, then tied a kerchief around her neck, adjusted her glasses, her hat, and crouched down over her square of earth. Wielding her trowel, she scraped the soil toward her, continually searching, picking up every pebble; sometimes she came upon small white specks of soil, small green specks, but Natalie said they were a natural ingredient of the soil.

Aaron found several rocks that he thought might be something, but they turned out not to be. He worked very quickly, very efficiently. Eleanor felt clumsy; her square was uneven. It was hard to reach the outer corners. Because her arms were short, she had to constantly shift her position. She thought of how as a child she had gone to the refrigerator to sneak spoonfuls of ice cream, carefully smoothing the surface so as not to be detected. But she always was.

Hoisting a rock, Aaron said, "What do you think?"

Eleanor considered it: a smooth stone, twice as big as her fist. "It's so hard to tell, isn't it? Natalie and Malcolm can just glance at things and know."

They called Natalie over, but she shook her head. "Just a rock. There's no chipping that I can see. It isn't a tool. If there were little chips all over the surface, it might be a hand ax."

Eleanor and Aaron crouched down again over their squares. "I'm just through the first layer," said Eleanor.

"That's good progress," he said.

Standing up, she brushed off her jeans and, glancing over at his plot, said, "But you've already made it through your first layer. You're on to the second layer."

"Yes."

"And you didn't say anything?"

"I'm just digging."

"I'm so slow." She looked back toward the house. Thank God for Joan. If she hadn't come up, Eleanor would be stuck inside with Charlotte all day instead of playing amateur archaeologist. And she needed to do something physical, to sweat, to forget herself.

"It's tiring, isn't it?" said Aaron. "Not that I mind, not at all."

Eleanor said, "I want to be tired."

"Oh?"

"I don't sleep well."

"No?"

"Troubles, you know."

"Your husband? Or ex-husband?"

She nodded. "And I worry about Charlotte."

"I like your sister. She's feisty and funny."

"She's very . . . determined." She meant difficult.

"I'm glad she didn't lose her baby." He took off his baseball cap, and she noticed how black and glossy his hair was. It was too sunny to remove her own hat. "She's never been married?" he asked.

"No, though a few men have wanted to marry her."

"That's not surprising. She's very beautiful."

"Yes," said Eleanor. "That she is."

"It must be hard for Charlotte, to be alone at a time like this. I mean, without the man who, well . . ."

So, she thought, Aaron had a thing for Charlotte. Everyone liked Charlotte—well, men did. She took out a tissue and blotted her face. She gazed at her dirty fingernails, at the splotches of paint on her hands. How could she have not showered this morning? She was really losing it. "I'm such a mess," she said.

"What? I'm sorry, I missed what you said."

"Nothing. Just that I'm a mess."

He looked at her. "Not at all."

They continued to drag their trowels across their squares. Eleanor noticed that the soil in the second layer was a few shades darker than the first. The best position to dig now was on her belly, with her arms dangling over the plot. Again and again she worked the trowel toward her, and in a forward stroke, she brushed up against something. She had struck an object. Peering into her plot, she expected to see the emerald remains of another Coke bottle, but instead she saw the scattered bits of something she recognized, but could not place at first. She thought of her grandfather's old jigsaw puzzles. Then it came to her: she was staring at the broken pieces of a bowl, or of a pot. The pieces were unmistakable; she had shattered so many similar things: plates, glasses, vases, bowls. Her mother said she was uncommonly clumsy.

"Aaron?" she said softly.

He stared hard. "Broken pieces of something. I don't know what."

"Pottery?"

"Maybe . . ."

Gingerly, she picked up several pieces. Each was incised with vertical and horizontal lines, a cross-stitch pattern. Aaron examined a piece. "Yeah, I guess it is pottery. Wait a minute, look," he said, handing it back to Eleanor.

She noted the pattern, and turning the pottery chard over, she saw the imprint of a thumb, a human thumb; the imprint was soft and round, a swirling whorl. She placed her own thumb on the thumb of the pottery maker. "Natalie!" she called. "Malcolm!"

Rushing over, Malcolm said, "What is it?" He gathered the pottery shards and placed them on the back of a legal pad, working them around like puzzle pieces until several shards locked together. "Do you see this impression?" Malcolm asked, pointing to the cross-stitch pattern. "This pottery vessel was probably pressed out on a reed mat which preserved the impression. It's very common to see that. This is a soapstone bowl, probably from about 1000 A.D."

"Did you see the thumbprint?" asked Eleanor.

"Ah," he said, turning the correct chard over. "You have touched the hand of a thousand-year-old woman. Women made the pottery, you see. They also gathered plants, skinned the animals, made the clothing. You see, men could not survive without women back then."

"They still can't," said Aaron.

—9—
The Rowboat

A few days later, Micah Silverman led Joan, Eleanor, and his brother Aaron to their table at the Silverman Hotel. Joan was a bit worried about leaving Charlotte at home alone. On the other hand, Charlotte deserved to be out of the limelight for a while, plus, Natalie would be checking in on her. And Joan deserved a night out on the town, even if the town was Tylerville.

"A bottle of the Asti Spumante, Johnny," Micah told the waiter. "I'm so glad you two ladies could make it. Oh yeah, and my brother, Mr. Green Acres."

On the table were four baskets of challah bread, three trays of what Micah called alpine slaw, plus apple sauce, packets of kosher margarine, and a silver pitcher of ice water. Standing against the red dining room walls were five-foot-high electric candelabra. The maroon curtains, which bordered no windows, were thick and lavishly draped.

"The place is nearly full," said Aaron, over the voice of Vic Damone, who crooned from the loudspeakers.

"Marketing," said Micah. "Very important. I'm steering the hotel into the future. Oh, I forgot," he said, slapping his head. "Open your menus. You'll get a kick out of my latest brainstorm."

Joan opened the menu and smiled.

Aaron said, "*Lenape soup?*"

"Is this an idea or what? You've got to be topical. All Tylerville is buzzing about the archaeological dig, so what better idea, huh? You people have been finding incredible artifacts. Pottery, bone, what next?"

"What *is* Lenape soup?" asked Aaron.

Micah whispered, "Borscht." Summoning the maître d'hôtel, Micah added, "Ladies, this is Sol; he practically runs the place. Sol, say hello to Eleanor and Joan."

Sol, who wore a wrinkled black tuxedo, said, in his raspy voice, "What beautiful women! Have you ever been to the Silverman? No, I'd have remembered. Welcome to our Imperial Dining Room. Are you here for the Thirty-five and Older Singles Weekend?"

"They're my guests," said Micah. "And I hope they'll enjoy the festivities. There's an after-dinner power walk with Gilda at nine. We could do that. And, let's see," he said, taking from his suit pocket a pink sheet of paper. "The itinerary," he said, waving the paper. "Later on, I'm going to the hair replacement lecture with Ralph Levine, an expert in the field."

Johnny the waiter approached the table, hoisting a tray of what Micah explained was cold sliced gefilte fish with "projectile point" horseradish. Micah grabbed a few "carrots Catskill" from the tray. "Hands off the merchandise!" said Johnny. Johnny then hugged Micah. "Micah is quite a guy. What a feeling in this place."

"If we could bottle it," said Micah.

"Buy me some stock!" said Sol. "I got to tell you something, boss, this hair replacement lecture, it's for the single stiffs. Everyone looks at your face, not at your head. Tell him, Aaron. Look at Telly Savalas. You tell me."

"I am a single stiff," said Micah.

Peering at his menu, Aaron said, "Paleo-Indian schmaltz herring?"

"Okay, genius," said Micah, "you think of something better. You find the ancient stuff, I market it. My brother, he got out of the business. Mr. Green Acres, what do you know?"

Joan was glad that she and Eleanor had opted for the Lighter Fare, a new twist on Catskills dining, according to Micah. "The new health wave," he said. The Lighter Fare consisted of tossed green salad with diet dressing and poached salmon with steamed rice and broccoli. Still, the portions were gigantic.

"This is so much to eat," said Joan. Fleetingly, she wished Frederick were here. She would nudge him and say, Frederick, I can't eat all this. And Frederick would clasp her hand and say, I will take care of it. He was good at handling mundane problems—but the difficult ones? He pretended they didn't exist.

"Don't you like the food?" asked Micah.

Taking a bite of broccoli, Joan said, "I love it. Really. It's great." Eleanor, for once, was actually eating.

"People come to the Silverman to eat!" said Sol. "Come on, you're skinny enough. We've added some new entrees—how about some ribs, or a BLT? We're not strictly kosher anymore."

"I like the food. Honestly," said Joan.

"Johnny," said Micah, "is the food hot? Did you deliver the food hot?"

"Of course, boss."

"I like the food. I do. Please don't go to any trouble—"

"Johnny, get a fork, a clean one, and taste the food. Check the temperature."

"What?" said Johnny.

"Check the temperature."

"Oh, Christ," said Aaron, covering his face.

Johnny, as instructed, took a bite of the fish and proclaimed it, "A-okay, boss."

"You don't have to cover up for them in the kitchen."

"No, it's perfect, boss. Not too hot, not too cold. Perfect."

"I like the food," said Joan.

Micah instructed Johnny to bring Eleanor and Joan some matzoh ball soup and a little stuffed derma.

Joan felt the need to explain why she didn't have much of an appetite. "I'm having a little problem with my son. It's hard to eat when you're unhappy—not that I'm very unhappy, I'm just a bit— Never mind," she said, forcing a smile. "Not that I'm unhappy being here at your fine hotel, Micah. I mean, I'm just a little down lately, what with my husband— Forget it, that's another issue."

"Your husband?" asked Micah. "I don't mean to pry, but is he seeing another woman?"

"Of course not."

"You can't be too sure."

"Really, he's not." But was he? "He's not like Eleanor's—husband." Joan sighed. Insert foot in mouth. What gall Micah had. Though, in a way, she liked people who said what they were thinking, which she was not particularly good at, and Frederick—he was hopeless at gut feelings.

Micah said, "This is the perfect weekend for you gals then—our Thirty-five and Over Singles Weekend. You two girls can meet new mates."

"My sister is thirty-four," said Joan.

"We bend the rules here," said Micah. "Do you like the soup? Is it hot enough?"

"It is the best soup I've ever had. In my life. My entire life," Joan said.

"Really?" asked Micah, as Dean Martin's wobbly singing voice came from the loudspeakers. "You really like it?"

"It's fine," said Joan. "Not that I know much about

matzoh ball soup. Dr. Eisenstadt lives down the block, but he's never had us over for dinner."

Just then, Don Juan, the DJ, ran around the room with a portable microphone shouting, "Clap Your Hands! Clap Your Hands!" Joan eyed Eleanor, who was at one time too shy to publicly clap for Tinkerbell. Eleanor was gently tapping her hands together.

"You see this jacket," Micah suddenly said. "Guess how old it is."

Joan shrugged. Eleanor stopped clapping.

Aaron groaned. "Not this again. He's always bragging about how old his clothes are. Why, I don't know."

"Sophomore in high school. Isn't that something? Sophomore in high school!"

"You were pretty fat then, too," said Aaron.

"Okay Mr. Skinny Guy. Mr. Brother with hair. Do you two fight sometimes?" he asked the sisters. "You know, did you take each other's clothes? Or better yet, take each other's men?"

Gulping her wine, Joan said, "Eleanor and I don't fight. Charlotte and I, well. She's my other sister." She was just a bit tipsy. Her forehead felt slightly numb. "Charlotte stole my boyfriend, years ago."

Eleanor said, "Are you sure about that? Are you sure they weren't just friends?"

"The old friend ploy," said Micah.

"She was lots more than his friend," said Joan.

Eleanor couldn't think of a response to that.

When Joan finally convinced Micah that she was through with dinner, the four of them strolled around the hotel. The Silverman was bustling with overdressed guests, and Joan realized that this was how the Catskills might have been thirty years ago. Time had lost all meaning within the confines of the Silverman Hotel. The past shimmered beneath the worn linoleum surface. Women in gold and silver lamé meandered in the lobby. A few gray-haired men lounged on some beat-up couches. In the corner, a woman wearing a lilac turban held another woman's hand, apparently reading her palm. "You will meet someone very soon, someone very rich, someone very tall, someone very handsome."

The gray-haired woman whose palm was extended wore a face of skepticism. "You're lying. I know it. My Morris always used to lie."

"You're married?" asked the palm-reader.

"No. My Morris is dead. Though not literally. He's dead in my mind."

Eleanor approached the woman whose palm was being read. "Excuse me, but aren't you . . . ?"

"Yes, yes," said the woman, barely looking up. "I know you. The girl on the train. The redhead on the train."

"That's right! How is the hotel? Is it all that you remembered?"

"Are you still depressed?" the woman asked. She pointed to Micah. "Girl on the train—are you going to marry him?"

"No, no—"

"He's got money," the woman said; then she explained to the others: "The redhead is depressed. She wanted to jump off a train, in the middle of nowhere."

"What?" said Eleanor.

"I wouldn't have allowed it," the woman said. "I wouldn't have let you throw your life away. Man trouble, that's what she's got."

"I *never* intended to jump off that train."

"You were going to do *what?*" Joan asked.

"I never—I wouldn't do something like that!"

"It's a good thing I was there," the gray-haired woman said. "I saved her life."

"You did not!"

"Are you okay, Eleanor?" Joan asked. "Why doesn't anyone confide in me?"

"She's crazy," Eleanor said.

"Everybody's crazy at the Silverman!" Micah shouted happily.

As if to prove him right, a wizened, mustachioed man appeared, flipping open his wallet. "I'm from the FBI," he said. "Don't tell anybody."

"Fine, Al," said Micah. "Go jump in a lake."

Leaning closer, the man said, "When I was in the jungle . . ." but Micah shooed him away.

"A real long ball hitter," Micah said. "Okay," he continued, "I'm off to the hair replacement lecture. Ladies, why don't you go over to the Night Owl Lounge. Aaron, you take them over there."

On the way, they passed the hair replacement lecture. Ralph Levine, who reminded Joan of the late Eddie Cantor, placed a toupee on a bald man's head. He explained, "There is nothing in this world more important than a head of natural-looking hair."

In the Night Owl Lounge, a five-piece band was playing "La Bamba." A woman with puffed-up platinum hair and a skintight red dress vibrated her ample body on the crowded dance floor. Around her, the cheek-to-cheek sequined couples made Joan think of sweet-smelling sardines.

Joan almost expected Desi Arnaz to suddenly materialize, along with his smiling, slick-haired orchestra, fresh from an engagement at the Copacabana. "Good evening ladies and gentlemen," he might have announced. "Tonight we'll begin with one of my personal favorites, 'Baba-loo.'" Joan felt as though she was somehow miraculously experiencing the fifties, 1957 perhaps—she could almost see her parents on the dance floor, her mother's red hair teased high, Ed in a black-and-white checkered dinner jacket mouthing the lyrics over his wife's pale, perfumed shoulder.

The singles were pressed against the walls—women with plunging necklines, arms heavy with bracelets, men with cigarettes dangling from their lips, wearing dinner jackets that didn't quite fit, or did not fit in the way they were supposed to fit here at the end of the twentieth century.

"What a sight," Joan murmured. She thought of Frederick, of dancing with him at their wedding, of holding him tight. He had finally made love to her in a tall hotel in the Bahamas, on the third day of their honeymoon. His cologne was powerful, for he lacked confidence. "Do you really love me?" he'd ask her. "Really? There's no one else?"

And she'd said, impatiently, "Of course I love you. Don't be silly. Who would I love more than you? Who would love me?"

He would never make love to her unless he had showered, brushed his teeth, combed his hair. Never. She used to think he was putting it off, but maybe he was just afraid.

"You don't have to do all that," Joan had told him a few months later, on an uncommonly hot April morning. Despite the heat, she felt luxurious, lying there naked on the cool flowery bedspread. "Can't it ever be spontaneous? Can't you ever just throw me on the bed and take me?"

He stepped out of the bathroom. He went to say something, then pointed to the toothbrush in his mouth, and he went back into the bathroom and ran the water. "What were you saying?"

"You don't have to 'prepare' yourself."

"But I want to. I want everything to be right." His smile was faint, wistful.

"Just throw me on the bed one day. Or on the kitchen floor."

"But isn't it more comfortable on the bed?"

"Forget it, I'm not in the mood anymore."

"No?"

"Forget it."

Aaron's voice interrupted her thoughts. "Joan, you look like you're a million miles away. How do you like the Silverman?"

"Everyone looks slightly . . . desperate."

Aaron said, "Everyone is looking for something—and yet they're happy being unhappy. They tell you about their gallstones, their operations, their divorces, how they were betrayed. People will talk to you. They don't have to know you. Talking does them some good, I think. There's a feeling of . . . I'm thinking of a Yiddish word, *haimish*. It means family, warmth, intimacy. Something like that. There isn't an English word quite like it."

When Aaron asked Eleanor to dance, she hesitated, but Joan pushed her forward. "Go ahead, Eleanor. Why not?" But as Aaron took her sister's hand, as they glided onto the crowded dance floor, Joan wondered: What is he really like? Why did his wife leave him? She'd had several glasses of wine and she felt herself swaying slightly, clutching the bar.

Aaron and Eleanor moved tentatively as the band slowly played, "When I Fall in Love." They danced politely, a bit stiffly. And then Aaron stopped. The lights still burned. The music still played. Other couples still swayed. Aaron and Eleanor, however, stood still on the dance floor.

Then he kissed her on the mouth.

After several more dances, Eleanor and Aaron returned to the bar. "Can I buy you a drink, Joan?" he asked. She thought: why not, why not another glass of wine? Eleanor was smiling, her face was flushed. She wasn't wearing her glasses and Joan felt a strange pity for her; her eyes were naked—she seemed so defenseless. Who was this man? This Aaron? Wasn't it too soon for Eleanor to have her heart broken again? For it seemed that Eleanor always had her heart broken. She had lived with that awful man who turned out to have a wife stashed away in Upper Montclair. And Rene. And before him, good-looking men who liked too many good-looking women. Women on the side.

In the ladies room, Joan told her sister, "I saw what happened."

"What do you mean?"

"Well, he kissed you."

She hesitated. "Oh, that."

Joan said, "Do you think it might be too soon?"

Eleanor was combing her hair. "Well, I—"

Joan put her arm around her sister. "You've been through a lot. I wouldn't want to see you rush into anything. Don't get mad. I just don't want to see you get hurt again. What was all that about the train? You were going to jump off a train?"

"Of course I wasn't."

"What do you really know about Aaron?"

"He's very nice—"

"But you're still technically married."

"Separated."

"Eleanor, be careful. I only say this because I don't want you to get hurt again so soon." And Joan wondered: was that really why? Or did she not want her sister to be happy, since she was not?

Stumbling into the kitchen in the early morning light, Eleanor came upon Mike and Veronica from down the road. And there was her soon-to-be-ex-husband, Rene.

He looked as though he hadn't shaved for a day or two. Still, he was beautiful. This had not changed. Not a strand of his shiny blond hair was out of place. He wore khaki pants, a pair Eleanor didn't recognize—they were obviously new—and a white T-shirt, which he, or someone, had recently ironed, for when he approached her, she smelled that freshly ironed scent. She was about to shake his hand when he kissed her full on the lips. His lips were warm. She thought of Aaron, and then she saw that it wouldn't work with him. Her husband was right here. He was not even her ex-husband yet. Joan was right: it was too soon.

"You look beautiful," he told her.

"Oh," she said, untangling her morning hair.

Sitting at the kitchen table, Veronica sipped peppermint tea. Her thin silver bracelets chimed as she lifted the cup. "I carry my own tea bags," she said, as if some explanation were necessary. She then picked up an aluminum decanter full of tea bags that Eleanor kept on the kitchen table. It was covered with rows of blue ducks.

"Quack, quack," Veronica said with a laugh.

Eleanor suddenly felt inadequate: she should have a shiny black decanter, an abstract decanter, a cool decanter.

"*Veronica*," Mike said.

"What? What did I do?"

Mike's eyes were wide with friendliness, or perhaps, nervous anticipation. "We picked up Rene from the train station," he explained.

"Was there much traffic?" asked Eleanor, heart pounding, attempting to make conversation.

"In Tylerville?" Veronica asked.

"Well, I suppose not. How is your play going?"

"Fine. Doesn't Rene look great?"

"Um, yes," said Eleanor, frowning.

"Are you okay, Eleanor?" Veronica asked. "You look like death."

Eleanor bit her lip. "I'm fine." She was going to cry, no doubt about it. She was due to cry, but she held it in. Rene was four days early—she wasn't prepared to see him. She felt disjointed. Why had he come so early? But wasn't that just like him?

"Eleanor," Rene said, rushing to her. "What's the matter?"

"Charlotte—she almost lost her baby the other day. We had to rush her to the hospital. The baby was saved, and Charlotte is fine, but she'll have to stay here until the baby is born. Although the doctor says maybe she can fly back to LA in a few months if there's absolutely no break-through bleeding."

"That's tough."

Mike, Veronica, and Rene poured themselves bowls of cereal, filled wineglasses with orange juice. Well, this was still Rene's house. Mike and Veronica were his friends—hers, too, she supposed, though she didn't feel too friendly.

"Oh," said Veronica suddenly. "Before I forget, the play's going to performed at the Catskills Theatre next week. A pre-Manhattan run-through. You might as well come."

"That sounds fine," said Eleanor. She excused herself for a minute and stepped into the hallway, where she looked up Aaron's number in the phone book. Nervously, she dialed, and when he answered, she said, "Oh, hello. It's me, Eleanor. I just wanted to tell you, I'm not going to be digging today. But you can come over. Feel free to come over." She felt rattled, as though she had done him an injustice.

"Did something happen?"

"No . . . Rene is here. He just stopped by. But feel free to dig."

He was silent for a moment, then said, "I wasn't going to come today anyway. I'm busy, the farm and all."

"I see we planted the tulips correctly this year," said Rene as he and Eleanor strolled down to the mailbox. He knelt down, scrutinizing the garden. "I can't believe we planted those bulbs upside down last year. No wonder they didn't bloom."

"No wonder." She hoped he wouldn't try to change her mind about the divorce.

Rene kissed her softly on the cheek, careful not to disturb her hat. "Remember, I still love you. And I always will."

Eleanor sighed. She pulled from the mailbox the cable television bill and a flyer advertising Veronica's play. "How's Veronica?"

"Well, you just saw her. They'd have stayed longer, but she and Mike had to go back to the city. But they'll be back for the play. It's going to be great. Veronica is really a remarkable playwright."

"Is she?"

"He, on the other hand," said Rene, pointing up the lawn toward Malcolm, "thinks he's remarkable, but I think he's a glorified ditch digger." Rene explained that he had spoken with Malcolm earlier. "I suppose he is smart. To some extent. And he tells me you've been digging. I can't picture you digging, not that you're helpless or anything. Do you like him? Oh, God. I'm upset about this divorce situation. I just don't understand— Why can't we just go back to the ways things were?" They strolled down to the pond. "Tranquillity Base, that's what I named it," he said, pointing.

"Hasn't been so tranquil."

They sat on the Adirondack chairs at the edge of the

pond. Four birds swooped down, dipping their tiny feet in the water. One of the birds chirped—a short tweet and a longer tweet, and another bird called back the same message.

"The divorce will go through in two weeks," Eleanor told him. "Maybe sooner."

"You're making a very big mistake."

She sighed. "How long are you staying?"

"I'd like to stay forever, but I see that's not possible, so how about two days?" He paused. "I can't believe this is happening, that I'm losing you."

"Where are you going to sleep?" she asked. "I mean, we should figure that out. Charlotte needs peace and quiet. We can't be fighting or anything."

Rene left his chair and sat on Eleanor's lap. He often did playful things like this, but now she didn't react, though he felt warm and smelled pleasant, like Ivory soap. "I'd like to sleep with you," he said. "It's been too long."

Pushing him off, she said, "You can sleep in the attic. There's a bed up there."

"If I die of heat prostration, you will be held accountable." He seemed to find his remark very amusing. "Oh God," he said. "I think I'm losing my mind." He sighed. "I'm losing you."

"Anyway," he continued, "no money in the archaeological dig. Oh well. You can't have everything. You wish you could. Still, at least we're doing our bit. When I finish the book I'm reading about Miró, I'm going to study up on archaeology. If that's okay with Malcolm."

She could tell he was angry. He wasn't getting what he wanted. He was really angry at his father, always had been. Once, he painted Sarah, one of the cows, instead of milking her. When his father caught him, he made him wear a sign that said "Faggot" for the rest of the day. He was eleven.

"Oh no," Rene was saying, "here's Joan."

Although Joan was well coiffed, wearing a gray pantsuit and black loafers, she seemed to have a bit of a hangover. She was pale, with dark circles under her eyes. "I just checked on Charlotte. What a mood she's in. How have you been, Rene? It's good to see you."

Rene said, "I could be better. What's that you're holding . . . ah, a book."

"A mystery."

"Good for you."

Joan said, "Is there something wrong?"

"No, not at all. Reading is fundamental."

Joan stared at Rene, then stomped away.

Eleanor called after her, "Joan?"

"Is she too much?" he asked. *The Mysterious Affair at Styles.* I read that when I was in the fifth grade."

"I'm going to read it after she's finished with it," said Eleanor. "For your information."

"I'm sorry," he said. "Joan's a good person. She really is. I'm just upset about you and me. I just wish—well, you know what I wish." She didn't expect it, but he began to cry. She wanted to put her arms around him, but she couldn't—that would be too dangerous. He would feel too sweet; she would never get away from him. Why, she wondered, couldn't she be the kind of woman who ignores her husband's affairs—a sophisticated world-weary woman? He did love her, in his way.

Later, Rene and Eleanor, dueling artists, set up their easels on the broad lawn at the east side of the house, which had not yet been dug up. The lawn was accented by a tangle of birch trees, and in the distance the mountains formed several peaks. Off to the right, the garden Eleanor had planted a few years before was a riot of pink peonies, spires of yellow foxgloves, spreading clumps of white geraniums. In spite of her allergies,

Eleanor had worked hard to get the garden going. Every chance she got, she hacked away at the brambles. It was like cutting a trail through the jungle. Each day she would see just a little more sunlight, a little more possibility.

Now she penciled in the birch trees, the pines, the small rectangle where she would lay in the colors of the garden. She sketched a small house, much like her own, though she replaced the narrow windows in the living room with one imposing, swirling, incongruous Palladian window, which would have pleased her ambitious mother. Next, she pressed curls of paint onto her palette. Staring at her empty canvas, she took a deep breath. The moment of truth. The other day she had painted so effortlessly, with such confidence, but now she felt the old fears. She took another deep breath, knew she would make a mess of things; still, with a large, flat brush, she stroked in the sky. As she outlined the house in soft gray with a liner brush, Rene, who now stood behind her, proclaimed, "Nicely done."

She ignored him.

"Don't you want to see what I'm doing?"

"Not really."

"You know you do," he said, pulling her over to his easel. Reluctantly, she followed.

He had not sketched in his painting at all—he had gone straight to the paint, which he had mixed furiously on his palette. She could tell how furiously he had been working by observing his palette. The messier it was, the better the painting.

On his canvas, cool ribbons of blue suggested the shapes of tree trunks and shadows, while wiggles of yellow-white became blades of sunlit grass. He had set the two of them in his painting. She knelt by the garden, a few dots of lilac. He knelt beside her. There was an ease of movement, of contentment, apparent in the figures: his hand rested upon her shoulder, her head was arched back slightly, as if someone had said something wonderfully amusing.

At first she didn't say anything. He could paint so quickly! But this was not them—had it ever been the two of them? Possibly at first—yes, admit it, certainly at first. It's easy at first.

"Well—?" he said.

This wasn't like his usual work; it wasn't abstract at all. What he had painted was the two of them as he might have liked them to be—if he didn't have to work at it. The couple they might have been if he had been different and she had been stronger, had insisted from the beginning that he stop seeing other women . . . but that wouldn't have worked.

Would it? she wondered.

When they finished their paintings, Eleanor and Rene strolled back up to the house to visit Charlotte.

"I don't think she'll want to see me," Rene said.

"Why?" asked Eleanor.

When they entered her room, Charlotte sat up in bed. "Oh Christ," she said, "it's you."

"You're looking well," said Rene.

"What the hell are you doing here? Eleanor doesn't need to see you. *I* don't need to see you."

"I haven't seen you since—last Thanksgiving. That was a great day, wasn't it?"

"You're a louse," Charlotte said, rubbing her eyes.

"I have one thing to tell you," he said. "And I mean it. I love your sister. In spite of everything."

Eleanor said, "In spite of what?"

He looked away. "In spite of all that you think I did, which I didn't."

—

Rene wanted to take Eleanor out on the rowboat. He always seemed to want her to do things she didn't feel comfortable doing: to smoke hashish, to hang-glide, to take up beekeeping—she had agreed to none of them.

"I'd rather not," she said.

"It's a lovely day. Why not? We can still be friends."

This time she gave in; going out on an aluminum rowboat was hardly daring, and they had gone out on the boat many times before. But now . . . She tucked herself at one end. Rene, at the other, rowed slowly toward the center of the pond. The wind surged, and Eleanor had to hold tightly to her big straw hat. Rene's blond hair fluttered. He carried his smile like a weapon.

Rene stopped paddling. The boat rocked when he stood up and glanced back toward shore, toward the house. "The place is going to seed." He sounded very British today. "Everything's all ripped up."

"Are you blaming me?" Eleanor adjusted her glasses. Part of her wanted to take off the glasses—it was her vanity—but she kept them on. Without them, the white house would have been a blur, the mountains in the distance a smudge, the horizon would have been missing. She would not have seen Malcolm and Natalie bent over working. She thought: *I should be working on my square. Not here, with this—this beautiful liar.*

"It's not your fault, I'm not saying it's your fault," he said.

"The house? It doesn't look good? I know it's not my fault."

"Come on. Please give me a smile."

She offered him a lame one; her smile went no farther than her mouth, it didn't ascend to her eyes. Though she did not like confrontations, bad blood, Eleanor said, "You were the one who wanted to buy this place."

Slowly he nodded.

Eleanor knew he had a different country in mind, a country of butterfly nets and badminton courts and picnicking. Eleanor had not much wanted to buy a country house in the first place. With her allergies, she didn't really like the outdoors. She didn't like the sun, the wind, the insects. Adventurous Rene, on the other hand, once said he'd like to travel to India. "I'd love to walk the teeming, steaming streets of Bombay. Observe the beggars."

Eleanor had grown to love the country, though she protected herself from it with allergy pills and her big straw hat.

"You know what's odd," he was saying.

"What?"

"You say you're allergic to flowers, and yet you planted a garden, and you were in the process of putting together this water garden."

Eleanor frowned. "Flowers bother me . . . in the house."

"But not outdoors?"

"Sometimes, I don't know. I take my pills."

With his paddle, he splashed water at her. Annoyed, she wiped droplets from her glasses. Her T-shirt, too, was wet, and her denim shorts were splotched a darker blue.

Laughing, he stumbled over to her end of the boat and tried to brush the water from her clothes. Eleanor stiffened. He felt so luxuriously good. *"Rene,"* she warned.

He smiled his glistening smile. "What?"

"Just . . . don't."

"I was just trying to help."

He sat beside her—his khaki thigh touched her bare one. She regretted wearing shorts because now he was stroking her thigh with his smooth hand. He still wore his wedding band.

"You better get over to your end of the boat," she told him.

"My end? Is this part of the settlement?" He lowered his voice. "Said Rene may not approach said Eleanor on a rowboat under penalty of law."

When she didn't say anything, when she just stared at the pale horizon, he climbed to the other side of the boat and began to paddle. Eleanor held her hat down in the breeze. She spotted a crimson flash in a tall oak tree at the far side of the pond—a cardinal.

They were moving closer to the far shore. He must have sensed her anxiety, because he explained, "We'll go for a walk." Looking over his shoulder toward the house, he shivered and said, "Your sisters."

Eleanor waved to Joan, a tiny figure on the shoreline.

"They hate me," he added.

"Not Joan, I don't think she does."

"But Charlotte does?"

"She called you a louse. Why did she call you that?"

Rene guided the boat through a pile of branches. The wind suddenly died, and they waited silently in the boat, which rocked several feet from shore. The only sound was the soft murmur of the wind high in the trees.

Whhaap!

"Rene!"

He had again struck the water with a paddle.

"It was a beaver!" he said. He held out his hand to help her to shore, but she stepped in the water; her canvas sneakers were drenched and her feet itched. Rene pulled the boat onto the grassy shore. They had taken this trip many times, when the sun was high and when the sun was low, when it was windy and when it was still.

Their footsteps were hushed by the thick spongy carpet of pine needles and ferns.

"We'll talk," said Eleanor, setting the ground rules. Then she held up a finger. "I'll get the pail from the boat, for blueberries."

"Sure."

Moments later, pail in hand, Eleanor strolled to the blueberry bushes. Concentrating, she picked the darkest berries. A black bird with an orange beak swooped down on a nearby bush, but in seconds, the bird alighted. Eleanor had the sense of vague contentment, which she knew was unwarranted. Still she was dealing with the situation, not giving in to Rene, and the country was especially beautiful—an extraordinary range of greens surrounded her: sunlit leaves, cool shadows.

But this vague sensation of happiness was fractured when Rene looped his arm through hers. She managed to wriggle away and went on plucking berries. Rene thrust his hand into the pail and grabbed some berries, shoving them greedily in his mouth.

Beyond him, Eleanor glimpsed Aaron's fields; his tall rows of corn swayed in the breeze. Just then, a bee hovered near and she ran around in a little circle, and then she dropped the pail, which since Rene's raid, held only half a dozen berries. "A bee!" she cried.

"Bzzzz," said Rene, who now sat cross-legged under the crooked limbs of an elm. She strolled over to him, though the grass was a bit too high for her comfort. She didn't like to walk in the tall grass; bugs and snakes and ticks and who knows what lurked in the tall grass. People had even written songs about what lurked in the tall grass.

Seeming to read her mind, he said, "Hold on," and ran back to the boat.

Eleanor stood there, as gnats and bees and flies and butterflies swirled around and made a crazy buzzing, clicking noise. The noise corresponded to what was going through her mind—she suddenly knew she should not be here, on the far side of the pond, with Rene.

He was soon back, blond hair sunlit, holding a small blanket over his head like a trophy.

She shook her head. "No, Rene."

"Why not?" He lay down on the blanket, elbows supporting him.

"No."

"Are you just going to stand there?"

Something crawled up her leg, a tiny caterpillar. She slapped her ankles.

"Stand if you want," he told her, "but I'll lie here and enjoy the country. My land. Land that I don't have to farm. I hated farming; it turned my father mean."

"It's our land," she corrected. "Which we have to sell."

"The land of the ancient Indians. It really is amazing. Spiritual somehow. And we're getting a divorce and we have to sell our land. It's a shame."

"Let's go back."

"Come on. Don't be absurd. Why stand in the grass with the insects? Don't be irrational."

When she didn't move, he gently pulled her arm. She shook him away, and he let her go.

"Who am I, a stranger?" He shook his head. "You have it all wrong. That's why we're getting this ridiculous divorce. You have really overreacted." He moved to an entirely prone position, face to the sun, hands folded on his chest. He looked up at her and smiled, a smile of appeal. "Eleanor," he said softly, in the voice she imagined was really his. She heard a farmboy in his voice. "I love you. I really do."

Standing up, he curled his arms around her. "Please, Eleanor."

She felt his warm mouth on her neck, on her lips. She hardened her mouth.

"Eleanor."

"What?"

"You love me, too. That's obvious."

"I don't love you," she said, turning her head, which

now rested in the fold of his arm and chest. No, she told herself. No. She stepped on his foot and he laughed a little.

"Are you trying to hurt me?" he said. And then he pulled her down on the blanket. Things happen so quickly. He removed her glasses and tossed them on the grass. He grabbed her hat and the hat pin scraped her scalp. She struggled free but he pulled her back down.

"Rene!"

Birds danced in the trees when he whispered, "I've missed you so much."

"Stop!" she said.

He maneuvered himself on top of her, pinning her to the blanket, and she remembered how he had once gingerly removed a splinter from the sole of her foot.

He kissed her eyelids, her forehead. "I've missed you."

"We can't." His chest was like metal.

"I've missed you," he whispered, grinding against her.

"Have you missed Marlena, too? I haven't forgotten."

He didn't seem to be listening. He pulled off his freshly laundered T-shirt. His back was like silk. It was odd to touch something so beautiful, so sensual, and to feel so badly.

"Marlena," she said.

"That was a mix-up." He moved her on top of him, holding her tightly against him. "Eleanor, you are the only woman I have ever loved. And that I swear is the truth."

"You're so . . . "

Smiling, licking her lips, he said, "I'm so what?"

"Beautiful." She said it listlessly—it was as if she had reported he had cancer.

"*You're* so beautiful, and now we don't have to get a divorce."

"We do."

"I love you," he said.

She struggled to free herself and, sighing heavily, he

let her go. She lay down on the blanket, a foot from him. She sighed. "I wish you were someone else."

"Why?"

"I can't trust you. And without that . . . "

Bare-chested, he knelt over her; his pale hair made her think of feathers. Small lines fanned out from his eyes. He was thirty-nine years old, but still he was boyish. "You can trust me," he said. "From now on you can."

"No."

He took her in his arms; his body was heavy and hard. He pulled at her shirt, and it strangled her a bit at the neck, and for a moment she was in darkness, and then her shirt slipped over her head, and her arms. He pulled at her bra, at the metal clasps, then at the zipper of her shorts.

"Rene, *stop it!*" He held her hands down, and she scratched his palm with her forefinger. She knew all of this was her fault. She should not have come here with him. She was wrong. For a second, he eased the weight of his hands, and she threw up her right hand, scratching him in the eye.

"You . . . bitch!" It was as if the thought had just come to him.

"Rene, how could you—!"

He held her shoulders down with his knees. "You bitch! You're like my father, you—you won't let me be happy! You want me to suffer!" His eyes were red in the corners. "Do you want to know something?"

She stared.

"I have something to tell you. Are you listening? *I never liked sex with you. I never did.*"

She went to scratch him again but let her arms fall.

"Sex is something you're not good at," he said. She thought—he's lying. Isn't he? He's lying. She recalled a soft summer evening a few years before, when they had made love right here, under the trees. Slow, tender love. "You are everything I will ever need," he had told her under the moon. She had been so gullible. Always so gullible. *I never liked sex with you.*

Abruptly, Rene turned to his right. He stood up. "Get up!" he commanded. At first she was confused and didn't move. He threw her clothes at her, and quickly she put them back on.

She heard a rustling in the trees. A quiet voice was saying, "Okay, Maddie, come on." A dog barked.

Her bra wasn't on right, the straps were twisted. She had put her shirt on inside out—the seams showed. The zipper of her shorts was broken; the zipper would only climb halfway.

Rene stared at the ground.

Eleanor heard something break. She had stood on her glasses. The idea of her glasses being broken, and all that had happened here . . . When she turned she saw Aaron Silverman.

No one said a word. Panting, Maddie ran around in a small circle.

"I'm her husband," Rene said.

"Yes," Aaron said calmly. "We're neighbors. I know."

Rene rolled his eyes. "Women."

Maddie ran to Eleanor, jumped up on her, muddying her shorts. "Maddie, come on," soothed Aaron, "leave Eleanor alone."

Rene laughed, "Well, everybody loves Eleanor."

Looking away, Aaron said, "Sorry, I didn't mean to—"

". . . My fault," Eleanor murmured, gazing at her broken glasses.

—10—
Prisoners

Joan checked the directions again, then stuffed them back in her bag. Could this be it? She parked her Porsche in a small lot and moved slowly toward the tiny church, peering at a crooked sign:

ST. ANTHONY OF PADUA—
ROMAN CATHOLIC CHURCH
MASSES—SUNDAYS, 10 A.M.

St. Anthony's had none of the stucco beauty of Our Lady of Perpetual Mercy in Florence. St. Anthony's did not make Joan think of a Spanish mission. Nor did the church bring to mind the granite grandeur of St. Bartholomew's in Hillside. Set on the banks of the Delaware, ten minutes from Tylerville, the unimposing brown wooden structure appeared at first glance Protestant, with a Bavarian twist. On the east and west sides of the church, gingerbread lattice bordered frosted windows, and overhead, the skinny steeple made Joan think of a precariously high heel. Brightly dressed women and children, men wearing crisp suits, motley couples clad in jeans who had not bothered to comb their hair, streamed into the church.

Inside, two stained-glass windows behind the altar depicted the Sacred Heart of Jesus and the Blessed Virgin. The two seemed to have been stripped of color—a thin wash of red and blue remained. Jesus and his mother appeared preoccupied, their eyes turned longingly toward the river.

Kneeling and standing in St. Anthony's Roman Catholic Church, Joan wiped beads of sweat from her upper lip. It was difficult to maneuver her elbows, pinned as she was between a man who wore overalls (a farmer, perhaps, or a hippie throwback) and a young woman in a linen suit (up from the city—the latest hairdo). Joan had gone to Mass and no one could fault her. Charlotte, of course, could not go to Mass as she was holed up in bed—not that she would have gone anyway. Charlotte believed in nothing but Charlotte. And Eleanor would not go. She would hardly speak, hardly move.

Earlier, Joan had asked her, "Aren't you going to work on your square?"

Eleanor sat curled on the couch, head on her knees. "No."

"Tomorrow maybe?"

"No."

"Then you'll go to Mass with me?"

"No." She did not elaborate.

Eleanor and Rene had gone out on the boat the other day, and when they returned, Eleanor was ashen. Rene, packing up his art supplies, told Eleanor, "You've exaggerated everything."

Eleanor shook her head. In her hands, she held her glasses, which were broken, and without them, her eyes, threaded red, were flat and unfocused. "I have not exaggerated." And then, without warning, Eleanor lunged at Rene, tearing his white T-shirt, ripping part of it away.

"What are you doing! I don't know what your problem is!" he said.

Eleanor drew back. "I hate you," she told him.

"You've lost your grip."

"Why did you say that? What you told me before—that was a lie."

Now the priest raised the Host, the Body of Christ, above his head, and Joan wondered: What did Eleanor mean? What was the lie?

She had never seen Eleanor so angry—in fact, she had never seen her angry at all. Eleanor wasn't human in some ways, thought Joan. She made excuses for everyone. Even Hart Tyler, that man she had lived with who neglected to tell her about his wife.

But after Rene left, when Mike and Veronica came to pick him up, Eleanor lost control. She kicked open the screen door, holding in one hand the painting she had worked on that morning, and in the other, a tube of paint and a brush. With a flourish, she hurled the painting on the lawn. Then she dug her brush into the tube and started destroying what she'd done. First the foxgloves disappeared in a thick sea of black, then the peonies, then the mountains in the distance. She then obliterated the house, taking the roof away, the front stoop, the door.

For two days she barely spoke. She hid in her bedroom. Joan brought her bowls of soup, oatmeal, boxes of crackers, bananas. She'd take a few mouthfuls, then say, "I'm not hungry."

Yesterday afternoon, Joan had said, "Come into Charlotte's room for a minute. We want to talk to you."

"What did that bastard do?" demanded Charlotte. "I don't know why you won't tell us."

"Who?"

"Rene."

"Nothing."

"Nothing?" Joan repeated.

"Nothing."

Charlotte said, "Nothing is so bad that you can't talk about it."

"Don't make me laugh," said Joan. "But Eleanor, really, anything can be forgotten, no matter how bad it is—the feelings of sadness will pass."

"Yes," said Charlotte. "The feelings of sadness will pass, or should pass, if you're mature enough, if you put the past behind you. Where it belongs. Just push it back deep, and forget."

Eleanor said, "I'm not sure why I won't say it. If I don't say it, maybe it won't be real." She sighed. "Maybe it isn't real."

Joan said, "But you're upset. Something was real enough to upset you."

"We went for a boat ride, and we took a walk, and he lay down on a blanket . . . "

"And?" said Charlotte.

"I may be making too much of this." She took a deep breath. "He tried to—to have sex with me . . . That's all."

"That asshole!" Charlotte said.

"But you didn't let him," said Joan. "Is that right? Nothing happened?"

"I didn't let him."

Joan grasped Eleanor's hand. "It's important to talk about it. He tried and failed. You talked him out of it."

"He just stopped. He heard Aaron walking our way. But, you know, if he had tried to have sex with me, say, eight months ago, I wouldn't feel badly, would I? Since he did the same thing, tried to have sex, then . . . well, if we were still—together . . ." She sat sullen, staring at her hands.

"He didn't succeed," said Joan. "You were too strong for him. You'll get over it. Won't she, Charlotte?"

Charlotte said, "He's a rapist!"

Joan said, "Don't say that. You're making it seem like he— She feels badly enough. Why are you saying he's a rapist? You always have to put the worst face on things."

"Attempted rapist. Is that better?"

Joan put her arm around Eleanor, who sobbed. "Now look what you've done."

"I didn't do it. *He* did it."

Eleanor thought: *I didn't tell them the worst thing.* She couldn't bring herself to say it. She sat alone in the living room, listening to the clock, though there was no place she wanted to be, no moment she needed to mark. Joan was at Mass. Charlotte was in bed reading. Natalie, Malcolm, and Mr. Simmons were digging.

The more hateful the words, the harder they are to forget. *I never liked sex with you, Eleanor. Never.* It couldn't be true—could it? Had she wrapped her legs around him incorrectly, kissed and stroked him the wrong way? Had she failed him? After all, somehow she knew that their marriage would fail. That she would fail. All along.

Had she somehow betrayed him with this knowledge?

A year or two before, when their old Valiant was still reliable, Eleanor and Rene had taken a drive. They'd had no particular destination; they wanted only to escape the traffic-snarled streets of Manhattan. Rene decided against going north to the country house. He wanted a change, so they headed south and eventually passed through Tinton Falls, New Jersey, where people drove pickups and russet horses galloped in stubby clearings.

"By the way," he said, "Beth and Tony are getting a divorce. Tony told me."

"Are you sure?"

"They're not like us, Eleanor. Their marriage has never been strong."

"I'm so surprised!"

"We love each other too much to ever part," he said, suddenly rummaging for a tape. "Where did I put that tape?" And it was at that point that she knew—exactly how, she couldn't say—that their marriage, too, would end.

Still, she said, "I love you, Rene," and she did; she watched his smooth hand on the wheel, crescents of blue paint under his nails. She thought: I will forget his hand, his smooth hand. A time will come and I will forget what he looks like, exactly.

"Did you see my tape?" he asked. "I make these tapes, and lose them."

Eleanor lifted herself off the couch and sat at the cluttered kitchen table now, where clumps of oatmeal clung to bowls. She should do the dishes, not leave them, as always, for Joan. A few blueberries had fallen on the floor, and, with great effort, she picked them up.

She should be with Natalie, Malcolm, and Mr. Simmons, working on her square. But she had lost her will. Digging up the earth—there seemed no sense in it. This morning, Mass would have been an easier option. Maybe she should have gone. God never gives us any cross that we cannot bear, the nuns used to insist. Eleanor wasn't religious, though at this moment, she wanted to be. But she knew she really didn't believe in it: she didn't believe that if you wore a scapular around your neck God would save you from the fires of hell, but if you didn't wear it, you would burn.

For a few years, long ago, Our Lady of Perpetual Mercy Grammar School had offered her a sure view of the world, but it didn't last. There, she wore a white short-sleeved cotton shirt, a plaid skirt and matching vest, green knee socks, saddle shoes, and the world had been comprehensible. She had looped perfect spirals across lined paper, diagrammed sentences. Subject, predicate, direct object, or—be alert students—predicate nominative. Everything, even pronouns, were accounted for.

Nothing was loose, not verbs and not sins.

Now nothing held its place. Eleanor forced herself to go for a swim, to wash him away. She pulled on a solid blue, one-piece swimsuit, and strolled to the edge of the pond. Her legs had been invaded by prickly hairs.

Slowly, she stepped into the water. It slapped against her toes, her ankles, her calves, her thighs. She shivered, held herself tight. The water lapped over her hips, and when it reached her waist, she winced. She pulled herself through the water, on her side. The only stroke she had mastered at the Florence Community Pool had been the sidestroke because she didn't have to put her head in the water.

Soon Eleanor felt winded—unhappy that this foray into the water hadn't soothed her. There was no redemption in this water. She knew she should not swim here: giardia, the parasite infection she had had—she didn't want to get that again. Rene had nursed her to health. Don't think about him. Forget him. Forget the first time they made love, when they lay entwined on the couch in the immense living room of his loft; their every gesture was satiny, their every kiss tender, and then their lovemaking grew ferocious. He bit her shoulder. He panted, "There's never been anyone like you. Never. This is almost . . . beyond sex. Yes, beyond sex. I've . . . been . . . waiting for you . . . Always."

Cupping her hands, kicking her legs from side to side, she glided through the black water. If she were brave, truly brave, she would sink beneath the surface and swallow the pond whole.

Instead she kicked toward shore.

As Joan drove back from Mass, she noticed that the pines lining the road looked like someone was shaking them. God was everywhere, watching her, watching everyone. The overpowering sky held huge white clouds; six of them floated side by side. They were near replicas of each other, billowy puzzle pieces, the shape of some undetermined country. A small propeller plane ambled beneath the clouds like a tiny dragonfly. Within the clouds, she spotted a plump foot, a thumb nuzzled at a mouth. She took a hard sigh and gripped the wheel. *Concentrate on the road,* she told herself, or listen to the radio. The D.J. announced the weekly school lunch menu: macaroni and cheese, tater tots, and apple sauce on Monday. On Tuesday, hamburger or hotdog and small green salad; on Wednesday, pizza, salad, Jell-O . . .

Joan stopped in town, parking on Main Street, in front of Harper's General Store. She planned to make a special Sunday dinner—roast chicken and potatoes, a huge green salad, summer squash, and an apple pie. At Mass, the priest, who wore long brown robes—a Franciscan—had proclaimed, "Go out and do good works for others." Well, she was doing her bit. She would cook—well, here in the country, she always cooked. A good meal, perhaps, would cheer Eleanor. Perhaps.

Bright-faced Walter Harper made up her order. "A first-class day," he told her.

"It's been so warm," said Joan, rummaging through a rack of cheap magazines. She picked up a copy of *True Confessions.* "I thought it was supposed to be cool up here in the mountains," she said, rubbing her foot against the gritty sloped floor. "This magazine is awful," she said. "Things don't happen in real life like this. White slave trade indeed."

Walter Harper, wrapping a chicken in brown paper, shook his head. "It's the ozone."

"Ozone?"

"You were talking about how it should be cool up here. It's the greenhouse effect. A damn shame."

Joan raised her eyebrows and Walter Harper said, "See—you don't think countryfolk watch science programs on the cable."

Struggling with the groceries, Joan loaded up the car. The trees bordering the village green jittered in the breeze. A man in a hard hat, thighs gripping a telephone pole, attended to some power lines. He shouted down to another hard-hatted man, "Egg salad sandwich! On rye!" A young woman, who wore an expression of benign neglect, negotiated a double baby carriage along Main Street. Joan thought of Jason and Diane, and then concentrated on Jason. In her mind, she heard him say, What's the big deal? Just then an engine turned over, and she noticed a white-haired man driving a tractor mower in the village green. The man atop the telephone pole called, "Jesus, the *flowers.* Jesus H. Christ, Otis. *Deaf and blind!*" What looked like orange confetti sputtered up as he drove. Someone named Otis was mowing down a line of marigolds.

The people walking along Main glanced over at the commotion. Well, nearly everyone. One man didn't. He did not look local. He stood beside a red compact with blue Jersey plates, rental plates. He was studying a map.

He was tall and wiry and his hair was black, truly black, with blue highlights. He did not look unhappy— merely confused; his brows were furrowed. He called softly to a couple walking by and they listened to him for a moment, then shrugged their shoulders, continuing along Main. The black-haired man sat on the curb, then stood up, pressing a center seam in his khaki pants. He moved slowly toward Harper's. There was something refined about him. His nose was long, aquiline. His mouth was thin. He took small stiff steps—there was nothing rangy about him, nothing loose-limbed. His long sleeves weren't rolled up, though it was warm. He wore a gleaming gold watch, an expensive watch. Joan, having loaded the Porsche with three bags of groceries, nodded to him. He nodded back. When he went to open Harper's heavy door, Joan smiled. "Lovely day."

He stopped. "Oh, yes. Quite."

He had an English accent—or perhaps he was Australian. Joan liked to talk to foreign people—to find out what they thought of Americans.

"Are you having a problem?" she asked. "You seem . . . confused."

"Well, yes. I am. Yes."

"And the problem is?"

He gazed off toward the green, half smiled when someone yelled, "Otis—you are a public menace! Enemy number one!"

"The problem, yes." He spoke very quickly. "The problem is, in short, I'm lost."

"Well," said Joan, noting his cramped, crooked teeth, "I'm not local either." She said this with some pride. "I don't live around here."

"But you're—here?"

"My sister has a house up here. Of course, she's not local either. She lives in the city. New York City. That's what we mean by that here—'The City.' "

"Ahh. I see. Yes." He took a breath. "What a lovely day." After a silence, he said, "Well, perhaps you can help me anyway. I'm looking for a—" He took a piece of crumpled paper from his pocket. "Miss Eleanor Powers. Though no, that wouldn't be her last name—Eleanor something or other. Oh, I just don't know." He smiled. "Do you ever think that you've really mucked it, done something . . . insane?"

Joan spread her arms wide. "You've found her!"

"Found her? Ah, yes. Yes indeed! Very pleased to meet you." The man put out his hand.

"No, no. I'm her sister. Eleanor's sister."

He frowned.

"Joan, her sister Joan."

"I'm actually looking for Charlotte. I should have rung ahead, but I thought she'd say, well, not to. You see, I'm Ian . . . Ian O'Toole. The director."

"Ah, the father!" said Joan.

He followed her back to the house in his rented car. Joan rapped on Charlotte's door; he waited quietly behind her. "Charlotte?" Joan called. No reply. Joan said, "She's in there. She's definitely in there. She's just—" Joan waved her hand. "Forget it."

"Oh," he said. "This is a bit of a muck-up." Joan was pleased that he did not say fuck-up. Charlotte would have said fuck-up.

Finally they had a reply: "I'm sleeping."

"I've got someone here to see you," said Joan.

"I'm sleeping."

"*Someone is here to see you.*"

Charlotte said nothing.

Opening the door, Joan said, "It's Ian."

"No problem," he said, though the situation did indeed appear, thought Joan, to be a problem.

Joan said, "Well, he is *the father*, isn't he? Why don't you talk to him? He's come thousands of miles!"

"Charlotte—?" Ian looked off toward the grapevine wreath on the wall. "Doing well?"

"You fuck! You fucking fuck! You FUCKING FUCK-ITY FUCK!"

"Charlotte," said Joan. "You're being childish."

"I'm childish? I almost lost my baby and I'm childish? I can't get out of bed for seven FUCKING MONTHS and I'm childish? I can't act, can't make movies, can't go home? FUCK YOU!"

Ian said, "She's a bit excited."

Eleanor, meanwhile, slipped into the room and introduced herself to Ian, shaking his hand. She was wearing a damp bathing suit, and Joan said, "You were swimming? Where?"

"The pond."

"But you said we weren't supposed to."

Eleanor ignored this comment and narrowed her eyes at Ian. "You're not staying here, are you?"

Odd, thought Joan. Eleanor's usual modus operandi would have compelled her to say, Please stay with us. There's a small room upstairs.

"Are you planning on staying here?" Eleanor repeated.

"Well, not actually—though it would be nice to keep Charlotte company."

"Wait a minute!" said Charlotte. "You're not staying here!"

"Why not?" Joan said. She thought it the only polite alternative. "Would you like a hamburger? A nice hot juicy burger? Being an Englishman, maybe that would be nice?"

Ian smiled weakly. "That would be wonderful."

Charlotte said, "You're making him a hamburger? While I lie in bed like this? In these circumstances? He put me in this circumstance. He doesn't give a flying fuck about me, or anybody."

Ian seemed to ignore this. Joan thought he was the pillar of understatement, so wonderfully British, so

Masterpiece Theatre, all good taste in the midst of American depravity. She decided that if a nuclear warhead wiped out Great Britain, Ian would describe the situation as "most inconvenient."

Ian said, "Oh, I've got quite a bit of equipment in the car, some film equipment—can I bring it in the house, for safekeeping?"

"I guess so," said Eleanor.

"Also," he said, "a film crew is arriving tomorrow. Just three people. Of course, they'll be staying in town, at a local hotel. Let's see, the Silverman Hotel."

Charlotte sat up in bed, a bold move, because she was supposed to lie still, except to shower and go to the bathroom. "A film crew! Why are you bringing a film crew here!"

"Well," he said, shifting back and forth, "I spoke to that chap, Sheldon."

"Seldon," corrected Charlotte.

"Well, I called your number in California—you didn't tell me where to call you back. I didn't know you were here. Anyway, this chap Shel—*Sel*-don answered." Ian cleared his throat. "And he told me all about you, of course. About how you were supposed to stay in bed for the duration of your pregnancy. Also, he spoke about this archaeological dig. I guess you told him. Well, yes, actually, you did tell him. And the BBC said, Why don't you go off and see what you come up with. I was going to call you, but I thought—"

Here Charlotte nearly got out of bed, but Joan pushed her back into position. "You're making a documentary? That's why you're here?"

"No, no. Of course not." He smiled, revealing his cramped, crooked teeth. "Absolutely not. Here to see you. Absolutely."

—

Later that afternoon, Ian rapped at Charlotte's window. He pressed his face against the glass, then opened the window. Placing his hand on his breast, he said, "But soft, what light through yonder window breaks? It is the east, and Juliet is the sun. Arise, fair sun, and kill the envious moon . . ."

Charlotte sat up. "You're no Romeo." She reached over and slammed the window shut.

Ian again jimmied it open. "I don't want you to think that directors can't act."

Charlotte said, "Oh Romeo, Romeo, wherefore art thou, Romeo? Honey, I've been looking, and you're no Romeo. You just want to make a stinking documentary. Anyway, I wish I could go home. Away from you!" She banged on the screen. "I get up to take a shower in the morning. That's the most interesting part of my day. It sucks."

"Must you speak like that?"

"Like what?"

He sighed. "I've been thinking. When you have the baby, we'll move to London."

"Excuse me?"

"We'll move to London. We'll start a new life."

"What kind of life?"

"You'll still act, if that's what's worrying you."

"I have to act."

"Of course. In England."

She had loved England. She and Ian had taken long drives around Bath, passing through the park in the center of the city, where the council had created, out of blue and red carnations, a mailman and mailwoman in commemoration of some postal triumph. The city proper behind them, Ian and Charlotte drove through patchwork hills, past the narrow river Avon, past cream-colored sheep, stone churches. They stopped for lunch in quaint pubs, like the Eight Bells, where one afternoon Ian leaned over a dark wooden table, and said, "I love you, Charlotte."

"I love you, Ian."

He held her face in his hands. "I love you."

They then shifted from love to work and discussed *Pride and Prejudice,* how well she was doing—how not so well others were doing, but Ian would wring good performances from them. He was the director; he controlled everything in the end.

They talked about the fall of Thatcher, the unfairness of a poll tax, the homeless in America and in Britain, her family (superficially, though—Charlotte avoided telling him too much). He told her about his mother, Gladys, a strong woman, though small, only four-foot-nine.

"Only four-foot-nine!" said Charlotte.

"Leave the north, Ian, my mother told me. Go south." He had lived in a small town near Manchester, a coal town. His father had worked the mines, as had his grandfather—and his father before him. His two brothers were miners, or had been, until the mines closed. "We're a town caught between the Industrial Revolution, and . . . what? Something—I don't know what."

"You've come a long way," said Charlotte.

"I have. And so have you. You've come a long way from Florence. I think of *the* Florence, but as you say, your Florence is no Florence."

Now he stood outside her window, and she longed to be outdoors as well, to soak up the country air, or—better yet—to travel again to England, to lie in a field under the heavy white sky. What a lovely day, she would say, when long slats of blue appeared. The blue of English skies, she decided, was different from the clear blue of American skies.

"The blue is slightly different here, isn't it?"

Ian squinted, looked up. "The sky? I suppose so. Yes."

"You don't think so."

He laughed. "I've never actually thought about it."

"I've only been locked up a few days, and already I'm going crazy. Me—thinking about the sky, the color of the sky. Our sky is more of a strong slate blue. Yours is a pastel blue."

"It's an interesting thing to consider."

"It's a stupid thing to consider!"

They were silent for a long while. "Will this work out?" she asked.

"What?"

"Us."

"Of course," he said.

"I don't know what to say to you, now that the movie is over."

He hesitated. "Well, that's natural. We don't really know each other."

"We should take a walk," Joan told Eleanor. "Do you hear the lawn mowers in the distance? I've always loved the buzz of lawn mowers. I suppose we should leave Ian and Charlotte to get reacquainted.

Eleanor sat curled on the couch, her chin on her knees. "A walk?"

"It's a beautiful day."

She sighed. "What's the sense?" But she gave in, after much prodding from Joan.

Joan said, "Aren't you going to wear your hat?"

"No."

Pointing at her own expensive Italian pumps, Joan asked, "Do you think my shoes will be okay, for walking?"

Eleanor shrugged. "I guess. I suppose."

"What are you talking about? My shoes are all wrong."
Joan put her arm around Eleanor. "Soon you'll be for-
mally divorced. I mean, that's what you want, isn't it?
Divorce isn't really a sin, you know. People always get
that wrong. It's remarrying that's the sin, I think.
Anyway, you'll forget all this. Aren't you going to wear
socks? I mean, you always wear socks when you go for a
walk. Lyme disease—what about that?"

"I don't care."

Joan slipped on a pair of sneakers, and the sisters
made their way along the path that circled the pond, passing the house, then the rock-shelter. There, Mr. Simmons
scribbled in a notebook. Malcolm and Natalie measured
rocks. "Archaeology is fascinating, don't you think?" Joan
said. "If you worked on your square, you might keep your
mind off, well, what happened. I thought you enjoyed all
that digging."

Eleanor sighed. "Not really."

As they moved toward the thick pines, Joan said,
"What do you think about Ian? I like a man with an
accent. Imagine, coming all this way just to see Charlotte.
It makes me— Well, it makes me angry. She treats him
terribly, and yet here he is. Don't you think that means
something?"

"I guess."

"If Frederick ever came up here, I'd have a heart
attack. He's never done an impulsive thing in his life."

Eleanor walked with her head down. "Oh."

"Do you want to go back for your hat?"

"No."

They walked in the shadows of the pines as the pond
shimmered in sunlight.

"Anyway," said Joan, "I love Frederick. I've got to love
him. Or I've got to put up with him. He's the only other
man besides— Forget it. Well, I slept with Stewart. There

was something very, I don't know, magnetic between us. I was drawn to him, God knows why. I saw a program the other day on PBS about love at first sight; they say it does exist—it's a physical thing, like hunger. It's sort of beyond our control. We recognize a certain scent, or something or other. Anyway, Stewart treated me very badly. I haven't slept with many men, have I?"

"I have no idea."

"Just the two."

Just then a peculiar sound could be heard, a water sound. Whoosh!

Joan froze, as did Eleanor. "What was that?" Joan said. The whoosh perhaps had been a beaver, a turtle, a bevy of frogs. Joan again heard something smack the water and, turning, she witnessed a rosy beige tentacle rising from the pond.

"Oh, no!" Joan said. She steered Eleanor into the deep shadow between two spruce trees, where they stood waiting for several minutes. Joan whispered, "Eleanor, do you think someone's there? Some weirdo! I thought there was no crime in the Catskills! Oh God, and I have to go to the bathroom." She always had to go to the bathroom when she stood too long concentrating.

In a loud silly voice, someone was singing "America the Beautiful."

"Oh, this is a strange area, Eleanor. I hate to think of you alone here."

"For pur-ple mountains ma-jesty. . . a-bove the fruited—"

Just then, emerging from behind a tree, a man appeared. He was naked; his feet were hidden in a bed of ferns, his pink penis, well, Joan didn't like to think about it.

"Oh, Christ!" the man said when he saw them. He covered his face with his hands, then, rethinking, covered his genitals. But he did not run. He appeared at first frightened, then suddenly grew giddy. "Well, what the hell! What the hell! There's nothing wrong with swimming nude in the great outdoors! Hey ladies! What's up?" He jumped up and down, laughing. "I'm freeeeeee!"

Joan said, "That's!— Oh God, it's Micah Silverman!" She waved him back but he stood his ground. "Get out of here! My God!"

"Isn't it the most glorious day?" He pointed to the sky, then quickly covered his private parts.

"What are you talking about? You're a pervert!" At least, Joan thought, in Micah's present state, he would not be able to tell them how old his clothes were.

Another voice, a softer voice, pleaded, "Get back in the water."

"Who's that?" Joan said.

"Nobody." The voice was near.

"Come on, Aaron!" Micah called. "He's shy, my brother."

"Oh *God!*" groaned the other voice.

"Pretend you don't see them," said Joan, guiding her sister back toward the house, but Eleanor did look back—Joan saw her. Okay, I was looking at Eleanor looking, Joan later said. As the sisters gazed back, Aaron Silverman arose, honey-toned, glistening, from the deep. He glanced quickly at Eleanor, and spotting her, jumped behind a bush.

Charlotte was reading the *New York Times.* She flipped the paper open to one of the special sections—she didn't really notice which one—and began to read an article titled, "The Lives and Worlds of Modern Cosmologists." It began, "Many agree that the more the universe seems comprehensible, the more it seems pointless." The article wasn't at all what she had expected. It did not focus on makeup artists who transform the stars with lipliners and blush. She wasn't stupid—she might have read the science piece, but her powers of concentration were limp.

Ian had arrived—to make a documentary. She knew she had been hard on him earlier, but he had caught her by surprise, and she had nearly lost the baby, and he didn't really care about her at all. He was just a horny director. She would make him stay in the upstairs room; she would not sleep with him. What was the point now?

When Ian slipped into the room, she didn't say a word. She wanted him to suffer. He leaned against the wall. "Charlotte," he smiled.

She looked up, sighed, tossed the *Times* overboard with the *Ladies Home Journal*s, the paperback novels, the puzzles and embroidery kits, which were supposed to make time race by.

"Doing well?" he asked. "I suppose it's obvious you're not doing all that well—but things will go smoothly from here on in. There won't be any further complications."

"*You're* here."

Ian sat at the foot of the bed. "I'm sorry about all of this. This—Well, you getting pregnant. And yet I'm happy, too. I want to be a father. I don't know why I didn't do it earlier. I know it's been hard for you, with me in England, and the two of us being, well, not . . . connected."

"Not connected."

"Exactly."

Ian smoothed the flowery bedspread. "I sense you're very angry."

"I am angry. But I realize this, well, situation is not entirely your fault, exactly. Or maybe it is. But it does me the world of good to be mean to you."

"Well, then—" He cleared his throat. "You were quite good in *Pride* by the way."

"Was I?"

"Very good indeed. Quite a convincing Miss Jane Bennet. Do you remember Longleat House? A lovely house, lovely."

"How could I forget?" She rubbed her stomach. "Who could forget having sex on that dining room table, such a long table. It seemed like a great idea at the time. I was horny in England. I wanted to be pregnant, I think I truly did. A death wish."

"Not at all," he said, vaguely. "Maybe I'll cast you in a new movie."

"What movie is that?"

"Well, this documentary, if it ever gets broadcast. Just kidding, though, there's no acting part in a documentary. I hope the documentary gets on the air. It all depends on how old the artifacts end up being. Simmons says the caribou bones will be at least eight thousand years old, and that's good enough for me. The charcoal is something I'm really looking forward to. I mean, how old will the charcoal be? You realize, the BBC has never really done a full-blown documentary on a North American archaeological dig. Though I personally did one on the Mayans, but that's Mexico. Sunny Me-hi-co. Anyway, you can stand around in the background and look beautiful, as you always do. Even now."

She felt fat and bloated and red and veiny and tired and hopeless. "I'm pregnant," she said.

Laughing: "Quite."

"I was very bad about this," she told him. "Really. I was terrible."

"Because you told me you were on the pill?" He frowned, then offered her a knowing, crooked smile.

She'd forgotten about that, put it out of her mind. "Well yes, that was wrong, but there were worse things."

"Worse?"

"I wasn't . . . smart."

"So you did something, less than ideal?"

"I pretended I wasn't pregnant. I drank and I tried not to gain any weight. Do you think there will be something very wrong with the baby?"

"Oh Christ, Charlotte. Why must you be so irresponsible? What are you trying to accomplish by making your life a muddle? Don't you want to be happy?"

"Of course I do," she said. But she wondered: do I deserve to be happy?

Ian's crew finally arrived, and they crammed into Charlotte's room to meet her. Colin, the cameraman, was very blond, with a small English mouth and watery blue eyes; Brad, the other cameraman, was large and fleshy, with broad features and straight black hair combed back from his square forehead. Ivy, the sound technician, was tiny, pert, and blond; in contrast to her sweet appearance, she was gruff, with a confident, accusing voice. "Brad is an idiot," she said. "Ignore him." And of course, there was Ian, with his wiry black hair, long nose, and slate blue eyes like the American sky.

"I wanted you to meet everyone," Ian told her.

Brad said, in his Cockney accent, "You look a bit like a high priestess, with the turban. Lying on your divan."

"My hair is wet," Charlotte said. "Therefore, the towel."

"You look brilliant, really. Like Cleopatra. Doesn't she, Colin?"

Ignoring him, Colin said, "You have a wonderful place here. A bit of the wild west. And a bit of Africa, too, with the ancient artifacts."

"It's not my place. It's my sister Eleanor's. I'm just here to rot."

Ian hugged her briefly. "Poor Charlotte. She's having a

tough time. But she's brave. I can't believe I'm going to be a father. Isn't it amazing? Ian O'Toole, at last to be a father."

"As far as he knows," said Brad.

"Leave it out!" said Ivy.

But Brad went on, "At least she doesn't have to stay at the, what is it, Silverman Hotel. Never stayed in a place like that before, and I've been everywhere—New Guinea and all. It's not the accommodations so much as the—clientele. Still, it's interesting, if you like to eat herring. A woman wanted to predict my future just as we were leaving, but I took a rain check."

Colin said, "He's a deep thinker, is our Brad."

"Well, I am! I've been thinking about the Indians. Imagine—they were here eight thousand years ago. Maybe longer! I shot some footage in Egypt a few years ago, and the pyramids were only about four thousand years old, tops."

"I think Charlotte wants to rest," said Ian, softly.

Charlotte was nearly asleep. She was always so tired. Lying in bed all day made her all the more exhausted. Pregnancy was draining her, as were the pills she had to take, which stopped her from losing her baby.

Ivy said, "Well, it was good to meet you. We better get to work, Ian. No time for slackers."

"Yes," he said, kissing Charlotte lightly on the cheek. "Back to work."

The day of Veronica's play finally arrived, and Joan insisted that Eleanor accompany her to the premiere. Eleanor didn't want to do a lot of things, but she usually did them anyway. She ended up doing what other people wanted her to do. So she sipped a Styrofoam cup of juice in the lobby of the Catskills Theatre in Hunter's Landing. What kind of juice was it, she wondered? Pineapple?

Banana? Or no—peach. Leave it to Veronica to choose the oddest juice available.

"This is really interesting," said Joan, looking around the newly renovated theater, once an old country picture house. Joan wore navy slacks and an ivory silk blouse, but in lieu of pumps and pantyhose, she had worn her sneakers. "Look at my feet," she said. "I'm liberated."

Charlotte was back at the country house, as was Ian, who had moved into the tiny workroom upstairs, while his crew stayed at the Silverman. Ian had started shooting the dig—and Malcolm, Natalie, and Mr. Simmons reveled in the attention. Eleanor did not revel in the chaos. Why were so many people around? She had wanted to be alone and now Charlotte, Joan, Ian, Natalie, and Malcolm were staying with her. And then there were Colin, Brad, and Ivy, staying at the Silverman, plus two graduate students were expected soon. She massaged her temples. A tiny nerve on her eyelid kept jumping. Why couldn't she say, Go home. Everyone go home. But she couldn't do that. She couldn't disrupt the dig; she couldn't tell Charlotte to leave in her condition, and she needed Joan's help. Maybe Ian and Charlotte would get married, and Charlotte would be happy for once. Certainly that wouldn't happen if she asked him to leave.

Examining the old movie posters in the lobby—*I Was a Prisoner of a Chain Gang,* Paul Muni's eyes wide with unbridled anger—it struck Eleanor clearly and suddenly: She despised Rene. She felt it between her eyes. Attempted rape—the words made her stop breathing for a moment. But wait—had she somehow exaggerated the whole thing? Could she have imagined it?

I never liked sex with you. Never. The words echoed in her mind.

Veronica and Mike Zaccari appeared. "Eleanor," Mike

said, offering her a small kiss on the right cheek. "And—"

"Joan," said Joan.

"Oh yes, we met the day we brought Rene over."

Eleanor, holding a cup of juice, said, "Styrofoam is not very environmentally correct, you know."

"I can't think of everything," Veronica said, adjusting her leopard hat.

"Where is he?" asked Mike.

"Who?" said Eleanor.

"Rene."

"He's dead," Eleanor said.

Joan touched her sister's arm. "What are you talking about?"

"Sorry, he's not dead."

"Eleanor, if you ever want to talk," Mike said, "I'll listen. Call me anytime."

When Mike and Veronica left them to talk to two skinny men, Eleanor spotted Micah Silverman and the thought of his hefty, glistening body made her turn away.

Micah said, "Eleanor! Joannie!"

"You are so sick!" said Joan. "I'm married and I have a son and I've seen it all, and I don't know what you were trying to do. Shock us?"

"You weren't shocked?" Micah took a sip of his peach juice and said, "What *is* this stuff? Some kind of lethal Kool Aid?"

When Aaron walked over, Eleanor stared at the ground. She had seen him naked, and felt sure he had seen what happened that awful day in the woods with Rene. And though she wanted an ally, someone to understand her, she felt guilty, dirty. He had kissed her on the dance floor of the Silverman Hotel, yet he didn't help her when she needed him, that afternoon with Rene. Eleanor gazed at his dark blue eyes, but then she looked away, this time at a poster of Virginia Mayo and Danny Kaye.

"How are you?" asked Aaron.

At first Eleanor didn't answer. "Fine," she finally told him.

Micah asked, pointing to his yellow button-down shirt, "How old do you think this shirt is? Just take a guess."

When no one said anything, he said, "Freshman year in college. Can you believe it? Freshman year in college!"

When they took their seats, Eleanor sat between Joan and Aaron. Aaron didn't say much—a vague comment about the theater, about the weather. He sighed several times, seemed about to say something more important, but didn't.

When the curtain rose, Joan squeezed Eleanor's hand. Eleanor felt the tremendous size of her sister's diamond anniversary ring. "Things will look up, kiddo," Joan whispered.

But they didn't. At least not in terms of the play.

On the darkened stage stood a young man wearing a woolen suit and horn-rimmed glasses. "How pale you are," he told the audience. "How lovely you look dressed in white."

"I'm not wearing white," said Micah.

Then, a woman dressed like a Buddhist monk was found, after some difficulty, by the lighting director. She said, "Do you hear the murmur of the Mississippi? Do you hear the voices of the Occidental tourists? Do you hear the rain over Bengal?"

Micah said, "Do you hear the moon over Miami!"

Then the woman disrobed. Underneath her monkish robes, she was clad in a blue corduroy cheerleading outfit with pleats. Inhaling deeply, she hurled herself into a cartwheel. Eleanor heard something crack. "Ouch!" Micah groaned. "I hope she doesn't do the splits. It looks deadly painful."

The strings of a guitar were struck, and a man made up to look like Stalin appeared. Eyebrows thick, accent thick, he said, "If I lived in Florida, I would never go to Disneyland. At first everyone's like her," he said, pointing at the cheerleader, who, gritting her teeth, slid into the splits.

"Jesus," said Micah.

In the lobby at intermission, Eleanor said, "I don't know how Veronica gets her plays produced. It's like the 'Emperor's New Clothes.' "

"I saw that as a kid," said Micah. "Done with puppets. Now that was a play."

"That's not what I meant about the Emperor's—" Eleanor shook her head. "Never mind."

Aaron leaned against the small bar. "I don't understand this play at all," he said.

Micah said, "This play is death. Is that what it's supposed to be about? I'd like to ask that Veronica: Honey, what is this play all about? That woman, she's a real long-ball hitter."

Joan said, "What's a long ball—?" But Micah cut in, "Do you know that woman? The playwright?"

Eleanor said, "We both live in SoHo. She's really a friend of my husband's."

Aaron said, "I'm going to get some air," and he slipped past Paul Muni and Danny Kaye, the ticket counter, and walked out the door. Something had gone wrong, thought Eleanor. A missed cue.

"Are we going to stay for the second act?" Joan asked.

"Are you kidding?" said Micah. "We won't give her the satisfaction. I predict you will never find her picture on the wall in Sardis."

"I'll be across the street, watching the river," Eleanor told them.

"What? Where are you going?"

"I'll just be outside."

Joan and Micah decided to stay for the second half of

the play. Micah said, "In truth, I cannot leave the worst play of all time. Let's face it, Joannie, we are prisoners of 'Prisoners'!"

Joan took a deep breath. "Does it ever strike you that?— Forget it."

"Strike me what?"

"Nothing."

"Out with it, already."

"Well, does it ever strike you that the Silverman is a very—well, unusual place? I mean, do you enjoy running the hotel? Do you ever think, its time has past?"

"No," he said, pulling the collar of his decades-old shirt. "You look very nice this evening, by the way."

"Really? Do I?"

Eleanor strolled across River Street. When a firefly passed, she flinched. She didn't want to see the rest of the play. Veronica and her awful play reminded her of Rene. Guilt by association. Plus, she was sure that Rene had slept with Veronica—not that she cared about Rene anymore. Rene was dead. The old Rene was dead—or the Rene she had believed in was dead; in fact, he never really existed. Still, she recalled that they had visited Hunter's Landing several times to watch the white water rafters streak by with cries of fear and delight. The rafters were delighted to be scared. But it was nearly eight-thirty. The last of the sun dipped into the silent Delaware.

Aaron was sitting on a bench at river's edge, gazing off to Pennsylvania on the other side.

Sitting beside him, Eleanor said, "What an awful play."

"Awful," he said, rubbing his curly hair. He thumped the ground with the rubber heels of his work boots.

"I hate her," Eleanor said, though she didn't really feel anything at all.

"Who?"

"Forget it. I don't know."

"Oh, the woman who wrote the play. The awful play."

"I think my ex-husband slept with her."

"Oh."

"But I don't care."

"No?"

"I really don't. I don't care about anything."

"Well—"

"Nothing interests me."

"Not the river?"

"Nothing. I think I'll have a cigarette."

"You don't smoke. I don't smoke. I don't have any matches."

"I'm going to start smoking."

"Suit yourself."

Eleanor gazed at the river, which curved shyly into town. She wished she could disappear into its gentle ripples. But she couldn't even relax right. A tiny insect climbed into her nose and she sneezed. The wind blew dust in her eye, despite the barrier her glasses posed; the dust must have slipped in at the sides. She hated wearing these thick old glasses; she couldn't see all that well out of them. Her newer glasses, of course, had been broken. That awful afternoon. Forget that afternoon. She cleaned these glasses on her sleeve, then put them back on. Everything was still blurry.

"You're having a tough time," Aaron said.

"Are you thirsty at all?" she asked. She'd been crying lately, and crying made her thirsty.

"Thirsty? No."

"So, you're not thirsty."

"I thought you said you didn't want anything, that nothing interested you."

"Well nothing does. Not even you."

She stomped back alone to the theater, and the manager, who had a long ponytail, had a message for her. He pulled from his jeans' pocket a crumpled note. Eleanor read it:

I'm staying for the rest of the play. Don't wait. I have a ride home. Okay?
Love, Joan.

Eleanor said, "She has a ride?"

The manager shrugged.

Eleanor drove the Valiant home alone.

Joan and Micah sat at a small shiny table in the Silverman's Night Owl Lounge. The table made her think of a lacquer box, but tapping her nails against it, she realized it was plastic.

"So," said Micah.

"So," said Joan.

"You have interesting eyes," he said.

"Interesting?"

"Very big. Very nice."

They were silent for a time, then Micah said, "I was sorry to hear about your husband."

"My husband?" Joan recalled that she had said something about her problems the night they had all gone to the Silverman for dinner. "It's nothing, really."

Micah sipped his scotch. "I'm an up-front person. Let me explain. I don't 'dance the dance.' I'm not into civility, not in place of the truth. I say what I mean, and I like others to tell the truth, too. It saves time."

Joan laughed. "You're a peculiar man."

"Odd?"

"You're a character, like someone I might have seen years ago on the *Ed Sullivan Show*."

"Are you saying I look old? Or are you saying I look like Shecky Greene? Or are you saying I'm funny? That's it, you think I'm funny. I can see the good in everything."

"What happened to your wife? I'm saving time—getting right at it."

"She left me for a dentist. Which is funny, because Aaron's wife also left him for a dentist. Two dentists from Long Island. My wife left me because she couldn't stand hotel life in the Catskills. Aaron's wife left him because she didn't want to be a farmer's wife. She wanted to be a Catskills' hotel wife. Aaron told her he'd go back to the hotel, but she said it was too late. You can't win for losing. So let me ask you, what's the problem with your husband? If he's not seeing another woman—that's what you told me the other night—what's the problem?"

"I'd rather not say."

"Let's not waste time."

And she thought: why not? Why not tell him? She ordered another glass of wine. "We haven't had sex in a year."

"That's a long time."

"Yes."

"Do you miss it? Sex?"

"No, not really. No." She drank up her wine. "It's something you get used to."

Micah clasped her hand. "Really?"

She twisted her diamond anniversary ring. "I miss it, sometimes."

"I have a proposition."

She shook her head. "No, forget it. No."

"You don't even know what I'm going to propose."

"You want us to sleep together."

"It's not a bad idea. Your proposal."

She followed him to Room 317, a suite. Joan took a deep breath. What kind of a nut was she turning into? The room smelled musty, like a hotel room. She thought, *well, this is a hotel room and it would.*

Micah stood by the window, fiddling with the blinds. Joan sat on the bed and took another deep breath. She picked up an empty ceramic ashtray that said, in a bold yellow script, "It's Better in the Catskills." She placed it down again on the table.

"So," he said. ·

"So," she said.

Had she lost her mind? Certainly, and yet she did not bolt from the room. She was free to leave. She had suggested this. Well, not actually suggested it, and yet the words, You want us to sleep together, came from her, not from him. She thought, oddly, or not so oddly, of the virgin martyrs she had read about in *Lives of the Saints* and waited for a stab of guilt to rise up in her. But she felt nothing. She felt nearly proud: well, Joan, you dutiful wife, look how adventurous you've become. She had never before done anything daring—unless quitting school at nineteen and a half to marry Frederick could be considered daring. She never missed Mass, had never cheated on Frederick and here she was, in a hotel room with a man she barely knew. A week away from her safe suburban home, a week away from driving Diane to piano lessons, from searing pork chops, from prodding Jason about algebra, and here she was: alone in a hotel room with a divorced man who wasn't even Catholic.

"Let me ask you something," Micah said. "Is this what you really want to do? I mean, I'm a ladies' man, a real, you know, horny guy, but I don't want you to be sorry."

Joan rummaged through her bag for nothing in particular. "You don't want to do it?" she said.

He waved his hand. "Don't call it that: It. I hate that."
He shook his head. "You're a real long-ball hitter."

"What in the world do you mean by that expression?
You called Veronica a long-ball hitter at that awful play. I
don't get it."

He straightened himself. "It means—I don't know.
You're something else."

"Good or bad?"

"It can go either way. It's one of those expressions that
depends on the situation. Like *aloha.*"

"I see."

"It's good, regarding you."

They waited, naked, under the sheets. Joan kept moving her pillow an inch to the right, an inch to the left. She
couldn't get it right. Her feet were very cold. She always
put her cold feet on Frederick's legs to warm them.

"Is there something wrong with the pillow? I can get a
new one from housekeeping."

"No, no. This is fine. Maybe I need two pillows. One
pillow isn't enough. My head feels too low."

He went to get up. "I'll call housekeeping."

"No, forget it. I'm nervous."

"Who isn't?" He picked up the phone and asked for
two new pillows and a box of condoms.

When everything arrived, he kissed her. He tasted like
waffles; she didn't know why. Waffles is what came to
her.

"Which way do you like it?" he asked, kissing her
neck.

"Which way?"

"You know, missionary—I suppose there are others."

"Missionary."

"Don't think about church . . . that'll ruin it."
Don't think about your husband.
Joan didn't have an orgasm. Well, she had a lot on her

mind and she'd come awfully close, and that was good enough.

Micah panted beside her.

"You're a real long-ball hitter," she told him.

"Listen," he said, out of breath. "What about you?"

"I came close." She always faked it with Frederick. He had had trouble maintaining an erection for years. Failed attempts. Afterward, he'd slouch in bed, head limp, penis limp. When he managed it, she felt he deserved a reward, so she'd arch her back and moan. "You should see a doctor," Joan would tell him and once he said, "I did."

"You did? What did the doctor say?"

"Nothing is physically wrong with me."

"Of course there isn't."

"Later on," Micah said, "we'll try it again. I'll try the way we just did it, or I can service you some other way if I can't get an erection. I'm forty-four, you know. When I was eighteen, I could do it seven times a night. There were a lot of singles weekends at the Silverman, and we didn't want the girls to leave with nothing."

"Seven times a night?"

"Forty-four is not old; I intend to have sex until I'm dead—maybe afterward if that can be arranged, and I don't see why not. Still, we can't forget your needs. You ought to have an orgasm. Sometimes with women, you start rubbing and it takes forever—women have to concentrate harder to have an orgasm, and, before you know it, the *Tonight Show* is over."

"You're certainly not into civilities."

"What I said before, about seven times a night? Sleeping with all the girls? I exaggerate. I don't know why. It saves time."

"Does Aaron have a thing for Eleanor?" Joan asked, propping herself up on her elbows.

Micah thought for a moment. "At first I thought yes. But I don't know. I mentioned her name the other day, and Aaron, in a highfalutin voice, tells me, What would he know about Eleanor?"

It was only nine o'clock when Ian kissed Charlotte good-night.

"This is going well, don't you think?" he told her, though he didn't look well. The pouches under his eyes looked like bruises.

"Is it going well?" she said.

"We're getting to know each other."

"We should already know each other."

"Nevertheless," he said, handing her a glass of water. She swallowed two large vitamin pills and ate three crackers. Taking pills without anything in her stomach made her feel queasy.

When Ian went upstairs to bed, she thought: *He isn't a bad guy. Not at all.* She thought: *I will learn to love him. Maybe I already love him. Yes, I already love him.* She yawned, patted her belly, and hoped she would have a girl. But no—it was too hard to be a girl. You have to be beautiful and you have to be kind, and who can be both? She therefore hoped for a boy, but really, she wanted a girl. She'd dress her beautifully in yellow hair ribbons, yellow cotton dresses, lacy white anklet socks, and frilly bloomers. She imagined her little girl's smooth, springy skin; her powdery scent, and she thought: *I am falling in love with my baby.*

She drifted off to sleep and dreamed that labor wasn't too bad at all. The white-starched nurse said, "You're finished?"

"Yes, it wasn't too bad, just like menstrual cramps, really."

"But where is the baby?"

"I thought you had her," Charlotte said, looking around, and then she spotted the baby; really the baby was a six-year-old boy. He had rumpled hair and wore dirty dungarees and a scowl. "There he is," said Charlotte.

"That's your baby? That's a little boy! How could you deliver a six-year-old boy?"

"You were there!"

The nurse shrugged. "Are you happy?"

"Yes, of course." But Charlotte didn't feel anything: pain or love.

Charlotte then dreamed that a dog was scratching at the front door, but sitting up, she thought: someone is opening the front door. When she glanced at her clock radio, 4:03 A.M., her heart began to pound. She called out, "Eleanor? Joan? Ian?" Who would be coming in at this hour? Her sisters would be in bed, sleeping. Ian would be in the upstairs room. She thought: just my luck, I'm pregnant, getting used to the idea of not being the center of the universe; I've stopped drinking, I have met a man I could learn to love, and someone is going to—

The footsteps came closer. Heart hammering, she slipped out of bed and pulled the door open a crack. Standing back, she saw a shadow dart across the hallway. She stood frozen near the door. Charlotte thought: *doesn't anyone else hear?* She took a deep breath and called: "Ian! Eleanor! Joan!" and finally she heard Eleanor's voice, "What? What is it—?" Upstairs she heard Ian knock into the furniture, calling out: "Charlotte? What now? Just hold on."

The bedroom door opened.

"Oh my God!" shouted Charlotte, stepping back.

"What's your problem?"

"It's you! I didn't recognize you! Your clothes—you're

all wrinkled. Your lipstick—it's smeared! Wait a minute, are you *drunk?*"

Joan steadied herself against the wall. "I am not *drunk.*"

Ian bounded into the room with disheveled hair and silk pajamas. Eleanor stood behind him, rubbing her eyes. Ian said, "This is quite inconvenient. It's very late."

"Joan is drunk!" said Charlotte.

"So what if I am," Joan said, weaving through the room. "Who are you to say I'm . . . immoral."

"Joan," Eleanor chided, "why don't you go off to bed." But her sister, arms crossed, stood her ground. Eleanor managed to guide Charlotte back to bed. "Charlotte, you shouldn't get out of bed. Please."

Joan said, "You always take Charlotte's side. Charlotte is everybody's *cream puff.* And Stewart. Remember Stewart, Charlotte? You slept with him, didn't you?"

"I never did!"

Ian said, "Why don't we all go off to bed now."

"That's Charlotte's favorite thing to do!" said Joan. "Her favorite thing!"

"Please go to bed, Joan," said Eleanor. "You don't mean what you're saying."

"The hell I don't!" Joan took Eleanor by the shoulders. "You let Rene treat you like, like . . . garbage. Why don't we demand—better!" Joan put her hand over her mouth. "I think I'm gonna throw up." Softly, she said, "You want to be a nice person, and then you get screwed."

In the morning, Ian sat at the edge of Charlotte's bed eating a bowl of cornflakes. "If you don't mind me asking, what was all that commotion last night with Joan?"

"When Joan's around, there's always a commotion."

In his understated way, Ian said, "She seemed a bit upset with you."

Charlotte sighed. "Years ago, she was pregnant and we had to do something about it."

"It must have been awful for her. But what does that have to do with you?"

Charlotte thought: what indeed? "I helped her out; she might have ruined her life without me. I've always been there for her. Joan—she just could never take control. She was always a coward."

"So what did you do for Joan—specifically?" asked Ian, finishing his cereal. "If you don't mind my asking."

—11—
The Strongbox

Charlotte had been the brave one, the one who had taken control. In the dark silence of the Florence house, she had slipped out of bed, careful not to awaken Joan, who had finally managed to drift off in the bed beside her. Charlotte slipped on a pair of socks to deaden the sound of her footsteps. Clutching a silver key and a small flashlight, which she'd stashed under the bed, she crept into the living room, carefully avoiding her father's recliner. With a blind hand touching the wall, she found the dining room; there, she slowly opened the lowboy, pulling out the strongbox. Layered over the pounding of her heart, she could hear the slow breathing of her mother, her father, Eleanor, Joan. With the tiny key, she turned the lock and pressed a tiny lever. The strongbox groaned open. Inside were various insurance policies, the title to the car, the birth certificates—the leather pouch. She opened the pouch, where she knew the money was. Ed handed over his meager earnings to Catherine every week, and Catherine placed the money, which accumulated for bills and daily expenses, in the pouch. Charlotte counted out three hundred of the three hundred and twenty-seven dollars in the pouch. She stuffed the money into the pocket of her bathrobe. Then, gritting her teeth, she twisted the lid of the strongbox back and forth on its hinges, managing to break the right hinge.

And then came the difficult part, the part she dreaded.

She placed the ravaged strongbox on the knobby carpet, then slowly made her way to her parents' bedroom. Gently, so gently, she twisted the doorknob. Her parents didn't stir. She tiptoed to her mother's jewelry box, which rested on her bureau on a long band of Irish lace. She opened it degree by degree, and when it was open, she placed the tiny silver key back in its place. She heard a quiet moan, but it was only her father, who lay with a forearm slung over his eyes. She thought: they must surely hear her wild heart, her rapid breathing. She closed her eyes for a moment, then tiptoed again to the door. She moved slowly to her own room and, waking Joan, whispered, "I've done it."

Her sister rubbed her eyes. "What?"

"It's done."

Charlotte pressed a finger to her lips. Then she ran toward the side door, pushing open the screen, the outer door, letting them slam. "Mom!" she cried. "Mom! Dad!"

"What is it! What is it! Charlotte! Joan!"

"We've been robbed! Look, here! Mom, look! The strongbox!"

Malcolm called a meeting. Things could get very chaotic with a film crew and archaeologists working for different goals, he said. So everyone gathered in Charlotte's room—Malcolm didn't want Charlotte to feel left out. For the occasion, Joan, who looked exceedingly pale, had whipped up a huge pot of chili and a gigantic green salad. In spite of her hangover, she had buzzed around all morning, cleaning, cooking, doing the laundry. And here, in Charlotte's room, she spooned out chili and salad on flowery plastic plates. Eleanor picked at her food. If only her appetite would come back; if only—

Clearing his throat, Malcolm said, "I'd like to introduce Sarah and Glenn—although I think they've already met everyone. They're graduate students at SUNY Albany, and they've been good enough to give us a hand—especially now that Eleanor and Aaron aren't working anymore. Eleanor has other responsibilities."

"I'm not stopping her from digging," said Charlotte.

"At any rate, Glenn and Sarah are working for college credit, not money."

"We're just so excited," said Sarah.

"This is, like, unreal," said Glenn.

"Here, here," said Brad. "By the way, Joan, this chili is brilliant."

"You don't know what I've been through."

Malcolm cleared his throat. "I'd like to take advantage of this meeting to review our goals. We're investigating a rich archaeological site. We've already found pottery shards from the Woodland era, plus charcoal from a hearth, a piece of a caribou antler, and a projectile point, which could be more than ten thousand years old—making them the oldest artifacts in New York State. The very oldest. But we can't be sure of it. I don't want anyone to get too disappointed if the artifacts are not as old as we hope they'll be. What we're doing is important, no matter what."

"I don't think they're going to be that old," said Charlotte.

"What do you know about it?" Joan asked.

"We all want the artifacts to be very old, so they probably won't be. That's the way I figure it."

"You're such a pessimist," said Joan. "I bet they're older than anyone can possibly imagine. Maybe a million years old."

"That's impossible," said Malcolm.

"How do you know?" Joan asked, massaging her temples. "You don't know everything. None of us really knows."

Charlotte said, "But the artifacts were found so close to the surface—it doesn't make sense that they'd be really old."

"Actually," said Natalie, "ancient artifacts are sometimes found right on the surface in a rock-shelter because there's protection—no wind or mud to sweep them away."

Eleanor said, "Please, Charlotte." Her voice was shaking; she might cry. "Just for one day, try not to be so—so—" She wanted to say selfish, but instead said, "negative. You're not the only one to be . . . afraid."

"What are you talking about? I'm not afraid. And Rene's gone—he's not going to hurt you again. I wouldn't let him."

"What happened with Rene?" asked Brad. "You're afraid of Rene? The bloke you're leaving?"

"Nothing happened," said Eleanor. "That's the thing. Nothing really happened."

"Charlotte," Mr. Simmons was saying, "beautiful though you are, you're forgetting one major point." He smoothed his invisible eyebrows. "We know the bone you found is from a caribou. Do you see any caribou around here? Do you often go caribou riding? No. Because there have been no caribou in this region for thousands of years. So we know the artifacts are old. Ancient, in fact. Why does no one believe?"

"Oh ye of little faith," said Brad.

"I still say the artifacts won't be that old," Charlotte said. "And if they are, what then? What does it really mean? We're the ones breathing now—we can't spend our lives thinking about dead people. I've got a baby to think about now—"

"Oh," said Joan, "*now* you're thinking about the baby."

Malcolm said, "But if we don't think about what went on before us—my God. What is the point of living if we're just, I don't know, plopped down on the earth for seventy years, without a thought for those who lived here before us, or who will live here afterward?"

Charlotte shrugged.

Ian said, "When will we find out about the artifacts—I mean, how old they'll be? I've promised the BBC they'll be at least eight thousand years old. If they end up being two thousand years old, they won't be pleased."

"We'll find out any day now," said Malcolm, pulling on his beard. "In the meantime, Ian, if I could ask your crew to be as careful as possible. Not to step on any of the squares that are being dug up. And we'll be as cooperative as we can be. And Eleanor, if you'd like to give us a hand, please do."

"Yes," said Joan, "why not help? I can handle everything in the house."

"There's one thing you can't handle," said Charlotte. "Me."

When everyone returned to work, Ian sat down on Charlotte's bed and placed his palm on her belly. "I'm glad you didn't lose the baby, and that you didn't have the—well, that you kept the baby."

"Is that what you wanted, at first? For me to get rid of it so you wouldn't have to feel responsible?"

He stared at his watch. "Charlotte, in truth, I hardly know you. I didn't know if fatherhood would be right for me. I'm a busy man; I'm just getting somewhere. People in England know who I am. Some people do. But I want a child, more than anything in the world—I know that now, and believe me, as parents, we'll get to know each other."

"You may not like what you find out."

"Don't be silly," he said, kissing her forehead.

Eleanor sat at the edge of the pond, looking up. The thick gray sky made her think of milk gone bad. The local newspaper was spread around her, but she had trouble absorbing even the headlines. She batted several flies away. "Beat it!" she said, more forcefully than she meant to. Beyond the pond, she could see Aaron's corn rippling in the breeze. He could have stopped Rene, couldn't he? But it was: Oh, hello, yes we've met. We're neighbors. She recalled Aaron's kiss at the Silverman Hotel, his warm hand on the small of her back. He had told her, "I can fit my hands around your waist."

Rene, Aaron. Why hadn't she found a man like Frederick? He was so loyal, so helpful; when he was going to be late, he called Joan to tell her. He never yelled at the kids. "How are you, Eleanor," he always said. "How is the job?" And he listened, seemed genuinely interested in the ad campaigns she worked on. "Good idea. Garbage bags on the moon. Very clever."

Joan walked over, wearing blue jeans and a T-shirt; her feet were bare. "It's good to see you're getting some fresh air," she said.

"Do you miss Frederick?" Eleanor suddenly asked.

"Oh yes, dear Frederick is the very best man in the entire world."

"Oh."

"He is the best—no doubt about it. The very best."

"You don't sound like you mean it."

Joan plopped herself down on the grass. "I could tell you things that would surprise you, about Frederick, about me."

"What kinds of things?"

"Nothing."

And Eleanor thought: *I could tell Joan some things as well.* She could repeat Rene's words, the words that had destroyed her sense of herself as a woman, as a desirable sexual being.

Joan stabbed the earth with a stick. "What the hell. Why not speak the truth? Isn't the truth what we're all afraid of?"

"I'm not afraid of the truth," said Eleanor. Rene should not have told her the truth. *I have never liked sex with you, Eleanor. Never.* And wasn't this very assertion a lie? He had nearly . . . nearly, he had pressed her down on the grass, she had gasped for air. He might have, he might have . . .

Joan was telling her: "Frederick and I have not had sex in over a year. What do you think about that?"

For a moment, Eleanor didn't speak. "I'm surprised," she finally said.

"I don't think he's seeing another woman, but how do I know?"

"That doesn't sound like Frederick. Maybe work has got him down. He's a workaholic."

"He ought to give me a workout in bed, that's all I can say. Still, maybe he's cheating on me. It would serve him right if I cheated on him, don't you think? I mean, why not? Do you think I should cheat on him?"

"That's not like you, Joan."

"Isn't it? I don't know why this family has so many secrets. We have to pretend everything is perfect. Yes, I'm wonderful. The children are wonderful. The house is wonderful. Why do we do that? I have a new attitude now: I'm not into civility in the place of truth. I'm going to tell the truth. It saves time."

Eleanor thought: *don't be a coward, tell her what Rene said.*

"Another thing," Joan was saying, "since I'm revealing family secrets. Jason is stealing."

"Stealing?"

"Taking money from me, from the kids at school. We've been seeing a therapist."

"I didn't know."

"How could you?" Joan stood up and with both hands tossed a rock into the pond, tearing its surface. "And, well, now that I'm telling the truth: I had—I lost—" She cleared her throat. "I'll say it. Why not say it? I had an abortion twenty years ago."

Eleanor was shocked. Joan? The perfect Catholic wife, with the perfect husband, the perfect children? This was a woman who never missed Mass and who sent birthday cards a week ahead, just in case. "I had no idea," Eleanor said.

"No, you didn't."

"Was it—? Well, when was it? If you don't mind talking about it."

"Of course I mind talking about it. That's why you don't know. I was seventeen. The father was Stewart."

"Is that when you got so sick?"

She hesitated. "Yes."

"Did Mom and Dad ever know?"

"Are you kidding? Of course not. If I could tell them I was having sex, I could have gone on the Pill or something. None of this would ever have happened."

"I just never knew."

"How could you? Anyway, life goes on. Or some semblance of it does. I'm making tuna for dinner. I know—tuna is not my typical dinner meal, but there are just too many people, and what can we do?" She counted off: "Mr. Simmons, Malcolm, Natalie, Glenn and Sarah, Ian, and what are those English people's names?—yes—Colin and Brad and Ivy. And then there's Charlotte, you and me. Twelve. Tuna for twelve. I don't mind. I really don't. It's good therapy. Still, Eleanor, it must be costing you a fortune."

"SUNY chips in seventy-five dollars a week," she said. "I'll help you out with the cooking."

"Really?"

"Why not?"

They strolled to the kitchen, where Eleanor chopped six stalks of celery, then sliced an onion. Joan had taught her how. "I now can cut an onion," said Eleanor. "This summer's triumph."

"It's something."

"One more thing that makes me cry."

"Don't be maudlin."

When the food was ready, Joan balanced a tray of sandwiches and a pitcher of lemonade while Eleanor held open the screen door. Joan arranged the food on the picnic table. The crew gathered around, ravenous as usual. When Brad grabbed some napkins, several flew away, though his straight black hair clung to his scalp.

"Look at them fly!" he said. "Like doves, they are!"

Joan said, "Brad, please! You're making more work for me!"

"Sorry," he said, staring at his sneakers. "I don't mean to be annoying."

"I'm sorry," said Joan, sighing. "I'm a little . . . on edge."

"Is it that time of the month?" he said. "If you don't mind my asking. Hormones can drive a woman wild."

Ivy said, "Brad! Bloody hell!"

After Joan caught the napkins, she and Eleanor walked back to the house. They sat down at the kitchen table.

"Do you want to talk about it?" Eleanor said.

"Talk about what?"

"You know, the—what you did."

"What's to discuss? What's done is done, right? I mean, isn't it? I've just had a brainstorm. To be honest, I want to keep busy—if I keep busy I won't think. We'll have dinner together. Just the sisters. I'll make us chicken cordon bleu and wild rice, and a nice salad, with endive and arugula. I can't cook gourmet for everybody. But we deserve better than tuna fish. Why don't you make the salad."

"Aren't you tired from last night?" said Eleanor. "You got in so late. Aren't you hung over?"

"Everyone should keep busy. Idle hands." She washed her hands at the kitchen sink; then she took some boneless chicken breasts from the refrigerator, rinsed them under cold water, then hammered them to paper thinness. "Oh, shit," she said, quickly frying the chicken in some oil. "Shit, shit shit."

"Is something wrong?" asked Eleanor, slicing a tomato.

"Shit."

"Come on, Joan."

Joan pulled on her hair, ripping out several thin dark strands; she then tossed them in the garbage. "I'm happy. That's what's wrong. Shit!"

Eleanor sat at the foot of Charlotte's bed and stared at the food. The chicken breasts were golden brown. Her salad hadn't turned out badly, either. She had garnished it with fat twirls of carrot. She wasn't able to manage thin twirls. Still, the food was magazine delectable.

"Ah," said Charlotte, "the sisters will dine together tonight. My sisters feel sorry for me."

"I don't feel sorry for you at all," said Joan, placing a tray in front of Charlotte. "Eat something." Joan then cleared Charlotte's bed of magazines and paperback novels and tissues and socks. "You're an incredible slob."

"I'm an *actress*. I'm creative, not anal-retentive, like certain suburban housewives I could name."

"How are you feeling, Charlotte?" asked Eleanor, forcing herself to swallow some rice.

"I'm fabulous," said Charlotte.

"Really?"

"Fabulous."

"She's lying," said Joan. "No one in this family tells the truth. We just stop speaking to each other. You used to make us tell you secrets, remember, Charlotte? The day's secret? I bet you have a few to unload."

Charlotte said, "Why don't you tell *me* a secret? What did you really do last night, Joan? You came home very late, about four as I recall. You said you had some drinks with Micah?"

"We had a few drinks. That's all." She hesitated. "Well, actually— Yes, I might as well tell you. I might as well." She took a deep breath. "Micah and I went to bed together."

Eleanor said, "Slept together? Had *sex?*"

"No," said Charlotte. "They took a *nap* together." Charlotte stared at Joan. "You cheated on Frederick? Do you want to ruin your marriage? Frederick is a great guy! Boring—but a great guy!"

"A great guy who hasn't had sex with me in over a year."

"Why not?"

"If I knew the answer to that!"

"I think he works too hard, that's all," said Eleanor.

"I don't even feel guilty," said Joan. "Isn't that awful? I mean, shouldn't a sense of overwhelming guilt have come over me by now? What's wrong with me? I don't even feel like going to confession. I suppose I'll call Frederick later. I hope infidelity isn't something that can be detected over the phone."

—

While everyone was busy digging, or cooking, or filming, Charlotte dreamed of Joan, of the statue of the Blessed Virgin flying toward her, an oily snake coiling around her neck, and finally she dreamed of Stewart, and in her haze, Stewart cupped her breasts and told her, I've only ever loved you, Charlotte. Only you.

Abruptly she sat up. Her mouth was dry. She had a terrible headache. She could hear Joan's voice outside. She was asking Ian if she could be in his documentary and he said, "Of course. Why not. Stand over there, near the rock-shelter." Joan was acting as if nothing had happened, as if she hadn't betrayed her husband. What nerve she had!

Charlotte rubbed her eyes and a memory came to the surface, like an artifact.

There had been so much blood. Screams. A neighbor called and Stewart said, "Everything is okay. My friend is a little sick. Abdominal pains." For hours, Joan screamed. And in brief quiet moments, she asked, "When will it be over? When?" And then, again, the screams.

Hours dragged by, and suddenly, as if a storm had passed overhead, the apartment was still. For a long while, Joan rocked gently on the toilet seat, pulling at the toilet paper dispenser. Charlotte handed Joan a sanitary napkin and a pair of clean underwear. "Am I okay?" Joan asked, shivering.

Charlotte guided her to the bedroom. "You're okay, I promise. I'm so sorry, Joannie. So sorry."

Stewart told Charlotte, "I didn't mean for this to happen. I loved her once. I really did."

Her sister lay shivering, staring. "Am I okay?"

"You're fine. I promise." Her sister was pale, her breathing was shallow. Charlotte placed her palm on

Joan's forehead. "Stewart, get the thermometer, in the medicine cabinet."

Handing her the thermometer, Stewart said, "I loved her. Honest. Once. I wanted to marry her once. Really."

Charlotte said, "Too bad you told her that."

He shrugged.

Charlotte slipped the thermometer under her sister's tongue. A red line climbed nearly the length of the thermometer, resting finally at 103.4 degrees. "You're okay. You're fine."

"We've got to call the doctor," Charlotte whispered to Stewart.

"We can't," he said. "They'll find out about the—the, you know. You know they'll find out. And Christ, they could *arrest* us."

Joan stared at the phone. Glancing up at the calendar, she noticed that Eleanor had penciled in "Divorce—Final" for next Monday. She, too, might be headed for court. She picked up the phone. She was shivering. She had become, in a week, someone else. She did not recognize her jeans and T-shirt, her dirty feet. She stared at her hand, wrapped hard around the receiver; she had filed her nails down and removed the coral nail polish. She thought of Micah. What had she done? She didn't love Micah; she didn't, in truth, even like him much.

"Frederick? Oh, you're there. Are you sure you're not busy? I can call back. You'll talk? You have a few moments? I just called to say hello, and to tell you I'll be home soon, in a few days. Give Jason and Diane my love. *What?* Frederick, I don't know if that's a good idea. For the weekend? Just the weekend? You and Jason? But there's no room here, there really isn't. No room at the inn . . . *The Silverman! I* really don't think you and Jason should stay there. It's—I'll be home soon. You made the reservation? No, there's no problem. No, I'm very happy that you're coming up. I really am."

Joan slammed the phone down. She bent over, rubbing her lower abdomen. Cramps. On top of everything else, she had just gotten her period—she wasn't menopausal, as Frederick had suggested. Well, she wasn't pregnant; here were the cramps to prove it, and, of course, Micah had used a condom—only the latex sheath had touched her. Yes—that was something.

Joan knocked at Charlotte's door. "Do you need anything?"

"What?"

"Do you need anything?"

Charlotte glanced up from her magazine. "No."

"Do you want some juice? A sandwich?"

Charlotte said, "Are you trying to make me feel guilty?"

"You're paranoid. If you want anything, give a holler."

"Wait a minute," said Charlotte, lowering the magazine. "Hold out your hands. My God, you're shaking. I don't know how you could have slept with a complete stranger."

Joan sat on the bed. "It's just my period. Cramps."

"That's it?" said Charlotte.

"Frederick and Jason are coming up for a few days. They're staying at the Silverman Hotel."

"You should think before you act."

"Oh, like you? I *have* been thinking. You should marry Ian. He seems nice. A good man. You'd be lucky to have him."

"Because I don't deserve a good man? Is that what you mean? Where are you going?"

"You said you didn't want anything."

"I do want something," said Charlotte. "I do. I just don't know what it is yet."

She wanted something, that was true. But what? A sense of . . . What? Peace, perhaps? Contentment? But how could she attain contentment with Joan hovering around? Charlotte had done so much for Joan. Joan should be grateful. Things might have been terribly different.

She remembered how Joan had shaken, her teeth chattering. It had been June when she slipped her sister's arms through the sleeves of her best winter coat. "I'm taking you back to Florence," Charlotte had said. She was worried about Joan, about her fever. She would have to bring her back home. They would make up a story. They would lie some more.

"No. Please," Joan moaned.

"We have to go home. Stewart will come with us."

"No. Not him. Just you."

Stewart stayed behind, and Charlotte made the long drive to Florence, past the silos, cow pastures, and cornfields, past the factories, pizzerias, and row houses, until at last Charlotte saw the steeple of Our Lady of Perpetual Mercy rising white against the blue sky. Charlotte said, "How are you? Are you okay?" And Joan, teeth chattering in the backseat, whispered, "No good. I'm scared."

In town, Charlotte drove past Dr. De Marsico's house, but there were so many cars out front that she had to park on Crescent. She strode toward the house, leaving Joan in the car.

Charlotte waited, arms crossed, at the side of the house, near the electric meter. The De Marsicos were having a barbecue. Pretty Mrs. De Marsico wore a yellow sundress. She was laughing, her head arched back. Her golden necklace gleamed. A group of children ran around the shuffleboard court, their arms extended like airplane wings. Dr. De Marsico stood talking to Walt Henderson, the baseball coach. The doctor glanced at her for a moment. Dr. De Marsico was a young man, or so her mother said. He was in his forties, which didn't seem so awfully young to Charlotte. Charlotte waved. He continued to stare, tilting his head to one side. Once again Charlotte waved her hand. Dr. De Marsico patted Walt Henderson on the back and, walking over, said, "Charlotte? Charlotte Powers, of course." He waited. "Come on back, have a hamburger."

"I've got a problem."

"I see."

"My sister is very sick. She's in the car."

"In the car? I don't understand."

"Please," she said, and he followed her to the car. Joan lay in the backseat, shivering, wearing Charlotte's best coat.

"Shall I call your mother? Where is your mother?"

"We'll meet you in the emergency room," Charlotte said. "Just you. Please."

Slowly, he nodded.

Charlotte drove around Florence for a few minutes to give Dr. De Marsico time to arrive at the hospital. She drove up Hayward, down Montrose, then, by force of habit, turned left onto Linden Street, their own street. How stupid could she be? She sped by the house; she didn't look. Then she drove along oak-lined Chancellor Avenue, toward Clara Maas Hospital, named for the young nurse, who, in the early 1900s in Panama, agreed to be stung by a mosquito infected with the yellow fever virus. Clara Maas allowed herself to be stung to aid the cause of research, so that the canal might be built. "She died," Sister James Delores had told Charlotte's fifth grade class. "She was a martyr. So much was learned about the disease because of her courage."

"My sister is sick," Charlotte told the ER receptionist. Charlotte signed several forms. "My mother will be here soon. My sister was with me down in Glassboro, and she felt a little sick, not too sick, so I agreed to drive her home, but now she's so sick. Very sick."

Charlotte held Joan's hand in the waiting room. Joan moaned softly. Dr. De Marsico finally appeared, looking very earnest with his glasses, his neat black hair, his crisp white coat. "Please," he told them. "Follow me."

"I didn't know you were on," said a nurse.

"I'm meeting a patient."

Dr. De Marsico closed the examining room curtain. Charlotte helped Joan put on the hospital gown, then eased her onto the cot. When a nurse opened the curtain, the doctor said, "It's okay, Barbara," and the nurse disappeared. Dr. De Marsico held Joan's wrist while he looked at his watch. He then slipped a thermometer under her tongue.

Charlotte said, "She's got a temperature."

When he pressed on her abdomen, Joan cried out. He pressed the tops of her thighs and said, "The underwear, the sanitary napkin. Please, take them off."

They were bloody, and Charlotte handled them gingerly, placing them gently on the floor.

"A botched job," said the doctor.

Charlotte said, "It's a bad period. Very bad—terrible cramps. And this fever—"

He took the thermometer from Joan's mouth. "Is your sister allergic to penicillin?"

"I don't think so," Joan whispered.

Dr. De Marsico said, "Charlotte, you've got to call your mother."

"I can't."

"You've got to."

"I can't tell her."

"What's the worst that could happen?" he said. "Joan is her daughter—you are her daughter."

Charlotte stared at the floor. "Please, I can't."

The doctor pressed his hands together. "I have to follow regulations. The law. If you went to Manhattan, you were very stupid. And I bet that's what you did. A few months ago, the law changed in New York. It can be done legally there now. But not in Jersey, not in most states. You girls are so stupid. It strains the imagination how stupid you girls can be. Or maybe you didn't have much money and you went for the best deal."

Charlotte caught her breath: she was stupid, so very stupid. But she didn't know! No one had told her! She closed her eyes; *deal with the issue at hand,* she told herself. Voice shaking, she said, "If my mother finds out, Joan will have no place to live. She's seventeen years old."

"She won't throw you out. You're underestimating her." He pulled on the curtain. "Do you know what could happen to me? If they find out? Have you any idea? Do you know what it costs to go to med school? Do you have any idea what debt is? When you have two daughters, a son, a wife?"

"He said he'd marry her. He lied."

He wouldn't look her in her eye; she tried to cling to his gaze, but he kept turning away. He said, "Why don't you girls just say no? You girls—you don't know how to say no. Boys can't help themselves; they are not to blame. I'll do a D & C. I can't stand around here haggling. There's probably some retained tissue."

"Please, don't tell my mother."

He stared at his watch.

"Please," Charlotte said. She nearly captured his gaze, but he looked away. She took his hand, pressing her pale pink nails into his palm. "What's it to you? What do you care?"

"Let go," he said.

"She did it to please him."

"Let go!" he said, shaking her away.

"She had an abortion. Are you happy? It costs us three hundred dollars and the man used a piece of wire. Yes, Joan is a terrible person who must be punished. You caught her! You're a big man! Why don't you call the police!" Charlotte stepped back. Softly, she said, "I could do something for you."

The doctor's face turned very white, with anger, shock, lust—she couldn't tell. He didn't say anything for a long while. Finally he cleared his throat. "Joan has very bad anemia. Does that sound okay? Is that what you want me to say?"

"Yes."

"Do you know what her temperature is? One hundred and four degrees. Do you know what that means?"

When Ed and Catherine Powers arrived at the hospital, Dr. De Marsico told them it was a good thing Charlotte had acted quickly. Joan's heavy periods had worsened the anemia, and a D & C was the only course. Her resistance was low, hence the fever.

Ed said, "Charlotte, you're a good kid. You got her here in time." Catherine clutched her rosary. Eleanor stood silently in the corner.

Joan's temperature did not go down that first night. Or the second. Catherine held Joan's hand, and told Charlotte, weeping, "You're my cream puff, dear. You go on home for a while. You've got to sleep."

But Charlotte couldn't sleep, and she couldn't sleep now. Her eyes were open in a room that was not her own, owing to the kindness of strangers; her sisters were strangers. Her sisters didn't understand her.

Eleanor strolled to the rock-shelter, and there, Natalie asked her, "Are you going to give us a hand?"

"I'm just so busy with Charlotte."

Pulling on his beard, Malcolm said, "Soon, Eleanor. A few days more and we'll know."

"The charcoal, the caribou bones, they're going to be more than ten thousand years old," said Mr. Simmons. "Trust me. The oldest in the region."

"But we're not sure of that," said Malcolm.

Just then, a monarch butterfly, wings like stained glass, nearly collided with Eleanor's nose, and Eleanor waved it away.

"It's only a butterfly," said Natalie. "That's the fun of working outdoors. It saved me, you know."

"Saved you?"

"Archaeology."

"Oh?" Eleanor looked off to the pond, which earlier had been black, but now was blue.

"Years ago, I got involved with one of my professors and—" She laughed. "I was a French major, at first. The professor, my lover, dumped me. And he *failed* me. That hurt the most. I did not deserve an F!" She shook her head. "Anyway, the next semester, I took Intro to Archaeology, and being outdoors lifted my spirits. The soil, the bright sun on my neck. I forgot about him. Malcolm says I would have forgotten him eventually, anyway. At any rate, I forgot how to speak French."

"I see."

"I just thought you might find the story interesting."

"Yes. But I'm fine. Really."

Just then Glenn ran across the lawn, waving his long arms over his head. He called, "Come here! You've got to see!" He and Sarah had been digging adjacent squares, the same squares Eleanor and Aaron had worked on. Everyone ran toward him, carefully avoiding the stakes and taut twine bordering each square.

Malcolm demanded, "What is it?"

Eleanor crouched down and saw something flat,

wooden and dusty, like an old desktop in an attic, buried in the earth. With a trowel, Glenn followed its long outlines.

Eleanor said, "A box? A storage box?"

Malcolm said, "Maybe."

Silently, Malcolm, Mr. Simmons, and Natalie, cleared away the debris. "A chest of drawers?" said Brad.

"A child's bed?" said Joan.

Finally the object was cleared of earth. No one said a word, for here, clearly, was a pentagonal pine coffin, the lid nailed tight with iron spikes. With great difficulty, Malcolm, Mr. Simmons, and Glenn lifted it from its resting place, setting it on the grass.

"Aren't you going to open it?" Ian asked. "This will make a wonderful segment, a lovely segment. And the sun is high: wonderful. Brilliant. Can you open it now? Brad, Colin, and Ivy, get into position."

"This is spooky," said Brad.

Malcolm pulled on his beard.

Eleanor said, "Opening it seems wrong somehow."

"It does," said Joan.

"It is wrong somehow," Malcolm said. "But we're archaeologists."

"Who could it be?" said Eleanor. "Is it a new coffin?" She wouldn't look inside if it was a new coffin—what must be inside a new coffin? She imagined a petrified body, limbs gnarled like the apple trees down the lawn. The coffin, however, did not appear new; it wasn't shiny and smooth like Whiskey Demon's had been.

Mr. Simmons, Glenn, and Malcolm hammered out the thick rusty nails.

Still no one opened the lid.

"Malcolm?" Eleanor asked. "Have you ever found a coffin before?"

"Only once."

Mr. Simmons said, "We've got to open it."

Eleanor turned away.

Mr. Simmons and Malcolm slowly lifted the lid. Eleanor's heart pounded.

She did not look, yet she knew that inside lay the remains of someone who had strolled her land, who had liked certain foods and disliked others, who had fallen in love. Eleanor told herself: don't be afraid, don't always be a coward. She opened her eyes. All that remained were old bones surrounded by beads and odd nuggets of gold. The chalky bones she had memorized in school lay cramped upon one another: the clavicle, the humerus, the tibia, the femur. With courage, she stared at the skull, at the hollow eye sockets, at the rise of the cheekbones, at the place where the nose should have been. The teeth were the most terrible feature of all—with the lips and gums gone, the teeth stretched long and deep into the skull.

Softly, Malcolm said, "Let me tell you what you're looking at." Brad and Colin's cameras whirred. "The body is completely decomposed." He crouched down and pointed to a ring, which had fallen below the blanched bones of the right hand. "I assume it's a woman, she's wearing a good many rings, but this is a Jesuit ring; note the letters IR. And here, around her neck, is a King George I medal. So we're talking, maybe 1750. Notice the fine white seed beads—they suggest she was wearing a blouse with a trimmed collar, and look, more beads, below her knees. A Lenape Indian woman, I imagine. She was probably buried in a trimmed, beaded skirt. And here, these dark blue glass beads are part of her ornamental head covering. Ah, and here," he said, pointing to the foot of the grave, "is . . . yes, a jewelry box, though the wood has rotted away. But here's the iron outline and inside are more beads, and here's some shell wampum."

It seemed as if hundreds of tiny yellow and green beads had scattered in one corner, as had a pair of tiny scissors, suggesting that the woman planned to spin and sew in the afterlife.

Eleanor spotted Aaron down the lawn. "Aaron!" she called. "Aaron! Come here! You've got to see!"

But, oddly, he disappeared into the house. Eleanor dashed down to the house, leaving everyone else crowded around the coffin. Hadn't Aaron heard her? Was Charlotte okay? Inside, she called, "Aaron?" She waited for his reply. "Aaron?" Silence. Eleanor moved past the rosy couch, the end table, and then she stepped into the kitchen. Finally, she opened Charlotte's door and found Aaron sitting at the foot of her sister's bed.

"Oh, Eleanor," he said, turning. "Were you calling me?" He was holding Charlotte's hand.

"What's up?" asked Charlotte.

Eleanor felt her eyes fill, her throat tighten. "They . . . found a coffin."

"Really?" asked Charlotte. "A coffin?"

Aaron moved toward Eleanor, but she punched the space between them. "Don't touch me!" she said. "Just don't touch me!"

He said, "I'm sorry, Eleanor, whose coffin? What are you talking about?"

Eleanor shook her head. "Forget it."

"Forget a coffin?" said Charlotte. "Are you crazy?"

"An Indian woman's coffin. They found it in the squares we were working on."

"Our squares?" said Aaron.

"Yes."

Charlotte made a face. "Is she . . . decomposed?"

"Malcolm says she died about 1750. She's a skeleton."

"You know," said Charlotte, "you'd better start eating."

"She looks fine," said Aaron. "Really."

Eleanor said, "Oh, thank you very, very much. Thanks for nothing."

"Are you angry?" said Charlotte. "Why are you angry? Why are you crying? She's been dead for years."

"I am not angry."

"You sound it," Charlotte said.

"Okay," said Eleanor. "I'm angry. At everybody. Including Aaron."

With that, she stormed from the bedroom, plopping herself at the kitchen table, arms crossed tightly against her chest.

"Eleanor," Aaron said softly, standing in the doorway. "Let's talk."

Grasping the tabletop tightly, she tilted her chair back. She felt rangy, drunk with anger. "About what?"

"You've got the wrong idea," Aaron told her.

She went to stand up, but her chair fell backward, and she found herself sprawled on the floor. She jumped up and went to the sink, where she began to wash dishes. The water was too hot, but she didn't bother to adjust the temperature.

"What's wrong?" he said.

"Nothing. I've got things to do. I'm under a great deal of stress—my sister. Well, you know my sister. Everybody knows my sister." She turned off the faucet and wiped her hands on a towel. "And they've found a coffin. They shouldn't have opened it. It isn't right. We're grave robbers."

"Are you okay?"

"We should have found that coffin."

"But you stopped digging—and then I got . . . busy."

Eleanor again sat on a kitchen chair. She took off her old, bulky glasses. "I was too busy. Too—distracted."

"Be careful on that chair now," he said, sitting beside her. "We could still dig."

"Yes—I suppose you do want to hang around here."

"Yes—I do want to hang around here. I've had a wonderful talk with your sister."

With that, she leaned over and grabbed his Yankees baseball hat. She hated the Yankees. She hated Aaron, she hated Rene. She kicked open the screen, then hurled his hat with all her might. "Get out!"

He shook his head, scratched his black curls.

— 12 —
The Edgar T. Hussey Sand Dune Cafe

Why was Frederick here now? lamented Joan. Why? Wasn't he busy? Didn't he have deadlines, a meeting with the chairman, a budget to put together? It wasn't like him to take off from work like this. Did he know? Had he found out that she—well, did he know what she had done? But no one would have told him—not even, she supposed, Charlotte.

Wearing big sunglasses and a kerchief tied around her head, Joan slipped in the side entrance of the Silverman Hotel. She mustn't run into Micah. She moved quickly, head down, arms hugging her body. Her head and heart pounded. Jason and Frederick were waiting in the lobby as if nothing was wrong. Frederick had his head in a newspaper and Jason was rolling his eyes at the scrawny bellhops. She thought: *I've escaped Micah.* She kissed Frederick on the cheek, and in doing so, felt a shock. "Oh!" she said.

"It's just the rug," he said. Eyes narrowing, he said: "I almost didn't recognize you. You look . . . different. I could be kissing a strange woman."

"But that's ridiculous!" she said, rubbing her temples. "I've missed you," Joan said—or lied, yes, she was lying.

"And I have missed *you.*"

Joan considered saying: I have betrayed you, but she smiled, waiting for a wave of undying love to sweep over her. Then she could say: my one-night stand has helped me; now I realize how much I truly love my husband. Cheating on him was the right thing to do, for now I love my husband more than ever.

But all she saw was the same old Frederick. As always, he had flattened his hair to his head. There were some tired lines around his eyes.

She hugged Jason, who reeked of after-shave, though he did not yet shave. He wore a T-shirt and dirty jeans. Joan told him, "I've missed you, too. You look a bit messy, but still, a sight for sore eyes."

"Mom, you look like a really messy Jackie Onassis."

"T-shirt and jeans, sneakers," Frederick said with a smile, though his eyes did not smile. "Look at you."

Then, to Joan's dismay, Micah appeared. "Is everything to your satisfaction?" he asked.

"Just fine," Frederick replied.

Joan's pulse raced. "Everything is fine. Please, just *go. Please.*"

"Are you all right, Joan?" Frederick asked. "Thank you, Micah, everything is fine. Joan, this is Micah Silverman, the owner of the hotel."

"I like to get to know my guests, to see if I can be of any assistance. We had a drink late last night, your husband, your son, and I."

"Oh? Jason, you had a drink?"

"Jack Daniel's, straight up."

"He had a seltzer," Frederick said. "Let's not upset your mother, Jason. We got in about eleven. I couldn't get away from the office earlier, and I didn't want to call you too late. Still, here we are."

Micah extended his hand but Joan merely stared at it.

When Frederick nudged her, she shook his hand. Micah said, "Pleased to meet you. I think your husband said your name was . . . let's see . . . Joan, that's it. Well, I'll let you get started with your day." With that, Micah disappeared up a staircase.

Joan said, "What did you talk about last night, with Micah?"

"Nothing interesting," said Jason, unwrapping a stick of gum and shoving it in his mouth. "Just, you know, hotel life, old Borscht Belt comics. Talking about Sid Caesar and Jack Carter is not my idea of a good time."

"Now, now," said Frederick. "Mr. Silverman is a charming man."

"Yes," said Joan.

"Oh, do you know him?" Frederick said, straightening his tie.

"No!"

Frederick wanted to eat lunch at the hotel, but Joan insisted they drive into town.

"But I thought we'd eat here. I have a craving for borscht," her husband said, "though I've never had borscht before."

"You hate beets," Joan told him, so they drove to Amanda's Diner, which teemed with men in jeans and baseball hats and women with fleshy arms in tank tops and culottes.

"This is so retro," said Jason, sliding beside his mother in a booth. "I love this stuff."

"I've missed you, Jason," Joan said, holding her son's face in her hands. "I really have."

"Okay, okay," he said, studying the plastic-coated menu. "Let's see. I'm going to have special number three: three scrambled eggs, hash browns, rye toast, and coffee. Christ, only $3.00. That's unreal. This is so cool."

Joan leaned over the table and kissed Frederick lightly

on the cheek. Then she took a deep breath and kissed him full on the mouth.

Frederick laughed. "Well, how about that."

Jason lowered his menu. "That's the first time I've seen you two kiss in a long time. On the mouth."

"Jason," his mother said.

"I'm just saying."

Joan took a deep breath; she tried to act natural. It was actually working. "So, Jason, did Nana and Grandpa take good care of you?"

"Nana mostly talked in Japanese. Do you think she could be faking it? I mean, how are we to know whether she's just making it all up?"

"Of course she's speaking Japanese," said Frederick. "She takes a class."

Joan said, "I hope you were well-behaved, that you didn't talk to Nana about religion—disputing the pope and all that. You know how that upsets her."

"Should I pretend I'm a good Catholic?"

"You're too young to know whether or not you're a good Catholic. You're just going through a phase." When Joan noticed a freckled little girl attacking a stack of pancakes, she added wistfully, "I miss Diane." She pointed to her heart. "I feel it here."

Jason said, "Diane practiced her piano every day. The 'March of the Gnomes' is coming along pretty good."

"That's a generous thing to say about your sister," said Frederick. "You're a good boy."

"I'm nearly a man."

Frederick and Joan laughed, and Jason said, "Well I am."

Just then, a woman sauntered over. Her red hair was piled high, and she wore a pink dress with a clip-on badge that said: Amanda, Owner. "Is this your family?" the woman asked.

Joan said, "Yes, yes, this is my brood."

"Brood? I'm sorry about the eggs the other day. We just don't get many orders for—what was it? poached eggs? Your wife came in the other day and ordered poached eggs, and the cook—well. He scrambled them."

"Honest mistake," said Frederick.

Joan said, "Poached eggs aren't fattening, that's why I order them."

Amanda said, "You? Fat? Come on, you're so thin! Isn't she thin?"

"My wife always looks wonderful," said Frederick, cleaning the table with a napkin he had dipped in his water glass.

"Well, you have a nice breakfast, now," Amanda said.

The diner was warm, and Jason's color was high. "You're a good-looking kid," Joan told him.

"Don't embarrass me, Mom." When the food arrived, Jason pressed his gum into an ashtray. "I met with Dr. Silberstein a few more times. I'm learning a lot."

"He really is," said Frederick.

"I'm learning that what you said before, Dad, was stupid."

"Stupid? I don't understand, son."

"That waitress—"

"That's Amanda, honey," said Joan. "She owns the diner."

"Whatever. That woman with the red wig—"

"I think it's her real hair," said Joan. "Dyed, of course."

"Amanda says that Mom looks thin, and she says to you, doesn't Mom look thin, and you say she looks wonderful."

Frederick squinted. "That was a mistake?"

"I'm not quite sure what you're saying," said Joan, sipping her coffee. She really shouldn't be drinking coffee, she thought. She was still shaking, just a bit.

"You should have been more specific, Dad. You should have said, Yes, my wife is thin."

"She's not . . . exactly thin. She's just right, in my opinion."

"You don't understand women, Dad."

After breakfast, they drove to Eleanor's. "I don't understand why you're wearing a suit, Dad," Jason said. "On your day off. It's kind of weird."

"Your mother looks very casual."

"Do I?"

"Are you wearing a, you know—?"

"Bra?" said Jason.

"Jason," said Joan.

They parked behind Glenn's orange van. "I hope we're not blocking anybody in," said Frederick. "Joan, are you sure it's okay to park here?"

"Where else can we park?"

Frederick gripped the wheel. "I see your point. I'll park here."

"Well, Eleanor," said Frederick, closing the car door. "Well, well."

"Well, what?" said Jason.

"This is quite an accomplishment—this archaeological dig. That water garden idea of yours—fantastic."

"I'm so glad you're here," Eleanor said absently. "Everyone is here."

Eleanor gave Jason a hug. "How's school?"

"It's over," he said. "I'll be a senior in the fall."

"That's fine," she told him. "You're a good kid."

"Tell *them,*" he said.

The four slowly made their way to the rock-shelter, talking disjointedly about the weather, the isolation of rural life, and the outlandish price of sneakers. Joan carried Jason's fishing rod. When they reached the shelter, Frederick shook Malcolm's hand. "Thanks for taking care of my Joan for a few days."

"She's really been taking care of us," Malcolm said,

stroking his beard. "She makes wonderful meals. You really must be proud of her. She's quite a cook."

Joan smiled, "Well, I do my best. Cooking is a skill not all of us possess." ·

Jason nudged Eleanor. "I think that's a put-down. Of you. I wouldn't stand for it."

Eleanor said, "Oh, no, Jason. That's not what Joan was suggesting at all. Not at all."

"Well, well," said Frederick. "This dig is quite an accomplishment. And these artifacts—the bone and all— might be the oldest in New York State? That's something to ponder."

Mr. Simmons said, "I'm convinced they are."

"We don't really know that," said Malcolm. "He's a little overoptimistic. We can't count our chickens."

Mr. Simmons broke in, "If you're interested in contributing in any way, say, dollars, to the Sullivan County Museum, just let me know. I understand you're quite a businessman. Your wife says you're always working."

"Well—I suppose so. I'm in cable TV. I do my best."

Joan sighed. "My husband has always tried to do his best. It just hasn't always worked out."

"Well, Jason," said Frederick, unperturbed, "are you going to go fishing? This is certainly the spot."

"I'll cook whatever you catch," said Joan, handing Jason his fishing pole. "You haven't gone fishing in a long while, have you?"

"No."

Frederick put his arm around Jason. "We used to fish at the park, remember?"

"Mostly you read reports," said Jason. "I fished."

"I'm going to fish with you in a few minutes. Father and son. But first I want to check in on Aunt Charlotte."

"First things first," said Jason.

—

"Well, well. How's my sister-in-law? How are you?"

"I think I'm getting bed sores on my butt," said Charlotte, "but thanks for asking. How's the Silverman?"

"The hotel? Fine, just fine."

"Meet anyone interesting there?"

Frederick scratched his head. "Um—gee. I don't know."

"Does the name Micah Silverman ring a bell?"

"Yes, of course. He had a drink with Jason and me last night. Very nice fellow."

Charlotte sat up and pointed at her brother-in-law. "Be warned."

"What?"

"Open your eyes. *Think.*"

"I always try to—think."

"Then don't think. Be emotional—feel. I swear, the Irish are the most repressed people on earth."

Frederick picked up a magazine. "Well, it must be nice to be able to catch up on your reading. I just have so little time. I barely have time to eat. I took off a few days and I can't imagine the chaos down at the office."

"It's good you took off. Important. I've had a lot of time to think, lying here, let me tell you." She frowned. "Do you love your wife?"

"You know, a few weeks ago, Jason asked me that. He pointed at Joan and said: 'Do you love her?' Well, he's a very sensitive kid. We've had a few problems with him lately. You might have heard. Overall, he's a wonderful kid, though. Wonderful. Of course I love my wife. Of course. It goes without saying."

"Does it?"

—

Jason caught four trout, but Joan could tell he was bored, or unhappy—he was something and it wasn't good. He didn't smile when he caught his fish. His silver trout wiggled for a few minutes on the grass, then gave in to death.

"You're quite a fisherman," said Joan.

"I'm a murderer."

Joan and Frederick took him back to the hotel. "You're always so difficult," Joan told him as they watched Frederick playing shuffleboard on a worn-out court in back of the hotel. He was losing.

"I'm not difficult at all," Jason told his mother. "It's just that I'm smart."

At dusk, while Jason watched a Mets game in his hotel room, Joan and Frederick had a drink on the deck behind the Silverman. A cloud of tiny insects hovered near, and Joan flicked them away.

Pointing heavenward, Frederick said, "Just look at that country sky, streaked with pink, and orange, and yellow. It reminds me of, yes, when I was a kid, and the Good Humor man came. My father occasionally let me get an ice cream. Very occasionally. I'd get the Hawaiian medley ice. I'd lick my ice and stare at the sky, at the sunset. I've always loved sunsets. But when have I ever had time to appreciate them, with school and then work and then with you and the kids?"

"*We* get in the way of your enjoying sunsets? Well, I can get out of your way if you'd like."

"No, that's not what I meant—"

"Do you have to stay here?" said Joan, pressing a glass of white wine against her forehead.

"It's too crowded at Eleanor's. Where else could Jason and I stay?"

"There are other hotels. It's very crowded here, too." But Joan looked around and only one other couple sat in the Siesta Outdoor Cafe: a woman with platinum hair, whom Joan had seen the other night in the Night Owl Lounge, and a man with bushy black hair and a wide yellow necktie. The two gazed into each other's eyes. They were obviously in love—newly in love.

Frederick said, "But I like it here, I like the Silverman, though I suppose it is a bit run-down. The carpets are threadbare; and the ambience is a bit—peculiar. A bit overdone, with the plush maroon drapes and all. The psychics in the lobby. Still, it's historic."

"Historic?"

"Micah was telling us the history of the hotel the other night. One night, Sophie Tucker sang here. Her voice shattered a wineglass. Are you all right?"

"Yes, fine."

"Are you sure?"

"Yes."

"You look a little pale. Oh, hello there, Micah. Sit down. Have a drink on us."

"I wouldn't want to interfere."

"Interfere?" said Frederick.

"I don't mind if I do," Micah said, sitting down.

Frederick said, "Joan, are you okay?"

Faintly, she said, "Yes."

"I was just telling my wife about the night Sophie Tucker sang that song about a Yiddish mother."

"That was back in the thirties. My grandfather talked about that until the day he died. Actually, he died at night." Micah called over a waiter. "Scotch on the rocks."

"Yes, Mr. Silverman."

"This is a famous place," said Frederick, wiping the table with a napkin. "I once saw a documentary about the Catskills on PBS, and they mentioned the Silverman. Apparently someone was rubbed out here?"

"Stop cleaning the tables!" snapped Joan. "Just—stop!"

Micah raised an eyebrow, then said, "The Catskills was a favorite resort area for bootleggers. In 1937, Louie Klein stabbed Murray Pindlestein in the chest thirty-seven times with an ice pick, then tied him to a pinball machine."

"Mr. Silverman, don't you have important things to do?" Joan asked.

"Not really."

"Don't you have a hair replacement lecture to attend? Or perhaps you should have your fortune told. Terrible things may be foretold. You'd better hurry."

Frederick said, "Joan, don't be so . . . rude."

"It's just, he's the owner of this hotel, and I don't want to keep him from his duties."

"Ah," said Micah, "there are duties, and then there are duties. You know, Frederick, your wife is a very lovely lady."

Joan buried her head in her hands.

Frederick said, "Joan, I don't think you're feeling well tonight. She's not usually this—I think her sister is getting her down. Her sister Charlotte is confined to bed; she nearly lost her baby. She's a few months pregnant, and Joan is up here helping out. That's the way Joan is."

"She's charitable," said Micah. "She gives of herself."

"You can tell just by looking at her, the kind of woman she is," said Frederick, giving Joan a little hug. She winced.

"I feel as if I know her. Really know her," Micah said.

Eleanor couldn't sleep—sleep was a state beyond her. She fluffed her pillows, but it was no good. She remade the bed. She dusted her bedroom bureaus. She slipped into bed again and stared at the fuzzy dark ceiling. No good. She made herself a cup of chamomile tea, which she slowly sipped. Then she went back to her room. She lay in bed, waiting. She had taken yoga lessons years before, so she tried a relaxation technique she had learned. She tried to relax her feet, then her ankles, then her knees, and on and on until she reached her shoulders, but they were like slabs of concrete. Shoulders—relax. But they would not budge. She kept seeing Rene in her mind's eye—his cold blue eyes, his angry mouth, his hard body on hers. She kept playing his words over and over again in her mind: he had never liked sex with her, he had never wanted her. And then there was Aaron, just ambling by— she was still angry with him. She tried to still her mind by focusing on the sounds of the night: the wind in the trees made a sound like cymbals, but it was no use.

Clutching a flashlight, stumbling in the darkness, for she was wearing an old pair of glasses, she made her way toward the rock-shelter. She must get herself a new pair that coincided with the present frailty of her vision. The crescent moon seemed to pulsate, to will itself to fullness. She could see the lights of Aaron's house in the distance. He wants Charlotte, Eleanor thought. What bliss it must be to feel wanted. Rene didn't want her, had never really wanted her. She thought: *Rene has never loved me.* She had learned an important lesson, however, from him: She was not special. She was replaceable by other women.

But it had not always been so; she didn't think so.

Surely not in Rome, where they ate as the Romans did—late and well. One evening, they shared a gigantic plate of veal scallopini in a tiny restaurant near the Spanish Steps, and then they took a taxi to the Colosseum, where, within its skeletal walls, her wedding band glinted in ancient moonlight. Rene drew her to him, rubbing the goose bumps on her arms.

"All this history," she said.

"You and I will always be together," he told her.

But their divorce would be final in a week. She thought: *I do not want him.* She waited for a contrary feeling, but it did not come. But oh, how lonely she was, even with all the people sleeping in her house and in the tents down the lawn. She lay down on the grass and cried. And finally, under the old moon, she drifted off.

In the morning, Eleanor was surprised to find Joan making breakfast. She thought she had planned to stay overnight with Frederick, but here she was, scrambling eggs.

Joan knocked a wooden fruit bowl off the table and when several peaches struck the floor, a rich aroma came up. "I never said I was staying with Frederick."

"Are you okay?" asked Eleanor.

"Of course. Why do you have grass in your hair?"

"I slept outside. I actually slept, for a few hours. I don't know why."

When two slices of blackened bread blasted from the toaster, Joan let go a small scream. "Sorry. I was startled."

Eleanor said, "I figured you would be with Frederick, at the hotel."

"You figured wrong. I came in very late. I guess you didn't hear me, sleeping outside like a homeless person. Do you want some eggs?"

"I think eggs would make me ill."

"You have to eat."

"I think I might try some pancakes, or one pancake. I might manage that. I'll make them."

"I'll make them. You'll ruin them."

Joan cracked two eggs into a bowl, poured in some Bisquick and milk, then she heated up a pan and threw in a slab of butter, which sizzled. "Charlotte's already eaten. She doesn't look well today. For once, she's not beautiful—imagine that. She's sleeping now, but take a look at her later—tell me what you think. I went out earlier and bought some donuts for everyone else. Brad and Colin and Ivy like cream donuts, but Malcolm and Natalie like croissants. Ian loves jelly donuts, he loves American junk food. I never saw a man who liked jelly donuts more than Ian. I wonder how much he likes Charlotte? Anyway, that's what I did today, already."

"Are you going to tell Frederick about Micah?"

"Of course not!"

"I thought you said that you were going to tell the truth from now on. Something about being truthful instead of being civil."

"Should I tell him? Should I? Dear Lord, if he can't have an erection now . . ." Joan placed a stack of pancakes in front of Eleanor. They were round and golden and steaming. Eleanor poured syrup on them. Dot Anderson from down the road made the syrup, tapping diligently into maple trees. "These taste great," said Eleanor, "but I hope you don't expect me to eat them all. I'll try to finish one."

"I feel like telling Charlotte off. Why did Frederick come up here in the first place? Charlotte might have told him something."

"She wouldn't do that."

"Like hell she wouldn't."

Joan stared at herself in the bathroom mirror. She was supposed to meet Frederick and Jason at noon. They would have lunch in town, or maybe they would drive over to Pennsylvania. She had begged him to meet her at Eleanor's, but he had insisted she meet them at the hotel. "We're eating in town—why drive out to Eleanor's only to drive back again? And the hotel is closer to 84 if we decide to drive to Pennsylvania."

Joan combed her hair. It was bone straight, and, admit it, thin. Her bangs were a bit too long, so she found a pair of scissors and trimmed them. Little hairs fell into her eyes. She tried to brush them away. They had fallen into the sink, too, and were difficult to clean up. She washed her face, though she had showered earlier. She patted wrinkle cream under her eyes—as if it would do any good. She opened her makeup case, but instead of applying it, she simply stared at the compacts, the beige foundation, the eyebrow pencil, the eyeliner, the lipsticks. Her face was clean, and if Frederick didn't like it, tough. Not that Frederick had ever insisted that she wear makeup. It was her idea. She had to make up for being plain, and makeup sure helped. Her long squared-off coral nails, too, had been her idea. But now they were naked, short and stubby.

Staring at her large eyes in the mirror, she decided: I will tell him the truth. Perhaps he would forgive her; at the least, something would change. She allowed her mouth and eyes to relax, and her face changed: her nose seemed less pronounced and the lines around her lips eased. Her chin, too, appeared less molted, smoother. She was a better-looking woman than she had thought.

When she arrived at the hotel, Jason was having his fortune told by a woman in a pink sweatsuit and matching turban. Frederick stood in the lobby reading a newspaper. "Honey," he said, offering her a smile.

"Frederick," she said. "That's better. What you're wearing. You don't need to wear a suit up here." Frederick had opted for khaki pants and a polo shirt, while Jason wore black jeans and a black T-shirt.

"You look a bit pale," her husband told her. "I don't understand why you didn't stay here with me. Why did you leave at three in the morning?"

"I told you, I didn't want you to catch what I have."

"Did you sleep okay at Eleanor's? I think you've come down with something."

"I think so, too."

"Mom isn't wearing any makeup," said Jason, strolling over. "She's a new woman. I hate it when you draw those black lines around your eyes. You look scary. By the way, I'm going to be an astronaut on the first manned mission to Mars, according to the lady in the turban."

Joan said, "Jason, I am not a new woman. Why would you say something like that?"

Jason pulled a pack of cigarettes from his back pocket. "Just a feeling."

"How dare you smoke!" cried Joan.

"I don't know about you, son," his father told him.

"Why can't you ever yell at him!" Joan demanded. "Don't you have any—I don't know—passion in you?"

"Oh, God," said Jason.

Micah appeared. Joan seemed unable to escape his old clothes and bald head. "How do you know when to find us?" Joan said.

"Did you tell me what time you'd be here? How could I know?"

Joan stared at the woman wearing the turban. "Micah," she said, "I believe you have something important to tell my husband."

Micah's mouth opened.

"I believe you have something to tell my husband."

"Let's see. A joke, how about a joke. Let's see. Many jokes have been told here at the Silverman Hotel. So many to choose from. How's this: What's the difference when a French lady, an English lady, and a Jewish lady have sex with their husbands?" Micah raised an eyebrow.

Jason said, "We have no idea."

Micah said, "The French lady swoons, 'Ah, Pierre, your kiss! You are the finest lover.' The Englishwoman says, 'By Jove, that was quite an excellent kiss, Reginald,' and the Jewish woman says, 'You know, Morris, the ceiling needs a good painting.' "

Frederick looked at his shoes. "A good joke. Yes. Very good."

Joan said, "That's the only story you're going to tell, isn't it, Micah?"

"Except for that your wife, Frederick, is like the French lady."

Holding the steering wheel at ten and two o'clock, Frederick said, "He's an odd fellow, that Micah. Very odd. Where do you suggest we eat?"

Joan thought her husband must surely be the densest successful man alive. On the other hand, maybe he wasn't so dumb. "Wherever," she said. "And Jason, please move your feet—don't stretch them out so that they hit me in the back of the head."

Jason said, "What was that all about, with Micah. Is he speaking in some kind of code?"

"Don't be ridiculous," said Joan, staring out the window at signs for "horse back rideing," and "tamatoes." *Dear Lord,* she thought, *on top of everything else, can no one spell?* They passed a billboard advertising a new development, Hemlock Estates. She said, "Now will you look at that. Hemlock Estates."

"Hemlock is poisonous," said Frederick. "Isn't that what Socrates drank?"

Joan said, "Can you imagine? A group of businessmen sit around a table and one says, 'How about Daffodil Estates,' and another businessman says, 'No, that's too nice a name, let's name the development after a poisonous substance, like hemlock.' You businessmen, you think you know it all."

"I don't know anything," said Frederick. "Or you don't think I know anything, so fine, I'll go along with that."

"Well, where should we eat?" asked Joan nervously. "Look, there's a diner . . . forget it. We've passed it. Frederick, where should we eat?" Just then they passed the Edgar T. Hussey Sand Dune Cafe, identified by its pink neon sign.

"Oh, there!" said Jason. "Let's eat there!"

"We've passed it, son," said Frederick.

"It looked like a terrible dump," his mother added. "Even for Pennsylvania. Let's eat somewhere nice. A colonial inn, maybe."

"Oh, please," Jason said, "let's eat at the—what was it?—Edgar T. Hussey Sand Dune Cafe. How can you resist a name like that? Let's do something different for a change. Let's experience America. I mean, New Jersey—it isn't really America."

The Edgar T. Hussey Sand Dune Cafe was not crowded. In fact, it was empty. A skinny man with dark oily hair and a thin mustache leaned on the greasy counter. "That section's closed," he said.

"But there's no one in this section, or any section," said Joan. "We are the only people here."

"It's closed."

Frederick frowned. "I see. I can understand that. Where do you suggest we sit?"

The skinny man pulled his fingers through his oily hair. "At the counter."

"But we'd like a table," Joan said.

"Tables are off-limits at the moment," he said. "You can't always have what you want."

Jason said, "That's from a Rolling Stones song," which he then started to sing.

"Please don't," Joan told him. "I already have a headache."

His father said, "Not that your mother means you're without talent. You're a talented boy."

They sat at the counter.

"I'm not a boy. I'm a man," said Jason. "Nearly a man, at the very least."

Joan gave him a hug. "But you'll always be my boy. Can we have some menus, please?"

The skinny man shuffled over with three laminated menus. "We don't have any more tuna fish," he said. "Or hamburgers."

"How about chicken salad sandwiches, all around," Joan said. "On whole wheat."

The skinny man said, "I wouldn't eat the chicken salad."

"BLTs all around," said Joan. "Is that okay? Are you out of lettuce?"

"You don't have to be nasty. Here I was, giving you a good tip."

Frederick said, "Edgar T. Hussey, would you be he?"

"I wouldn't."

"It's an interesting name," Frederick went on. "Is he your father?"

"Never met the man. Don't know who he is, or was."

The BLTs arrived, with potato chips on the side. Frederick and Joan had coffee; Jason had a coke. "I really shouldn't drink any more coffee," said Joan. "I'm a little jumpy."

"Really?" said Frederick. "Why would that be? That Micah fellow is a bit strange. Do you think he was insulting you, Joan? Or was he just trying to be funny? I don't always understand comedians. Sometimes I laugh because everyone else is laughing. Take my wife, I don't know."

"Who would want to take your wife?" said Joan. "Who would want me? Micah was just trying to be funny. That's all."

"Maybe he thinks she looks French," said Jason. "Anyway, it's good to be out of Grandma and Grandpa's house. I know they mean well, but Grandpa's always watching programs like *Green Acres,* and then he complains that Arnold the pig could not actually go to school. And Grandma keeps going on and on about Kennedy, and plots, and, to tell the truth, I'm glad to be here at the Edgar T. Hussey Sand Dune Cafe, even if there are no sand dunes in hundreds of miles." He gulped his soda. "Oh, by the way. I'm supposed to tell you that I'm not a virgin anymore. Dr. Silberstein said it was something I should tell you."

Joan dropped her spoon into her coffee. Frederick cleared his throat. "I see," he said softly. "I see. Well, that's good."

Joan said, "That's good?"

"I mean, that he told the truth. Thank you, Jason—that must not have been an easy thing to say."

"It wasn't too bad," he said, munching his chips.

"Boys will be boys," said the skinny man. "Can't fight nature. Boys are different than girls. They have needs, they can't control their needs. But girls don't care for sex, much."

Joan said, "Women, for your information, do like sex. Though not when they're young. Not when they're seventeen."

The man said, "My wife doesn't like sex."

"I am not surprised," Joan said, getting up. Frederick and Jason followed her out.

Ian sat on Charlotte's bed. "And how is the mother-to-be today?"

"Okay, I guess."

"You look a bit knackered."

Charlotte felt heavy and slow. "Can you stay with me?" she said. "Talk?"

Ian glanced at his golden watch. "Certainly."

"I think you're wasting your time out there. I don't think the artifacts will be that old . . . Do you mind talking to me? Am I really that awful?"

"Of course not. I don't know what you mean. You told me you were on the pill, but that's okay. Maybe you forgot your pills when you went to England. That's possible, isn't it?" he said, grimly. "Anyway, what shall we talk about?"

"I don't know, anything. You have some broccoli between your teeth."

"Do I?" He worked his tongue around his teeth. Neither of them spoke for several minutes. "Well," he said, "I must see what Brad, Colin, and Ivy are up to. Who knows what Brad is up to. We'll have another nice conversation later on."

"I don't want to lose the baby," she blurted out. All she could do these days was imagine its fishlike claws plumping into baby arms inside her, its stunned eyes growing round, sweet, and beloved. She deserved to lose the baby, though; she didn't deserve a child. She had only wanted the baby because she didn't want to be alone, and she didn't need a man. Her mother had always told her: don't rely upon the kindness of strangers. Don't live your life waiting for Mr. Right; the best any woman can find is Mr. Close-Enough.

"You're the only man I've ever slept with who wasn't circumcised," she suddenly said, a fact easier to reveal than what she had just been thinking.

He laughed. "I see. I guess you can't say I'm the only man you ever slept with."

"And you can't say I'm the only woman you ever slept with."

"As I told you, I've been married. Thrice."

"Three times. Too many times. Well, don't let me hold you up. God forbid I should take up too much of your time."

When Eleanor ran into Ian coming from Charlotte's room she said, "How is she today?"

"Fine, I suppose. Just tired."

"Joan said she doesn't look well."

"She can't always be beautiful. She's under a great deal of stress"—he glanced at his watch—"and to be honest, so am I. I have to send some footage back to London. Just some preliminary footage. What time does the post close?"

"Five-thirty, but they like people to come by five, especially if they're sending something complicated."

Ian touched Eleanor's arm. "I'll see you a bit later." And then he walked his elegant stiff steps toward the front door. He seemed a bit confused by the screen. "Not used to these . . . nets." He paused. "I do care for your sister, by the way. I do."

Eleanor, too, cared for Charlotte, but she needed to find out something from her. She went into the room and opened the blinds. "Joan said you looked a little off."

"Well, she should mind her own business."

"She's just concerned."

"I know she's a good person, but I don't feel it. It's something I know in my head. I'm a terrible person."

"Why do you say things like that?"

"See—you can't say, No. Charlotte, you are a wonderful person."

Eleanor cleared her throat. "You're a wonderful person. Why do you say things like that—that you're terrible?"

"I've had too much time to think. Joan is a good person, but she's still wrong on a few points. For example, I did not steal Stewart away."

"I don't think she's thinking about him right now. She's worrying about Frederick. Do you think she should tell him about Micah?"

"No." Then she said, "Yes." Then she said, "I don't know."

"Can I ask you something?"

"Sure."

"What did Aaron want?"

Charlotte picked up a magazine. "Aaron?"

"The other day, he was sitting on your bed."

"Oh, yeah. I really don't remember. It wasn't anything important."

"Do you think he's . . . in love with you?"

Charlotte bolted upright. "Christ, don't tell me you think I'm taking *your* man away, too! Everybody has it in for me! Even my little sister!"

"Aaron isn't my man. You wouldn't be taking my man away."

"If you say so. But I'm not interested in him." Charlotte shook her head. "You are so dense."

Back at the Silverman, Joan told her son, "Why don't you play shuffleboard?"

"I don't know how to play."

"Why not learn?"

A gray-haired couple strolled by. They were laughing, playfully punching each other on the arms. Jason said, "Shuffleboard? Are you kidding? I'm not old enough."

"Jason, please cooperate."

"Mom, level with me. Be honest. Christ, why is that so difficult? You want to be alone with Dad. Why don't you just say so?"

"Shuffleboard is a fine game. It will serve you well in retirement years."

"Sure, I'll play," he said, stepping into the shadows. "Go have your talk with Dad."

Joan sat her husband down on the thin polyester bedspread. The forest green material had been quilted with clear sturdy thread, though no fluffiness resulted—the quilting had been a useless exercise. Frederick edged forward, holding his hands so tightly that his knuckles went white.

"Well," he said.

"Well," she said.

She stared at the artificial woodgrain dresser in the corner, at the old Zenith television set on a shiny table, at the garish cardboard painting of Catskills foliage hanging over a dusty tabletop. "I have something to tell you," she said.

"Maybe we should forget it," he said. "No use bringing up anything—troublesome."

And she thought: *maybe. Why not whisk the truth under the threadbare carpet? Why not forget it?* But then she thought: *No.* She gripped the bedpost. "For once, we should talk."

Frederick stood up and stared out the window. "Can I ask you something?"

"Of course," she said.

He sighed. "Forget it."

"No, what?"

He took a breath. "You slept with him, didn't you?"

"What are you talking about? I don't know what you're talking about."

He touched his temple. "I know."

Frantically, she said, "I don't know what you mean."

"Where did you sleep with him? It might help to know."

She said nothing.

"Please answer me," he said.

Slowly, she said, "Oh God, does it matter?"

"To me, yes."

". . . In a hotel room."

He turned to her. His dimples were lines, deep lines. "Here?"

"I don't know if this is the room."

He turned away. She noticed how evenly his hair had been cut in the back. Abruptly, he tried to open the window, but it wouldn't budge. He punched the wall. Then he turned back to her. "Your son can have sex, but your husband can't. Jason and I will leave tomorrow morning. I'll tell him I have urgent business at work. You and I will talk to a lawyer." He took a long hard sigh. "You've never really loved me. I know that. You loved Stewart. Why, I can't say. I've loved you, but I'm not dangerous enough, maybe. I can't get your heart racing like Stewart, or the memory of him."

"I don't love him. That's completely illogical."

"What does logic have to do with it?"

"Stewart—he was so—so cruel. He didn't care about me—he loved her, all along. If it weren't for her . . . "

"If it weren't for her—what?"

"I don't know. I might have— Forget it."

"You might have had the baby?"

"I might have. I might have gotten over my—I don't know what to call it. It's something hard inside me. My guilt. My Catholic guilt."

He sat back down on the bed. She went to put her arms around him, but he drew back.

"Why don't you want me?" she asked. "Am I that grotesque? Do you have another woman on the side, like Rene? Like Stewart?"

"God how I wish you would stop thinking about him."

SISTERS *and* STRANGERS — 299

"I don't think about him."

"You don't think about me."

She did, though. She thought about how his eyes shone after she gave birth to Jason. "Oh, Joannie. Look what we've made," he had told her, voice breaking.

She was saying, "I slept with Micah last week, not with Stewart. It's you who can't stop thinking about Stewart."

"You carry him around with you, he's living in our house, a nineteen-year-old ghost." He added, "I'll call the lawyer."

As Joan made her way to the parking lot, an elderly couple, clutching tennis racquets, nodded to her. She couldn't nod back. She felt suspended, outside of herself somehow; she was living someone else's life: pretend you are a woman who has just cheated on her husband—how would you walk away from him? She was unsure now if she had slept with Micah at all. It must have been some-one else. She would never do a thing like that. Her life— it had been fine, hadn't it? Beautiful? Everything had been fine—well, nearly fine; you couldn't have everything. Trudging up Eleanor's dusty driveway, she began to cry, and by the time she opened Charlotte's bedroom door, her face burned. "What have I done?" she said.

"What are you talking about?" said Charlotte.

"He's going to divorce me."

"What? You told him? You told him you slept with Micah?"

"He knew. How did he know?" And then she said: "Did you tell him?"

"Round up the usual suspects," said Charlotte. "If an evil deed's been done, it must have been done by Charlotte."

"Well, did you?"

"Why would I tell him?"

"I don't know—to take everything away from me."

"Joan—I didn't tell him. I didn't."

She thought for a moment. "Micah dropped hints. Your wife is like the French lady. I'm going to kill Micah. He's ruined my life."

"Has he?" asked Charlotte.

Joan shrugged. "I don't know. Not yet."

"Things aren't always as straightforward as you think they are."

Joan rubbed her eyes. "What do you mean?"

"Nothing."

"No—what are you getting at?"

"Just that maybe you're not as morally superior as you thought."

"Does this mean we're even? I slept with Micah, you slept with Stewart? Sleeping with Micah didn't hurt you. I know you slept with Stewart. Why won't you just admit it? I don't even care anymore. I really don't."

"You won't lose Frederick. Not if you don't want to lose him."

Charlotte thought, Frederick won't leave Joan. He loves her. Her sister was just stupid. She had a wonderful husband. He was having trouble with sexual matters. Well, there are more important things in life. There are worse things. Ian was the father of her unborn child, and she didn't really know him—she didn't know if she liked him. She leaned close to the window and in the distance she could see him talking to Brad and Colin. Now he was walking under the apple trees, motioning to Malcolm and Mr. Simmons. Now he was bending over, looking at something, some artifact, perhaps. Charlotte called, "Ian! Ian!" Her throat was hoarse from the yelling. Calling him made her feel for the moment like she loved him.

Standing under her window, he asked, "Is there a

problem? Are you all right?" He carefully rolled up his sleeves. "What can I do for you, Charlotte?"

"We need to talk."

"You have to be patient," he said, "I'm under the proverbial gun. I've got work to do." He was fuzzy through the screen, like an imprecise newspaper image made of dots.

"I see. Work to do," she said.

"Precisely."

"I want to talk to you about my sister."

He squinted. "Eleanor?"

"Joan."

"Ah. More problems?"

She waved a hand. "Forget it." He stared at her for a minute, offered her a vague smile, then he returned to his cameras, to Ivy and Brad and Colin, to Natalie and Malcolm and Mr. Simmons and the two graduate students, to people who were active, who were getting things done, making their mark, as she was not.

Ian didn't love her either. She knew it.

Charlotte opened a book about Hollywood. She tried to read, but kept thinking about Joan, about the past. She willed herself to stop. But she couldn't. And she thought: *why not investigate the past?* She had nothing to hide. Some memories were actually pleasant—of the ocean, of ice-skating, of summers at the Florence Community Pool.

Joan had once run away from home, packing all her belongings in a 45 record case.

"No one believes in Miranda!" she had sobbed.

Eleanor shrugged. "I don't think it could be true."

Catherine said, "Nobody has imaginary friends, Joan. It's a nice idea, but nobody has imaginary, invisible friends. You do, of course, have your guardian angel."

Charlotte said nothing, but she followed Joan at a safe

distance as she shuffled past a cluster of old office buildings, then marched on to the pool.

In the steamy locker room, where Joan planned to live,
Charlotte said, "I believe in Miranda."

"Really?"

"I do. She's real." Big sister and middle sister made
their way to the diving board; middle sister went first, big
sister followed. Middle sister wasn't allowed to dive,
according to their mother. But Joan said, "Watch me! I'm
going to do the sailor dive!" Feet first, she sliced the
water, her right hand shading her brow, saluting.
Charlotte mounted the board, feeling the warm eyes of
the boys upon her. Her breasts had appeared six months
before; her hips had curved a bit. When she jumped, the
board fluttered beneath her; she rose weightlessly in the
air, deftly touching her hands to her calves—then, grace-
fully, perfectly, punctured the surface of the pool. In the
depths, she observed the purple-veined legs of fat women,
the hairy legs of gross men, and finally the skinny legs of
Joan flapping for dear life. Joan's legs made her think of a
skinny chicken. Joan was not a great swimmer; well, she
was only in the sixth grade, while Charlotte was an eighth
grader. Charlotte put her arms around Joan's waist and
pulled her to the surface, past the fat ladies' legs, the stiff
hairy calves of old men, the flapping skirts of the mothers
she knew, to the bright sun of Florence.

Charlotte saved her. Joan would have made it anyway,
probably. But a few years later, Joan nearly died.

Charlotte closed her eyes. Joan had been in the hospital, while she, Charlotte, had prayed in their Florence
bedroom: "Dear Lord, please make Joan all right. Please
let her live." Her parents and Eleanor were still at the
hospital.

And then the doorbell rang. She had no idea the doorbell would ring. That wasn't her idea. She opened the

door and there he was. What was he doing? What was he up to? Stewart said, "I had to see you. I couldn't just wait for you in Glassboro."

"What are you doing here? Have you been to the hospital?"

He opened the screen door and stepped inside. "I can't go," he said. Charlotte backed away. She had the best of intentions.

Stewart took a step forward.

Charlotte felt the blood drain from her head. The right response.

But what did Stewart want, after all? Perhaps he only wanted to comfort her. He took another step forward and she saw that his eyes were rimmed red, that his nose, too, was red, raw, running.

"Stewart," she said. A long, slow anxiety rose in her.

His eyes were heavy-lidded, his veins were like purple ropes at his temples. She stood in the doorframe between the living room and the hallway that led to three tiny bedrooms. The house seemed incredibly small, a house for tiny, insubstantial people.

Now he was very near, breathing hard. He smelled of beer. "Charlotte," he said, "will she make it? God, she's so sick! What if she dies?"

"She'll make it."

"You're sure?"

". . . Yes."

He put his right hand on her shoulder, then gently twisted a plait of her long golden hair.

"Stewart, no."

"Will she make it?"

He put his arms around her tiny waist. He listed back and forth. He was drunk.

"You were nice," he said, "to let me stay with you. In Glassboro."

"You should have told me you were coming."

He smiled. "Well . . . yeah." He cupped her breasts and she did not stop him. She thought: *Stop him.* He lifted her T-shirt and placed his hands under her lacy bra. "Charlotte," he murmured.

She pushed his hands away.

"I'm sorry, Charlotte. It's just— Is she gonna die?"

What if she did die? Charlotte felt a weakening in her legs. "She can't die." Stewart knelt and sucked her left breast. She held his head, as if he were a baby. "If she dies, I will die," Charlotte said.

Stewart guided her to her own bedroom—Joan's bedroom, too—his hands gripping her shoulders. He positioned her on the bed and lay on top of her. "I've only ever loved you," he said. "Only you."

"No," she said, as he pulled down her denim shorts, her pink cotton panties. He entered her silently.

She thought: he is a knife, he is killing me.

I have killed my own sister. And then she thought: no, she hadn't. Really not.

"It's always been you," he panted. "I didn't admit it . . . to myself . . . at first."

He came quickly and kissed her lovingly on the lips. Coated with shame, she went to the bathroom. There she pulled a tiny Dixie cup from its blue plastic dispenser and sipped some water. Her mother thought the Dixie cup dispenser one of the triumphs of the twentieth century. "No more germs passing from person to person!" Charlotte glanced at her face in the mirror. She was beautiful, which, she thought, was ironic.

Stewart, still naked on her bed, said, "I love you, Charlotte. Does that make me the worst kind of person?"

She dressed quickly, and, sitting at her frilly pink vanity, she pulled a brush through her long golden hair. She powdered her shiny face.

"Charlotte?"

Turning, she said, "I don't love you."

He sat up. "But we just made love!"

"I don't love you."

"Charlotte! How can you say that?"

"I let you do it because . . . I don't know why. To make things as bad as they can be. You said you loved Joan, that you'd marry her. You lied."

"Charlotte, I love *you*."

"And I don't love you back. How does it feel?"

He pulled from the pocket of his jeans a letter. "What difference does it make?" he said. "In the end?"

She read the letter. It was from the draft board.

Charlotte told herself now: *Don't remember. Don't think. Go back to the present, to the everyday.* Seeing Joan might break the spell, for Joan was here and that meant everything was all right. She was alive, she hadn't died.

Maniacally, Charlotte called, "Joan! Eleanor! Let's—!" Let's what? What? Charlotte, desperate for diversion, completed her thought: "Let's play cards!"

"Cards?" said Joan, peering into the room.

"Cards. Gin rummy."

Joan sighed. "Okay. As long as you don't drink it. The rum, I mean."

"I told you, I'm not drinking anymore. Christ, what kind of person do you think I am?" Charlotte pressed her face against the screen. "Ian! Ian!" she called. "Forget it. He doesn't hear me."

"He's working on his documentary," said Joan, sitting with Eleanor at the foot of Charlotte's bed.

Charlotte said, "He's not who I thought he'd be."

"No?" Joan asked.

"He's not what I expected."

"Are you what *he* expected?"

"I thought he'd be more attentive." Charlotte quickly shuffled the cards. "Wait. I've got to get rid of these jokers." She dealt the cards. "Don't worry, Eleanor, I won't make you play fifty-two card pick-up."

Joan said, "You were mean, making her pick up all those cards."

Charlotte arranged her hand. She held three diamonds—an ace, a Jack, and a five—a seven and Queen of clubs, plus a six and seven of spades. Not a bad hand. And yet she had the feeling that for once she would not win.

Joan nudged Charlotte: "Tell Eleanor what you used to do."

"What?"

"You used to cheat Eleanor in crazy eights."

"I don't even remember how to play that game," said Charlotte, biting on a card.

"Eleanor," Joan said, "Charlotte used to cheat you in cards. She was mean."

"I was a normal older sister. That's normal behavior."

"That's not normal," said Joan. "At least, I don't think so. I, for one, never made Eleanor play fifty-two-card pick-up."

"It doesn't matter," said Eleanor. "I didn't mind picking up the cards. Not really." She thought for a moment. "That's not true. I did mind. I hated picking up all those cards on my hands and knees, counting to make sure I'd found them all. Still, it was a long time ago. What does it matter now?"

"Again, I am the evil sister," said Charlotte, suddenly hurling her cards in the air. Five landed on the bed; two fell on the rag rug.

"What are you doing?" said Joan.

"You're saying I'm not a good sister. That I was never a good sister. And I was."

"All I said was that you used to cheat Eleanor at cards."

"You're trying to make me out to be the biggest monster in the world."

"Eleanor, what is she talking about?" Joan retrieved the cards. "Fine, if you don't want to play, we won't play. Your hormones are on a roller coaster ride. You need to rest."

"I believed in Miranda! I saved you."

Joan said, "What are you talking about?"

"The pool—remember? Miranda!"

Joan squinted. "The pool? What pool? Miranda? Oh, I remember, yes, my imaginary friend. I haven't thought about her in such a long time."

"I saved you."

"I don't know what you're getting at. You're tired. Go to sleep."

—13—
The Ice Age

Charlotte was aware of someone hovering over her. A glinting-eyed shadow. A man. Without warning, he pressed a knife into her abdomen, and she thought— could one even call it thinking?—stop him. But she was unable to speak. She was unable to move. She thought: do not stop breathing. That is the last step. She sat up in bed, and there was no man, just the fuzzy darkness. Just the feeling that something was wrong. Something terrible. *I am in pain, yes, it is pain. The worst kind of pain.* When she tried to stand, her knees buckled. Grasping the bedpost, she called: "Ian? Eleanor? Joan?

"Eleanor? Ian? Joan? Joan? Joan?"

Someone switched on the light. Pink light flooded the room. Charlotte whispered, "Look at me."

Joan said, "Charlotte? Can you hear me?"

Yes, she thought, *but I cannot speak.*

Ian carried Charlotte to the car, while Eleanor followed.

Ian said, "Has she lost the baby? Are you sure? Perhaps it's something else. Is it possible? Women can bleed during pregnancy, I know that. We don't know anything yet."

Joan stayed behind—she had to do the hardest thing. She had read about the proper course of action in books, had heard girlfriends talk about it.

She picked up what Charlotte had lost, placed it in the plastic bag, and drove to the hospital.

"Charlotte? Can you hear me?" said the dark-haired doctor. Dr. Levine was very young. He reminded Charlotte of Dr. De Marsico.

She nodded.

"You can hear me. Good. How are you feeling?"

Charlotte gazed at him and laughed.

"The miscarriage was not your fault," he told her. "You're wrong to think it was—you misunderstand medicine. Do you think it's your fault?"

"Yes."

A nurse rubbed her arm with alcohol. The doctor said, "You'll feel a pinprick, and then you'll relax. It's only Valium." The doctor went on, "Yes, you might have taken better care of yourself; still, I'm sure our laboratory tests will confirm that it was a genetic abnormality. If you had eaten better and had not drunk wine, you still would have lost the baby."

Charlotte heard him, but her mouth would not open.

The doctor repeated, "There was a genetic abnormality. I'm sure there was. You assume you lost something wonderful, not something defective."

Joan sat at the foot of Charlotte's hospital bed. The Valium had coaxed her troubled sister to sleep. The hospital smelled like beef soup—salty and hot.

Eleanor said, "I'm going to get some tea. Do you want some?"

"Some tea would be nice," said Joan.

Ian said, "So that's it, I suppose. That's it." His mouth was tight. "I thought I would be a father. I spoke to the doctor. They'll do a—what is it? Yes, a D & C. In a few hours. Is it very warm in here? Bloody hell, do they have the heat on? Eleanor, I think I'll go with you. I need a bit of air." He glanced at Charlotte. "I really thought—"

Eleanor said, "We'll be back in a little while."

When they were gone, Joan stroked Charlotte's forehead. In the harsh light, her sister's hair had a greenish cast, as did her skin. Her eyes were closed and Joan could make out small swirling veins on the shiny lids; under the lids her eyeballs flicked back and forth—jittery dream eyes. Joan, too, had dreamed, years before, when she was pregnant—strange and sometimes joyous dreams about precious babies, about plump, boneless feet.

Charlotte stirred, licking her lips. "No baby," she murmured.

Joan had had dreams of her own. A hospital bed of her own. Before she had even met Frederick, before her babies, Jason and Diane. In Clara Maas Hospital in Florence, Joan's mind had swirled from thought to thought. She had known that she was sick, terribly sick, that she might die, and yet . . .

Her mother, was it her mother, said, "My poor Joan. My poor Joan. Sleep."

She dreamed of a boy, a blond boy, eyes clear and blue. She dreamed of Stewart, the boy she loved. They kissed on a Saturday afternoon. "Joannie. Joannie," he whispered. She felt a warm glow, the breeze at her back, crisp leaves at her feet.

People can sleep through a thunderstorm, but they awaken when they hear their names. Joan opened her eyes a degree. She was no longer kissing Stewart. Her sister was speaking: She was crying. Her sister never cried.

Charlotte was saying, "I let him, Joan. I let him have sex with me. You did, too. You told me it hurt. You let him use you—like a toaster, an iron. But I punished him. He took my body and then I told him I didn't love him. *I used him. . .* Do you hear me Joan? I punished him." And then: "Please don't hear me, You'll get better, and you'll forget. Do you think I'll forget?"

Now Joan told her sleeping sister, her greenish sister, "You see, you told me. I was awake. I remember."

The following day, Ian drove Charlotte home from the hospital. The silos and farmhouses quivered. She was still queasy from the D & C. "You'll be going back soon, I guess, to England."

Ian said, "I don't want to think about that now. I want you to know that you'll get over this."

"Will I?"

"The doctor told you about your hormones—they're out of balance. That's why you're crying, why you can't stop."

"Stop the car," she said.

"What?"

"Pull over."

He parked on the side of the dusty road, which was bordered by a fence. He said, "What are you doing?"

Charlotte ducked under the fence and moved toward a stretch of dry grass covered with dandelions.

Ian, too, crouched under the fence. "Do you need some air? Are you ill?"

"I'm remembering my grandfather's lawn," she told him, panting.

"His lawn?"

"Whiskey Demon never took care of his lawn, and my mother hated that. 'You've got to do something about these dandelions,' she told him. But Whiskey Demon couldn't give two shits. Still, my mother moaned about the state of his lawn. Nana had given up on the lawn. She was too busy trying to save his soul. One day my mother was ripping out dandelions and Whiskey Demon said, 'They'll just be back.' My mother said that you had to fight them. 'No,' my grandfather told her, 'you have to learn to love dandelions.' "

Charlotte stood in the living room, arms dangling empty at her side.

"I'm so sorry," Eleanor said softly, holding Charlotte in her skinny arms.

Joan stopped sweeping the kitchen floor and, resting the broom in a corner, said, "Charlotte, don't blame yourself. That would be a mistake." But she thought: *Isn't Charlotte to blame? Isn't she?*

"Joan cleaned your room for you," said Eleanor.

On the fluffy bed, lacy pillows were propped up invitingly. Sunlight fell on a small bowl of apples set on the bureau. Lavender from Eleanor's garden scented the room. There were no bloodstains.

"We'll let you two get settled again," said Joan, motioning Ian into the room. "Ian, maybe you'd like to stay down here with Charlotte. I don't know why you two didn't stay together in the first place."

Ian's face was expressionless.

"Maybe you'd like to stay down here with Charlotte," Joan repeated.

Ian said, "Oh, please don't go to any trouble. Not on my account."

When Joan and Eleanor left the room, Charlotte told Ian, "I can't stop crying."

"I'm sorry," he said.

"Sure you are."

"You will feel better. Soon."

She placed her palms on her breasts. "They're not swollen anymore. My stomach was hard, now it's soft again. Already." She took his hand, which was cold.

He offered her a small smile. "I thought I'd be a father." His teeth crowded in upon each other. Charlotte wondered whether it hurt, having such crooked teeth. "You need to rest," he went on. "I'll just be outside, supervising the crew. They feel terrible about what happened. You need to rest."

"I'm not tired."

"But you must rest."

"All I've done is rest."

He said, "What more is there to say?"

When he was gone, Brad bounded in with a bouquet of white aster and dandelions cradled in thick green leaves. "Tough luck, Charlotte," he said.

"Thank you," she said flatly.

"Ivy said not to give you weeds, but I think the dandelions are pretty. I suppose it's how you look at things."

In turn, everyone came to see her: Malcolm, Mr. Simmons, Natalie, Colin, Ivy, Sarah, and Glenn. They each stayed for a minute or two and said they were sorry, looking not at her but at the shadowed hollows of the room.

"Thanks," she told them. "For nothing. Or no—for something. Thank you."

Joan was always there to offer her something. "Do you want anything? Some toast? An English muffin? Some tea?"

"Thanks, but no."

"Are you sure?"

Charlotte said, "How many times do I have to answer you? Anyway, I'm sorry."

"For what?"

"For everything."

"The miscarriage wasn't your fault. You have to accept that." But it was her fault, wasn't it? In part? Charlotte had acted as if she wasn't even pregnant. At least Joan had had the nerve to end the situation, to take the bus into the city, to act. To decide. She stopped for a moment. She had always blamed Charlotte for forcing her into it—because if her sister had forced her into it, then none of it was her fault. She could still be a good Catholic, a penitent one. Perhaps she *had* decided, after all.

Frederick would want to know that Charlotte had lost the baby. But Joan had other motives. She admitted it. She was human. She had proved it with Micah. She wanted Frederick's—what? sympathy? love? attention? Gripping the receiver, she said, "I have something to tell you. Something terrible. Charlotte lost the baby." She began to cry, though she hadn't planned to.

"Should I talk to her, or is it too soon?"

Joan blew her nose. "She's resting now. Give it a few days." She wanted to tell him how she had picked up the remains, how she had thought about that day in Glassboro, when she had finally—when it was over. He had never really wanted to hear the unpleasant details. He never wanted to hear about Stewart. She wanted to tell him how awful she had felt driving to the hospital with—well, with whatever it was, a baby or not a baby; she wanted to describe the peculiar weight in her throat. She wanted to tell him how her brake lights had illuminated the darkness, in the hour when there is no hint of light in the east, and yet one looks. She wanted to tell him about the hour when there are no people, when the corn, weighted down with dew, does not grow. "Charlotte lost the baby," was all she could tell him. She waited for Frederick to say, I forgive you. Come back. She waited to care about what he said. "Hold on," he said, "Jason wants to talk."

Jason said, "Are you guys getting a divorce? The whole thing sucks."

"Jason, please, your language."

"Divorce is worse than cursing, Mom." Joan could hear Diane crying in the background, clamoring for the phone.

"Mommy," she said, voice quivering, "when are you coming home? I can play the 'March of the Gnomes' without looking at the music once. And I want to get a pocketbook." She took a deep breath. "Are you and Daddy getting a divorce?"

"Of course not, honey. We love you. I can't wait to hear you play. I'll be home very soon."

"Do you love Daddy?"

"Well, why wouldn't I? Of course, we both love you. We will always love you. You know that."

She hesitated. "Oh."

When Frederick got back on the phone, she demanded, "Why did you tell the children we were getting a divorce? How could you!"

"I didn't tell them anything. Jason—you know how he picks up on things."

"Don't tell the kids about Charlotte. Wait until I get home. They don't need to hear any more bad news."

"You're coming home?"

"I don't know. Eventually."

"I called Max Levin." Max Levin was the preeminent divorce lawyer in Hillside.

Joan couldn't think of what to say in response.

At noon, Malcolm gathered everyone under the apple trees, which cast a net of shadows on the grass. There was a sense of expectancy. "Everyone. Please, I have something to say." He moved his hand along the horizon. "Imagine that everything is covered with snow and ice. The last ice age has not yet retreated. There are no trees. Barely any animals. But a hunter is here—he shouldn't be here. He is too far north. He should be dead. But he is not. He wears a parka made of caribou skin; trousers, boots, and mittens. His boots have been soaked in animal oils to keep out the snow.

"In the distance, the hunter spots a caribou. He is starving—he is always starving. He needs the meat and marrow, the skins, the sinew and the gut. He stalks the animal, making deep footprints in the snow. It is difficult to move in the deep snow—the hunter's thighs burn. He waits for the best shot. He is always waiting. And then he seizes his moment. He hurls his spear through the silent, frozen air. The spear catches the caribou; there is a blunt sound. Blood stains the snow; the caribou falls in a heap. Legs searing, the hunter hauls the animal to the rock-shelter. It takes him some time; the caribou is heavy. He builds a fire and roasts the animal. He eats and he is warm."

"And what you're trying to tell us is—?" said Ian.

"What I'm trying to tell you is that the charcoal from the fire and the collagen from the caribou bone were dated at nineteen thousand years before the present time, plus or minus 370 years."

Jumping up, Mr. Simmons cried, "I knew I was right! I knew it!" But several deep wrinkles soon lined his forehead. "But it's so old that no one will believe it. The last ice age had not yet retreated—it didn't retreat until fifteen thousand years ago. It's impossible, they'll say. And it *seems* impossible, even to me. How could a man live through an ice age?"

Malcolm said, "But we have charcoal, and bone, and a

projectile point. In Pennsylvania, they only found a few charred rocks and some charcoal. How can they refute us? What we found—or what Eleanor, Aaron, and Charlotte found—are the oldest artifacts of man east of the Mississippi."

"They'll find a way to refute us," said Mr. Simmons.

"Well," said Charlotte, rubbing her eyes, "how could someone live through the ice age?"

"It is sort of unbelievable," said Eleanor. "What do you think, Joan?"

"What do I think? I don't know. I don't know anything. My mind is a muddle."

Everyone moved to the rock-shelter in a silent procession. To Eleanor, it was difficult to fathom that a hunter had lived here nineteen thousand years ago in a world she had always thought of as new—the New World. Yet her hunter had sat crouched in her rock-shelter, warmed by a fire, thousands of years before the pyramids had been built, before the rise of the Sumerian city-states, before the Babylonians, the Minoans, the Chang civilization in China. She thought of the book her father had bought her years ago, bursting with treasures of the ancient world—frescoes of noble Egyptian women in flat profile, eyes wide as hands, the golden mask of Tutankhamen, the leafy golden headdress of the oldest Sumerian queen. Her hunter had left no bangles, no towers, no statuettes of bare-breasted women clutching snakes. Just a projectile point, pieces of bone, an old extinguished fire. Malcolm said he was not part of a developed civilization. He was only a hunter, and that was something even more amazing. He had breathed her frozen air.

She decided she must tell Aaron. He should know— even if he was interested in Charlotte, even if he had not helped her when Rene ha. . . *Forget Rene*, she told her-

self. She, Charlotte, and Aaron had discovered the projectile point, the piece of caribou antler; they had uncovered
the ancient fire. She supposed he should know about
Charlotte.

She left the others behind and made her way around
the pond, past Aaron's cornfields and the old rusted
plow, until she finally rapped on his door. She was out of
breath, for it was a warm day. She opened the door; it did
not occur to her to wait—it was as if she had forgotten
that when one knocks on a door, one waits until someone
opens it.

He was sitting in his yellow kitchen, sipping a mug of
coffee. A stack of dishes rose from the sink.

"Eleanor?" he said, standing. "Come in."

She tried to still her breathing. "Malcolm has the
results," she said.

He placed his mug on the kitchen table and stared at
her, seeming afraid to speak.

"The bone and the charcoal have been dated at nineteen thousand years before the present time."

Slowly, he said, "Nineteen thousand years . . . ago?"

"I thought you should know. You and I found the artifacts. And Charlotte, too."

"Could anything be so old?"

"Malcolm says everything here was covered with ice
and snow then. The ice age and all. Still, the hunter was
here. Though it seems impossible."

He took off his baseball cap.

She said, "You don't have to worry about your hat.
Your hat is safe."

"My hat? Oh, yes, you threw it on the lawn. That's
nothing." He gazed out his kitchen window. Two small
plants sat perched on the narrow ledge.

"What are you looking at?" she asked.

"I always thought of this land as my great-grandfather's.

Aaron the Jew. But of course the land is older than he was."

"Of course it is."

"I know, I'm just saying. I wonder what he would make of it all. He used to own eighty acres, including the land that your house now stands on. But he sold it off. He wasn't much of a farmer." He pulled open a drawer and took out a pile of curling photographs. "Here," he said. "This is him." Eleanor peered at the photo. A bearded dark-haired man wearing a black hat and a crumpled bow tie sat stiffly on a small chair. A woman, his wife, presumably, stood behind him. Her hair was pulled back tightly. Her mouth was thin but wide. She wore a long black dress with a stiff lacy collar.

"Your great-grandmother?" she asked.

"Yes."

She stared at the photograph and could think of nothing to say, though her brain was electric with activity— she could not make sense of her own thoughts. "I should go. I have to take care of Charlotte." She handed him the photo. "I have to tell you something, about Charlotte."

He sat down at the kitchen table. "Is she okay? I was planning on seeing her this afternoon."

"It's bad news. Charlotte lost the baby."

His lips parted. "Should I still go see her?"

"Only you know that."

"Eleanor, you've misunderstood," he said, moving near. The buttons on his shirt gleamed. She noticed a small thin line next to his left eyebrow. Worries. He, too, had worries.

She stood rigidly still. "I thought you'd like to know. Everything is going wrong."

He hesitated for a moment. "I'd like to ask you something. I'm not much good at asking things. I should talk more. That's my mistake. Have you seen Rene?"

"Of course not. I think you know why I haven't seen him. What a thing to ask—!"

"I had to find out—"

"I've got to go," she said, turning. She had a strange ache in her head.

"Eleanor?"

She stopped hearing his voice as she ran past the rusted plow. When she came upon Malcolm he tried to stop her, but she shook her head and kept going. "Are you okay?" he called after her. Finally, she stomped up the steps, hurried through the living room, and rapped on Charlotte's door.

Charlotte had deep circles under her eyes. The tip of her nose was red. Still, Eleanor said, "I know you're upset—you've been through a lot. I'm sorry to ask you this, but I have to know what he talked to you about."

"Who?"

"Aaron."

"Oh, Eleanor. I promised him I wouldn't tell you."

"Please."

"He wanted to talk about you."

"Oh, really? He was holding your hand."

"Aaron—he wanted to know if you're still in love with Rene."

"But he saw Rene trying to . . . well, you know!"

"But what did he see? Eleanor, I have broken so many promises, so many confidences, fractured so many loyalties, that I'd rather not go on. Can you understand that? Do you understand?"

Joan stopped cooking. She was on strike. So even though it was five o'clock, when normally she would be transfixed in a cloud of steam, she sat idly near the rock-shelter. She watched a thin man with an expensive haircut motion to a fat man, who balanced a video camera on his shoulder.

The cameraman said, "Go."

"Hello, Susan. Yes, I can hear you. I'm here live in the Catskills, the old Borscht Belt, and what archaeologists have found is the oldest evidence of man east of the Mississippi. Experts date caribou bones and charcoal found in this cave to nineteen thousand years before the present time. Susan, that's old! The residue of an ancient fire and an arrow were also found. No caribou in these parts, Susan. Not anymore. And yes, so many of the old comics are gone. Danny Kaye, Georgie Jessel, the list goes on . . . That's a good question, Susan. Archaeologists cannot reconcile that fact. The last ice age retreated fifteen thousand years ago from this part of New York State. How could man survive an ice age? You've got me. Yes, right again, Susan, perhaps our hunter was a woman. But that would be unusual. Experts tell us that women didn't hunt . . . Maybe I will, Susan. Maybe I'll take in a show at the Concord. Good suggestion. This is Alan Pierce, Eyewitness News, reporting live from Tylerville, New York."

The reporter strolled over to Joan. "Hi, I'm Alan Pierce, Eyewitness News. Got any coffee on the burner?"

"I do not. Do I look like the cook?"

He shrugged and walked off.

Later, Malcolm said, "Joan, I'm going to order some pizzas. You seem a bit distracted. It's none of my business why. It was kind of you to cook for us for as long as you did. My question is merely this: how many pizzas should I order?"

"If you people can figure out how old those ancient artifacts are, I think you can figure out how many pizzas to order."

"I'm sorry."

She sighed. "No, I'm sorry. You're a good egg, Malcolm. It's just, Charlotte lost her baby. And I'm losing—well, I don't know what I'm losing. Why did I sleep with Micah?"

"Who?"

"When I was small, if I got a bad bounce playing kickball, I shouted, 'Do over.' I wish I could do that now."

"Who is Micah? Never mind. You're a fine woman, Joan."

"I didn't even like Micah. He wasn't the greatest sexual experience in my life. He was a real long-ball hitter. When I kissed Frederick for the very first time, at Columbia, when it was autumn, when we were young, when his face was smooth, that was something."

"I'll just go order the pizzas."

And then she saw someone she didn't think she'd ever see again. She didn't want to see this person, and when he sat down beside her, she smacked the top of his hairless head.

"One question, Micah," she said. "Why?"

"Why what?"

"Why did you tell Frederick!"

"I didn't tell Frederick."

"Your wife is like the French lady?"

"That's not telling him. You told him."

"I didn't tell him!"

"It's the only logical solution. You don't have to tell someone something, to tell them."

Joan ripped fistfuls of grass from the lawn.

He said, "You're ruining the environment."

"You've ruined my life."

"Have I? You don't believe that. You had your fun with me, didn't you?" He buttoned the blazer. "Guess how old this blazer is. Just take a guess."

"I don't know and I don't care. Maybe you bought it

SISTERS *and* STRANGERS — 323

yesterday, or maybe it was purchased during the last ice age. Carbon-dating your clothes is not my interest."

"Junior year in college. Still fits. I did you a favor," he told her.

Joan threw grass in his face.

"I'm not allergic," he told her. "Anyway, I did you a favor. I freed you."

"Freed me from what?"

"That I don't quite know. The other day, one of the psychics—actually, it was Miriam, our best—she told me I would be forgiven for my sins."

"You're making that up."

He went to hug her, but she swatted him away. He said, "You're a different person now."

"That's for sure. Soon I'll be single. Excommunicated from the Church. Alone. Though maybe I want to be alone."

"Do you or don't you? I mean, that's the question, right? I gotta go," he said, glancing up at the sky. "The beautiful, beautiful Catskills. Just think, a caveman and Eddie Fisher both admired this sky. Anyway, I'm left with nothing. As usual, I didn't get the girl. Still, I played my part."

Charlotte climbed the winding stairs to Ian's room. She felt as though she was doing something she should not be doing; she had been imprisoned in bed for so long, and now she was free to prowl about the house.

"Oh, Charlotte," he said, glancing up from a script. "Good to see you. The BBC is very pleased by the way. Very pleased indeed." He quickly made the bed. The room smelled faintly of turpentine. It had been Rene's workroom.

"Turpentine," she said absently, "erases paint. Removes what was painted by mistake."

Ian said, "Sorry about the mess. The BBC is excited about this documentary. I'm just about through shooting. The archaeologists did the digging, we filmed, and now we know how old everything is."

"How wonderful."

"You look better, incidentally. Much better. Your face is very beautiful, but you must know that."

She sat beside him. "I was hoping. I had been hoping."

"I thought you said the artifacts wouldn't be so old."

"Not about that. About us. I was hoping a lot of things, but I'm a fool."

"Not at all."

She grabbed his script. *"The Waiting Years,"* she said, flipping through the pages. "What an interesting script. Set in Japan. You're going to Japan?"

"I'm just reading the script. Nothing is set."

"Is anything ever set?"

"Some things are."

"But not for long," she said, hurling the script across the room. "You don't listen," she told him.

He sat silently.

"You were never going to marry me."

"I thought you'd have the baby, and then we'd see. I wanted you to come with me to London. To move in with me. With the baby. Definitely with the baby."

"And now?"

"That's up to you."

"Is it?"

"I wanted to be a father," he said. "Something is"—he frowned—"missing." He stared at his shiny loafers for a long time. "My brothers don't have jobs, but they have children. Their kids play together. They live in the same village. It's dark and grimy there; the mines have been closed for years. The children play soccer in the empty streets and spill their tea and giggle, squirming at sticky tables. I don't know what I'm trying to say. I wanted a child. What we had in Bath was special. But I have had three wives, and three divorces."

"So you're saying—"

He took her hand. "Let's suppose you had not gotten pregnant, would I be here? Would you care?"

"I wanted that baby, too."

"Did you? Did you really?" His eyes narrowed. "You're a selfish woman, Charlotte. You're a selfish liar. You used me—you wanted to get pregnant, didn't you? You lied about being on the pill, and a relationship that is built upon a lie—"

She grabbed a pillow and pressed it against his face. Flailing, he kicked his legs and arms, yet she knew he was not really dying. Before he had been a director, he had been an actor.

There was no more script left. She let go, rolling beside him.

"Charlotte, my God! You are the most destructive woman I have ever met. You need help! You need counseling!"

She stared at the ceiling.

"I'll be going back to London soon. Very soon."

"Whatever," she said.

Joan was aware of an unearthly noise, a high-pitched wail that might be human—or might come from a sloe-eyed cat, a coyote. She wondered what sound bears make when they're terrified. Joan felt the wails in her stomach, between her eyes. She pressed her face to the window, where she saw nothing unusual, just moonlight on trees. She nudged Eleanor, sleeping in the bed beside her. "What is that terrible noise?" She listened harder. "Could it be Charlotte?"

Joan went into Charlotte's room and flicked on the light. She felt a weight beneath her ribs. Her sister's head was arched back; her neck was long and white; her mouth was a wide slash. Joan said, "Stop screaming!"

When Ian came in and sat beside Charlotte, her wails swelled louder. "I think we should call a doctor," he said.

Joan touched Charlotte's forehead. "She doesn't have a fever . . . Stop screaming! You're just—you're just pretending. You're acting! Just stop!"

Eleanor said, "We should call the doctor—"

"She doesn't need a doctor. She just needs to go on with her life. She's not the only woman on earth to have a miscarriage. Charlotte, get ahold of yourself!" Joan pressed her hand on Charlotte's mouth; it was Joan who cried out. She stared at her palm—Charlotte's teeth had sliced the skin.

Eleanor said, "I'm going to call the doctor."

Joan stared at her right hand, the uninjured hand, the hand without the large diamond anniversary ring. Then she slapped Charlotte hard across the face. She slapped her sister so she would stop screaming, so she would snap out of it, but really, that wasn't why. She slapped her sister because she had slept with Stewart, the boy whom she had loved—whom she still loved, if love can be defined as a habit of regret, that ghost of a boy. The boy she had never forgotten. If only Joan had slapped her sister that day in Glassboro when Stewart strolled out of her bedroom, if only she had demanded what she deserved: attention, respect, instead of closing down, of cramping in upon herself.

Ian said, "I'm leaving. Day after tomorrow."

Joan sighed.

"It's for the best," he said.

———

The sun was high. Joan and Charlotte sat in the rowboat in the middle of the pond. It was not a particularly warm or cool day. The air seemed to make no impression one way or the other. Though Charlotte's screams had vanished, she was left with a singular stiffness. She might have appeared serene had Joan not known her so well. There were the knitted brows, the tight mouth, the hands folded stiffly.

Joan let the paddles hang in the water. For a long while, the sisters said nothing. Joan wanted to say something, but what? I should never have let you get away with it. *I* should have screamed. I should have screamed until you told me you were sorry. She sat silently, aware of birds high in the trees. "I hear an awful ringing in my ears," said Joan, "from last night. An echo."

"Oh yeah?" Charlotte's voice was hoarse and soft.

"Last night—I didn't know what to make of it. You've never lost control. I always thought you knew what you were doing."

Charlotte rubbed her throat. "I am not a perfect person."

"You merely look perfect. You didn't look perfect to the doctor."

"He said I was fine, basically fine."

"That's not what he said. He said you had postpartum depression. I had it too, you know, after—well, after we did what we did."

"But how can one have postpartum depression without a baby? I feel so empty. I feel like I might disappear."

"You—disappear? The great actress? Anyway, I think you should see somebody."

"I already saw the doctor."

"I mean a counselor, a psychiatrist. We should do what's best for you."

"There's nothing wrong with me that anyone can cure.

Last night, I simply realized that something dark was stuck to me, worse than original sin because it can't be washed away."

"You're delirious."

"Can I ask you something?" Charlotte paused. "Have you always hated me? I could understand it, your hating me. When we were very young, I don't think you did. Not when we played with our Barbies, when I helped you with your math homework."

Joan sighed.

"You hated me."

"I wanted to." And then, with sudden courage: "I did." She waited. "Do you think lightning will strike me? For hating my sister?"

"I slept with Stewart," Charlotte said.

She caught her breath. "You've said it. Imagine. The truth—I've waited a long time for it." Joan closed her eyes. "I can't picture Stewart in my mind at the moment. Which is odd, because I've never really stopped seeing him. He's fading somehow."

Charlotte was saying, "Cream puff. What bullshit. I rise to the top. I sink to the bottom." She stood in the small aluminum rowboat—she did not list.

Joan said, "Sit down. You're going to fall." But Charlotte, hands in the air, her pink prairie skirt fluttering, paid Joan no mind.

Suddenly, but with great drama, she cast her body into the water.

Joan threw out her arm; Charlotte's splash hit her in the chest.

A stone striking the water—Joan's first thought. A stone ripping the water. She stood, waving her arms about. She meant to scream but could not—her voice was stuck.

Joan, too, jumped. The cold water enveloped her.

Down and down and down. She willed herself to open her eyes in the brackish water. Flecks of dead leaves clung to her mouth. Vines clung to her feet. Her sneakers were weights. She saw nothing—just weeds ambling by. When her chest burned, she clawed to the surface, gulping a long breath as the sun warmed her aching ears. She called, "Eleanor!" No one heard her; no one ever heard her.

She descended again, swinging off to the right—nothing, just gritty earth swirling—then off to the left, every which way, until again she kicked toward the surface, mouth panting at the sun. Once again she dived, beating her feet against the water, maneuvering her arms first this way, then that. More leaves, a boot, someone's boot, and then she saw something otherworldly, a strange floating creature with a billowy pink shell. A corn-colored tuft on its head. It was not human, and yet it was human.

It was her sister—she had known it and not known it.

As if suddenly changing her mind, rethinking her stillness, this will for the water, Charlotte thrashed her arms, her legs; her head shook. She clawed desperately, catching a leaf, a piece of twine. Then, seeing Joan, a peculiar smile appeared, a smile of benign discovery—perhaps she never meant to die; she meant merely to make things as bad as they could be. Joan tugged at Charlotte's pink skirt but Charlotte was frantic—an arm swung out right, then left. Drawing back, Joan thrust out her palms out, then pointed upward, casting her eyes toward the surface. At last cooperating, Charlotte allowed Joan to cling to her waist, and the two at last floated toward the sun.

Charlotte tried to breathe but she didn't know where her mouth was. She put her head back and yes, there was something, the arms of the sun, long warm arms. She could feel more arms, solid arms, and she thought of the Pietà; they had seen the statue at the World's Fair, in Queens, in 1964; they had come so far—imagine, she told Joan, it's 1964! Age of the sun, of gleaming Chevrolets.

Charlotte forgot the sun—there's no sun; her hands itched and burned as she slid across the water and was pulled into something high off the ground. An altar? Hands pushed her onto her belly and pressed hard on her back. Too hard. *My ribs are gone,* she thought. *My ribs are gone. My lungs, yes, here they are, sacks of ice.* With all her might, Charlotte reached for a breath, a small breath—*my breath is my life,* she thought, *my life is my breath.* She clasped Joan's hand—she felt the ring, a diamond for Jason, a diamond for Diane; she felt Joan's long thin fingers; her own were dying and she thought: *Joan. My sister, Joan. I am sorry. Tough luck, I am sorry, and what does it matter. Nothing matters— you are my sister, always, nothing can tear the tie.* Then Charlotte felt a cold burst in her chest, like an explosion, and she thought: *this is the last moment. The last.* She gasped and spit and churned and retched and moaned. Water and mucus oozed from her mouth, her ears. Something in her brain buzzed and she didn't care, anyway it went, she didn't care. Is this not what she deserved? What she wanted? She was working hard for this, wasn't she?

There was something in her throat, a whirl, the wind. Someone was kissing her—well, she'll let them, why not. She was using them, stealing their breath. Turn the lock, find the breath; it's there—somewhere. The pressing on her lips stopped, and she realized that she was breathing, in and out, in and out, and it felt like a new process, one she had known and forgotten.

Charlotte stared into the wet gleaming face of her sister. Her clothes were crepy, like the clothes of the dead.

Aaron crouched beside them in the boat. The water from his hair fell into her eyes.

Aaron said, "I saw you from the other side of the pond. I saw you."

At shore, everyone crowded around Charlotte, who lay on a smooth patch of grass. Joan said, "Aaron saved her," but Charlotte said, "No, Joan saved me. My sister Joan saved me."

Eleanor knelt beside Charlotte, who lay shivering on the grass.

She felt something loosen inside her. Her sister had nearly . . . it did no good to consider it. And Joan—what might have happened to Joan?

"Arisen from the dead," Charlotte finally said, sitting up slowly.

Ian said, "Did you fall? Did you slip? What happened?" Charlotte shrugged. She allowed Eleanor and Natalie to guide her toward the house.

Ian said, "Let me carry you."

Charlotte said, "No. I can walk. Let me walk."

Joan stood at the shoreline, arms hugging her body. "I'm fine," she kept saying. Aaron, soaking wet, helped her to the house.

In the bedroom, Eleanor pulled off Charlotte's heavy clothes. She rubbed Charlotte dry—vigorously scrubbing her hands and feet—and all the while Charlotte kept saying, "Joan saved me." Eleanor slipped a flannel nightgown over Charlotte's head and helped her into bed, placing two flowery comforters over her.

"Joan saved me," said Charlotte.

Eleanor said, "Did you slip?"

"I don't know. No."

"Then why?"

Charlotte said, "Because I'm an asshole."

"No," said Eleanor. And it took all her courage,

because Eleanor could not say the things that needed to be said: they were the hardest things to say. "I love you."

"Why?"

"Because you're my sister."

"You have to love me."

"Of course there's more—you're—"

"A good person? That couldn't be it."

"We grew up together. We lived in the same tiny house."

Joan, eyes wide and bright, sat on a kitchen chair.

"Let's get those clothes off," Eleanor said.

"I'm fine. Really. Fine."

Eleanor guided Joan to the other bedroom, toweled her off, and put her to bed.

"Should I call Frederick?" Eleanor asked.

"What does he care?" Joan said.

"He should know."

"No, don't tell him. Don't."

"Are you sure?"

"I'm fine."

"I'm going to call him."

Joan grabbed Eleanor's arm. "Out there, I thought, if Charlotte dies . . . I used to want her to, when I found out about Stewart. I hoped she'd be run over by a bus, the 68 to Times Square. But then . . ."

Eleanor saw to Aaron, who stood dripping in the hallway. Taking charge, she said, "Go upstairs. Take some of Ian's clothes. I don't think he's finished packing. Hold on." She handed him two rosy towels. "Here."

"Will Ian mind?"

"Of course not," said Ian, stepping into the hallway. "I hope I didn't cause all of this. We've all been so careless."

"The room upstairs, you'll see which one," Eleanor said.

Aaron nodded.

Eleanor said, "By the way, thank you. I meant to say that. Thank you."

Charlotte slammed the mattress with her fist. She had lost three things she could never replace: the baby, Ian, and herself. Though perhaps it wasn't so bad to lose herself, to feel so empty. It had scared her, to feel so hollow, to feel as deep and black as the pond. The other night she felt as though she did not exist, that she was not alive and not dead; she felt panic worse than death. But was it so bad, truly, to feel obliterated, for wasn't there hope in that very obliteration, in becoming someone better? She went to the window and stood in a bright wedge of sun. She stood there until the wedge narrowed half an inch. She scanned the property and her eyes locked onto the rock-shelter, which gleamed white.

She was still standing there when Ian entered the room. "Charlotte," he said, "did you get any rest?"

"Don't meet anyone else like me."

"I wouldn't mind."

"Sure. You love women who try to suffocate you."

"I must go back to London. I may be back, most likely. You seem better." He rubbed her hands. "You've warmed a bit."

"I'm going back to LA in a few days," she told him.

"I'm sorry."

"We're all sorry."

Charlotte stood at the window in a smaller wedge of light and at last Ian appeared, holding two suitcases, which he set on the dusty driveway. His hair looked blue under the sun. Brad and Colin and Ivy were leaving, too. The four glanced back at the house. Ian gently kicked a suitcase, though it never fell. He waved to her, offered her a timid smile. Everything was small from this distance, not as big as it should have been, as real as it should have been. There was something strange about his mouth. Again he waved. Charlotte did not wave back. But as he turned and stiffly made his way to the car— when he could no longer see her—she opened her hand. The tips of her fingers ached.

Staring at her flower garden, Eleanor felt for a moment like a general surveying the battle scene when the battle is over. The garden was a tumble of debris; everything seemed to have blown in: candy wrappers, bits of cut grass, the long dead stems of maverick flowers. There were dead buds to snip, weeds to pull. She continued on down the lawn and stared for a moment at the mailbox; she grabbed several letters, and there it was. She slipped her little finger under a narrow gap on the underside of the envelope. She felt something weighty in her stomach, something airy in her legs.

The letter was typed on heavy white paper; there was a round embossed seal in the upper right-hand corner. The State of New York: Albany. She was divorced. Her name had been legally changed; she had requested that. She thought: *I am Eleanor Powers again*. She had taken a long journey back to her original name. When she returned to the house, she waved the letter.

Joan, who was manicuring Charlotte's nails, said, "What's that?"

"It's final."

Charlotte said, "The divorce? Don't be upset. Please don't be."

"I am and I'm not," said Eleanor.

"Well, he was a terrible person," said Joan, hugging her. "You'll forget, won't she, Charlotte."

"She shouldn't forget. Rene was an asshole. In fact, on Thanksgiving, he—"

"What?" said Eleanor quickly. "What did he do on Thanksgiving?"

"Oh, nothing. He insulted me. He said I wasn't that pretty. He said I wasn't as pretty as you."

Joan stroked red polish on Charlotte's thumbnail. "She's not perfect, you see. She's really not. She has many faults. Eleanor, you're going to be okay, aren't you? Because I could stay. Frederick doesn't want me. But my children do. At least I hope they do." She looked up. "I've run away from my children, too, not just from Frederick. Anyway, I'm leaving on Tuesday. Charlotte figured she'd leave then, too. Unless you need me here. We sort of forgot about you."

"I'm okay." She pointed to her eyes. "I've got an appointment today with the optometrist."

—14—
Culacino

Eleanor offered to make her sisters dinner on the eve of their departure. "Let me help you out," Joan said, washing her hands at the sink.

"I can do it," Eleanor said. "I'm not helpless. I'm really not. Don't treat me like a child."

"Okay, if you say so. But if you need any help—"

She was starving. She decided to make fettucini Alfredo; it was possible, she told herself; she could read directions, even if they came from the cookbook Rene had given her. She chopped the onions, stirred the sauce, a butter, flour, and heavy cream roux; she tossed in the Parmesan cheese, the parsley. She set the table with her best dishes—or the best dishes that she had in the country: beige stoneware covered with tiny pastel roses and daisies.

"This is good," Joan said, twirling the creamy pasta around her fork.

"You know," Charlotte said, "you're right. Not bad, Eleanor."

"Last night," Eleanor told her sisters, "I had the strangest dream. I don't usually remember my dreams. Anyway, the three of us were back at Our Lady of Perpetual Mercy Grammar School. We were wearing our plaid uniforms, green knee socks, and saddle shoes. In the school yard, all the girls were playing baseball with a hardball and a huge plastic bat, though the nuns never allowed us to play baseball. Not the girls. The pitcher was a big girl with red hair and buckteeth. She hurled the ball past me twice. But finally my bat struck the ball. It flew over the school, I hit it so hard. And both of you told me, 'It's been a long time since we had a victory.'"

"Which means—?" said Charlotte.

"That things have to look up. I mean, they do, don't they?"

In the morning, Malcolm gave them special permission to go into the rock-shelter, to sit where the hunter sat. The sisters crouched down and slowly crawled toward the back, where it was cool and dim, like a cathedral.

Eleanor sneezed. "There's something in here I'm allergic to, mold or something."

"I wonder what kind of guy he was," said Charlotte, crouched between her sisters. "You know, the caveman."

"I'm sure he would have had a thing for you," Joan said. "Best-looking cavewoman east of the Mississippi."

"Are you suggesting that I'm looking old?"

"Oh God, Charlotte. You can dish it out, but you can't take it."

Eleanor said, "Are you still going to lie on your résumé about your age?"

"Of course I am," said Charlotte. "I'll be forty next week, but remember, I'm thirty-two. I'm going back there, to LA. I'm going to—oh Christ, I don't know what I'm going to do. Anyway, what's today's secret?"

Joan said, "That we don't have any."

"But that's impossible," said Charlotte. "That's not natural."

"You're right," said Eleanor, sneezing. "We've got to keep something to ourselves. Something—I don't know."

Even here in this shelter, pressed against her sisters, she still could not reveal what Rene had told her; she could not repeat his words, hard and mean, like rocks. Not yet, and maybe never. "But we shouldn't be strangers. I mean, that's the thing. Don't feel you have to leave. You can stay as long as you want."

"Well, it's not exactly comfortable in here," said Joan.

"You know what she means," said Charlotte.

They finally crawled out of the shelter, showered, made up their faces.

"Why do we waste our time covering up our flaws?" Joan complained. "Still, I'm not drawing those lines around my eyes anymore. Forget it."

"We do it because we're idiots," said Charlotte. "Because we still aren't brave enough."

Finally they were ready. Joan drew an invisible circle on the grass with her sneaker. "It's time," she said. "I'm dropping Charlotte off at the airport. And then I'll drive home. And see what happens. I still don't know what I should do. I'm hoping it will come to me when I get there."

Charlotte was dressed beautifully: she wore a pink cotton shift and sandals. Her skin was golden, which seemed miraculous to Eleanor since Charlotte had spent so much time indoors. Joan wore jeans and a T-shirt. She must have sensed Eleanor's gaze, because she said, "I know. I look awful."

"No, you look great. I'm staring because—you look so different than when you first arrived. That's all."

"I wish I could stay. You might still need me. But I've got to get back." Joan kissed Eleanor good-bye. "Wish me luck," she said.

"Eleanor, thank you for everything," Charlotte said with tears she did not wipe away. "Thanks."

Joan said, "We used to live together. All of us,

together." She said it happily, though it seemed to Eleanor a sad thing.

"I wish you didn't have to go," said Eleanor, coiling her arms around her sisters, and yet, really, it was time; she had to figure out her own life. Charlotte left a moist mark on Eleanor's shoulder. Eleanor thought again of the Italian word, *culacino*—the mark left on a table by a wet glass. There was no comparable word in English, as there was no word to describe what her sisters were leaving behind.

Charlotte trudged up her front walkway, dragging her luggage. She always brought too much luggage; in this case, pajamas would have sufficed. She set her bags on the walkway and rubbed the indentations on her palms. The Culver City air was hot and sulfury, like when you first light a match. Little Oliver Lowell from next door was still following himself around and around on his red tricycle. Mr. Lowell was still making huge splashes in their pool. "Hey kids, watch this!"

She had brushed her teeth on the plane, but her mouth was sticky, and the first thing she did, after dropping her luggage in the living room, was brush them again. She had not seen herself in her own bathroom mirror in a long while. It was the familiar face, in the familiar light, and yet there was something different around the eyes— something steadier and sadder.

She stepped into the kitchen. Her toaster was cleared of crumbs; the porcelain sink shone. She did not remember leaving the house so spotless. She sat down on the living room floor, which smelled of lemons. She stared at her nails, manicured by Joan. She knew they would soon chip—still they were a gift. She sat there for a long time, thinking of Tylerville, of Eleanor and Joan. She rubbed her palms, still indented from her luggage, and thought of Joan's huge anniversary ring, of swirling in the depths of Eleanor's pond. A banging on the door roused her. For a moment, she hoped it might be Joan: I came to see you! As promised!

But it was Seldon. "What are you doing *home?* My God, Charlotte! What's going on? You're supposed to be in *bed!*"

"Come on in," she said.

"I saw the lights on and I hoped you weren't being *robbed.*"

"I lost the baby."

Seldon's eyes widened. "I'm so *sorry.* Here, sit down. Was it very painful?"

"It hurt like hell. But what's done is done and all that. Still, I don't want to forget. To forget is a mistake. Anyway, I must concentrate on the mundane, on the details. I've got to get some more furniture. I've got some money coming from *Pride.*"

"It's on TV next week. I saw an ad in the paper. Sorry again, about the baby." Seldon cleared his throat. "How's Ian?"

"He's gone. Back to London."

"Oh."

"It's not his fault. Though he is an asshole." Charlotte scanned the living room. "Did you clean the place?"

"It's just you're such a *slob,*" he said. "I hope it was okay."

She leaned over and kissed him. "Thank you, Seldon."

He rubbed his cheek. "If only I—"

"Liked women," she said.

He shrugged. "I like you. But, Anthony—I love him, though he's such a pain. Still, I love you, too—differently."

Charlotte smiled. "I love you, too. Differently."

"The old friend thing," he said. His eyes narrowed. "You haven't yelled at me yet. Are you okay?"

"I'm just warming up."

"How did things go with Joan?"

"Okay, in the end. The old sister thing. It's an ancient phenomenon, goes back forever."

Joan drove past the cool Doric columns of the Hillside Art Museum, past the golf club, past the spacious Georgian homes covered with ivy, past the clock tower in the center of town, past the men with graying temples, the women in the flowery dresses. She meant to make a left on McKenzie Street, where Frederick and her children lived—where she still lived, she supposed—but she kept driving. She gripped the wheel tightly. She had dropped off Charlotte earlier at Newark Airport. They had peered at the departure screen: Newark to Los Angeles, Flight 187, 3:35 P.M.

"Time for coffee?" Charlotte had asked, clutching her ticket.

Joan glanced at her watch. "We've got ten minutes."

"No coffee, then."

Joan shook her head. She wanted to say, I forgive you, or at the least, I don't think I can hate you anymore. A few minutes later, Charlotte's pocketbook slipped by on a conveyor belt. Her sister walked through the metal detector. The woman from security said, "Go ahead, now. Don't just stand there."

"Come see me soon," Charlotte said. "Promise me."

Joan wiped her eyes. "Save me some of that sun."

Joan found herself driving to Florence. It wasn't far, a memory of turns. Her parents' house was just up ahead, the house with the red trim. She remembered the day she had come home from the hospital, all those years ago.

When her fever finally returned to normal, six days after she entered the hospital, she was discharged. She sat, dressed in baggy jeans and a T-shirt, on her hospital bed, waiting for her father to pick her up. She half wanted to be rolled out on a wheelchair, but the nurses hadn't offered, and she didn't really want to be conspicuous, so she sat waiting on the clean white sheets.

Her father had said, "Poor Joannie. You poor kid."

"I'm okay now, Dad." She had a strange taste in her mouth, like tin.

"Your mother sure has missed you. Me, too. You're my favorite little girl."

"You say that to all your girls."

"Do I?" he said, scratching his head.

"So Mom wanted me to live. How about that. Such a plain girl like me."

"Of course she did. No one in the world loves you like your mother. Nobody wants the ultimate for you like that lady does."

"Dad, if I told you something . . ."

He stared at the shiny hospital floor. "We love you no matter what. That's the upshot. That's the tall and short of it."

"There are things I'd never tell Mom."

"Joannie," he said, "there are things she'd never hear."

Now her mother was complaining, "I just called Eleanor! Charlotte is gone! Why doesn't anyone tell me anything?"

Diane ran into the hallway. Joan kissed the top of her head, which smelled vaguely like bread. "Mommy, I can play 'March of the Gnomes,'" she said, retiring to the living room to play it, a slow recitation of notes very close to each other.

Jason appeared, peeling a banana. "Dad's home, alone. He wanted to be alone."

Catherine said, "Charlotte lost her baby! Can't I be trusted to know what's going on? *Domo komarimashita!* That means, I am in a fix! My own daughter, and no one tells me! My cream puff! Why would you keep something like losing a baby from me?" She fell back onto Ed's recliner.

"I'm sorry, Mom," Joan said. "We meant to tell you, but we thought you'd be so upset. Of course we would have told you eventually."

"You don't give me enough credit. You never did."

Ed arrived, lugging a bag of groceries. "Oh, Joannie," he said. "Poor Charlotte. You're mother's—we're both—"

"Charlotte is going to be okay," Joan said.

"How do you know?" Catherine said. "How can anyone but Jesus know?" She then led Joan to her old bedroom, where a tiny mahogany rocker rested in the corner. Though it was very small, it seemed very empty. "Your father made it."

Ed said, "It was no trouble to make it. Charlotte will have another baby, though her biorhythmic clock is clicking pretty hard. These things happen."

Joan said, "How did you find out about Charlotte anyway?"

"Jason told us," said Catherine. "At least my grandson feels I'm worthy of information."

Joan didn't ask how Jason had found out.

"I'm going to go see Frederick now," said Joan.

"She's headed toward Divorce City," said Jason, as she slipped out the front door.

Her mother shouted, "Divorce!"

Joan was drawn to the light, to the curve of pond she could just make out. Hillside Community Park—she found herself there. She found him sitting on a lawn chair, surrounded by a trail of papers, which had come undone. Some had fallen into the nearby stream, others clung desperately to tree trunks.

She walked over and tapped him on the shoulder.

She expected him to say, Joan. My loving wife, Joan. But he stared, expressionless. "I was just going over some reports," Frederick said.

"They've flown the coop, your reports."

"I was holding them, then I let them go."

"You've got that right. You were holding me, and then you let me go."

"I don't know what you're saying."

"You're such a stupid man."

He kept reading his reports.

"Do you hear me? You're a stupid man. I don't know why I married you. I really don't."

He was silent for a time, and then he said, "Let me tell you why you married me. You were scared. You'd just had an abortion and you were scared."

"I was not scared."

"You didn't want to fall in love again. Stewart—you didn't want that to happen again."

"I did love you."

"Did you? You were content. And that was fine. I thought that was fine. But after a while, I couldn't—I just couldn't. I needed to make love to a woman who loved me."

Joan's heart pounded. "Did you find one? A woman who loved you? Is that what this has been all about?"

He sighed. "Would you love me then? You probably would. When Stewart didn't love you anymore, you couldn't get him out of your mind. But I didn't look for another woman. Like a stupid man, I kept waiting for you. I thought, one of these days, the tide will turn. And it did, but not the way I thought it would. You slept with

Micah." He walked over to some bushes near the pond. She followed.

She told him, "You're so distant, even now—you lack passion. Why can't you ever yell? Why couldn't you ever confront me? Don't you ever get angry?"

"Of course I do! That's—that's why I'm leaving you!" He was no longer pale; his veins were purple ropes at his temples. "Does it help when I scream! Do you only listen to screaming! Can you only love someone when they're cruel? Like him? Just admit it—you loved him, you never forgot him."

"I *did* forget him."

He shook his head.

"I wanted to."

"Who the hell are you remembering anyway? Damnit, he's a ghost!" He stomped his foot. "I'm standing right here! I'm your husband!"

"You were always working," she said. "You were never here."

"I'm here now!" He kissed her hard on the mouth.

"But soon you'll check your watch," she said. "You'll say, Got to be up at five."

"I don't have to get up." He sat on the ground. "I've taken a three-month leave—that's why I'm working here, trying to put things in order. If I just have some time. If I can just relax . . ." He sighed. "I should confess something—I never talked to the divorce lawyer."

She was angry. "You lied to me!"

He shrugged. "As did you."

They were quiet for a long while. Finally, she said, "Frederick?"

"Yes?"

She took him by the hand and they walked to the edge of the pond, where a narrow stream flows for a few feet before sliding through a tunnel. She had never before walked through the tunnel. Jason had wanted to, years ago. Jason—he was brave. Stared trouble down. She wasn't sure what was on the other side, how long the tunnel would be. She wasn't sure if she could ever feel the passion for Frederick that she had felt for Stewart, or for his ghost, but she understood that she, too, was culpable for the near death of her marriage. "Let's go through," she said.

"What?"

"Let's go through the tunnel."

"But how long will it take us?" he asked. And then he said, "Yes, let's go."

"Jason wanted to go through once," she said.

They had to duck their heads a bit. Their whispers echoed off the curved walls and Joan thought of the rock-shelter, of all that had been discovered in Tylerville. They were all explorers, all hunting for something—her husband, her sisters, her children, her parents, herself. Though it was dark, she suspected they would soon see light on the other side.

In fact, she could see something now, just up ahead, gleaming.

Eleanor considered driving to Monticello to see a movie, but to wear something presentable, just to walk down to the car seemed too much. She sat on the couch for a long time, watching the living room curtains flutter in the breeze. Light was fading. She thought of the day she had first come to the country to get over Rene. Had she managed it?

She must have fallen asleep because at first she didn't hear the knocking at the door. And when she did hear it, she stood up, startled. She cleared her throat several times before opening the door.

Aaron waited, standing loose-limbed in the darkness, under the stars. He had not worn his baseball cap. He was holding a small brown box. "Scrabble," he said.

She tried to clear her head. Scrabble? It was as if he were speaking another language. Then it came to her: a board game. "You want to play Scrabble?" she said, leaning against the screen.

"If you do."

"Scrabble?" *Wake up,* she told herself. "I'm just sitting here," she said. "I can't concentrate."

"So will you play?"

She frowned. "I suppose so. Why not?"

Eleanor motioned him to the couch. She cleared the coffee table of the magazines Charlotte had left behind and arranged the board. She thought: Why a board game? If he was interested in her, why not take her to the movies? To dinner? But it was too soon. She didn't even care that she wore dirty sweatpants or that her T-shirt was too big. Her hands seemed squarer than usual. Her nails were plain and short. She had the hands of an older woman, one she had lost track of.

Eleanor was losing—she just couldn't put words together. W-N-R-L-O-P-C. What could be made of that? Aaron led by 197 points. She felt something floating in the center of her—she tried to pull it back into place but it was no use. She didn't know what she was reaching for. Another seven letters—maybe she'd see something this time. And yes, there it was. A word. She placed five tiles, S-I-L-L-Y, onto the tiny squares of the board. She was embarrassed about the word; she longed for a word like ZIGZAG or XENON. She wanted to rack up some points. Suddenly she didn't want to lose. "You're not cheating, are you?" she asked. "My sister used to cheat me in cards."

Aaron cleared his throat. Her "S" had slipped onto

another square, as had the "L." The other "L," too, was nearly upside-down, and with his right forefinger, Aaron went to push the tiles back into place. She, too, had seen her letters askew, and with her right hand went to straighten them. When they touched hands a thrill ran through her.

And then they weren't touching anymore. She wasn't sure if she had let her hand slip, or if it had been him.

He said, "I'm going back to work tomorrow on our squares. Malcolm, Natalie, and Mr. Simmons are going to keep digging."

"I may start digging again."

He scratched his head. "I want to explain something, about why I was talking to Charlotte."

"You don't have to explain," she said, staring at a jumble of tiles. "You were holding her hand."

"She'd been crying, about Ian, about how she seemed destined to be alone. I wanted to talk to her about you. I wanted to know if you were still with Rene."

"But you *saw* what happened."

He stared at his work boots. "Yes."

"You didn't even try to help me."

"You were doing fine without me. You were making love, weren't you?"

"Making love?"

"You heard me coming and put your clothes back on. I thought you still loved him. Charlotte said you didn't. But I wondered."

"I don't love him!" In a softer voice, she said, "He was never who I thought he was. I just didn't see it."

"What was going on then?" he asked. "That afternoon, with Rene?"

"I don't want to talk about it."

"Charlotte didn't want to either. You should tell me everything," he said.

"Should I?"

He leaned over the coffee table and kissed her; his left hand pressed softly against the small of her back.

Several days later, Eleanor knelt over a square of earth. Carefully, she pulled dusty layer after dusty layer toward her. Who knew what she might find? Overhead, the sun was fierce, though it faded white into the hazy sky. There was a certain density to the air. The earth, the sky, were layered—there was more to them than one might think. She adjusted her hat, then slipped her finger under the kerchief tied around her neck and waited for a breeze.

"Found anything yet?" Aaron asked.

"Not yet. But we probably will. I mean, we've got to keep looking. We can't stop searching."

He nodded.

Putting down her trowel, she wiped her brow. "Do you think you can forget people? When they're gone? Just forget them completely?"

"I'm not sure I know what you mean."

"Can you forget people?"

His eyes were soft. "I still remember my grandfather, though he died years ago. When I smell a cigar, I remember. When I see an old man with gnarled fingers, I remember. When I step inside the Silverman Hotel, I remember."

"But can you forget people you'd like to forget. For instance, say someone said and did something awful to you, can you forget?"

"Do you want to talk about him?"

She wanted to ask him if he had figured it out about Rene—about what had been going on that day. Perhaps he saw the invisible scars on her body where Rene had hurt her, though no one else could see them. She hadn't yet told him. She wasn't ready. Still, she wanted to ask him what would become of them, of her and Aaron. How it would all turn out. But she knew she must wait and see. Or not just wait passively—she would have to be vigilant; she would have to sift things through.

She took off her hat and kissed him. It was something she chose to do.

EVERYTHING TO GAIN
by Barbara Taylor Bradford

Life seems almost perfect until an act of random violence tears apart the fabric of one woman's happiness. Here is a remarkable woman who thinks she has lost all, but by virtue of her own strength and courage, has everything to gain.

SWIMMING WITH DOLPHINS
by Erin Pizzey

Pandora escapes a series of abusive relationships to the captivating Caribbean island of Little Egg where she finds Ben, a passionate lover, and begins to discover an inner peace that will finally lead her to happiness.